THE
SWORD
OF
CYRUS

JC RYAN

BOOKS

By JC Ryan

Rossler Foundation Mysteries

The Tenth Cycle

Ninth Cycle Antarctica

Genetic Bullets

The Sword of Cyrus

The Skywalkers

The Phoenix Agenda

The Rowen

Termination

Vinci Books

vinci-books.com

Published by Vinci Books Ltd in 2025

1

Copyright © JC Ryan 2014

The author has asserted their moral right to be identified as the author of this work in accordance with the Copyright, Designs and Patents Act 1988. This work is a work of fiction. Names, characters, places and incidents are the product of the author's imagination or are used fictitiously. Any resemblance to actual persons, living or dead, places and incidents is entirely coincidental.

All rights reserved. No part of this publication may be copied, reproduced, distributed, stored in any retrieval system, or transmitted in any form or by any means, including photocopying, recording, or other electronic or mechanical methods, nor used as a source for any form of machine learning including AI datasets, without the prior written permission of the publisher.

The publisher and the author have made every effort to obtain permissions for any third party material used in this book and to comply with copyright law. Any queries in this respect should be brought to the attention of the publisher and any omissions will be corrected in future editions.

A CIP catalogue record for this book is available from the British Library.

Paperback ISBN: 9781036700416

The EU GPSR authorised representative is Logos Europe, 9 rue Nicolas Poussion, 17000 La Rochelle, France
contact@logoseurope.eu

Prologue

October 12, 539 BC, the ancient city of Babylon, 55 miles south of modern-day Baghdad

From the lofty walls of the great city, guards and civilians alike looked down upon the invaders, mocking them. Babylon was known by all to be impenetrable, yet these foolish Medes set up camp outside the walls. Perhaps they didn't know that there were provisions for a siege lasting twenty years. Jokes were hurled into the air. "Don't you know that you will have to wait there for twenty years to make us open our gates?" A few even taunted, "Want some fresh bread and wine?"

None of the taunts reached the ears of the Medes, for they were too far away. But occasionally a soldier broke discipline and lofted an arrow toward the heads he could see above the ramparts. Seeing the mockers duck was well worth the mild disciplinary action that resulted.

None of Cyrus's soldiers knew of the holy book of the Hebrews, where prophecy regarding their leader spoke of the favor of their one god, known to the Hebrews as YHVH, toward Cyrus. Perhaps Cyrus himself was unaware of it, but he was about to fulfill the prophecy in Isaiah and again in Jeremiah of the holy book, made 90 years before his birth. *"I will dry up thy rivers...I will dry up her sea."* Babylon's vulnerability was the Euphrates River, where it entered and exited below the transverse walls that bridged it. Cyrus diverted the river upstream, forming a lake and causing the river to become shallow enough for his men to wade, passing *under* the walls into the center of the city.

Even this would not have afforded them access to the city itself, except that the citizens had been celebrating their cleverness with wine and rich food, secure in the belief that no one could gain entry to the city. Once again, Jeremiah's prophecy had predicted what would happen. *"Thus saith the Lord to...Cyrus...I will...open before him the two leaved gates; and the gates shall not be shut."*

So had the prophets prophesied, and so it came to pass. The enormous gates that barred entrance from the riverbed to the streets that crossed the river were carelessly left open.

While the Babylonians feasted and drank, once again fulfilling prophecy, Cyrus and his invaders casually walked into the city without challenge. *"I will make drunk her princes, and her wise men, and her captains, and her rulers, and her mighty men, and they shall sleep a perpetual sleep, and not wake, saith the King, whose name is the Lord of hosts."*

No one noticed the subsidence of the river, and the gates were left open to allow the citizens to cross at will. By morning, the city had fallen without a fight. *"The mighty men of Babylon have forborne to fight, they have remained in their holds: their might hath failed; they became as women... One post shall run to meet another, and one messenger to meet another, to show the king of Babylon that his city is taken at one end."*

July 5th, 2019; Tehran, the day of the Ayatollah Kazemi's attack on Washington, D.C.

Dalir Jahandar sat at his desk late in the afternoon. He had watched the coverage of the attacks around the world, and as he'd expected, the Ayatollah had failed. They had not been as prepared as they should have been. One mistake was to time the attacks for the same moment, which meant that most people in Europe were asleep at the time. Little loss of life meant that there was little stir in those countries. Anger at the destruction and the threat, yes, but little outrage. It was almost as if they had expected it.

When he was tired of the disappointing TV coverage, he turned off the set and took up a manuscript that he'd had made in his early adulthood, a transcript of the Cylinder of Cyrus, which he'd read many times every year since he had learned the art of reading. Dalir thought of his father's words, repeated throughout his youth and right up until the older man's death from the accursed 9th Cycle virus.

"My son, you are destined to wield the Sword of Cyrus. There will be a great king of Persia once more, and he will rule an empire that encompasses the whole world. That destiny belongs to you. Use the knowledge wisely."

As he did each day, usually several times a day, Dalir repeated his oath. He then opened the transcript and read the familiar words again, supplying the interpretation he put on each point.

"Nabonidus the ruler of Babylon has displeased Marduk, the lord of the gods. By his own plan, he did away with the worship of Marduk, the king of the gods, he continually did evil against Marduk's

city. Daily, without interruption, he imposed the corvée upon its inhabitants unrelentingly, ruining them all."

"The governments of the West have displeased Allah, they are doing evil against the people of Allah, they are ruining them all," murmured Dalir, mesmerized by the words full of portent for his future.

"Upon hearing their cries, Marduk, the lord of the gods became furiously angry and decided to find a new king for Babylon."

"Allah has heard the cries of his people, he is angry and he wants to have a new king in the west," repeated Dalir, under his breath.

"Marduk surveyed and looked throughout the lands, searching for a righteous king, his favorite. He called out his name: Cyrus, king of Anšan; he pronounced his name to be king all over the world."

"Allah has looked all over the world for a righteous man. He has found his favorite and called his name: Dalir Jahandar, the Brave, the Valiant." Dalir's lips moved as he spoke the proud words without sound.

"He ordered him to go to his city Babylon. He set him on the road to Babylon and like a companion and a friend, he went at his side. His vast army, whose number, like water of the river, cannot be known, marched at his side fully armed. He made him enter his city Babylon without fighting or battle; he saved Babylon from hardship. He delivered Nabonidus, the king who did not revere him, into his hands. All the people of Babylon, all the land of Sumer and Akkad, princes and governors, bowed to him and kissed his feet. They rejoiced at his kingship and their faces shone. Lord by whose aid the dead were revived and who had all been redeemed from hardship and difficulty, they greeted him with gladness and praised his name."

'*Allah will be with him, at his side, he will save the world from hardship. The leaders of the world will bow and kiss the feet of Dalir Jahandar, the greatest leader of all.*' Dalir repeated these words only in his mind, as his eyes glazed and visions of the greatness to come replaced the words on the page.

"Cyrus, king of the world, great king, mighty king, king of Babylon, king of Sumer and Akkad, king of the four quarters, the son of Cambyses, great king, king of Anšan, grandson of Cyrus, great king, king of Anšan, descendant of Teispes, great king, king of Anšan, of an eternal line of kingship, whose rule Bêl and Nabu love, whose kingship they desire for their hearts' pleasure."

Dalir Jahandar, to his certain knowledge the rightful heir of Cyrus the Great, the liberator, the conqueror, the favorite of Allah, considered his destiny.

Chapter One

THE OATH

Three months earlier...

Dalir Jahandar stumbled out of the Erfan Grand Hospital, Abad, no longer conscious that it was the best private hospital in all of Tehran. His beloved father, Dariush, named for one of the great kings of Persia, was gone, a victim of the infidel's virus. Not only Father, but Dalir's beloved wife Roxana, chosen for him with great care and sealed to him with two children and growing love and respect over the years. Remembering his children, his two sons Dariush, the eight-year-old, proud of being named for his grandfather, and Basir, the four-year old, so small and yet eager to learn, anguish swept him again. All gone, all dead, one by one, as he watched. It was more than a man should be made to bear.

He'd hardly noticed the stinging shower of disinfectant, the hospital staff who directed him to leave by way of a door that had no hindrances of sick and dying bodies. His thoughts circled again and again to the actions he'd taken to protect them. All for naught. If it hadn't been for the mission his heart and mind whispered to him, he would have begged Allah to take him as well. But, that was not to be. He would have to wait to find his family again in Paradise, for first he had a sacred task; one that had been handed down to him in the blood of his forebears.

The present

He swore an oath that day, and had repeated it many times every day since then. Under his breath when he was in public; aloud with tears streaming down his face in mourning for his loved ones when he was alone. It became his sole reason for living.

Yesterday's bombings in Washington, D.C. on July 4th were to have been part of his revenge, even though he had doubts that they would be effective the way Ayatollah Kazemi set them up. Today, US President Harper was to address his nation and the world in the wake of the attack. Contrary to what Dalir expected, perhaps what even the world expected, the president's speech was conciliatory. Harper cited the high feelings about the medical disaster only recently contained as a possible reason for the attack. But then, he said that violence never solved anything and urged all countries to work toward peace. In particular, he pledged to work out a reconstruction project for the Middle East. To Jahandar, it was like a slap in the face, that this man he hated would so blatantly try to buy the good will of the people his countrymen had all but destroyed.

Now, as US President Harper's speech was being broadcast to billions of people globally, Dalir Jahandar listened, his lip curled and eyes flashing. At some point, he jumped to his feet and paced, tearing at his hair as he answered Harper, at first mentally and then spewing forth in violent Farsi. What did this infidel know of peace? A peaceful man did not murder millions of people with an engineered virus designed to attack only his enemies. A peaceful man did not kill millions, making Hitler and Stalin look like saints.

Had there been a watcher, his conclusion might have been that Jahandar had taken leave of his senses, driven insane by the war of hate in his mind against the people whose evil plan had taken his father, his wife and two small children. His loved ones had died in the most horrific pain and agony he could imagine, and he wasn't even allowed to go to them to offer comfort. He could only watch from behind a glass barrier as, one by one, they succumbed to the demon-spawned virus like millions of other men, women and children of his blood. Almost two hundred million in all. The mind balked at the numbers. Surely the earth would cry out in protest at so many dead, and yet it did not.

His oath, wrenched from his agonized mind as he left the hospital that day and a constant refrain in his head ever since, came into his consciousness now as he heard and rejected the falsehoods of the American president. *May Allah let me die a death a thousand times worse than this if I do not avenge the death of my loved ones on the evil one who did this.* By now, the faceless evil one of that day had found more than one face. One was the very man on his TV screen, Nigel Harper, with his honeyed words of poison and lies.

Another was Daniel Rossler, whose organization's meddling in things that had no business being dug up had resulted in the virus being unleashed. Each face of the fateful expedition was also burned into his brain. These people had been responsible for the physical fact of the virus, if they had not engineered it themselves. They sent sick people home to the Middle East to infect others, much as the American government had sent blankets infected with deadly smallpox to wipe out the indigenous peoples who claimed the same land. It was a well-known trick of the Americans.

Now as Harper quoted from the infidel's holy book, Jahandar, sickened beyond measure at the hypocrisy, added prayer to oath as he turned toward Mecca.

"Allah, I beseech you, please grant me my wish. Allah, keep me alive to be the Sword of Cyrus. If you grant my wish, I will kill millions of infidels for you. Allah, bless me in my undertaking, that the infidels may be wiped from the face of the earth and no longer offend you."

His prayer complete, he spared one last glance at the TV screen, where Harper was answering the questions the foolish reporters had been fed to ask him.

"Peace, you want, infidel? Peace you shall have, *in your grave*. There will only be peace when my revenge is complete."

Jahandar considered his options. He could join the thousands of suicide bomber volunteers who remained committed to the cause under the Ayatollah Kazemi, but that would exact his revenge on only one, or at most a few, of his targets, even if collateral damage was great. His despair in his personal life was enough to drive him to it; if not for the greater mission, he would pack his car full of explosives and drive it into the nearest Western embassy this very night. However, a plan was forming in his mind that held better promise. It would take all of the influence he'd built up among the ranks of the righteous of the rebellion. It would also take his most eloquent powers of persuasion.

Jahandar grew up with a father who practically revered

Persia's greatest king, Cyrus the Great. Over and over, he told his young son, Dalir, of the exploits of Cyrus, and that the great king's blood ran in his veins. Now, he, Dalir Jahandar, would gather influential and wealthy ethnic Persians under one banner to restore the ancient kingdom in all its glory, people who, like he, could trace their lineage back to the glory that was once Persia, in the time of the great king Cyrus. People who understood their history and were proud of it. When they were ready, they would once more conquer the known world.

This time, however, instead of flinging themselves in reckless abandon against the superior military strength of the enemy as the rebels had been doing for decades, they would do as Cyrus had done to Babylon. While the infidel world reveled in its sin, drinking and whoring its way to perdition, he, Dalir Jahandar, chosen by birth and by fate to wield the Sword of Cyrus, would find his way into their stronghold by stealth and conquer the infidel from within.

Chapter Two

WE'VE GOT TO DO SOMETHING ABOUT THIS!

July 6, 2019; Tehran

Jahandar wasted no time in making good on one promise of his oath. The President of the United States may be impossible to get to while in office, but Daniel Rossler was vulnerable. For a job so important, no one would do but the best, Adam al Gadahn, who happened to be the number two terrorist on hit lists of both Mossad and CIA. The man was known to be resourceful and clever, well worth the $150,000 that Dalir offered him to kill Daniel. They met in a coffeehouse, away from prying eyes.

"I will pay you one-third today, my friend, and the rest when I hear in the media that it is done. Daniel Rossler, above all, must die. If before he dies he sees that his wife and friends will also die, I will be more than satisfied. I will pay you an additional $50,000 for each member of the Rossler Foundation that dies with him, but your payment depends on Daniel Rossler dying, above all." Jahandar's eyes glittered in the dark room as he thought of his pleasure when Rossler was dead.

"I will see to it." The assassin took no pleasure in death, only in his skill at it, and the money it brought him.

"Do not contact me again. You are on your own from now on. When I see the reports in the media, I will pay the rest of the money into your account."

"That will be satisfactory."

"I want this done as soon as possible."

Annoyed, al Gadahn allowed himself to express his displeasure, though the words were mild. It was his eyes that told Jahandar he'd gone too far. "Allow me to do my job in the most efficient way. It will be soon, I promise you."

Al Gadahn left the coffeehouse with a bulge under his robes that had nothing to do with the state of his emotions. He went straight to a bank to deposit the cash. From there, he went home to contact his network in the US.

"Get me all the information you can on the Rossler Foundation, Daniel Rossler, and any of the other founders you can. This is urgent; you must report back to me within two weeks at the maximum." His orders conveyed, he made to disconnect the call, only to hear the response faintly as he took the phone away from his ear.

"As you wish, Aqa al Gadahn."

While he waited for the information, al Gadahn made his way to Puerto Vallarta, Mexico, where for a payment of only ten thousand dollars, he bought safe conduct through one of the tunnels controlled by the drug cartel Sinaloa Federation. From there, he found conveyance through friends of his network, up through New Mexico into Colorado and eventually to Aurora, where he was the guest of a prominent Muslim cleric. By the time he arrived via this circuitous route, his henchman had the information he required.

Pictures of Daniel Rossler, Sarah Rossler, their toddler, Nicholas, and various friends and founding members of the Foundation along with their families were given to him. Most important, the information that these people would undoubtedly gather for the birthday of the Rossler patriarch, Nicholas, who would be eighty-six on July 25th. With the younger Rossler, JR, and his wife Rebecca back from their honeymoon, everyone, even the parents from North Carolina, would be in attendance. In addition, close friends Sinclair and Martha O'Reilly, Rajan and Sushma Sankaran, along with most of the important Antarctica expedition members, would also be at the party. He would be able to please Jahandar, collect a fortune in bounties and virtually wipe out the Rossler Foundation in one blow.

Al Gadahn contacted a network member, a sleeper who had long been in place for just such an occasion. The man had pledged his life as a suicide bomber in case such would be needed, many years ago. It was time for him to earn his martyrdom. The making of the bomb was al Gadahn's task alone. It was one of the skills that had landed him on the most-wanted lists of most of the major European nations, as well as the CIA and the Mossad. His signature was the use of a Pakistani-made lithium-ion battery in his IED. Though it was largely destroyed in the blast, enough remained to twist the noses of investigators, his version of 'Kilroy was here'.

To make his bomb, al Gadahn purchased an inexpensive cell phone with prepaid minutes, replaced the battery, and wrapped the whole thing in plastic explosive, with the battery attached to the circuit that previously controlled the vibration function. The battery was set up to short-circuit when the vibration circuit energized it, because his Pakistani-made battery did not have the fail-safe circuits that American-made batteries did. His bomber would walk toward the Rossler party with the package concealed beneath his clothing, carrying a remote control device that would also trigger the bomb. When he was as near to the table as he could get, he would presumably trigger the IED. However, if that did not occur, al Gadahn would be nearby with the phone number queued up, and would trigger it himself from a position of safety.

Because the Rosslers now had no detectable protection according to his informants, it would be a simple matter. Once he learned the location and time of the party, he would reconnoiter a safe place from which to observe.

Stupid Americans, he observed two days before the birthday, to so readily give away their plans. By now he had moved to the Boulder area and was staying in a hotel that the decadent citizens of this country would probably think beneath them. For him, it was a luxury compared to those of his native land, one of the poorest countries in the world, Eretria on the west bank of the Red Sea. Shaking his thoughts from the bitterness this disadvantaged start usually engendered in him, he read the announcement of the party honoring Nicholas Rossler. If al Gadahn had anything to do with it, and he would, this Rossler and all the others would celebrate no more birthdays.

July 25, 2019; Boulder

On the day of the party, al Gadahn and his bomber arrived and parked as near to the restaurant as they could.

To his satisfaction, al Gadahn had ascertained that the restaurant where the party would be held had a large plate glass window in front, where he would be able to easily observe the bombing. A generous donation to the restaurant owner through a Turkish ex-pat friend had assured him that the party would be seated in the front, the excuse being that the friend wanted to do something nice for the Rosslers. The local Muslim community had unjustly accused them of engineering the virus, when in fact they had been instrumental in stopping it, he told the restaurant owner. After performing his part, the friend and his family slipped away quietly, telling no one where they were moving.

Al Gadahn shook himself from his thoughts as he saw one of the targets enter the restaurant. Young JR Rossler was easy to spot, a freakishly tall man with a stunning woman at his side. In short order, others began to arrive, and all were seated at closely-gathered tables near the front window as arranged. Al Gadahn could see them burying their noses in the flowers his friend had ordered delivered and then talking excitedly among themselves. When he had ticked off all of the important targets on his list and the new arrivals had stopped, he turned to his silent passenger.

"Allahu Akbar," he intoned, embracing the man.

"Allahu Akbar," the other replied, a mournful tone coloring his words. Al Gadahn went on alert. As soon as the bomber got out and started across the street, he pulled out his cell phone and scrolled to the speed dial number he'd prepared.

Inside the restaurant, the bomber paused at the door to get his bearings, then turned left and made his way toward the Rossler party. He could see Daniel Rossler seated in his straight path, a few yards away. Meeting Daniel's eyes, he put his hand in his pocket, noticing that the eyes on which his were trained suddenly widened.

For his part, Daniel had watched the man enter, casually observing that he was wearing a jacket in spite of the warm July evening. As the man walked toward him, Daniel noticed that he was the apparent focus of the guy's attention, and switched his own focus to meet the man's eyes. Something about him kept Daniel raptly attendant on the man's moves, and when his hand entered his pocket, Daniel knew.

At that moment, the man screamed "Death to the Rosslerites! May you all burn in hell! Allahu Akbar!"

Daniel yelled, "Get down! Get down! Get down!" as he swept Sarah off her chair in a full-body tackle and covered her with his body. JR reacted immediately, knocking his own wife to the floor and looking around wildly for his parents and grandparents. Others hesitated, and paid for their confusion. As friends and family hit the floor, Daniel had a split second to brace for the blast. What he couldn't see from his position was that, instead of using whatever was in his pocket to detonate his bomb, the man had turned and run for the door. Two seconds later, the front of the restaurant was demolished as al Gadahn's detonator triggered the bomb.

Al Gadahn had watched as his bomber's steps grew slower and suspected that he was having second thoughts. In the seven seconds it took for his phone to dial the other's and detonate the explosives, the bomber had delivered his crazed message to the Rosslers and turned away, making for the door. As a result, the blast that tore through the restaurant was largely directed away from the Rossler party. There were injuries, of course, among them. Sarah was bruised, not from the bomb, but from Daniel's desperate bid to save her, and she had been hit in the upper arm by shrapnel from a wooden table in the form of a good-sized splinter that would have to be removed at the emergency room of the local hospital. Daniel had cuts from flying glass and bruises. JR and Rebecca had been sitting in the center of the group, and were largely unhurt as overturned tables and the bodies of others in the party took the brunt of the blast.

The rest of the Rossler party were more or less intact, although bruises would appear later. The worst of the injuries were cuts from flying glass. Nicholas, shaken but mostly unhurt, held a napkin to Bess's face, where a shard of glass had narrowly missed her eye.

The scene was chaotic as children shrieked their fright and adults realized their hearing was affected. Daniel could see Sarah mouthing words, and from the expression on her face, she was screaming them, but he couldn't make out the sound. His ears were ringing and all sounds were muffled, as if he had earplugs in. At last, he calmed her enough with his hands cupping her face that he could read her lips.

"Where's Daddy?"

Immediately, he turned and started helping the others from the party up, searching for Sarah's dad, Ryan. Thank God that her mom, Emma, had excused herself from the party to babysit little Nick, who didn't always do well in restaurants, being a typical two-year-old. Finding Ryan, Daniel gestured for the older man to go to his daughter, while he continued helping the injured up from the floor as best he could.

The unlucky ones were the patrons sitting at the tables between the bomber and the door. Fifteen were killed, and others received maiming injuries. Screams of pain from that area led Rebecca and JR there, as soon as they had shaken off their shock. They immediately went into action triaging the injured. Rebecca directed JR to cover the dead with any tablecloths he could find, while she comforted the horrendously wounded as best she could. When she'd done what she could for them, she sorted the disembodied limbs that lay in a bloody stew near ground zero. Few would be able to be reattached; they were too damaged. Bits of the bomber, based on the leather attached to the bloody gobs, clung to walls, tables, and the occasional nearby victim. Adding to the mess and the stench, several people had lost their recently-consumed dinners.

Ten minutes after the blast, dust still hung in the air, adding to the general confusion. No one could hear, and the dim lighting in the restaurant coupled with the dust kept them from seeing clearly as well. For many, that was a blessing. In addition to the smell of blood and vomit, a hint of bitter almond hung in the air with the dust. Disoriented, Rebecca was at first alarmed by the odor. When she was able to make JR understand her, he assured her that it was almost certainly from the explosive, no doubt plastique. She stopped worrying about cyanide gas and continued to check her patients.

Sirens could be heard coming closer, and to save some of the victims would require that they be the first to be treated. Those who would survive would later feel fortunate that a doctor was on the scene. Once the EMTs took over helping Rebecca, JR looked around in barely-contained rage.

The demolished restaurant looked like the war zone he was far too familiar with and that had caused him countless nightmares. Sounded like it too, through the blanket of fuzziness that was hindering his hearing.

"Daniel, we've got to do something about this. Look at Grandma!"

Daniel was angry, too, but knew that there was no immediate target for his rage. This was undoubtedly Middle Eastern retaliation, based on the appearance of the bomber. His task at the moment was to lead, and leading required a cool head. "Calm down, JR. We don't know for sure who initiated it, though we both have our suspicions. Let the cops do their jobs. We'll figure out what to do about it when we know more."

Luke walked up to the pair at that moment, having settled a weeping Sally in one of the few intact chairs.

"Boulder PD will be here soon, but I've called Sam Lewis. He's going to get on the horn to the FBI and have an investigative team here ASAP. I told Lewis I thought it could be Al Qaeda, or one of the other terrorist organizations. He'll send a CIA team, too."

"I hope they can all play nicely together for a change," Daniel said, barely beginning to regain enough hearing to understand Luke's statements. He wasn't joking. The situation didn't call for jokes.

July 26, 2019; Boulder

It was well past midnight when a weary but angry Daniel Rossler arrived home. Sarah had been treated and released at the ER, and he'd put her in a taxi to go home to Nick and her mother. Emma was shaken but grateful that Ryan had come straight from the restaurant to give her the news himself, and to report that there were no life-threatening injuries among their family or friends. Still, it was awful to think of what might have been, if the bomber hadn't apparently had second thoughts. Witnesses from the back of the restaurant had reported his sudden move to run back toward the door.

If only he'd made it. Perhaps fewer or even none of those who were killed or badly injured would have been hurt at all. Daniel couldn't fathom why the man had turned, but each time his restless mind lit on the question, he breathed a prayer of thanks that he had. And each time, a wave of guilt for the innocent bystanders who'd lost life or limb engulfed him. Daniel was not a heavy drinker, but after checking on a sweetly-sleeping Nick and dropping a light-as-air kiss on Sarah's head, he returned to the dining room and found a bottle of fifteen-year-old Scotch. Pouring a stiff drink, he carried it with him into the living room and heaved himself into his favorite easy chair.

Had he missed anything? Boulder PD were hot on the heels of the ambulances, and he'd promised to return to the scene as soon as he could get his wife some medical attention. There weren't enough ambulances, he'd need to drive her. Daniel was well-known in Boulder; the cop was okay with the plan. Once he'd put Sarah in the taxi at the hospital, he'd returned as promised to submit to as many interviews as they or anyone else wanted. He would do everything he could to help.

Did he know the bomber, they asked. No. What made him start yelling even before the bomber screamed his threat? The eyes, he answered. The eyes were flat, black, full of hatred. And then the hand moved. He didn't see any more, he was covering his wife to save her if he could. Did he know that the bomber had turned and run away?

"Is that what happened?" Daniel asked in response. He'd been surprised not to wake up dead. The man was so close…

"Witnesses say that as soon as he yelled 'Allahu Akbar',

he turned and ran like a scared rabbit toward the door. Why do you think he would have done that?"

Daniel shrugged. "Changed his mind?" He didn't have a clue, and speculation was of no use.

"But then the bomb detonated." The officer was observing him closely as he made the statement.

Daniel tilted his head. "There was another one. He triggered the bomb." The certainty came an instant after the thought.

The officer alerted to the bald statement, not conjecture but assurance. "How do you know?"

"Afghanistan. IEDs. The FBI and CIA are on their way, they'll know." Daniel was emotionally and mentally exhausted. He couldn't even form a complete sentence. He'd be of no more help.

He'd waited for them, watching the clean-up efforts, every able-bodied witness pitching in to pick up scattered furniture, make a pile of the hopelessly broken pieces and sweep up broken crockery, glasses and other detritus. When he talked to the feds, repeating the answers he'd given to the same questions from Boulder PD, their voices batted at his ears like someone clapping their hands over them and releasing them, rapidly, over and over.

Now, at home, his Scotch almost gone and his ears still ringing, Daniel felt the weight of mind-destroying guilt. People were dead because someone wanted him dead, him and his family. He didn't know how he would come to terms with that. Perhaps a way would come to him in the morning.

Daniel staggered slightly as he rose and made his way to his bed. Only Sarah's arms could comfort him now.

Morning came very early, as the phone rang at five a.m.

Momentarily forgetting what had happened the night

before, Daniel felt a flash of irritation. Who the hell was calling at this ungodly hour? He fumbled for his phone and answered churlishly, "Do you know what time it is?"

"Sure do, Daniel," answered Harper. "Calling to tell you how sorry I am about what happened last night." Memory came flooding back as Daniel sat up in bed.

"Nigel," Daniel said, alerting Sarah that President Harper was on the phone. She sat up and brushed her hair back with her fingers.

Harper had noticed that Daniel was confused. "Did I wake you up? Didn't figure you'd be sleeping. What's going on back there?"

Daniel was alert now, answering as if he hadn't been rudely awakened from too short a slumber. "Looks like radicals from our friends in the Middle East. Fifteen innocent bystanders blown to bits. And who knows how many of the critically injured will have died of their wounds since I left the scene a few hours ago." Daniel said in a tired voice.

"When is this going to end? When will these people have seen enough bloodshed, death and destruction? " Harper had caught Daniel's angst and was asking questions that had no answer.

Daniel revealed his despair in his answer. "I don't know. I'd say when we've mopped up the terrorists, but that seems to be like pulling weeds. For every one you pull, three spring up in the same place."

"My assistant is calling me into a meeting. Take care Daniel. I just wanted to call and offer you my condolences and to also tell you I am making arrangements for better security for you, your family and the staff of the Rossler Foundation" Harper was gone before Daniel could get out his response.

"Thanks, Nigel."

Chapter Three

PERSIAN SUPREMACY

Mid-July, 2019; Tehran

Dalir's task in creating his secret society was made a little more difficult by the fact that several of the people he had in mind to invite to his party did not live in Iran at all. In fact, the wealthiest Persians had fled to the far corners of the earth during the overthrow of the Shah fifty years previously. However, their roots in Islam had brought many of the younger generation into the fold of the Islamic Republic on a stealth basis. How the stupid Americans would squirm if they knew that a famous and popular search engine's profits might fund retribution against them, or that the clothing that turned their wealthy young women into harlots, baring their skin for all to see, might purchase guns and ammunition to be used to destroy their sinful way of life.

What fun it would be to reveal to the Americans just how much of the most costly and prestigious real estate in their great cities belonged to expatriate Persians. But, that would come later, much later. For now, Dalir decided to contact men he knew to be wealthy, and invite an elite twelve of them to form a committee to put his plan into motion, both by their influence and with their funds. Three Americans, a pair of brothers from the UK, four Iranian citizens who had managed to amass some wealth under the iron rule of the Ayatollahs, and one each from France, Greece and Italy were the ones who agreed to meet with Dalir in Tehran to hear his plan.

On a day only three weeks after the speech that had galvanized him to action, Dalir met with these men to lay out his plan.

"Gentlemen, you know that my goal is to restore the Persian Empire in all its glory in the present day. Do I have your commitment to work together for this goal?" Jahandar had explained it to each of them, once he had their assurance that his words would go no further. He didn't expect to have to explain it again.

The eldest of the group, a man of sixty-eight, who was the only representative of the first generation of expatriates who'd fled Iran in the late 1970s, spoke for all when he interrupted.

"How do you propose to do this? Assuming we are all here because your goal intrigued us when you stated it, we would like to see this come to pass. But, history has showed us that we cannot do it by military might. Some of us resorted to conquering through economic superiority." A ripple of laughter ran around the table. Everyone there knew that this man owned significant real estate holdings in New York City and had an estimated net worth of nearly one billion dollars.

"Don't worry, Massoud, we will not be bombing your precious buildings," Dalir joked in return. Seeing that the others had deferred to the older man and that all seemed to be willing to commit only after they had heard the plan, Dalir explained.

"I think we are in agreement that radicalism has cost us our finest young men, while gaining nothing," he began. "Between economic sanctions and wars that we cannot win, and now this demonic virus, we have been brought to the brink of extinction." The nods around the table encouraged him to lay out his bold plan. "There is an American saying, 'if you can't beat them, join them.' This is how I propose to do it."

Dalir went on to marshal his arguments, as the twelve listened avidly, encouraging him with expressions of agreement.

"The quality of life of our people has deteriorated, even before this latest blow. The Ayatollahs established the Islamic Republic with the support of the people because of the inequality in distribution of wealth under the Shah. Can it now be said that the Ayatollahs went too far? That their repression and extreme measures all but returned our great nation to the Dark Ages? Many of our best minds fled with their wealth, some of your families among them. Are you now ready to join with me to reverse these errors?

"Where would we be today if we had signed the 10th Cycle Treaty and reaped the benefits of technology and modern medical practice that other countries have seen? Our riches in oil did not benefit our people; for two decades, our people have suffered because the greatest consumer of oil in the world would not buy ours. Now it is of little use, since the 10th Cycle cold fusion technology was discovered. Of course we use it for ourselves, but does the government supply its benefits to the people at little or no cost? No!"

Dalir paused in his speech, looking around the table to judge the effect of his words.

"Our people still die of diseases that have been wiped out in the rest of the world. Because the Ayatollah Kazemi declared that the secrets of the library belonged to Egypt and must be delivered back there before Muslims may take part in those miracles, we have become a third-world nation. And the toll of this virus!"

"Dalir, surely you no longer believe that the virus was engineered by America," another of the American members of the committee interrupted.

"It does not matter if America engineered it or merely let it loose," Dalir said, his eyes darkening to black with the intensity of his emotion. "We died in our millions. Our hospitals were not equipped, our medics not trained. America could have helped more than it did, and that was partly because the Ayatollah would not allow it." Dalir failed to mention that he had been in perfect agreement with the decision at the time. Nor did he reveal that his entire family had been wiped out. It was critical that he forge these twelve men into one fist to do two things: first, to rid him of the Ayatollah to pave the way for the second. And second, to back his bid to infiltrate the Rossler Foundation by professing a new, peace-loving regime in Iran.

"Before I go any further, I must insist that, if you are with us, you swear a solemn oath to do everything in your power, using your influence, your wealth, and if necessary your life, to restore Persia to its former glory. If you are not, leave now, but know that you are bound by honor and by blood not to reveal our plans. Swear it!"

As Dalir moved his gaze from one to the next, each

followed the lead of the eldest in fisting his right hand and clapping it to his left shoulder as he said, "I so swear." When all twelve had followed suit, Dalir thanked them.

"I propose that we name ourselves The Sword of Cyrus. You will be richly rewarded when we have prevailed. If your wealth has been spent, it will be returned to you. If you have died, your families will be well cared for. In due time, the world will know and revere your names. I, Dalir Jahandar, descendant of Cyrus the Great of Persia, swear it to you in return." Jahandar's passion swept through his chosen, binding them to him in spirit as well as honor. As the twelve stood, applauding in agreement to the name of the group, Dalir motioned for them to sit down. There was still urgent business to attend to.

"This is what we must do. Does any one of you believe that the Ayatollah Kazemi is fit to govern in the wake of his refusal to allow treatment for the infidel's virus?" Once more, Dalir scanned the room. Seeing no dissent, he continued. "What, then, shall we do with this man? I attest to you, because I have had occasion to be in his presence, that he is deluded, perhaps insane. He believes himself to be the Twelfth Imam, and yet he was powerless to stop what was happening to our people. My suggestion is that we remove him by whatever means necessary."

"What of the government when he is gone, Dalir?" asked Massoud. In spite of the fact that he'd been a mere lad when his family left Iran, he knew that the Ayatollah was the real leader of Iran's government.

"There is of course the actual government. Certainly they have no power at this time, nor do we wish to give them any. Let us call for elections and put our own men in power, those who will support us in our mission." Dalir's plan had already called for this.

"You, Dalir?"

"No, not at this time, although I thank you for your faith in me," he answered. "It is my opinion that we, the Sword of Cyrus, must stay out of the public eye in both political and religious capacities. We must use our influence in a measured and logical way, not get caught up in populist agendas.

"I propose that we work toward making the West believe that Iran has become a nation of those who would support peace and democracy. Let us work to bring our people into the modern world of technology and medical advancement. When we are fully accepted and have had the opportunity to fully exploit the technology in that library, we will strike. They will never see it coming, because their decadence keeps them complacent. They do not learn from their errors." Dalir took up a ceremonial dagger that had lain on the table in front of him the entire time, and stroked it, his eyes darting from one of the twelve to another.

"When you say remove..." started the member from Italy.

"I mean he must die," Dalir finished for him, with a firm emphasis on 'must'. With a swift motion, he stabbed the dagger into the table.

Each of the Twelve had an assignment to consider the manner of death of the Ayatollah. They were to meet by videoconference link in three days to discuss how to assassinate the most heavily-guarded man in all of Iran. It was one of the four Iranian members who came up with the best plan.

"I have learned that Kazemi will be attended by his

personal physician next week, on Wednesday," he explained. "Once the physical exam is complete, a physician's assistant will hand the doctor several syringes, containing some regular inoculations. It seems our Ayatollah reserves for himself the best of Western medicine." His sneer was easily visible to the others, who shared his disdain for a hypocrite.

"What inoculations are these?" asked Dalir.

"Some vitamin shots, as I understand it. Also, a flu vaccine." Once again, Saman could not hide his disgust.

"That son of a goat!" Dalir exclaimed. The others raised their heads in surprise, but Dalir did not explain that his family had died for lack of the gene therapy treatment, and that Kazemi's use of a vaccine against seasonal flu was one of the worst betrayals he could imagine. Instead, he remarked that it was a direct contradiction of Kazemi's own policies.

"Just so," said Saman. "May I continue?"

"Of course."

Saman said the rest in a rush, unwilling to be interrupted again. "This physician's assistant has a vulnerability we may exploit. He is known to love his family very much. I do not propose to harm them, but he need not know that. On my signal, men in my employ will snatch them from their home and convey them to mine, to be my guests until this man performs our mission. We will have him substitute a substance we give him for the flu shot. You'll appreciate the irony, Dalir. This substance will mimic a heart attack, and Kazemi will die with no one the wiser that it was an assassination."

"An excellent plan, Saman! Are we in agreement?" Dalir smoothly took control of the conference with his question.

With the others all nodding, Dalir asked a follow-up

question. "Saman, have you determined the substance to use?" *If not*, he thought, *I have a few ideas of my own.*

However, Saman had apparently thought of everything. "After much research, I believe that the best would be eight grams of potassium chloride. The substance breaks down immediately in the body into potassium and chlorine. The chlorine bonds to the body's naturally occurring sodium, forming sodium chloride - ordinary salt. The freed potassium, however, will result in a potassium overload, which will create tachycardia, leading to a heart attack." His self-satisfied smile revealed that he'd taken pride in the thoroughness of his research.

Dalir stated the obvious, while toying with the dagger he'd taken to carrying with him everywhere. "So, it will appear to be natural causes." He would have preferred to stab the traitor through the heart, but that would not be prudent.

"Yes, Dalir. Death will occur within half an hour at most, and the method will be undetectable." Saman was certain; he'd made sure of it before bringing it to the table.

"Excellent! Nothing can be found upon autopsy?" This from Massoud, who had a fondness for the TV show, CSI, and prided himself on his knowledge of criminal investigation in America.

"Perhaps an elevated level of sodium chloride - nothing that should raise suspicion," Saman returned.

"How soon can you arrange to have this man's family detained?" Dalir asked.

"I have taken the liberty of doing so already, Dalir. They should be arriving as my guests at my home right now. Every precaution has been taken. I even did my research into the method of death on computers than cannot be traced to me. Everything is in readiness except for gaining the physician's assistant's cooperation. Shall I make the call?"

"Make it from an anonymous location. Purchase a prepaid phone for the purpose." Dalir was well-versed in fieldcraft, though he would not reveal the nature of his experience to these men.

"Certainly, Dalir."

Two hours later, a frightened man was shown into the conference room, where only Dalir and his colleague were waiting for him, both with their faces obscured by cloths covering their lower faces. He had been brought blindfolded to this place, but the blindfold had been removed so that he could see the grandeur of the room and be impressed by the importance of the anonymous men in front of him.

"Kasra Turani, do you know why you are here?" The voice was stern and regal.

"*Bebakhshid Agha.* Excuse me, sir, I do not. The voice on the phone, it said my wife and children..." The frightened man could not finish his sentence, and his legs were about to betray him.

"Are safe, Kasra, I assure you. They will remain safe as our guests until you have accepted our mission and carried it out. Then they will be returned to you, none the worse for wear." The voice was kinder now, and Kasra began to take heart.

"Please, sir, I know nothing of missions. I am a simple man, a physician's assistant. What could I do for a man of wealth and discernment such as yourself? A special medication, perhaps? Something Dr. Abbasi could prescribe for you?" He feared to name it, for use of illicit drugs was punishable by death.

"Thank you, but that will not be required. You will be given a syringe with a special medication for the Ayatollah

Kazemi next week. You will substitute this syringe for the medication you usually give that most resembles the appearance of our special medicine. Do you have questions?" Dalir's voice had gone stern again, guessing what the man offered. For that, he would change the plan for the man's fate.

"Yes, please sir. What is this special medication?" His voice quavered, a sign that he had a good idea.

"That does not concern you. Do you accept this mission?"

"Will the Ayatollah be harmed, sir?" Once more, he tried, and once more, was rebuffed.

"Again, that is not your concern. Do you understand what will happen to your wife and beautiful young daughters if you refuse?"

"Yes, sir, I think so, sir." Resigned.

"To whom do you owe your allegiance?"

"To my family, sir."

"Then your choice is clear, is it not? Do you have any more foolish questions?" Dalir was now out of patience. The man's immediate fate hung in the balance.

"No, sir. I accept the assignment, sir."

"Very good. This medicine will be handed to you when you make an excuse to leave the examining room briefly. Make sure to conceal the unused syringe with the vitamin injection in your clothes, and get rid of it outside the palace somewhere within half an hour of Kazemi's injections. Do you understand?"

"Yes, sir."

"Excellent. You will be well rewarded. Not only will your family be returned to you, but you will receive generous payment besides. You will never have to work again if you choose not to, and you will be free to choose where you wish to live." At the moment, Dalir fully believed what he was saying.

"Will I not wish to live here in Tehran after this mission, sir? This is my home."

"Certainly, if you wish."

Chapter Four

MEETING WITH AN OLD FRIEND

August 15, 2019; Boulder

"Luke, how's it going?" Luke Clarke, ex-CIA agent, head of security for the Rossler Foundation and uncle to Sarah Rossler, knew the voice, but couldn't place it, nor the slight accent.

"Fine. I believe you have me at a disadvantage."

"Luke, I am wounded! You do not recognize your old friend, Arsalan?"

Luke froze, an expression of wonder flashing across his countenance. "I'm glad to hear from you, Arsalan. Congratulations on escaping the flu." It had been so long since he'd heard from Arsalan, before his retirement from the CIA. Luke didn't even know if his old sleeper agent was still in the Middle East. Of course, he should be. When someone agreed to lie low and be activated when needed, it was expected that they'd stay put.

"It was not easy, my friend. I have some information for you," Arsalan continued.

Luke had a question first. "Wait just a minute. You know we thought you dead? Why have you been silent all this time?"

"It was not safe to contact you before. I am in New York right now. When can we meet?" *New York?*

Luke thought fast as he answered, "Hold on, buddy. I'm retired. You'll have to give it to someone else."

"I think not, Luke. Your government will want to hear this. I trust only you. You must broker a meeting with someone of importance, and very soon. Time is critical."

Shit, Sally's going to kill me. Aloud, Luke answered, "I'll get hold of Sam Lewis. Remember him? He's now the head of the CIA. Will you talk to him?"

"Only if you are present," Arsalan twisted the knife.

"Man, you don't know how much trouble I'm going to be in with my wife," Luke said, hoping to get off the hook.

"Ah, you have my sympathy. Wives can indeed be difficult. Nevertheless, I must insist." Arsalan sounded more amused than sympathetic.

Luke took a number where he could reach Arsalan and wasted no time before calling Sam Lewis.

"Sam, Luke. We've heard from an old friend. Thought you'd be interested to know he survived the epidemic." Luke wanted Sam to nibble at the bait before he set the hook.

"Oh?" *There's my nibble.*

"Yes. I just got a call from New York. Interestingly, it came to my direct number. I don't know how he found me." *Tease him a little, so he'll bite strong.*

"I haven't the slightest idea what you're talking about, Luke. Who was it?" Sam's exasperation with the game was beginning to show. Just one more flick of the line, and Luke would have him.

"He didn't contact you?" *Flick.*

"Who didn't? Stop talking in riddles, man." *Ha, took it, hook, line and sinker.*

"Arsalan. Ahmad Ahmadi, remember? Besides me, you're the only man who knows he was ever CIA," Luke said, through with the tease. He knew Sam would be interested now.

"You're kidding! We haven't heard from him in ten years! He made it through the flu, huh?"

"Seems so," Luke answered.

"What's he want?"

"A face-to-face meeting, soonest. Says he has some information our government will want to know. I'll get on a red-eye as soon as I calm Sally down. She's about to draw and quarter me."

Sally, Luke's wife, had taken more than enough of Luke's abrupt departures and worrying about his safety. She didn't want him in the forefront of any more of what she called CIA stuff, especially not dangerous CIA stuff. And, Luke had to admit, *all* CIA stuff was dangerous.

While Sam made the relatively simple preparations to hop from Washington, D.C. to New York City the next morning, Luke's task was more complex, requiring among other things that Sally or someone else drive him to Denver International Airport in the middle of the night. To his dismay, Sally insisted on the honor. He was in for forty-five minutes of hen-pecking on the trip from Boulder. If he didn't love her so much, he'd consider sneaking away in a taxi instead.

Before going to Arsalan's hotel the next morning, Luke met Sam at a restaurant for breakfast to discuss how they'd play it.

"Remind me what we had in mind for this guy, Luke. You recruited him, yes?"

"Yeah. Harvard-educated, comes from a well-placed family in Iran, speaks flawless English. We picked him up and then waited to see what he'd make of himself back home. Figured we'd activate him if and when some crisis came along. This was right after the fall of Saddam Hussein, if you'll remember. I tried to locate him when this virus crisis started, but he was nowhere to be found. That's why I never reminded you about him while that crazy leader of theirs was trying to throw nukes at us."

"Oh, yeah. Got it. Man, I'm slipping."

"You've been just a bit busy, I'd say. So have I."

"Well, let's go see him."

Ahmad greeted Luke and Sam in the sitting room of his New York hotel suite.

"Nice digs, buddy," Luke remarked. "We always thought you'd make something of yourself. What brings you to New York?"

"I'm here with an urgent message. Our lines of communication are broken, so I had to come in person."

Luke's frown of puzzlement cleared as the second half of the explanation registered with him.

"It must be important! What can we do for you?"

"My friend, I contacted you because I believe I can do something for you. Please, may I explain?"

"Sure, go ahead."

"When I returned to my country with your instructions, I did as you suggested. I made myself useful to certain persons in power, and waited for your signal, watching the places where you told me I would see it in good time. After several years, I became known as someone who could get things done, if you understand me."

Luke and Sam nodded, though Luke wasn't sure he wanted to imagine what Ahmad was implying.

"I married, had a family. No one could have known that I was an agent for your CIA. This is important."

"Hey, congratulations! They came through the medical crisis okay, I assume?" Luke said.

"Oh, yes, by the grace of Allah, they are safe and well."

"Good to hear. Sorry to interrupt; you were saying?"

"When the medical crisis, as you call it, began, I was summoned to the headquarters of the Ayatollah Kazemi, along with others, and placed in quarantine. I am sorry that at that time, it was no longer safe to contact you. We all watched each other; no one could have gotten so much as a note out to his family without the Ayatollah knowing it."

"Sounds tense," Sam Lewis interjected.

"Indeed. I was one of the Ayatollah's most trusted lieutenants, but even I had to be careful what advice I gave. The man has gone quite mad, and those who disagree with him meet unfortunate fates, especially since he has started to believe he is the Twelfth Imam. Those who don't agree just disappear or lose their heads. Messy business."

"I'm sure. What can you tell us about this Twelfth Imam business?"

"It is a belief of devout Shias. The Twelfth Imam, a Muslim leader in the ninth century of your Christian era, disappeared from this earth without death. Prophecy has it that he will return in a time of crisis, and that he will destroy the infidels and restore Islam to its rightful place, bringing all into Allah's fold."

"And Kazemi thinks he's that guy?" Lewis asked.

"He believes it with all his heart. It is for this reason that Kazemi has resisted efforts to modernize Iran, and it is why he instructed his followers to reject Western medicine when the crisis began. He is responsible for much unnecessary suffering of my people. As I said, I was unable to warn you of his plans, but he was broadcasting them in any case. I think that nothing was lost by my failure."

"Perhaps a few minutes, nothing more. Don't beat yourself up, man, we understand. What now?"

"In return for the information I have brought you, I want your cooperation in convincing your president and other leaders that some of us in Iran want nothing more than peace and the opportunity to rebuild our nation. We will also use our influence to bring other Middle Eastern countries into the fold."

"What's your intention, Ahmad? Do you want political leadership in Iran?"

"No indeed! I feel my best efforts are behind the scenes, as you say. Leaders are constrained by the need to please everyone. I can be more efficient by being one of those who must be pleased." Ahmad flashed white teeth in a predatory smile. "Above all, I wish to be instrumental in achieving peace with Israel. We have thrown the flower of our youth at Israel in hatred for too long. It must stop, if we are to bring about an end to the hardship that our stubbornness has caused us."

Luke looked at Sam, a dubious expression in his eyes. Sam took the lead with the obvious question.

"How do you propose to bring all this about, Ahmad? Your entire culture has been at war with Israel, in principle if not in fact, for thousands of years. Many have sought to end it, and all of them have failed."

"Many outsiders have sought to force peace upon us,"

answered Ahmad. "Western governments, in fact, have attempted to impose their own cultures and standards upon us. This will never work. We are a proud people, with traditions that predate your country by thousands of years. Only we ourselves, working from inside our culture, will be able to bring this about. Until now, there has never been sufficient motivation."

"What are you asking us to do?"

"Back my effort," Ahmad said. "The only way to bring this to pass is through technological advancement. If my country and the other countries in the Middle East can be brought up to equal technological standards with the West, our people will be more content, and a more content populace is less vulnerable to rabble-rousing. However, we must be clever about it. Technology imposed from outside will meet the same fate as anything else. But if important advances are seen to be 'discovered' or 'developed' from within the Middle East, it will be better accepted. Do you see?"

"Makes a weird kind of sense. But again, what do you want us to do?"

"Luke, you are in a position to facilitate my plans. What I want is to see Iran become part of the 10th Cycle treaty. Everyone knows that most of the technological advancement that has occurred in the past five years is thanks to the information found there."

"Wait a minute, buddy," said Luke. "Even if I could do that, and I'm not saying I can, your Ayatollah has already made his feelings well-known on that score. One minute he says the whole thing belongs to Egypt and has to be given back. The next he's saying that the US invented the whole story, and that everything coming out of the library is a satanic plot of infidels to enslave Muslims. How are you planning to overcome that?"

"As I said, it must seem to come from within the Middle East. If our best minds can have access to the library as other scientists do, we can feed the advancements slowly into our culture and soon there will be fewer differences between us. Furthermore, the Rossler Foundation has great influence among manufacturers and researchers now. If they would put us in touch with these entities so that we might negotiate with them to bring their factories and laboratories to our lands, it will put our people to work in well-paying jobs and bring them out of poverty. Soon there will be no resistance at all to the improved technology, for our citizens will be able to afford it through their own labor. They will no longer be enslaved by an ideology that urges them to hate others."

"You're forgetting that the Ayatollah and others are radically opposed to the kind of change you're proposing, Ahmad. How will you persuade them?"

"Here is the crux of why I asked you to meet so quickly. There is much dissatisfaction in my country with the way the Ayatollah handled the virus crisis. Some very influential men now question whether much of the mayhem caused by the virus would have happened, if the Ayatollah had not been delusional about his power and violently opposed to what the West tried to do to help. I have a friend who has told me of a secret group of leaders who have decided that they need to rid the country of Kazemi and those who would follow him. He is a dangerous man, intent on the destruction of the US, which you must agree with me will lead to the destruction of the Middle East."

"They're going to call for an election?" Luke asked.

"They are going to assassinate the Ayatollah," Ahmad

stated. "Within the next twenty-four hours, which is why you must be prepared. Don't bother to ask for details, I don't know them. I know this much only because my lifelong friend, from my schooldays, felt I should know. He believes there may be a reaction that could be dangerous to me while I'm here. I do not know what he thinks may happen, but if I need to know in order to protect myself, then you must need to know as well. I have a deep affection for your President Harper, whose integrity I believe will support my plan for reconstruction of my country. Perhaps his safety is at risk as well."

Luke examined the dapper Persian closely, trying to discern whether that last sentence had been a threat. He could detect no hidden agenda, however. He turned to Lewis and shrugged.

"All I can do is put a bug in Daniel's ear. It will be up to him, whether to cooperate with Ahmad or not. After all, people from his country were trying to blow Daniel up just a couple of weeks ago. But I don't see any downside to an Arab world that is no longer trying to wipe the rest of us out."

Luke failed to notice the look of distaste that Ahmad quickly suppressed when he said 'Arab world'. Had he still been an active field agent, Luke might have remembered that Persians, Ahmad among them, were not Arabs. A common religion lumped them together as Middle Eastern, and a closely-shared genetic heritage had made them all vulnerable to the virus, but Persians were as Caucasian as he himself; those whose blood ran pure.

Lewis was more agitated. Why hadn't Ahmad revealed this information at the beginning of their meeting? There wasn't a moment to spare. He had to inform the president, like *yesterday*.

"I'm sorry, Ahmad, Luke, but I need to leave right now. If Kazemi is assassinated, you know it's going to come home to roost in the White House. It won't matter who takes credit, Iranian leadership and other Arab countries are going to blame either the Israelis or us, and it won't matter which. We're in deep shit."

"Wait, Sam. When can we meet again?" Luke called to a retreating Lewis.

"Can't talk now, I'll be in touch. We'll set it up when this mess is over and if we have survived it."

By the time Sam Lewis was able to catch a commuter hop back to D.C., it was nearly lunchtime and the president's appointments secretary was in no mood to accommodate an emergency request to see him. Lewis arrived in person to demand that the secretary put him through, and Harper happened to hear the commotion.

"What's going on out there?" he called, just before arriving on the scene himself.

"Mr. President, we have another problem." Sam's urgency was manifest; surely the president would take five minutes for him.

"Sam, am I ever going to get to see you when we *don't* have another problem? Come with me. Have you had lunch yet?" Despite his first words, Harper was jovial. He and Sam Lewis had been through some rough times together, and he trusted the man to be truthful when it came to the importance of his errand.

"No, sir," Sam replied. He'd skipped breakfast, too, which thought made his stomach growl in that moment. Harper suppressed a grin.

"Well, you can tell me all about this problem over lunch. We both have to eat, problem or no problem," he said, clapping Sam on the back.

Lewis composed himself to be patient as he followed Harper down the hall into a private dining room. There he found that Mrs. Harper was waiting for her husband.

"Why, hello, Sam," she said. "I didn't know you were joining us. Let me have another place set." Always gracious, she smiled at Sam in welcome.

"I'm sorry to barge in on you, Mrs. Harper. I have a matter of the utmost urgency to convey to the president, and then I'll leave you to have your lunch in peace. No need to set a place for me," Sam said, more than a little embarrassed by the fuss.

"Nonsense, there's plenty. Please sit down." Esther Harper busied herself in directing a server to bring another place setting, as her husband pulled out a chair at her right.

Reluctantly, Lewis took a seat on Mrs. Harper's left, across from the president, knowing that arguing further would just waste more time. He schooled himself to patience again as Harper said grace, and then launched in eagerly as soon as Harper looked at him with raised eyebrows.

"Mr. President, we have information that the Ayatollah Kazemi of Iran is going to be assassinated within the next 24 hours. Probably more like 18, now."

If he had exploded a pipe bomb at the table, it could not have made a bigger impact. Harper jumped to his feet.

"Hank," he yelled to the Secret Service agent at the door. "Get the Chief of Staff in here immediately. Tell him to call the Security Council in on the double."

"Yes, sir," the agent replied, before disappearing through the door, only to be replaced by another agent.

"Lewis, I don't want you to have to repeat yourself. Eat, while you have a chance."

President Harper followed his own advice, eating as quickly as possible as his wife looked on in concern. This happened far too often. Not for the first time, Esther Harper worried that her husband's health was being irreversibly harmed by these constant crises. She did know that his temper was growing shorter, though he seldom let her see it. As he and Sam Lewis finished their hasty meal and left for the conference room where the National Security Council was gathering, Esther prayed for her husband, her nation and the world, in that order.

When his National Security Council was assembled, Harper indicated that Lewis should now repeat his bombshell, and finish telling the story. Lewis began by announcing that they had probably fewer than 18 hours to prevent an assassination attempt on the Ayatollah Kazemi. Before he could go on, the Chairman of the Joint Chiefs of Staff lived up to his reputation by asking why in the world they'd want to prevent it. Harper restrained himself, barely, from calling the man an idiot to his face.

"Who do you think they'll blame?" he asked, in a deceptively mild tone. One more idiotic outburst from this man and he'd have his general's stars.

"Sir, please," said Lewis, impatient to get the rest of it out.

"Go ahead, we'll take that up later," answered the president, staring balefully at the general.

Lewis continued. "We have been informed of a plot planned and to be executed by a new group of men of influence in Iran and possibly other Middle Eastern nations. They have a legitimate beef with Kazemi, but their plan to assassinate him is short-sighted. Unfortunately, we didn't learn of it until today, and it's to take place within the next eighteen hours or sooner. We don't have enough information to intercept the assassin. I suggest we inform the Ayatollah."

Complete silence greeted his words, and then the Secretary of State spoke.

"I doubt that would help," she began, thinking aloud. "They'll consider it a threat rather than a warning. It could even be counterproductive." Sam had to concede the truth in that statement. He was learning that the Secretary of State had a cool and intelligent head on her shoulders.

"Lewis, do we have assets in-country who can be sent as a protective detail?" This from Harper.

"No, sir, not like you mean. Even if we did, I doubt we could get them anywhere near the Ayatollah," Sam said, acutely aware that the best asset they had was at the conference in New York City at the moment, rather than where they needed him.

"Anyone have any ideas? Any at all, even silly ones?" the president asked, looking around the conference table.

"Do we know how this assassination is to take place?" someone asked.

"No," Lewis replied. "Our informant was given the information on a very basic level. He said an old friend told him, so that he could protect himself from any blowback. He's in the States right now, part of the reconstruction conference that you called, sir." The last sentence was directed to Harper.

"Just who is this informant?" blustered the general, who had seen the word 'idiot' on the face of the president, even if the man didn't say it aloud.

"I'm sorry, sir, the man is our asset, and his identity is strictly need-to-know. I don't see any purpose in revealing it." Sam set his jaw. He'd reveal it to this hothead over his own dead body.

The general bristled, but was forestalled from speaking by Harper, who had inherited the Chairman from a predecessor. "I asked for ideas, not a pissing contest." Harper's threat was clear. Stop jockeying for king of the mountain and *think*.

The Secretary of State said, "Sir, I don't think we have time to do anything about this, but it wouldn't hurt to call Israel and warn them. This is going to come back on them or us, and maybe both. All we can do is be prepared and give them a chance to be equally prepared." She had a very good point, which Harper acted on at once.

"Make the arrangements," he directed his own Chief of Staff, who excused himself to do so.

"The way I see it," Harper stated, "our hands are tied. We can't stop it, and if we warn Iran, it looks like a threat. Who else besides Israel needs to know? And will any of them try to warn Iran and make it look like we're the threat anyway? Ideas, people! I need ideas." Not even in the thick of the 9th Cycle virus that had brought the Middle East to the brink of extinction and the world to the brink of nuclear war had the time been so short to act.

A few months previously, a chance encounter with a virus that had survived for millennia in an algae bloom in the depths of a hidden Antarctic valley had resulted in a pandemic that killed nearly two hundred million people across the globe, all of Middle Eastern descent. In the countries comprising the Middle East, almost half of the total population was lost, some countries being harder-hit than others.

The devastation wasn't only to the population; economies were in shambles, infrastructure had failed or was about to. It couldn't have been much worse if nuclear bombs had been dropped on them. In fact, near Iran's border with Afghanistan, several nukes *had* been detonated, the result of an ill-fated attempt on the part of Ayatollah Kazemi of Iran to launch missiles at the US. Losses of life from that disaster and the mass of suicide bombings that took place on the recent Fourth of July accounted for another fifty thousand or more.

Though the virus had been stopped virtually in its tracks by the gene therapy solution found by the Rossler Foundation's virologist, the world was still reeling from the near apocalypse. Harper's hair, a rich brown when he took office six years before, had turned completely white in the past four months. More than anyone, except perhaps Daniel Rossler, he felt the weight of responsibility on his shoulders. He had fewer than two years to bring his country out of the deepest recession since the Great Depression. But, he was fully aware that the fissure between the West and the Middle East was deeper than ever and must be bridged before the peace required for a rebuilding effort to be successful would come to pass.

As the world recovered slowly from the devastation of what came universally to be known as the 9th Cycle Virus, after the nickname the Rossler Foundation expedition to Antarctica used, President Nigel Harper had found himself in the forefront of the call for reconstruction of the hardest-hit countries. The conference in New York City was one of his initiatives to move things in that direction. Now, all that was once again threatened by the new crisis.

"I'm not sure anyone else needs to know, Mr. President. It's highly unlikely that anyone but Israel or the US would be blamed. We may as well get ready for retaliation, rather than worrying about pulling someone else's bacon out of the fire." This came from the Secretary of Defense, with expressions of agreement coming from most of the others in the room.

"Very well. Do we wait until they throw a nuke at us and shoot it out of the air, like last time?" Harper asked, referring to the close call of a few months past.

"Sir," the general said, "with all due respect, I don't like to leave it to luck like that. We've recently installed new technology in our geosynchronous satellites, thanks to your friends the Rosslers. We now have the capability to knock out their electronics so their birds can't fly. Without any harm to life," he hastened to add. The international ban on weaponization of space had tied his hands to a large extent, but he felt that he could justify this technology if called on it.

"What's all this?" Harper asked. He knew he wasn't briefed on every little thing, it would have been impossible to keep up. But this was something he should have known.

"It's called a SEMP," the general answered. "Sustained Electromagnetic Pulse. As I understand it, it doesn't destroy the electronics, unfortunately. But it does confuse them for several minutes each time it's used. We can send a series of these pulses to prevent them launching their missiles. It's a lot less invasive and aggressive, they would in all likelihood not know that we caused the malfunction and will have no reason to direct aggression towards us."

"What'll they think of next?" asked the president, expecting no answer. "Will this protect Israel, too?"

"As long as we can prevent launch of any missile, yes. But, you can't tell them, sir." Blanching at the president's expression, he amended his statement. "Excuse me, sir, I should have said it's classified."

"I won't tell them," growled Harper. Even though he had a good personal relationship with President David Yedidiyah, of Israel, it was fun to rub the man's nose in America's superior technology now and then. Harper still hadn't gotten over the slight that Israel had handed the US a few months before by refusing to allow him to reestablish embassies in Israel after the US embassy in Tel Aviv had been reduced to rubble by a suicide bomber. On the other hand, there was no question that the Mossad was the premier security agency in the world, surpassing even that of the US, though they were darn good, too. He would have liked to brag about this new defense item. *Oh, well, guess I won't get to have fun this time.*

Once again, they were relying on largely untested technology, but the backup plan was the laser technology employed a few months previously. And the back-up plan to that was a preemptive strike with his own nukes. Harper figured he had it covered.

Chapter Five

THIS IS NANOTECHNOLOGY

August 15, 2019; Boulder

In the aftermath of the 9th Cycle virus, when the expedition members returned home, the mood was at first subdued. The Middle East was still in the grip of the virus, although it was loosening. Robert Cartwright had accepted an invitation to join the Foundation on a permanent basis, and had returned to Australia only to get his belongings and say farewell to his mother, who was looking forward to a visit to her son in the US for Christmas. Robert and the electronics engineer and IT specialist for the expedition, Cyndi Self, were living together for the time being.

JR Rossler's bride, Rebecca, who had been the expedition's medical director, had also accepted a permanent position with the Foundation. The four of them spent quite a bit of their leisure time together, as well as working together at headquarters. JR and Robert had become fast friends, and Rebecca and Cyndi liked each other as well. Events in the Middle East seemed far removed from their daily lives in

Boulder after the shock of the suicide bomber had been put behind them.

One night as the four were barbecuing in the Rosslers' back yard, JR asked Robert if he'd ever heard back from his Chilean contact about the strange, light-emitting substance found in Paradise Valley, Antarctica.

"No, and I've lost touch with him. I can't find out what happened, but the rock was returned to me a week or so ago, after being sent to Australia and forwarded here. I'd still like to know what that thing is. I've never seen anything like it." He handed JR the plate of brats to put on the grill.

"It seems a shame to just drop it. Why don't you ask Daniel if you can do some more digging?" JR asked, placing each brat carefully across the grill sideways.

"Maybe I will. I'll give it some thought first, try to come up with someone who may be able to suss it out," said Robert, while watching the flames dance.

A few days later, Robert knocked on Daniel's open door.

"Boss, you got a minute?" he asked, leaning against the doorframe.

"Sure, Robert. What's on your mind? I could use a break from all of this virus paperwork headache." Daniel put down his pen and focused on the Aussie geologist.

"Well, it's kind of trivial in that context, but do you remember that Nyree Dasgupta and I found that crazy rock that shot out laser-like light? The stuff that's lighting the valley?" Robert asked, stepping inside the office.

"Oh, yes, of course. Didn't you send your sample off somewhere?" Daniel gestured for Robert to sit down, but he remained standing.

"Yeah, but I got it back with no explanation, and I still don't have an answer. JR and I were talking about it the other night. Since we didn't get much about 9th Cycle technology out of the ruins, and this stuff might have already been there when the 10th Cyclers got there, we're thinking we maybe should follow up on this. It may be the only thing of value we get out of those two very expensive expeditions." Robert's characterization was an understatement. The expeditions had cost human lives, not just dollars.

"You have a point," Daniel responded. "What did you have in mind?"

"I've an old friend from CalTech, met him while he was on an exchange at the University of Sydney a while back. Name of Mark Hoskins. He's back in Pasadena, and I'd like to show it to him in person and get his recommendation of someone who can take a look at it and figure it out." Now that they were at the crux of the matter, Robert got it all out in one breath.

"You need a place to stay while you're out there, or just the airfare?" Daniel's question revealed that he'd already tacitly approved the plan.

"Let me give him a call and find out," Robert grinned.

"Okay, let Traci, my assistant know. I'll approve it out of discretionary funds, at least until you've got a formal proposal about it."

"Thanks, Daniel. I'll keep you in the loop."

The next day, Robert sat in Mark Hoskins' CalTech office explaining the provenance of the ordinary-looking rock he'd brought with him. When he swore that the rock had been emitting a strong, focused beam of light before Nyree picked it up, and that it had stopped doing so as soon as she touched it, Mark expressed doubt.

"You know, Rob, it isn't April Fool's day. What really brought you out here? Just wanting to see an old friend?"

"You can count on that, mate. But what I'm telling you about this rock is no joke. I'm looking for someone who can explain it, maybe even turn it back on," Robert insisted, turning the rock over and over in his hand.

"This isn't my area of expertise," Hoskins said. "Your guess is as good as mine. This 'rock' looks manmade. I wonder if the light doesn't have something to do with subatomic manipulation of some kind. Let's show it to a kid the physics department recruited for the upcoming semester. He knows more about nanotechnology than anyone on earth, I think." Hoskins reached out his hand and Robert deposited the rock in it.

"Nanotechnology? You really think it could have something to do with that?" Robert asked, inclining his head in the rock's direction.

"We'll never know if we don't ask. Come on, I think he should be in his office." Hoskins got up to lead the way.

A few minutes later, Robert was being introduced to a Roy James, newly-minted PhD out of MIT. Robert knew they were getting younger and younger, but this guy couldn't have been more than about 26 - 28 at the outside.

Even though physics wasn't Robert's specialty, he had a decent understanding of the atomic table. It was his job to know the more common minerals when he saw them, and he understood that some of them differed only by a few protons or electrons from the others. That, however was the extent of it. When it came to creating new elements, which scientists have been doing since 1940, and lining atoms up to miniaturize sophisticated functions on the molecular level, he was in far over his head.

It quickly became apparent that young Roy James was one of the most brilliant people Robert had ever met, even if he was also one of the most socially awkward. In their initial meeting, Roy seemed nervous and gawky, unable to look Robert in the eye or speak without stuttering. Until he heard the story of the rock that Robert and Mark had brought with them. Then he transformed almost miraculously. He asked to examine the rock under the 10th Cycle microscope that had been provided for his lab, and became very excited.

Exhibiting a new ability to speak precisely, he asked Robert to repeat the story. "Where did you say this came from again?"

Robert repeated his explanation, emphasizing that when Nyree picked it up, the light emission stopped, but that before that this small sample was part of a larger pile of the same substance that was emitting thousands of candlepower of focused light which, upon striking the unique mist layer created by the extreme difference between the warmth and humidity of the Antarctic valley and the cold, arid air above the volcanic cone, illuminated the entire valley with reflected light.

"We think there were probably dozens of them located on the shelf level where we found this one, but the discovery was so startling that we decided to bring this one back down and study it rather than try to locate others. It seemed more important at the time," Robert explained. "We think it might have been 9th Cycle technology, but we don't really know. Could have been 10th. I don't know how the valley would have been inhabitable without some kind of light source for the 9th Cyclers, though. It would have to be pitch dark in there except in the height of summer when the sun is high enough overhead to shine down into the valley. And even then, it would be like a cloudy day."

"We have nothing like this today!" Roy enthused. "We couldn't even come close to it! Your physics researchers haven't found anything about it in the 10th Cycle library?" He'd heard of the library, of course. You'd have to have been completely cut off from modern society not to have heard of it by now. But, he'd never had the chance to see the archives.

"Don't know that they're looking for it." Robert responded. "Research is pretty much hit and miss even now. The library is so vast that there don't seem to be enough people to dig everything out quickly. Why?"

"Why?! You're kidding! Do you know what nanotech could do for us?" Roy asked. When he went on, it was clear it had been a rhetorical question. "Just the efficient use of existing resources alone could save billions of dollars! Take my dissertation, for example, 'Nanotechnology: Exploring the Practical Boundaries of Increasing the Capabilities of Electronics Devices While Reducing Weight and Power Consumption'. I speculate that we may be able to create a cell phone that can be inserted in your ear, no larger than a hearing aid that will operate on its initial charge for up to a year. You won't even know it's there until someone speaks in your ear."

Roy seemed so excited by that possibility that Robert hated to point out that something like that could cause traffic accidents galore as startled drivers suddenly heard their wives calling them with a grocery list, or worse, yelling at them for not remembering to take out the garbage. Obviously, there were many gadgets that nanotech could improve; Robert just wasn't sure that a cell phone was one of them. Nevertheless, he caught the gist of Roy's enthusiasm as the other man went on to extol the many benefits of nanotech. That gave Robert an idea.

"When do your classes start, and are you ready?" he asked Roy. Hoskins started to interrupt, but Robert waved him down.

"Middle of September. Yes, all of my lectures are

prepared. I'm just waiting for my research funding to come through before I start my next project. Why?" Roy was still turning the rock over under the microscope, seeking anything that looked like an on-off switch.

"I'd like to arrange to bring you to the Rossler Foundation for a few days. Maybe if you gave a presentation about how important it would be to find 10th Cycle information on this, if any is to be found, someone would start looking for it. We've got a whiz of a data specialist that knows his way around the index better than anyone, name of Raj. You two would get along like a house afire." Hoskins was shaking his head, but neither of the other men noticed.

"I'd love to. Let me make sure it wouldn't violate my contract with the university, and if it can be set up in time for me to start the semester on time, I'll be there." Roy was looking forward to exploring the marvelous 10th Cycle library. Hoskins had a bad feeling about the whole thing. The university may not have their whiz kid for long.

Exchanging contact information, Robert and Roy lost no time in making the visit a reality, with Robert expressing gratitude to Mark for introducing him to the young genius.

"Glad I could do it, Rob. Say, I wouldn't mind an invitation to hear that presentation," Hoskins said, doubting that he'd ever hear it at CalTech, the way things were going.

"Consider yourself invited. I'm sure Daniel and the rest would have no objection. I'll shoot you an email to confirm."

With that, Robert headed back to Boulder, sure that he had just been instrumental in bringing a potentially important line of study to the Foundation.

Robert saw Daniel in his office the next morning with the news that one of the most brilliant nanotech researchers in the country, if not the world, had identified this ancient rock as the most advanced piece of nanotechnology in the world. He was gratified to see that Daniel was suitably impressed.

"I wonder if the manufacturing method is hiding in the library somewhere." Daniel mused. Robert understood him to mean the 10th Cycle library, the only library in which Daniel had interest these days.

"I wouldn't be surprised. JR and I thought it might be 9th Cycle, but even if so, those 10th Cycle blokes would have figured it out, wouldn't they?" Robert was still a little shaky on the history of the 10th Cycle, since it violated a lot of his concepts of time on the historical scale. Geological scale was a different matter. Even the supposed 260,000 year scope of human history was nothing compared to geological epochs.

"Maybe," Daniel said, bringing Robert's attention back to the present. "Do you think there's any value in looking for it, Robert?"

"Roy James certainly thinks so. He's brimming with ideas about the benefits of nanotechnology," Robert hadn't told Daniel yet that he and Roy were already planning for Roy to visit the Foundation headquarters.

"Do you think he'd come and talk to us about that, if you invited him?" Daniel asked.

Robert had a decision to make. Tell Daniel he'd already set that in motion? Or let him believe that it was his idea only and go through the motions of inviting Roy? Everything he knew about Daniel suggested he had no pretentious ego, though, so his answer was easy.

"Already invited him. He's waiting on us to give him a date, but it will have to be in the next couple of weeks. He needs to be back at CalTech for the first day of classes in the new semester." Robert swallowed a nervous gulp. Had he overstepped his authority?

"Good man, Robert. Let me check my calendar."

Daniel named a date in the first week of September, and that worked fine for Roy, so it was set. They invited select scientists in electronics engineering, chemistry, physics and a few who were interested in anything new at all, including Robert himself, JR, Sinclair and Nicholas, plus Robert's friend Mark. Because of its implications for medicine, Rebecca also asked to sit in and to invite Hannah to fly out from Atlanta. Sarah would be there, though her field had no interest in nanotech, as an official representative of the Foundation along with Daniel. Raj, of course, since he would be doing the first search through the translated index for anything related. Sinclair, Nicholas and a few of the staff in the translation and research departments were also invited.

Chapter Six

ALLAH'S HAND HAS STOPPED US TWICE

August 16, 2019; Tehran

Dr. Abbasi was called to the Niavaran Palace, home and headquarters of the Ayatollah Kazemi, at just past midnight, Tehran time, on the morning after his scheduled visit. There, he found Kazemi unresponsive and without a pulse. Alarmed, he attempted resuscitation methods, then called for an ambulance. The Ayatollah had suffered a massive heart attack and must be rushed to a hospital and intensive care immediately.

Three hours later, a weary Abbasi entered a waiting room where many of the Ayatollah's closest followers and lieutenants were pacing. One of them rose to meet him.

"Will he recover?" Dr. Abbasi would have preferred to give the news he must give in his own time and on his own terms. Because he was caught unprepared, the news came baldly.

"No, I'm afraid not. The Ayatollah has passed to another plane. Which of you will contact the media?"

Abbasi looked around the room at the group of people who had suddenly grown silent.

His question went unanswered as those of the faithful who believed Kazemi to be the 12th Imam sent up a ululation of grief. Confusion reigned. Some individuals among those closest to Kazemi automatically began to plan and prepare for burial, since Shariah law required burial to take place as soon as possible. Others felt that it was entirely possible the Ayatollah would rise from the dead, if he were indeed the 12th Imam, and therefore nothing should be done for several days, even though it would break with tradition. Dr. Abbasi was horrified at the thought, particularly because embalming was forbidden. In any case, embalming would have corrupted the body so that if Kazemi did, against all reason, return to life - no, it was impossible.

In the midst of the unseemly arguments taking place at the hospital, the Ayatollah Khorasani, the person most likely to step into Kazemi's nominal role as adviser to the government, arrived. As soon as he had taken in the situation, he took the doctor aside.

"Is it possible that my brother was poisoned?" he asked. Dr. Abbasi paled, realizing that he had been the last to administer medicines to Kazemi and would come under suspicion.

"No, surely not, Aqa," he said, affording the other the title of respect. "I examined him myself not twelve hours ago. He showed no sign of distress at that time. This sort of cardiac event cannot be predicted accurately. I have told the Ayatollah in the past that he must avoid stress, but, as you know, he has been unable to do so."

"How can we be sure?" answered Khorasani.

"Sure of what?" one of Kazemi's followers asked, approaching just in time to hear the question.

"Sure that the master has not been poisoned," answered Khorasani, well aware that once the notion was out, some would take up the cry.

"Poisoned!" said the follower, loud enough for others to hear. Within minutes, the doctor was beset with demands to answer Khorasani's question. "How can we be sure?"

With dread, Abbasi answered the only way he could. "An autopsy would tell us." Abbasi knew full well that the idea would not be well received. It would be considered a desecration of the body, even more so when the body was that of a religious leader. Nevertheless, the question had been raised, and the only way to dispel it would be to autopsy the great man's body.

Khorasani, anticipating the answer, had a follow-up question. "Would it not be possible to perform blood tests without an autopsy?"

Abbasi pounced on the suggestion with alacrity. "Oh, yes, Aqa, that would be a way to begin. I will order it immediately." Later, he would wonder why he had volunteered to hasten the time of his interrogation.

It took no time at all to run the tests Abbasi ordered, since the lab was instructed to put these tests ahead of all others. When the results were made known, there was little of interest. However, a sharp-eyed lab technician did note that there was a higher level of sodium chloride in the blood than he would have expected. Unfortunately for Abbasi, the technician took his results directly to Khorasani, who, since Kazemi had yet to rise from the dead, hoped to succeed him. Khorasani questioned the technician closely.

"What does this result mean?" Khorasani asked, watching closely for any sign of untruth in the technician.

"It could mean nothing. Or it could mean that an overdose of potassium chloride was administered to the Ayatollah. The substance would break down in the blood stream, causing a heart attack from the overdose of potassium. Meanwhile, the chlorine molecules would join with the body's naturally-occurring sodium to form sodium chloride, hence an elevated level in the blood." The technician spoke theoretically, unaware of the storm that his words would stir up.

Khorasani took a few moments to consider this. By now he had learned that Abbasi had attended Kazemi the previous afternoon to give him various routine injections. It would have been easy for one of them to be the substance that would kill Kazemi within twelve hours. There was only one way to find out.

"Bring Abbasi to me," he ordered his new followers.

Abbasi begged to be spared. His thought that he would be blamed had turned out to be prophetic, but he had no defense. It was he who had injected the Ayatollah. It was probably by his hand that the poison had been administered, but how? His desperate mental search for answers was made more difficult by the torture. If he had known, he would have given the information as soon as he was tied to the chair and struck repeatedly, but he didn't know.

It was only hours later, after having several toenails forcibly ripped out while chained spread-eagled to a table, that the doctor transcended his agony long enough to remember. The syringes had been prepared and handed to him by his assistant. Had the doctor not been tortured, he may have declined to throw his assistant under the bus, but he had no other ideas, and the pain of the treatment drove all thoughts but those of self-preservation from his mind.

The relief obtained from giving an answer didn't last

long. Although the torture ceased, the doctor was left to remain chained to the table without medical attention while his assistant was located and brought to the Palace. His condition was intended to frighten the assistant into talking without resorting to the same methods, though the questioners wouldn't hesitate to use them if necessary.

Kasra Turani entered the torture chamber with apprehension, which turned to terror when he saw his employer strapped to a table by means of iron chains. Those who gave him his instructions did not warn him that the doctor would probably be tortured. However, they had provided him with the means to an end to his own torture. As soon as the beating stopped, he pled for mercy and said what he had been told to say.

"Yes, I gave the doctor a syringe that someone else gave to me. I did not know that the Ayatollah would die! Please, they threatened my wife and children." His terror lent truth to his words, and he was believed.

"What did you think would happen to the Ayatollah?" the questioners asked. The stern voices left Kasra no doubt what would happen to him.

"I did not know! I asked, and they would not say - only that my wife and daughters would be harmed if I did not. What was I supposed to do?" Kasra's wails fell on unsympathetic ears.

"Has your family been returned to you?" they asked. One of them knew the answer. It had been he who took the man's family in the first place.

"Not yet. Please, allow me to leave. I must be there when my family returns." Tears fell from Kasra's eyes as he pictured his wife, defenseless after he was gone. Only the same denial of certain death that allows a man to live his life in peace maintained the glimmer of hope that it would be all right.

"Of course. We'll escort you there. First, we must take care of a small matter."

Turani did not ask what came next. He was too frightened by the doctor's condition to do anything but what his handlers had told him to do, and now what the men who held him prisoner wanted. If he was surprised when they took him to the headquarters of NIRT, National Iranian Radio and Television, he did not say so. Nor did he question it when he was put on a sound stage in handcuffs and told to look at a red dot.

One of his questioners took his place beside Turani. When the signal came that the feed was live, the questioner began his interview. Turani followed the leading questions without hesitation.

"Kasra Turani, you are here under arrest because of your actions of yesterday at the Niavaran Palace. You have previously confessed your crimes to us, is that correct?" A bright light was in his eyes, so Kasra could not see his questioner.

"Yes, sir. I have begged mercy, because I was forced to do what I did." He'd been told to say these words, and he followed his instructions to the letter.

"And what did you do, exactly, for the record?"

Kasra hung his head, terribly ashamed of his actions, though he'd felt he had no choice. "I substituted a syringe with a liquid that was unknown to me for one of Ayatollah Kazemi's regular injections."

"And did you expect that liquid to cause the Ayatollah's death?" The questions were now sterner, and this one hadn't been asked in this way before. He wasn't sure what to say. He settled for the truth.

"No sir! I asked the purpose, but the people who forced me to do this would not say."

"How did they force you?"

"They threatened my wife and children, sir. I could not let them be harmed," he said, understanding belatedly that by putting his wife and children ahead of the Twelfth Imam, he'd signed his own death warrant. What could he have done otherwise, though? If someone were to die for his actions, better himself than them.

"You acted on the order of others, is that correct?" On and on came the questions. Kasra wanted to close his eyes, lie down and forget what he'd done, but they wouldn't let him.

"Yes sir," he answered.

"And these others, did you know them? Would you be able to identify them?" This had been asked before. They knew the answer. Why were they asking him all these questions again?

"No sir, they wore masks," he answered, barely loud enough to be heard.

"Did this not make you wonder if the Ayatollah would be harmed?" Yes, of course it did. But that wasn't the correct answer.

"Please, sir, no, I was too worried about my wife and family." And because of his love for them, he was surely going to die. He only hoped he would be able to see them once again before his execution.

"Very well. Was Dr. Abbasi aware of this substitution?"

"No sir. I concealed the real medicine in my clothing, and handed him a syringe that looked like the normal medicine."

"Are you prepared to answer for your crimes?"

Turani wondered briefly what answer would be required

of him, but since he was following the lead of the questioner, he answered after only a brief hesitation.

"Yes sir."

"Then you shall be reunited with your wife and children," the questioner said at last. Hope surged in Turani's heart.

Watching the TV screen from his table, Abbasi's eyes widened in terror as he saw the man with the sword approach from behind Turani, but in the torture chamber, surrounded by other secret police, he did not make a sound, fearful for his own life.

On hearing the words of his questioner, Turani's relief was evident, right up until the time his head flew from his shoulders. Turani didn't even have time to wonder if those who had captured his family would make good on their promise of payment, so that his wife would be compensated for his death. The live feed from NIRT was broadcast immediately, and then uploaded on YouTube for the repeat viewing of those who could stomach it.

Abbasi was now a loose end. He met his fate only half an hour later, and by the same sword. However, the man who had ordered Kazemi's death was a man of honor in his own way. Turani's widow and children received sufficient payment to live in luxury wherever they wanted.

Before the hour was up, Ayatollah Khorasani also made a live broadcast. To no one's surprise, he immediately pointed his finger at the United States and Israel as the potential culprits who put the unfortunate physician's assistant up to his crime. His rhetoric was even more extreme and bombastic than the late Ayatollah Kazemi's had been, though Khorasani did not attempt to claim the title of the Twelfth Imam at that time. By the time he had stopped speaking, he had mortally offended most of the non-Middle Eastern countries in the world, and had half-committed Iran and its allies to a declaration of war.

Khorasani's words and actions ignored the unfortunate fact that the 9th Cycle virus had wiped out over half of the population of his country before it could be stopped through the generosity of Western countries that had supplied a gene therapy for it. The government was in chaos because many key officials had succumbed to the virus, and others were still recuperating from being near death. The President had been one of the victims, and elections were due to be held in a few weeks. However, an even more important election must now be held. The Assembly of Experts, the body of Islamic theologians that was charged with electing, and if necessary removing, the Supreme Leader of Iran, must name a replacement for the late Ayatollah Kazemi. No one doubted that Khorasani aspired to the post, and few doubted that he would achieve it.

It is a fact that may seem peculiar to citizens of the West. The President of Iran, although the highest official that is elected by popular vote, is not the head of state. He answers, in fact, to the Supreme Leader. Having both offices empty at once in this case was a disaster. To fill the gap before elections could take place, Parliament took it upon itself to name General Ali Armand, the Chief of Defense, interim president, rather than follow the constitutional line of succession. Since war with the West seemed inevitable if not imminent, it was considered prudent to have a man of war heading the interim government.

The first election to take place was within the Assembly

of Experts, naturally, since it didn't require campaigning, a decision of the general populace or the attendant bureaucratic hubbub. By Iranian constitution, the Assembly met every six months to perform various administrative functions, among them to maintain a list of potential candidates for the office of Supreme Leader in the case of death, disability to perform the functions of the office, or removal of the incumbent. Consequently, they had a ready pool of candidates. It only remained to consult among themselves and take a vote.

Constitutionally, candidates for Supreme Leader must possess qualities of Islamic scholarship, justice, piety, right political and social perspicacity, prudence, courage, administrative facilities and adequate capability for leadership. The Assembly must elect anyone who meets these criteria but also stands out in one or more of the qualifications. Because of Khorasani's quick actions to determine Kazemi's true cause of death and his proactive political leadership, he was the natural candidate and was already on the list from the last meeting of the Assembly. It was quick work for the Assembly to meet in emergency session and elect him, which took place only a few days after Kazemi's death.

Khorasani wasted no time in taking over the reins of government. He approved the appointment of General Armand and called the man into his office to direct him to declare war on 'all enemies of Islam', a vague term he intended to mean anyone who wasn't Muslim. Armand was no match for Khorasani on any front. His initial protest was that Iran was in no shape to wage war against even an army of children fighting with wooden swords, after the virus and the nuclear incident that had taken place several months before. Seeing that his words fell on deaf ears and being a soldier rather than a politician, however, Armand followed orders. That very day, he ordered what was left of his military to prepare for war, and to take up the offers of replacement nuclear warheads and missiles from their allies, North Korea and Pakistan.

September 1, 2019; Iran

The rag-tag assembly of nuclear specialists in the Iranian Army, their numbers also halved at least by the virus, took inventory. Half of their former inventory had been expended in the futile attack on Israel and the US during the height of the medical crisis. Another fifteen percent had failed at launch, causing the nuclear explosions to occur over their own territory. Now only one-third of their former inventory was left; not enough to seriously threaten even Israel, their first target.

When this was reported to Armand, he contacted North Korea and Pakistan, requesting that they make good on their promises to supply extra weapons. The attack he intended to launch was put off to give their allies time to transport the necessary items to Sirjan, where emergency construction of launch facilities were taking place, Qom having been destroyed when the missiles there had blown up just before launch during the previous attempt to nuke Israel.

Armand had a bad feeling about all of this, but, being fond of his head, he kept his opinions to himself. All he could do was place the missile site prudently far away from Tehran. Although it was relatively convenient to the Pakistani border, it was far enough away from the Afghan border to avoid a repeat of the embarrassing and disastrous failure of one of the missiles that had managed to launch in the spring. Diplomatic relations with Afghanistan had been seriously strained by that incident, which rendered the Iranian city of Tayyebat and much of the western area of northern Afghanistan uninhabitable for decades to come.

Naturally, it was almost impossible to keep Iran's intentions secret. No sooner than the nature of the construction project in Sirjan was detected, The US moved its counter-strike satellites into geosynchronous orbit. Other satellites were tasked to follow the progress of certain heavily-laden trains heading southeast from North Korea toward the Middle East. Iran might manage to deploy nuclear weapons, but they would not be able to do so undetected. Ironically, Iran's military did not know it.

A massive effort among Iranian workers and others imported from allied countries made the launch site ready in only six weeks, just in time to receive the materiel. Before they could deploy, the nuclear specialists insisted upon a dry run to test the missiles without warheads or fuel. In other words, they would test the electronics only, in order to preserve what numbers they had. On the day of the test, the specialists were baffled to see that nothing worked. From the ignition sequence to the electronics that would deploy the warhead when the target was reached, everything was as dead as the late lamented Ayatollah Kazemi.

They were at a loss to explain it. Other experts were sent for, from as far away as North Korea and Russia. Several days after the test failures, foreign experts arrived to inspect the electronics. After running several more sophisticated tests, the experts agreed that the only explanation was that the equipment had been damaged by electromagnetic interference, such as a massive solar flare. What didn't make sense was that the surrounding countryside and the city had escaped the same damage. If it had been a solar flare, the experts would have expected that the power grid would also be knocked out, at the very least. Moreover, no record of such a flare existed.

Exasperated at this setback, the military set about replacing the damaged parts as quickly as they could obtain supplies. Word of the failure was suppressed, except in certain circles. The administrative members of Ayatollah Khorasani's household were among those who were informed, among them Ahmad Ahmadi, a holdover from Kazemi's tenure. Ahmad had certain suspicions about not only this failure, but the disasters that overtook the previous spring's nuclear launch. He had no doubt that the US had found a way to deflect the blowback from Kazemi's assassination, thanks to his early warning. However, as maddening as it was that his assessment of the relative military strength of his country to the US was correct, it afforded him an opportunity to set his agenda in motion.

His first visit was to his leader, Ayatollah Khorasani. Carefully, he explained his belief that a war against the West would not have a successful outcome, citing as an example the debacle at Sirjan. Then he explained his vision of duping the West into reconstructing Iran and the rest of the Middle East while giving over the secrets and educational opportunities that would bring them firmly into the twenty-first century. Khorasani was an intelligent man despite his rigid religious views. What Ahmadi was saying made perfect sense. With his permission and encouragement, Ahmadi was ushered into the presence of General Armand and other political leaders to lay out his plans once more.

"Mr. President-General Armand, distinguished gentlemen. I am here today to convey a message from Ayatollah

Khorasani. He bade me tell you that Allah has spoken. Twice we have attempted to visit jihad upon our enemies, Israel and America. Twice, Allah's hand has stopped us. We must now listen with our brains instead of with our hearts. Allah wants us to concentrate on building up our strength, rebuilding our lands and infrastructure, raising our people from poverty and deprivation. Only when we have achieved equality with the West will we be in a position to challenge their greed and apostasy. We must now humble ourselves to seek alliance with the West instead of fighting."

Expressions of shock were all that Ahmadi could see on the faces of his audience. It would take more than this one speech to bring them on board, but with the authority of the Supreme Leader behind him, a vote to call a hiatus to the war was passed overwhelmingly. Now Ahmad would have time to persuade them individually to his cause. Armed with a letter from Khorasani, he first met with key individuals within the eighty members of the Assembly of Experts, to assure them that his plan did not represent turning away from the teachings of the Quran, but rather adoption of certain strategies that, carefully restricted to those whose heads would not be turned, would bring prosperity to their country. That prosperity would in turn feed the preparations for the real agenda: total world dominance. With approval from the most influential members, assuring him that Khorasani would remain in power for the foreseeable future, he next went to General Armand.

Ahmad Ahmadi was received as an honored guest by Armand. His reputation as a valuable asset to the late Ayatollah Kazemi preceded him, and Armand was pleased to host the spokesman of the current Supreme Leader. Ahmad set Armand's mind at ease by telling him first that he didn't bring instructions from the Supreme Leader, but rather more information about the plan of which he'd spoken in his speech to Parliament. Armand composed himself to listen, though his expertise was in matters of military implications, not those of peace and subterfuge.

"General Armand, my congratulations on your appointment as interim president. May I ask if you aspire to the election on a more permanent basis?"

"Not at all. I'm no politician, and if you and the Supreme Leader have your way, my presence in this office will be of no value. I do not say this in bitterness. On the contrary, I will be glad to get back to the business that I understand best, even if that business has no immediate relevance."

"Do not worry, General Armand. I can assure you that within a few years, your assistance in rebuilding our military strength will be of the utmost importance. Let me tell you of our plans."

Ahmad began by stating his belief that Iran must find a way to modernize everything except those things dictated by Sharia law, that is, the manner of dress of women and so forth. As for the rest, they must allow their scientists to explore the most up-to-date discoveries, including those associated with the 10th Cycle Library. They must attract foreign investment by inviting international corporations to move their operations into Iran, and assure them that their facilities and administrators would be safe and that they would receive big tax incentives to do so. They must encourage the education of both children and adults to a standard equal to those of Western nations.

"You want to westernize our country?" asked Armand, shocked.

"Not at all. I want to adopt such technology as we require to achieve prosperity. Once that is achieved, I want to Islamize the West, to coin a phrase." Ahmad stopped talking to let the general's understanding catch up.

Armand's shock turned to admiration as he beheld the big picture. "This will require a level of intrigue that would rival any harem of old," he joked.

"Indeed. Only certain people will be granted the knowledge of our eventual intentions. We must carefully select those who will lead these efforts, for it will be tempting to them to wholeheartedly adopt a Western way of life. They must be beyond such temptation, devout Muslims who understand our purpose and can carry it out without becoming seduced. Janaab, you are the first to receive this honor." The flattery would keep Armand from the temptation of talking to people he shouldn't. If not, he and anyone who shouldn't be privy to the plans were expendable.

One by one, Ahmad visited other members of Parliament until he had the buy-in required to set the next step in motion. He then requested that Khorasani direct Armand to name him Director of Reconstruction, giving him plenary power to act on his plans.

Chapter Seven

THIS IS WHAT YOU CAN DO WITH NANOTECHNOLOGY

1st week of September, 2019; the Rossler Foundation in Boulder

Roy arrived the evening before his presentation and was entertained at dinner by the Rosslers, Daniel and Sarah, with the other guests being JR and Rebecca, and Robert and Cyndi. Seated between Sarah and Rebecca, Roy seemed uncomfortable despite the best efforts of the women to draw him out. Rebecca, with an interest in psychology watched him carefully for clues to his behavior. When she or Sarah addressed Roy, he seemed to freeze for a moment, before stammering a reply without looking at them. However, when one of the men brought up a topic, he conversed easily. Rebecca decided Roy was extremely shy, especially around women. Roy could have told her that it was worse than that, if only he could have brought himself to speak to her.

Roy's presentation the next morning began with the history of nanotechnology, which to the surprise of everyone else in the room began centuries ago, with the processes that artists used to create stained glass windows. Of course, those artists had no idea that the processes actually changed the molecular structure of the gold and silver particles they used to enhance their colors. In fact, he went on to say, the modern notion of manipulating matter on an atomic or molecular level was introduced in 1959, by a scientist named Richard Feynman speaking at his own university, CalTech. It was during that speech that he described the process he envisioned. However, it wasn't until 1981 that scientists had a tool to even see anything as small as an individual atom.

As his audience began to shift in their seats, Roy finally got to the exciting part. Taking out the rock that Robert had showed him, he did something with his hands that no one could see. To the shock and amazement of his audience, a bright blue-white light shot out of the top of the rock and splashed across the ceiling.

"You are looking at an ancient form of nanotechnology, the light source from Paradise Valley in Antarctica. I appreciate Robert Cartwright bringing it to my attention, along with the thought that there may well be important information about this fascinating field within the 10th Cycle library. This is only a sample of what nanotechnology can do," Roy said, switching on the overhead projector to display his slide show.

With slide after slide in the PowerPoint presentation, Roy described the multitude of uses envisioned for nanotech. In medicine, countless applications that required something small enough to target damaged cells without further damaging healthy ones, as well as delivery methods that could cross the blood/brain barrier without harm. In delivery of electronic charges to devices as diverse as cell phones, solar cells and fuel cells at a higher level and lower cost. Batteries that would remain fully charged for decades, or that could be recharged in a matter of seconds. Each time he mentioned a different field, one or two or several scientists sat up, intrigued at the implications to their own research. Better air quality? Cleaner water? More economical exploration of space? Nanotechnology, claimed Roy, had an application for all of them, and more.

Basically, he said, they could group the current research into three categories; real and already in use nanotech, ideas in the making which would most probably be developed over the next few years, and science fiction - ideas which could be possible, but no one knew how yet. Then he reminded them that many scientific discoveries started off just in that way. After looking at the rock he got from Robert, in fact, he wasn't sure what was sci-fi and what wasn't anymore.

Perhaps the most surprising was the part of his presentation where he explained where nanotech was already in use, over 1,300 applications and growing at three to four per week. Not everyone was happy at all of the uses. Nanotech in manipulation of food was something that Sarah and a few others deeply distrusted, but the mothers among them couldn't fault using carbon nanotubes for stain-resistant clothing that needed no ironing. Nano-medicine had some controversy surrounding it, Rebecca knew, but Hannah was highly intrigued about the use of nanomaterials to deliver therapies to only diseased cells. Perhaps the same method could be used to deliver gene therapy, her pet cause.

It was a tribute to his breadth of knowledge and enthusiasm for the subject that Roy was able to hold the attention of his entire audience for a full three hours. By the end of the presentation, both he and the audience were emotionally wrung out by the dazzling implications. Daniel knew that there would be no stopping some of the Foundation-employed scientists from abandoning their current projects or enhancing them with nanotech research. Roy invited questions from the audience, which he answered as best he could, although he was not an expert in many of the fields represented and he had difficulty forming a sentence when he was answering a query from a woman.

The bombshell came, as usual, from JR. "How can nanotechnology be used in warfare?" he asked.

A ripple went through the room as the shocked Rosslerite scientists considered what he was saying. The world had settled down somewhat in the two months since the 4th of July attacks, as well as the suicide bombing attempt of the Rossler Family on the 25th July and the terrorist groups responsible had been largely dismantled to the best of their knowledge. No one wanted to contemplate war, much less be involved in research concerning military applications. Seeing that his question had been misunderstood, JR clarified.

"I know that the Rossler Foundation will only pursue peaceful research and development," he said. "But, we aren't the only ones doing research, obviously. There may be others out there already doing research along those lines. Wouldn't it be better to know what it may be? What's possible, so we can be prepared?"

Roy was glad to have the chance to talk longer about his favorite subject.

"Well, there are already some applications being developed that may interest you. Is anyone here a Trekkie?" Many of the scientists laughed at the reference to fans of the old TV series Star Trek, and a few sheepishly raised their hands. Fans of the series were known to be nerds and kooks, but the truth was that many a science career was born of an interest in the fabulous devices and concepts of the future that the writers had introduced. What Roy had to say next wowed them.

"How about a cloaking device? Nanotechnology has the potential to make it possible, and it is common knowledge that military research is focusing on such things as cloaking technology, laser-type weapons that resemble phasers and even replicators. After all, Feynman's original idea was that millions of tiny manufacturing devices would be able to make anything they were programmed to. Why not replicate food out of its component atoms, for example? Or even Earl Grey tea? DARPA is already working on a truck that will reconfigure itself into a helicopter, like the Transformers in the movies.

"Most chilling is this. When you manipulate molecular and atomic structure, the resulting material exhibits new properties. It may soon be possible to manufacture a nuclear weapon the size of a can of Coke that has the destructive capability of a Hiroshima-type bomb. The same capability to deploy medicine could be used to deploy toxic substances."

The formerly exuberant mood in the room was changed almost immediately to discomfort and dread. How would the Foundation be able to research beneficial applications of nanotechnology without potentially letting more deadly capability out into the world? Obviously, it was a matter for Board discussion before any research projects were approved.

Daniel was grateful that Raj had suggested filming the presentation. Luke wasn't there, but he needed to know what had been discussed. Security for super-sensitive research would obviously have to be beefed up or invented.

The whole question could wait until the next meeting of the Board, though. They were to take up several proposals from scientists who were seeking Foundation funding, and those would be considered first. Daniel had no doubt that a couple of them would be modifying their requests after this presentation. In anticipation of finding something in the library that pertained to nanotech, he called Luke in.

"Luke, I'd like you to watch the recording of the presentation of that young hotshot scientist that Robert brought in. As usual, JR has opened a can of worms, but he's right. We need to be prepared. Let me know what you think."

Four hours later, Luke was at Daniel's door, white as the snow that would soon cover the nearby 14,000-foot peaks. "Is he kidding? Nuclear weapons the size of a can of Coke?"

"I'm afraid not, Luke. So here's where you come in. I doubt that we should prevent all nanotech research. From what Dr. James said, there are just too many benefits. If we find anything in the library, we're going to have to allow research to exploit it. But, as you saw, some of it will be a double-edged sword, especially the medical stuff. I need you to come up with a protocol that will keep the dangerous stuff out of the hands of anyone but those with the highest security clearance we have. And we need to develop a system of clearances like the government has. How quickly can you put that in place?"

"I've got some ideas, let me think on it for a day or two and give you a proposal."

"You've got it," Daniel said. "I can see this blowing up in our faces if we aren't on top of it."

Chapter Eight

THE PRESIDENT'S SPEECH

November 11, Veteran's Day, 2019; Washington, D.C.

Despite the unrest in the Middle East, the continuing annoyance of an underground regime intent on throwing their inadequate munitions against the West and even a personal attack on a close friend of Harper's, things had been quiet for nearly six weeks now. Delegations of Iranian leaders with milder words had traveled to D.C. to speak with Harper and offer conciliation.

On a day that was sacred to Americans, especially the military, the president was expected to make a speech. He had thought long and hard about it, and had even called his friend Daniel Rossler to give him a heads-up about what it would contain. Daniel had been aghast.

"Nigel, are you kidding? Those people can't be trusted! Why, it's only been a couple of months since they tried to blow me up, along with my family and dozens of innocent bystanders. They did kill over two dozen! What are you thinking?" Daniel's agitated pacing made his words jerky, and Harper could visualize his friend as he strode from one end of his office to the other.

"I'm thinking that it has to come to an end, Daniel. I've spoken to the leaders that are in power now. Those things happened on someone else's watch. We need to be the bigger man. Will you trust me?" Harper, arguably the most powerful man in the country, held his breath. It was important to him that Rossler agreed.

"Nigel, you've been a friend for years. We've been through a lot together. I know you're a good man, and I trust your judgment. You know I won't oppose you, but can I just say I'll take it under advisement?"

"Of course, Daniel. I hope you'll be listening." Harper figured that Daniel would come around, because he knew his friend to be a man of reason and good will. Asking him to forgive the recent attack on his family may be premature, but the time was right for this announcement. He'd just have to wait and see whether his friend was ready or not.

Harper took the podium in the room reserved for news media, the deep blue of the background contrasting with his silver hair to good advantage. World response to the next few minutes' communication would dictate whether his administration would be seen by posterity as the greatest recovery in US history, or the greatest failure. That didn't concern him, though. Harper was of a breed not seen since early in the country's youth, a man whose principles were unwavering, who truly put the good of the people before political advantage.

"My fellow Americans, members of the press, citizens of the world. As you know, we are just beginning to emerge from the most disastrous double crisis in history. Even now, people are still dying from either the last vestiges of the H10N7 virus, nuclear radiation, or injuries sustained in suicide bombings all over the world. My brothers and sisters in humanity, this did not need to happen.

"It is true that the virus was set loose by accident, and that we might not have been able to prevent great loss of life. However, we all made grave mistakes in the wake of the panic. Had we worked together from the beginning, much of the pain and suffering might have been avoided. Had we been less willing, even eager, to take up arms against each other, those who died from causes other than the virus might be alive today. None of that matters now; we cannot change what has occurred, only what may occur in the future. Casting blame will not cure our broken world."

Harper paused for a moment, to sip the water that had been placed on the podium for that purpose. A small stir in the audience caught his attention as he drew breath to continue, but the would-be interrupters were quelled by their neighbors, or perhaps by the stern look he gave them. The next part of his speech contained the meat, as well as some hard-fought quotes from the Bible, which his speech-writers had advised him to leave out. He no longer had patience for the political correctness that had all but erased the 'under God' from the Pledge of Allegiance. Nor did he any longer have to answer to petty groups who sought to gain their freedom of speech at the cost of his. He would speak his mind unfettered by those constraints.

"I am here today, with the full support of my counterparts in the major European nations as well as Canada and Australia, to call for a global effort to put an end to the skirmishes that continue to plague world peace. I call on Muslims and Christians, Hindus and Buddhists, all the religions of the world, in fact, to examine the core of their teachings and find charity in their hearts for those whose religion may be different, but whose humanity is the same. I call on East, West and every nation of the world to lay down their arms, their ideologies and their resentments, to work instead to build up those of our neighbors and fellow travelers on this globe who have lost everything. Let it be as Isaiah prophesied: '*And they will hammer their swords into plowshares and their spears into pruning hooks. Nation will not lift up sword against nation, and never again will they learn war.*'"

Once again Harper was forced to pause, this time by thunderous applause in the media room. He would not realize until he saw the recorded playback of his live speech that, in the final sentence he uttered, his voice had taken on the tones of a great orator, ringing out richly in his conviction that this was the right thing to do. Moments passed before the applause died down enough for him to continue.

"Only months ago, I asked you, my fellow Americans, to rise to the occasion, to do the right thing. You have worked tirelessly. Your sacrifices will continue as we dig deeply into our pockets to rebuild those who would destroy us. And yet, we must. If we turn our backs now, we are not the great nation our forefathers envisioned. We must lead the way. And we will reap the reward, for Isaiah also said, "*The fruit of that righteousness will be peace; its effect will be quietness and confidence forever.*" And again, "*My people will live in peaceful dwelling places, in secure homes, in undisturbed places of rest.*" This I desire for you, for all of us. This shall we accomplish if we put our hearts into it."

A smattering of applause threatened to break out, but Harper held up his hand for silence.

"I have just one more thing to say. I urge all peace-loving nations, all nations who want to see an end to endless warfare and to destruction of their lands and people and even nations whose ideology has previously led them in the direction of war; lay down your arms and send your representatives to the UN. Even those who are not members will be welcome if they come in peace and good faith. Together, let us work to devise a global reconstruction plan that is fair and balanced, without regard for ideologies. Let us all go forward in peace and prosperity, that we may no longer have hatred for each other."

Harper stood, his head bowed, remaining at the podium while applause buffeted him. Many of the very nations he knew needed the most help were not members of the UN. Others, perhaps, had lost faith in that institution, but he knew of no other with the required infrastructure to pull off this summit meeting to end all summit meetings. Had he succeeded in his mission? The final arbiter of the success of his Administration would be the way it was written in the history books, and then he would know.

When the last echo of applause had died away, and the last question had been answered, Harper made his way heavily to his quarters within the White House, where he was met by his wife of three decades, Esther. She put her hand along his cheek and examined his face closely.

"You were magnificent," she whispered.

Chapter Nine

LET US BE FRIENDS

November 18, 2019; Washington, D.C.

Toward the end of the most disastrous year in human history, Ahmad Ahmadi, CIA code named "Arsalan", contacted Director Lewis of the CIA, not in his capacity as a CIA asset, but in his new role as Director of Reconstruction of Iran.

"It's good to hear from you, Arsalan. You've done well for yourself since we last spoke. To what do I owe the honor?" Lewis asked. The last time he'd spoken to this man, Arsalan had declared his intention of working in the background. Now he was calling as an important government official.

"If only I had been able to keep to my intention of staying in the background," Arsalan answered. "These new duties limit my capacity to work for reform in some ways. However, in others, it helps to have the power bestowed upon me. It's just that I have to work twice as hard to persuade key players that my suggestions are to

The Sword of Cyrus

our advantage." It was almost as if he'd read Lewis's mind.

Lewis didn't see how there were any limits to Arsalan's reform efforts. Already, those efforts had resulted in quite a few international corporations planning to situate manufacturing facilities in Iran. Nevertheless, he was willing to wait patiently for Arsalan to get to his reason for calling.

"I'm sure you're doing all you can, Arsalan," he said, hoping it would move the smooth preliminaries along and make Arsalan get to his point.

"I am doing my best. This brings me to the reason for my call. You are aware that our reconstruction efforts are hindered in many ways by the lack of new technology coming out of the 10th Cycle Library?" Arsalan's tone made it a question.

"I hadn't thought much about it. Why is that?" Lewis was genuinely puzzled.

"Only nations that have signed the 10th Cycle Treaty and sent representatives to the Rossler Foundation Board are given the technology. Surely you must know this." Now Arsalan sounded impatient, as if Lewis's ignorance was wasting his time.

"I suppose I did. As I said, I haven't thought much about it."

"And surely you know that countries belonging to the region you call the Middle East were not given the opportunity to sign the treaty," Arsalan persisted. Lewis began to get an inkling of what the call was about.

"And why was that, Arsalan? Do you recall what leaders in your country were saying and doing back then?" The accusation put him back on even ground.

"Of course, Director Lewis. However, times have changed. We have eliminated the radicals and our new leaders are favorably disposed toward the West. Even your president has urged the cooperation of the Western nations in helping us to rebuild. We come now with our hands outstretched in friendship, to humbly beg the opportunity to join the treaty members. Other nations in my region are similarly disposed." Arsalan had rehearsed the last two sentences until they didn't sound like a plea, but more of an expectation.

"Of course you know it isn't up to me," said Lewis. Why was Arsalan calling him in the first place?

"Yes, of course. But you have the president's ear, and he is a friend of Daniel Rossler. Perhaps you can hint to the president that his assistance would be most appreciated." Ah, the reason, finally. Lewis wondered if Arsalan was unaware that his old handler Luke was the uncle of Rossler's wife. That would have been a more direct route. Although, it may not have had the desired result.

"That's all?" Lewis asked.

"Yes, sir. That is all I can ask. You will have my lasting gratitude if you will grant this favor," Arsalan said, humble now, more like the agent Luke Clarke had recruited all those years ago.

"I'll do what I can. Take care, Arsalan. You're treading waters that have always been very dangerous. I admire you for your courage to do that to improve the lives of your people."

"I shall indeed, and thank you."

Lewis requested a meeting with the president at his earliest opportunity, stressing that the matter was not an emergency. Harper's secretary found a slot for him three days later, at ten a.m. When Lewis arrived at the Oval Office, he found the president sitting, not behind his desk, but in a comfortable chair with a coffee table in front of it.

Harper gestured to the matched chair and offered Lewis a cup of his special brew. Lewis had never gotten used to the president being so down-to-earth, but he concealed his discomfort and accepted the coffee, which Harper poured by his own hand. If Lewis had mentioned it, Harper would have gruffly explained that he wasn't the Queen of Sheba and had no use for formalities among friends.

"What can I do for you, Sam?" Harper asked, handing him his coffee.

"It isn't for me, Mr. President, but for a former CIA asset. You know him as Ahmad Ahmadi, Director of Reconstruction for Iran." Lewis noted that Harper was taken aback by the information that Ahmadi had been a CIA asset.

"Why didn't I know this?" the president asked. His tone of voice was milder than the words implied, as if he were genuinely curious, rather than disturbed.

Lewis answered carefully. "Mr. President, in matters of international espionage, every person who knows the identity of an asset, no matter how important or well-intentioned, represents a risk to that asset's life. Therefore, we operate on a strict need-to-know basis. If there had ever been a need for you to know his identity, we would naturally have told you." To Lewis's relief, the president retained control over his famous temper.

"I can understand that. I am surprised that you didn't say anything when the man rose to his current office."

"It didn't seem important then, sir. Naturally, he no longer considers himself in the employ of the CIA. It wouldn't be appropriate. However, it does give him a way to unofficially request a favor that has no business going through diplomatic circles, since it involves a private foundation." Lewis took a sip of the hot coffee, and decided to ask the president where he got the beans. It was some of the best coffee he'd ever had.

"Foundation," said Harper. "You have to be talking about the Rosslers. What does he want from them?"

"He wants Iran and a couple of other Middle Eastern countries to be given the opportunity to sign the treaty," Lewis answered. The direct question deserved a direct answer, even though it was a shocking one.

"They weren't given that opportunity in the first place because of the danger that terrorists would get hold of sensitive information. Why should they have it now?" Harper demanded. He, too took a sip of the coffee, but seemed not to notice how good it was.

"It isn't my place to say they should or shouldn't, sir," said Lewis. "I'm just the messenger boy. Ahmadi would appreciate it if you'll put a bug in the ear of the Rosslers, and then they can decide. He did say that they, Iran that is, are now favorably disposed toward the West. I should also tell you that this isn't a new claim. It was Ahmadi that gave us the tip about Kazemi's assassination. At that time, he discussed with Luke Clarke and me how he'd like to change the Middle East from within, even make friends with the Israelis."

"And you trust him?" Harper's glance was sharp, evaluating Lewis's body language as well as his words.

"Let's say that he has given me no reason not to trust him. I don't absolutely trust many people, sir." Lewis would make no recommendation. In truth, he didn't trust Ahmadi, or any other Middle Easterner, for that matter. But times had changed.

"You and me both. Well, I'll have a talk with Daniel and see what he thinks."

A few hours later, after all his daily obligations had been

met and while his dinner was settling, President Harper interrupted Daniel's dinner with a call to his cell phone.

"Daniel, did I catch you at dinner? Should I call later?" the president said, certain that Daniel would speak to him now no matter what. After all, you don't ask the president to call back at a more convenient time, even if he is your personal friend.

"I always have time for you, Nigel. My waistline will thank you for it," Daniel said, laughing.

"I remember! Sarah has no business being such a good cook for a PhD." Harper remembered a batch of her cookies with particular fondness.

"What can I say, Nigel? It's like a hobby for her, and she enjoys it. I'd hire a cook, but she won't let me," Daniel said, in no hurry to get down to business. It wasn't often he and the president had time to just exchange pleasantries.

"I envy you. Listen, Daniel, I didn't just call to shoot the shit. I've had a request from the Director of the CIA, Sam Lewis. You know him?"

"We're acquainted. He's a good friend of Sarah's uncle, Luke Clarke," Daniel said, on alert now.

"Yep. Anyway, he got hold of Sam, and Sam brought the request to me. Seems the guy knows you and I are friends, and he wanted me to approach you about letting Iran into the 10th Cycle Treaty." Harper's mild delivery did nothing to cushion the shock Daniel felt at the request. Hadn't the Foundation made it clear that they wouldn't deal with countries that harbored terrorists? He said as much to Harper.

"Well, I understand, and I agree. But haven't you noticed that Iran's cleaned up its act in recent weeks? And several other Middle Eastern countries have followed Iran's lead. I'm not going to argue in favor of it, but don't you think the idea bears some discussion?" After what terrorist groups had done to his family, Harper wouldn't blame Daniel for flatly refusing. But, he had to ask.

"I suppose it does. Tell me, Nigel, do a few months' worth of reform make up for a thousand years of hate?" Daniel asked, sitting down at the desk in his home office with a sigh.

"I wish I had an answer to that. Or to the question of when we drop our guard and let them demonstrate their sincerity. I'm a simple man, Daniel. If a man points a gun at me, I consider him an enemy. If he puts away the gun and smiles, I consider him a friend. Now, I know as well as the next man that he could easily pull the gun again. But, if I don't give him an opportunity to leave it in its holster and be a friend, doesn't that make me as much a bad guy as he was in the first place?" Daniel did his best to follow Harper's cowboy logic, but he had grave doubts. Instead of expressing them, he did his friend the honor of considering his request.

Harper threw in one more strong argument. "Apart from that Daniel, the Rossler Foundation has always said that the information from the 10th Cycle Library is for the benefit of all humanity. Here is one more opportunity to practice what you preach".

"Nigel, let me talk to my advisers and my Board. I'll get back to you as soon as I can. Will that do?"

"Can't ask for more, Daniel. Remember what I said, though."

The next morning, Daniel called a meeting of his core group of advisers. Sarah was with him when he arrived at work, alerted the night before when Daniel finished his call from the president. The others came as soon as they could get there, each finding an email upon their arrival at their offices. Nicholas was the first, and wanted to know the subject of the meeting right away, but Daniel persuaded him to wait for the others. Sinclair and Luke arrived together a few minutes later.

"I suppose you're wondering why I called you all together," deadpanned Daniel, who had always wanted to utter the cliché. These days his quirky sense of humor had to be suppressed in the interest of clear communications. After the others groaned and rolled their eyes, he smiled and got down to business.

"I had a call from President Harper last night," he explained. "It was in the nature of a request for a personal favor. I'll take it as a personal favor if you'll all give me your honest and considered opinions. At the request of Iran's Director of Reconstruction, Nigel has asked us to consider allowing Iran and a couple of other Middle Eastern countries to join the 10th Cycle treaty."

His words dropped into the assembled group like a cherry bomb in a punchbowl. Sarah of course already knew what he would say, but didn't expect it to be so baldly stated. She observed as Nicholas and Sinclair dropped their jaws. Luke's expression became grim, and he pressed his lips together.

Daniel wasn't finished, though. "I know it's a shock. My first thought was not unless hell has frozen over, but Nigel pointed out, very colorfully I might add, that even God gives a man a chance to repent. Iran has given every indication of turning over a new leaf since the Ayatollah Kazemi was assassinated. Moderates are now in charge of the government. The new Ayatollah has made no bombastic statements against the US since the killers confessed, and I've read that he has changed his stance because he might otherwise be removed from office. Iran has made guarantees of safety to industries that will locate facilities there. They seem to be fully engaged in reconstruction of their country, with no time for saber-rattling. They're even allowing women to be educated there or abroad." Daniel looked each of his advisors in the eyes as he made his speech.

As Daniel wound down, everyone but Luke became neutral in his expression. Luke, however, had something to say. "You're saying that a zebra can change its stripes. I disagree. I'm sure he believes his reforms are taking hold. But believe me, they have shallow roots. You can't change an entire culture in a few months." Luke's expression indicated that if a vote were taken now, he'd come down as an emphatic no.

"I don't disagree, Luke. On the other hand, we of all people should be anxious to help these poor folks, especially the rank and file populace. What would be the harm if they had cheap electricity? Have we made any progress in the weaponization of 10th Cycle cold fusion, Grandpa?" Daniel's eyes went to Nicholas.

Nicholas Rossler, Daniel's grandfather and head of the Research department, didn't know much about cold fusion. His lifelong profession was archaeology. But, he had surrounded himself with the best minds in the world for the investigation of 10th Cycle technology for any potential as a weapon. The result was that before any new technology was licensed by the Foundation, it was thoroughly tested and proven harmless. The one exception was cold fusion, because of its potential to relieve the burden of expense from third world energy production and the environment from the harmful effects of coal-fired electrical plants. As a result, the investigation was still ongoing, and the cold-fusion plants worldwide were constantly monitored for signs of tampering.

"No, not at this time. But any time you're dealing with nuclear energy, there's a potential," he answered, shrugging his shoulders.

"Anyway, I told Nigel we would keep open minds and discuss it rationally, rather than speculating emotionally. What do you say, Luke, do you have any specific concerns?" Daniel had experienced a change of heart overnight, and was leaning in favor of the idea at this time.

"Nothing specific, no. But, if we do this, we need to perform the most thorough background checks possible before we let their scientists in here. And there should be some new security measures in place, which I'll discuss with Nicholas and Sinclair both." Sinclair O'Reilly, the head of the translation department, also oversaw some sensitive information.

"Fair enough. Grandpa? Thoughts?" Of all his advisors, even those with a professional background in security like Sarah's Uncle Luke, he placed the most value on his grandfather's thoughts. The old man had been his hero when Daniel was a child, and hadn't slipped from that pedestal in the years since. His intelligence was legendary, and his ability to reason things through was a priceless asset.

"I have to admit, I hadn't thought about it the way President Harper put it to you. But he's right. The danger of refusing to accept that a man or a country has changed is that he might regress. We've had several months of peace in the Middle East except for the actions of a terrorist group that's lost its leader. If we allow this, could it be possible to make that permanent? People have been trying to make that happen for hundreds of years. What if we could achieve it?" Nicholas nodded. "I think we take the chance, with the precautions that Luke has mentioned.

"Noted. Sinclair?" It was time for Daniel's old ally, his grandfather's student and the man who'd broken the 10th Cycle code in the first place, to weigh in.

"Sure, and I've got no problem workin' with them," Sinclair said, revealing his nerves with his famous affectation of an Irish brogue though he was second-generation American. "I'll take Luke's advice about how to be sure they're behavin', though." He rapped his knuckles on the table in assent.

Daniel and Sarah had already discussed the idea at length the night before after putting little Nick to bed. Both had misgivings. They had speculated on the answers of the others, and it had gone pretty much as they expected. Their own decision, by mutual agreement, was to move forward with a proposal to the Board if Luke could assure them that he could filter out anyone who had past ties to terrorist organizations. Accordingly, they thanked Nicholas and Sinclair for their time and asked Luke to remain behind.

"So, you think this Ahmadi dude is sincere," Daniel asked.

"I have no reason to think otherwise," Luke said, unconsciously echoing Sam Lewis's answer to the president. "Trust but verify - that's my motto," he added.

"Then it's settled. If you can put strict controls in place, extra background investigation and whatever you have in mind for internal security, we'll put it to the Board." Daniel's gaze at Luke indicated that an assurance was wanted.

"I can't guarantee that nothing can slip through," said Luke. "But we've learned a thing or two in the past couple of years that I think can make it ninety-nine percent certain. I can't do better than that." Luke shook his head as he spoke the last sentence, as if he regretted not being able to assure perfection. In fact, he'd do his best to insure it.

"Nothing's certain in this life," Daniel said, speaking from personal experience. "That will have to do."

Daniel reported back to Harper that they were going to put the request to the Board. At Harper's request, he called an immediate meeting, though the regular meeting was several weeks away. Harper believed that the sooner Iran was allowed to join the treaty, the sooner they could count on a lasting peace in the region.

By now, Daniel was in agreement, if wary. When he made his presentation to the Foundation Board of Directors, he marshaled all the positive arguments he could think of. Equality of opportunity would make the Middle East less contentious. Improving the quality of life for the people of the region would be humane, and would go a long way toward restoring personal dignity, long repressed by radical Muslim clerics. There would be an opportunity to broaden the scope of investigation into the secrets of the library, with scholars from a radically different culture on board. Surely they would have a different way of thinking that would enhance investigative efforts. And more. Because he knew it would be on the minds of his Board anyway, he glossed over the risk. There was no need to call attention to it.

By a narrow margin, the vote was in favor of including Iran and two other countries, Saudi Arabia and Turkey, since they were nominal allies of the US despite strained relations over the 9th Cycle virus. Persuaded that it was in the best interest of the country as well as the world, the Rossler Foundation would open their doors to carefully vetted Iranian researchers after the 10th Cycle treaty was amended to include them, but only on a trial basis, for a year. After that, the arrangement could be renewed if everything worked out.

The terms of their inclusion were that the Middle Eastern countries could send scientists to study what had already been discovered in the library, except for certain discoveries that had been declared off-limits to everyone. The Middle Eastern scientists would also be free to conduct their own research, provided they in turn shared it with the rest of the treaty members. It was left open what could be shared with other Middle Eastern countries, to be taken on a case-by-case basis.

It was a matter of a few months only to turn the tide of public opinion to that of hope for the future. No longer were there daily rallies condemning the US for its assumed role in loosing the 9th Cycle virus on the world. The term 'genetic bullet' fell into disuse and disfavor, with the power of peer pressure to stop using such a politically charged phrase. Even mullahs and ayatollahs were heard to embrace the idea. Only behind closed doors and among those of the inner circle of the Sword of Cyrus were words of anger spoken against Israel, the United States, and the rest of the Western world. These elite kept the fires of hatred burning, so that when their plan had come to fruition, once more jihad would be brought to bear on the infidels.

In the United States also, public opinion turned from suspicion against Muslims in general and Iran specifically to cautious optimism that a new era had indeed begun. Harper pushed his support of the international committee charged with rebuilding the Middle East, encouraging both

US and international corporations to invest in the Middle East, particularly Iran. Director of Reconstruction Ahmad Ahmadi of Iran instigated negotiations to provide tax breaks and subsidies from oil production to companies that would invest in Iran, if the US would follow suit. Harper appreciated that both Sam Lewis and his friend Luke Clarke, who was related by marriage to Harper's good friend Daniel Rossler, endorsed Ahmadi as one of the good guys.

Best of all, Ahmadi's influence brokered an agreement of Iran's military to give up their nuclear weapons. Experts from the US, Great Britain, Germany and France were invited to supervise the dismantling of all warheads and launch facilities. The entire process was transparent, as the appointed experts would attest.

By the end of the year in which the world had gone from the brink of nuclear war between Iran and the US not once, but twice, the political climate between the two countries had changed radically. So radically, in fact, that anyone somehow going into complete seclusion at the end of March and not emerging until December would have sworn he'd come back to an alternate reality. In this, Iran was leading the rest of the Middle East, whose various countries' leadership were content to sit back and see if the detente between Iran and the US would last, and who got the better end of the stick.

On the last meeting of the year according to the Western calendar, members of the Sword of Cyrus congratulated themselves on a job well done. They had used the despair of the people and leadership of Iran in the aftermath of the virus to turn the tide of public opinion, winning their bid for change with nary a shot fired. It was an impressive feat, to overcome centuries of distrust and religious strife in only a few short months. Their leader, Dalir Jahandar, was largely to be credited with both the strategy and the implementation of the social engineering. Seeing that their agenda was about to succeed, they had good reason to celebrate.

"What is the next step, Dalir?" one of his friends asked, as Dalir had instructed him to.

"You must all do everything in your power to cooperate with Western industry and research. Those who own land must lease it to companies to build warehouses and manufacturing facilities. Those who are involved in transport must make your trucks and railway cars available to them. Do I need to say more?" Seeing no questions from his followers, Dalir was satisfied that his society understood the requirements of the plan. Now he turned to the most important element of all.

"You all know that Iran has not been allowed to share in the marvelous discoveries within the 10th Cycle library. The Rossler Foundation has now agreed to open its doors to us, as well as to a couple of other Middle Eastern nations. That way, when we betray their trust, it will be more difficult for them to discern who has done it. Bear in mind that, although this plan may take years to implement, we will be searching all the while for a method by which to eliminate the West as a dominant force. The Sword of Cyrus will then re-establish the glory and the empire of ancient Persia."

With the cooperation of a few members of the Sword of Cyrus, who had contacts and resources not just in Iran but globally, Dalir had been preparing for the time when the trend toward more cooperation with the West would open an opportunity for something he'd long aspired to. Placing several spies within the Rossler Foundation scientific community would give him the wherewithal to put his plan for restoring the glory of the Persian Empire in motion, and would furthermore open opportunities to make good on the oath that he swore at his family's deathbeds. The time was almost ripe, and he would be ready.

Chapter Ten

THE RECRUITS

Back when the news had reached Dalir Jahandar that the Rossler Foundation had been opened to Iran, Saudi Arabia and Turkey, a thrill of victory went through him. Now it would be a simple thing to have some of his prepared agents considered among the candidates for the Board position as well as research fellowships within the library archives. He had been anticipating this moment for some months, combing not only Middle Eastern countries for the brightest and best scientific minds, but also searching out Muslims who were ethnic Persians now living elsewhere.

Those he had recruited were examined for clean backgrounds, so that false ones wouldn't have to be prepared for them. Some, the Sword of Cyrus were able to persuade to their mission without threat or bribe. Others turned out to be corrupt enough to cooperate for money, but had not previously had the opportunity to use their intellect in such a way. Still others, those whose expertise was most desired but who could not be persuaded or bribed, were blackmailed by various means into cooperating. All were well aware of the price of betrayal.

Among the recruits were several stunningly beautiful women, chosen for their roles in the tradition of the mystique of Mata Hari. They were assured that the purpose for which they were to be groomed was permitted under Sharia law, and that they could not be stoned or punished in any other way for engaging in 'pleasure marriages', that is temporary liaisons for sexual purposes, with men from whom they expected to learn secrets otherwise hidden. The practice of muta'a, or temporary marriage for pleasure in return for money or other gain, was allowed by Mohammed, and the higher purpose, to restore the Persian Empire, served as the required necessity. The secrets uncovered would be the payment. Thus assured, the women entered training in the arts of seduction willingly.

When it was time to choose a representative to the Rossler Foundation Board, the twelve members of the Sword of Cyrus expected Dalir to put forth his own name, as was his right. However, he demurred, saying that his work would not permit him to spare the time. Instead, Reza Mokri, an industrialist of sufficient wealth to permit him the leisure required, was chosen, and groomed also for his role. His bid for the position was readily accepted by the Ayatollah Khorasani, who directed the newly-elected president to appoint him.

Mokri was an urbane Shi'ite whose English was impeccable, honed as it was at Oxford, though retaining a slight British accent. He was also quite handsome, tall and well-built, with caramel-colored skin, eyes that shifted from amber to coffee-colored in different light, and an audacious smile that had come close to leading more than one woman astray. Appearing young and lighthearted, he made friends easily and just as easily took advantage of them at every turn. Reza was the perfect candidate for the purpose the Sword of Cyrus had in mind; that is, to obtain by persuasion, stealth or subterfuge every advantage he could for their cause. Fortunately, he was not a particularly devout Muslim, so his potential seduction of female members of the Rossler Foundation board would not be a moral burden to him.

Until the time he was appointed to the Board of Directors, Mokri honed his negotiation skills by traveling the world to recruit major corporations to situate facilities in Iran in the name of reconstruction. With many members of Parliament in his pocket, he could offer favorable terms with regard to taxation, and somehow he always seemed to have the perfect site in mind for whatever type of facility he was courting. His best work, of course, was with companies who were headed or strongly influenced by women.

In the five months between the inception of the Sword of Cyrus and his call to report to the US for his appointment to the Rossler Foundation board, Mokri had persuaded a pharmaceutical company to relocate or build research facilities in Iran on the strength of the availability of subjects carrying the gene responsible for the vulnerability of Middle Easterners to the 9th Cycle virus. Because of the new discovery, the company hoped to corner the market on a seasonal flu vaccine marketed strictly to Middle Eastern people. Mokri had also attracted two electronics companies, a cosmetic company that wanted to develop cosmetics for brown-skinned women, and a manufacturer of ready-to-eat and convenience mixes of Middle Eastern cuisine. He had also made a small fortune personally, by selling some land that he controlled to several of these companies. He almost hated to leave the fun to infiltrate the Rossler Foundation.

Mokri's companions and colleagues from Saudi Arabia and Turkey were to join him en route. One, he knew, the Saudi, was an older man who was deeply distrustful of having a woman from Turkey within their circle. She, in turn, was contemptuous of the man, whose intellect she did not consider equal to her own. These two would spoil the plan if Mokri did not persuade them to vote as a bloc. To his delight, the woman was young, single and not ugly. He would be able to get around her easily. Therefore, he turned his charm on full-force for the man. Before the three reached Denver, he had been elected as their spokesperson in all matters, and they had pledged to back him for the opportunity to share in whatever he could get from the other board members.

The three were met at Denver International Airport by Daniel and Sarah in person. They were determined to make up for their misgivings by treating the new members of the board as well as they could, and this was the first step. On the way back to Boulder, Sarah attempted to make conversation while Daniel concentrated on driving.

While Ibrahim was mostly silent, both Reza and Deniz readily answered questions about their homelands and the conditions there. Sarah hesitated to ask what she really wanted to, which was how the ordinary people of the Middle East were faring after the 9th Cycle virus swept through their countries. Since many Middle Easterners were still confused about the origin of the virus, and the Rossler Foundation had played a pivotal role in unintentionally releasing it from its long dormancy, Sarah decided that discretion was the better part of valor and had determined not to bring it up.

However, Reza, in a surprisingly insouciant manner, brought it up himself, and his words were surprising.

"You know, that virus your expedition let loose has caused a lot of damage and human suffering but in a certain sense it may also turn out to be as you say, a blessing in disguise. It could very well have been the best thing that could have happened in Iran." His companions had been warned that he was going to do this, so they betrayed no shock. Not so Sarah, whose first thought was 'who does he think he's kidding?' Her eyes widened perceptibly as Daniel met them in the rear view mirror.

"What makes you say that?" Daniel asked, his tone as mild as he could make it.

"It has forced us to change a way of thinking that hasn't served us well in the last thousand years. My people and even our leaders are now open to modern ideas and technology. We will be too busy bringing ourselves out of this disaster to wage war on our neighbors."

Daniel didn't respond to that. Like Luke, he was glad to hear it. Luke had told him of the conversation with Ahmad Ahmadi, without revealing how he knew him. Now someone else who evidently had the ear of the highest offices in Iran was saying the same thing. He was still wary of these old enemies, but he was beginning to be encouraged.

Chapter Eleven

A VALUABLE ACQUISITION

One of Dalir Jahandar's most valuable acquisitions to his cause, Oleg Zlatovski, was found through one of the twelve Sword of Cyrus directors, a man whose gun-running operation was masked by oil interests. In both enterprises, having a retired KGB/MI6 double agent in his pocket was a valuable resource. As soon as Zlatovski understood the mission that Dalir explained, he agreed to set up the network that the Sword of Cyrus would need for communicating with their agents, as well as to train the agents for their roles. In this, he had no ideological interest. However, the billion dollar payout in technology and cash was of high interest.

Oleg, who was going by the name Andreas Dimitriou when he met and began offering his consulting services to Jahandar's man, had retired from the KGB in a time-honored manner. He had faked his own death. Now he was living in Greece with a new appearance and a dwindling bank account, though he had several properties that he could sell if needed. A little plastic surgery, carefully up-kept blond dye for his hair and beard, and not even his brother would recognize him, fortunately.

Zlatovski's allegiance was to no one but himself, and in his area of expertise he carried a wealth of knowledge of the weak spots in Russia and the West. Oleg's personality was deceptively mild, but in truth he had no scruples, was morally bankrupt and cared only for his own desires and comfort. He had no idea how his gun-running contact had learned his true identity, but there was no danger. Their enterprise was illegal, and they had as much to lose as he did.

Had they believed him alive, Zlatovski would have been wanted by every security agency in Europe, the USA and Israel and a few others besides. If his brother had known he was alive, his life would be worth nothing as well. His options were limited in Europe, but he was very open to financial gain wherever it could be found, no matter who it harmed in the long run. For this reason, he was perfect for what Dalir had in mind.

Oleg was well-versed in creating blind networks, where each agent was only aware of one other, and not by the other's real name. His initial brief was to train each of the dozen or so scientist recruits and a handful of recruits who were experienced administrators individually, so that they would not know each other when they met at Rossler Foundation headquarters. Each type of recruit would have similar assignments to the others of their type, and it was hoped that they would be allowed to work on a broad variety of projects, so that they could steal as much as possible across the entire scope of the 10th Cycle library. However, if one was caught, he or she would not be able to bring down the entire network. Their handlers would be employed in ordinary jobs in Boulder, and again, none would know the other. Each scientist would report to his handler, each handler to a single person in Tehran, who in turn would report to the Sword of Cyrus. One weak link would not break the chain - only shorten it.

Oleg thought it a clever touch to use the method of communication that the Rosslers had made famous while they were hiding their activities from both the now-defunct Orion Society and their own CIA, back when they were trying to crack the Giza Pyramid's code. What was so clever was that you could actually tell someone you were using that methodology, and as long as you were communicating from anonymous IP addresses, such as those found at internet cafes, that someone would never be able to find your communications. If you further confounded them by using a single text document such as a common paperback book, among several, with a skip sequence for coding the messages, even if they found your communications they would not be able to read them. It was the most secure method he'd ever utilized, and it tickled his well-developed sense of humor that it made use, not only of methods known to the Rossler Foundation, but a mixture of quite primitive and very sophisticated methods.

The best thing about it was that it was much simpler than it sounded. The method included making use of one or a series of throwaway email accounts, not to email in the clear, but to leave a message in the draft folder. In this way, even the NSA's broad sweep of metadata, intended to capture every email and every phone call for who contacted whom, would be foiled, since nothing was ever transmitted. Brilliant, really, Oleg mused. Even more brilliant when he asked for a dozen popular Arabic texts that would not raise suspicion if found among the possessions of the scientists. The handler's security would be even less at risk, since he would not be employed by the Rosslers. Each pair, the researcher and the handler, would be assigned a different text. They would apply a randomly-selected Fibonacci number to create the coded message and break the code. It would only require that one thing be embedded in the message in the clear; the chosen Fibonacci number. Naturally, every scientist would be supplied with several Arabic books, so as not to raise suspicion if rooms were ever searched. Each was required to memorize a selection of Fibonacci numbers - that is, numbers that can be developed by adding the last two numbers in the sequence to form the next.

In addition to training the recruits on the use of this communication method, each was put through a rigorous regimen of hand-to-hand combat training, memory improvement training, and acculturation training. For the men, this amounted to grooming and sensitivity training. They were instructed to curb their natural male superiority when dealing with Western women. They were shown films culled from sex therapy libraries that taught them how to please a woman in the bedroom, a concept several found so foreign as to be ludicrous. Whoever heard of a woman's feelings in the bedroom being important?

Conversely, the women were sent to European finishing schools, taught how to dress, groom themselves as American women did, converse with men without lowering their eyes, and yes, how to please a man in the bedroom, since American men would expect them to know rather than having to show them. In the case of the women, the concept of muta'a was thoroughly discussed by mullahs, brought in to break down the female recruits' natural reticence toward lovemaking outside of marriage. After that task had been accomplished, Oleg himself made sure that each had learned her lessons well, instructing a few more than once. It was also his privilege and his entertainment to help the women attain a level of tolerance of alcohol that would allow them to remain fully functional even after the man one was seducing had met his limit. In these matters, Oleg was happy to travel from city to city and stay a week or more in pursuit of perfection.

By the time the announcement came that their long-awaited hope had been answered, every recruit that was still on board, a few having washed out, was as ready as they could be and eager to get started. Those who were scientific researchers, in particular, were looking forward to making great strides in their own fields while still carrying out their missions. Not everyone's application was accepted, but more than half a dozen scientists were given their one-year appointments, and three or four administrative professionals were also selected.

Zlatovski was given his cash payment and returned to his comfortable retirement in a village on the coast of Greece, but told to remain available in case he was needed again. The rest went to their respective homes to await the signal to apply for new positions opening at the Rossler Foundation specifically for Middle Easterners.

Chapter Twelve

THE ROSSLER FOUNDATION NANOTECHNOLOGY PROGRAM

By the time the new positions within the translation and research departments had been filled with Middle Eastern candidates, initial efforts made by the translation department and Raj to find references in the 10th Cycle library to nanotechnology had already borne fruit. Of course, the term wasn't found in direct translation, but with Raj's thorough understanding of search terminology, enough turned up to warrant a proposal to the Board for a special program to seek it all out, translate it and sort it into lines of inquiry that were ranked by importance.

Roy had been invited to spend his Christmas and semester breaks helping the latter phase, and was primed to take an early sabbatical if anything of high interest could be found. CalTech wasn't pleased by the prospect of losing its new recruit so quickly, but the advantage to the university of having one of its best and brightest in the forefront of a new line of inquiry at the prestigious Rossler Foundation made up for it to some extent.

As Christmas rapidly approached, Daniel and Roy

worked feverishly on a proposal to the Board for funding the initial phase of the program; that is, the initial search and translation. With Roy's expertise on hand, it was a slam-dunk to get the funding. As always, the Board was encouraged to nominate experts from its member countries for carrying out the work. The recruiting process was arduous, particularly once it was decided to allow Iran, Saudi Arabia and Turkey into the Foundation membership, even for a limited time. The new Middle Eastern members of the Board took full advantage of this perk. After thorough background checks, a team was formed.

The role of nanotech program lead went to Karsten Adler, a Swiss-born scientist with a PhD in molecular mechanics who had been living and working in the US for several years. He was chosen as much for his proven administrative ability as for his background in CERN, the European Organization for Nuclear Research, working on the Large Hadron Collider. This freed Roy to do what he did best, research. He was given the role of senior researcher. Among the rest of the team were a few scientists from the Middle East and one or two of those were nuclear scientists. However, Luke could find no ties to terrorist organizations among the lot of them.

Luke had given a great deal of thought to the increased security measures required by the program to investigate nanotechnology. He had the idea that all of it was potentially dangerous, this nanotech stuff. Partly he was influenced by half-remembered warnings of the dangers from thirty or forty years ago. Even though development of the technology hadn't kept up with the speculation about it, he still had a gut-level distrust of it, particularly after watching Roy's first presentation. To enhance the regular security they had in place, he decided that the program manager should be instructed to segment the research, even the translation.

The nanotech program would be set up a little differently from other programs already running at Rossler Foundation headquarters. Each program had a committee that evaluated information coming out of the translation and research for potential danger, consisting of the program manager, one or two Board members, and such other experts as were deemed necessary. In the case of the nanotech program, because of the breadth of scope in fields to which it would pertain, Luke suggested that no one person, except the program manager himself and the evaluation committee, would have the whole picture. In that way, anything with the potential to be used as a weapon would be hidden from the rank and file.

When it went to the committee charged with allowing it or suppressing it, it would be out of Luke's hands for the most part. For this particular program, he asked that Daniel himself, Karsten Adler as the program manager, Roy James as the expert in the investigative subject and Sarah if she so desired, be appointed to the committee. In addition, he recommended Raj as the data expert, so that he could recommend ways to keep the data compartmentalized and Sinclair, who had a keen understanding of his translators' personalities and trustworthiness.

When it came to the research, Karsten and Roy were found by virtue of their background checks to be 100% trustworthy. As they brought on research assistants, further steps might need to be taken, but this was already going to be a burden on the time and duties of the committee members, so Luke felt it would be best to start this way and go from there as needed. Roy was interested mainly in the theoretical rather than the applied properties of nanotechnology, although he had a boyish delight in playing with ideas for useful gadgets. Karsten came with the highest of recommendations from his former employers. In addition, by birth he was Swiss, long recognized as a neutral nation with no ax to grind with anyone. As such, he was considered above suspicion.

Luke had a private conversation with Raj and with Sinclair about his security measures, as well as explaining the necessity to Karsten, who agreed. Roy also understood, but didn't have much to add, since he only cared about his research, not anything that he considered political.

Roy went home for just a couple of days for Christmas, blissfully unaware that Karsten had planted a bombshell in their office that he would discover on his return - he'd hired a *woman* as the program administrator. Alica Cindric would be responsible for organizing meetings, taking minutes, keeping all program and project documentation up to date, and keeping the budget on track. Essentially, she would be Karsten's right hand, freeing him from what was basically housekeeping drudgery. For Roy it meant having to go through Alica to get Karsten's ear, a distinctly unpleasant hassle for the painfully shy man, who had trouble even speaking in any woman's presence let alone a beautiful one.

Alica was perfect for the job, a lovely Croatian widow whose application came through Iranian diplomatic sources. As an ethnic Persian, her plight after her husband, a high-level aide to the Croatian ambassador to Iran, and her son died in the 9th Cycle flu pandemic, was of interest to both Croatia and Iran. That of course would not be found in her documentation. Her cover story was that her husband and child were killed in a car accident. Slipping that into the public record and the real story out of it was not the least of Oleg Zlatovski's talents.

Finding her work at the Rossler Foundation, was easy. She passed the background check with flying colors, had never had any contact under the name on her documents with anyone who had terrorist links. But, unbeknown to the selection committee, she had never been convinced that the virus was naturally occurring. An abiding hatred of America and especially of the Rossler Foundation had led her to answer the recruitment ad placed by Oleg Zlatovski. In matters of seduction, she was his best student ever.

In fact, all of the new Middle Eastern employees fit into the Foundation staff's social activities nicely. In spite of quickly-held training on sensitivity to matters of Muslim culture and religious observance, the Foundation staff welcomed them matter-of-factly for the most part. The Middle Easterners were good studies and took their lessons to heart. American and European employees found them to be very easy-going. No one ever noticed one of them asking about the food or turning up their noses at a drink after work. There were even some short-lived hookups between the men and some of the American women, nothing serious occurred, and the liaisons didn't last long.

Alica was circumspect at first. She had a very special mission, but it had to wait until the time was right. She would be activated at the right time, and then someone was going to have his world rocked. For now, she amused herself by torturing Roy James as if she were innocent of the knowledge that he was paralyzed in the presence of women.

Before too many weeks passed, little separated the Middle Eastern staff from any of the others. They rapidly learned the company culture, one of tolerance and laid-back social interaction combined with a strong work ethic in most employees. No one worked harder than they, but no one played harder, either. The snow-covered peaks of the Rockies beckoned everyone to get outside for hiking and skiing at every opportunity, leading to organized outings on the weekends for those who cared to be with their co-workers seven days a week.

Daniel was pleasantly surprised. During the height of the flu crisis, when rhetoric was flying and nukes were deployed, he'd imagined a swarthy face with black hair, mustache and beard as the face of the enemy. Now, he recognized similar faces in the halls every day, but they no longer looked sinister to him. Their expressions were open, their greetings friendly. When he mentioned it to Sarah or others, they agreed. This was working out very nicely.

Daniel and some of the others who'd had the most misgivings began to relax. A feeling of optimism pervaded the halls of Rossler Foundation headquarters, a shared belief among the founders that perhaps they'd gotten through the bad times and would enjoy peace from then on.

Roy found that working with Raj on locating references to anything that could be classified as nanotech to be very refreshing. He understood Raj's work, and Raj was a quick study in the nuances of nanotech. The original meaning of the word had morphed into a broader concept. Now anything that was very small, in other words, microscopic, or that utilized manipulation of atoms on the subatomic level, might have the moniker attached to it. In the 10th Cycle, there was a direct translation of the word technology, but 'nano' was unknown. To focus his search, Raj asked for

Arabic words for tiny, infinitesimal, delicate and precise. If those turned up no records for similar words in the index, he would go to Aramaic. Though the 10th Cycle language wasn't actually Arabic, but rather resembled Sumerian, Raj had learned that Arabic was a good start when he wanted to search the index. Pronouncing the words he located was a different matter. The word that was closest to all of those concepts looked like a squiggle to Roy, and sounded, to both of them, like 'dufokik'.

"Let's stick with calling it nanotech," suggested Roy, rolling his eyes at the unfamiliar sound.

"Of course. There is no reason to call it anything else," replied Raj. "But, we must now ask Sinclair to translate this word into the Linear A symbols, and then we can find the references in the database." His offhand use of the linguistics term caused Roy's brain to hiccup.

"Whatever you say, Raj. You lost me up until you said database," Roy said, laughing. He put his finger close to the computer screen, almost touching the squiggle. "Is this the word?"

"That's funny, my friend. I lose most people *when* I say database. Yes, that's it." Raj wasn't as dumbfounded as Roy that a squiggle and a few dots could convey a sophisticated meaning. His own native language was usually written in Devanagari script, a series of 54 phonemes with inherent vowels, many of which would have looked like variants of an upside-down and backwards lowercase H to the American beside him.

When he'd had Sinclair transliterate the Arabic into Linear A, he searched the database for relevant references. In the end, there were hundreds of them, and they were scattered across many sections of the library.

"What do you want to study first?" Raj asked Roy, after

he'd prepared an index of the potential subjects. Roy looked up from the article he was reading on his tablet to see the printout in Raj's hand.

"The way I understand it, I don't get to choose. It has to go through the committee that determines what may be dangerous, before they turn us loose with it." In fact, Roy was on that committee, but because he was working with known translations until Raj finished his search, it had yet to meet.

"Ah, yes, the security committee. I am a member of this one, as are you. We can run a report by section, and let the others know we have some leads. So, take a look at this and let me know where you'd like to start, assuming the committee okays it." Raj handed the stack of papers to Roy, who handled them reverently. He was still in awe of the fact that he would be allowed to work with 10th Cycle material. Only the elite of the scientific world had free run of this stuff.

"Sounds good. Oh, are you going to give me an internal invoice for your time here and the report printouts? Karsten has me reporting everything to that woman, and she'll have my hide if I don't remember everything." Roy shuddered as he thought of Alica. He was screwed either way. If he reported this expense to her, she'd taunt him with her flashing black eyes, and if he didn't report to her, she'd come after him. Either way, he was likely to make a fool of himself with his stammering and rubber legs.

"I can do that. Usually I run a monthly report," Raj answered, the question unasked but implied in his tone.

"I'll see if that will do, or whether she wants it every time I spend part of the budget. I'll tell you, Raj, that woman's going to be the death of me." Roy shuddered again, breaking a sweat this time.

"Why do you say that?"

"I'll be sitting quietly at my desk, minding my own business, and all of a sudden, she's there, patting my shoulder, or peering into my face while she asks me a question. Which I can't answer, because she makes me forget what I'm doing." The look on Roy's face was comical, but Raj was sympathetic.

Raj laughed. "I know that feeling. At least I did until my Sushma decided I was the one for her. Then there was no escape. You must learn to control your emotions, my friend."

"That's easier said than done. I get nervous around women." The understatement was laughable just by itself. The truth was, Roy dissolved like wet tissue around women.

"My sympathies are with you, my friend," Raj said, with sincerity. There'd been a time when he was almost as bad.

The security committee found a number of worthwhile projects to fund under the nanotech program. They decided to focus on those that would best support the reconstruction programs taking place in the Middle East. Since they had all this funding for the special researchers, and since everyone was interested in modernizing their countries, why not give them the newest and best technology? All under the safeguards that Luke had put in place, of course. They decided on three initial projects; air quality, water quality and electronics. The last came after some debate. There would of course be some military applications for electronics, and they didn't know exactly what the library would contain. Luke reminded them of the safeguard – no single translator or researcher would get all of the information. It was relatively safe, and they'd be under regular security safeguards as well. With that assurance, the projects were funded and research into these three areas began.

Roy's mind wasn't on the discussion, or he might have reminded the committee that rearranging atoms and molecules on this scale leads to new properties, as he'd mentioned in the presentation five months ago. It was an oversight that would lead to disaster.

Sinclair was as pleasantly surprised as anyone else by the demeanor of the Middle Easterners. However, he didn't know them as well as he knew the translators who had been with him for years. Accordingly, he thought it prudent to initially put only one new employee on each section of the nanotech files, similar to Luke's plan to break up the research phase. The way that the translators worked was that each one had a block of symbols which had been first decoded by computer into Sumerian with the proper skip sequence indicated in the index. It was still a marvel to Sinclair that the 10th Cyclers had packed so much information into so little physical space by the use of skip sequences governing which words were formed. That they had done so with Fibonacci numbers was a miracle, something far beyond his ability to do, though he could easily grasp the concept.

Once the clear texts were generated, the translators had to do something similar to what the Navajo code-talkers of the Second World War had done. That is, they applied the ancient words to modern concepts. The 10th Cyclers had obviously expected the dominant language of the current cycle to evolve along the same lines as theirs had, but that hadn't happened. So translating their words was as much an art as a science, even after all the decoding had taken place. It was slow, painstaking work, and the translators had to have a working knowledge of whatever scientific field of study that they were working on to make any sense of it at all. Sinclair was proud of his team. No one could have made more progress than they, in the few short years since the library was discovered.

When the first translator had finished a section, a second one was often assigned to check the work and make sure there had been no errors. After the translation was finalized, it would normally be turned over to the researcher who had requested it. In the case of the nanotech files, however, a second determination of the security committee would be required.

Roy found the process too slow for his requirements, but was gratified to be included on the security committee so that he at least was one of the first to get a look at the translated sections. He was interested in all nanotechnology on a theoretical level, less so in the applied concepts. It wasn't surprising, then, that he had less interest in the method for removing harmful substances, from industrial waste to human waste, from groundwater, or new catalysts for transforming airborne hydrocarbon particles into harmless gasses, than the electronic applications he was seeing coming out of that project. To keep him happy, Raj suggested that Roy be allowed to experiment with the new information.

The planted agents of the Sword of Cyrus, however, were already at work undermining the security of the data. Even though they could only get pieces of it, they were each instructed to go ahead and get what they could. They weren't told that somewhere in Iran, scientists were working to see if they could put the pieces together. If it hadn't been so dangerous, it would have been funny. Computers on the Boulder end taking an ancient set of data, decoding it, giving it over to human beings to figure out the meaning, and then some of those human beings coding it again and sending it to distant computers, who then gave it back to human beings to figure out the meaning again. There was so much room for error, particularly when the data was so fragmented. But, as with a partially-revealed picture, some of the missing parts could be guessed from the surrounding context.

Roy and JR were taking a lunch break off-campus one day shortly after the first security committee meeting for the Nanotechnology Program, during which Raj had moved that Roy be given carte blanche to experiment with any information found. Raj's point was that someone with Roy's level of curiosity and broad interest in nanotech could easily become bored if his expertise weren't called upon sooner rather than later. To avoid that, Raj thought something in the nature of a nanotech hobby would help, and might even find applications that would be useful to either the Foundation, or could even be licensed to manufacturers if it had broad appeal. To Roy's delight, the motion had carried.

"They even gave me a small budget for materials and such," Roy told JR, while juggling his enormous and very juicy hamburger.

"No way! I need to get Raj to propose something like that for me," JR responded. His hamburger was just as big and juicy, but at the moment it was resting on its plate while JR wolfed down one French fry after another.

"Oh? Are you interested in nanotechnology?" Roy asked.

"No, archaeology. I've got a few ideas I'd like to explore, but since they don't have anything to do with the 10th Cycle library, I doubt I can get funding for them. I'd like to have been a fly on the wall at that meeting, to hear what Raj said to get yours."

"Oh." Roy wanted to be polite, but ancient mysteries held no interest for him. Rather than pursue that line of conversation, he brightened. "JR, I've always wanted a 3-D printer, wouldn't that be cool?"

A little lost at the turn the conversation had taken, JR frowned. "I guess. Why?"

"Because I could design a cool gadget and fill it with nanotech electronics, of course."

"Oh, of course." JR was now completely lost.

"You just gave me an idea. I'm going to order a 3-D printer and make it," Roy said, his mouth full of burger so that the words came out a bit muffled.

"What is it?" JR had looked away from the unappealing sight of Roy talking while eating.

"A surprise. Can't tell you until it's done." Roy took another huge bite of burger, just as JR changed the subject.

"Whatever, man. Hey, you want to get a date and see a movie with Rebecca and me this weekend?" JR hadn't yet learned of Roy's not-so-secret paralysis around women. Rebecca was one of the few who put Roy at ease and could interact with him without triggering his panic button.

"Uh, date? I don't think so. Thanks for the invitation, though." Roy failed to suppress a shiver of apprehension. *Date? What woman will go out with a stupid and clumsy idiot like me? I won't even be able to talk to her. No way!!*

"Okay, maybe hiking or something another time," suggested JR, taking up his burger again now that the fries were gone.

"Sure, I'd like that," Roy answered. He liked JR, a tall drink of water for sure, but all accounts indicated he had some amazing stories. Roy would like to hear them from the horse's mouth sometime. Damn, he should have explained his woman problem. Maybe next time.

The Sword of Cyrus

JR went about his business, while Roy started searching out the most powerful 3-D printer that would fit within his budget. Like most tech devices, the first personal-use ones cost more than a thousand dollars and printed only in plastic, while industrial application printers were out of reach for most hobbyists. Now, though, they were more sophisticated, used several different materials including plastic, metal and yes, carbon nanotubes. And the price had dropped dramatically. Roy found a 'gently used' RepliBot Gen5X for only $2,000, well within his budget. While he waited for it to be delivered, he delved into the information he could find both in the 10th Cycle library and in published papers about nanotechnology and created an AutoCAD drawing of his device.

After the printer was delivered, and when it was ready, he tested it during a meeting he requested with Daniel for the purpose of doing so. Speaking in very general terms, he asked Daniel about patents.

"This is probably in my contract, but could you explain to me again about patentable concepts that come out of the 10th Cycle library?" he asked.

"Do you mean, whether you have any financial interest in them?" Daniel countered.

"Yes, I suppose that's what I mean. If I invent something, and part of the information I used to develop it comes from the library, can I patent it myself, or does it belong to the Foundation?" Roy was just making conversation. He was pretty sure the patent would belong to the Foundation. He'd invented his gadget on Foundation time, with Foundation funds and materials.

"Okay, yes, that is in your contract. It's on the honor system. If you develop it strictly on your own time, even if information comes out of privileged material, you patent it and we ask for twenty percent of earnings as a royalty for that material. Are you with me so far?"

"I think so," Roy said, fiddling with something in his pocket.

"Okay. If you develop it strictly during working hours, we patent it and the royalty is reversed; we have first refusal on licensing it and you get twenty percent of our royalties as a bonus for inventing something that's financially valuable." It was a very generous deal. Most companies would claim all rights to it under those circumstances.

"All right. That seems more than fair," Roy said, now anxious to demonstrate his gadget, which had been unobtrusively operating in the room as they spoke.

"Hold on, there's one more scenario. You develop it partly during working hours and partly on your own time. Then we patent it, but we prorate the royalties, based on how much of your own time you spent. So, if you're working on something during working hours and come back to do something with it after hours, it's worth keeping track of the time. Does that make sense?"

"Yes," Roy said, unable to wait any longer for the reveal of his toy. "I have something to show you, and I spent only my working hours on it. I think it could have several uses. Want to see it?"

"Sure! You mean you already have it done?"

"Well, I needed a test run. You and I are about to find out how well it works." Roy sent a homing command through the tiny remote he had in his pocket, and a small black object flew toward him and landed on his shoulder. Daniel followed its flight with interest.

"Allow me to present the Spyfly," said Roy with a big smile on his face, picking it up and handing it to Daniel.

Daniel held the tiny black plastic device in the palm of

his hand. No bigger than a common housefly, it was very realistic, but on closer inspection, Daniel could see that it was made of plastic, with a material he couldn't identify for eyes. The tiny wings whirred into action at Roy's command on the remote, and it flew up and hovered just an inch above Daniel's palm.

"Well, I'll be a monkey's uncle," Daniel said, surprised into North Carolina slang he hadn't used in years. "What does it do, besides impersonating a fly?"

"Let's see," answered Roy, who had come prepared with his laptop. After opening it and queuing up a media streaming program, another click of a button on the remote sent the video the fly had collected, complete with audio, during the meeting.

Daniel watched open-mouthed as the video perfectly captured his explanation of the Foundation's work-product and patent policy. The picture was clearer than most surveillance video from commercial applications. Good enough, in fact, for government work, he thought, though he didn't mean it in the way that cliché had been meant for more than fifty years. What Daniel meant was that he could think of a few people, starting with Luke and including Luke's friend Sam Lewis, head of the CIA, the police the FBI and a few others who would love to have a supply of these gadgets.

"What would a thing like this cost?" he asked Roy.

"Mass-produced? Maybe fifty dollars," was the nonchalant answer.

"No kidding! Do you have any more?"

"No, but it wouldn't take me more than a couple of hours to make another one. That 3-D printer I bought is fast."

"Roy, I think you just earned enough to pay your salary

for the foreseeable future. If you want to stick around here instead of going back to CalTech, just say the word. Could you whip up three or four of those for me?" Daniel was as excited as a kid with a new science lab setup to have a little fun with one of his own. He could imagine several of his closest friends would want their own, too, as soon as they saw it.

"Sure. I'll have them ready by tomorrow afternoon. I've got some other ideas, too," Roy answered, pleased that his invention had made such a good impression.

"Great. Can you come back here tomorrow, say at 3 p.m.? I'll clear my schedule. I've got some people I'd like to surprise." Daniel couldn't stop grinning. This was going to be fun!

"Yep. Oh, and I promised to show it to JR. After all he gave me the idea." Roy wasn't sure if JR was one of the people Daniel referred to. He didn't want to spoil the surprise, if so.

"Okay, I'll invite him too. Thanks for bringing this to me, Roy. Write up a proposal for the next idea you have, and I'll make sure you don't run out of funds. Oh and let me know if you need more equipment and tools in your lab. I am happy to fund a lab that can produce stuff like this."

Roy set off down the hall to his own lab, whistling. On the way he met Alica, who greeted him with a cheery, "Hi, Roy!"

Roy stumbled, not expecting the walking vision in front of him to address him directly. He blushed as if he'd been caught thinking impure thoughts about her, and that wasn't far from the truth. Alica was one of the most beautiful women he'd ever had the opportunity to talk to, and he had more than once kicked himself for blowing it every time. He just couldn't seem to get out more than an incoherent stammer.

"Uh, hi, Alica."

Roy ducked his head and kept walking, but he stopped whistling. Alica stopped and turned to look at his retreating back. "What are you so happy about, Roy?" she said, barely containing her giggle.

He stopped and turned back to her, losing his grip on his laptop and juggling for a moment to keep from dropping it.

"J-just got some g-good news winged a-a-things," he stuttered. Alica gave him a brilliant smile that almost buckled his knees.

"That's nice!" she said.

"Uh, er, y-yes. Thanks." Words failing him again, he turned and almost ran for his lab, leaving Alica shaking her head behind him. She'd never had a man act like that in her presence. Concluding he must be gay, Alica dismissed him from her mind and went into her own office.

Roy closed the door to his lab and slapped himself on the forehead with the heel of his hand. For the hundredth time, he told himself he needed to get hold of himself and stop being a moron any time a woman was around. Especially a beautiful woman like Alica! She liked him, at least she acted like she did. Maybe it was time to get help, or he was going to end up single for the rest of his life.

The following afternoon, Roy was happy again as he showed his toy to the assembled guests in Daniel's office, fortunately all male. Luke, Sinclair, Nicholas and special guest JR were all there to see the remarkable little device that JR's offhand remark had led to. The Spyfly was a big hit, each man wanting one for himself. Daniel had Roy hand out the three he had on hand to Luke, Sinclair and

Nicholas, suggesting that they put them to good use, without specifying what exactly to do with them. Roy did so, showing them how to stream the video to their computers, make the fly do random fly-type activity, and recall it to their locations. No one could believe that such a tiny object could do what Roy had made it do. All he had to say about it was 'that's nanotechnology'.

Luke stayed behind as the others left, wanting to point out to Daniel how useful such a thing would be to law enforcement, and even more so to the CIA.

"Is it okay with you if I show this to Sam Lewis next time I talk to him?" he asked. "And, for that matter, what about Ryan? I'll bet he'd like to license it for mass production if any government agency wants it. I can't imagine them not wanting it, either."

"Good idea, Luke. Go ahead," Daniel responded.

It wasn't long before Raj appeared in Roy's office, begging for a Spyfly for his use. He wasn't sure how he was going to deploy it where it needed to be, but it seemed to him that this was a way to finally get the truth about Area 51 and aliens. Roy detained him to talk about his next idea, a nanocomputer. Virtually everyone who had an interest in technology was aware that computers had been getting smaller and smaller, beginning with the room-sized computers of the 1950s, to the desktops of the late 1960s and finally the wristwatch-sized models introduced after the turn of the century. Raj was well aware that nanotechnology would represent another level of miniaturization, but he hadn't spent much time researching how the interface between a dust-mote sized nanoprocessor and a human being would work.

"It wouldn't be something you'd interact with," explained Roy. "You'd build the programming into it and incorporate it into something you wanted to act on its own. For example, you could make a smart bullet with it, which could correct its path in flight, so you'd never miss. Or you could release a bunch of them like dust into a building to monitor activity in the building."

"Wow, I don't know if the Foundation would support that kind of research. Bullets, definitely not. Nothing that could be used for warfare. And probably not smart dust, either. The only thing I can think of to use that for would be industrial espionage, or maybe spying on your country's enemies," Raj said, though his eyes had lit up at the thought of smart dust in Area 51. That would be the way to do it!

"They seemed to like the Spyfly. That's just a bigger model," Roy objected.

"Hmm, you have a point. Let's put that one on the shelf for now. Got any other ideas?"

"Yes. How about a sniffer that could detect harmful chemicals, or biological indicators?" Roy answered.

"That might fly. It would be used for self-defense, so the prohibition on warfare technology shouldn't apply."

"What you're talking about is already being manufactured. I'm talking about other applications. Like, a monitor in the kitchen, where most accidents involving mixing two cleaning products together happen. It would be like a smoke detector, only it would detect harmful gasses like chloramine vapor, and alert the housewife to get out of the kitchen. Like that. Or biological. How many people can afford an assistive animal? Or might be allergic to them? Instead of a dog to alert you when your insulin is too low, you could have a nanotech sniffer in your pocket to do it."

"That sounds like a winner. Why don't you work on that? Would the same device be able to sniff everything?"

"No, it would have to be programmed to recognize

different things, but maybe I could make it do several things. Like, the one that would sniff low insulin could maybe detect cancer, or a seizure that's about to happen, or a heart attack. And the other one, for detection of harmful vapors in homes, maybe several different chemicals, or gas or smoke, just smaller."

"Well, give it some thought. I'll think about applications for microscopic computers and get back to you." Raj was already absent in everything but body. He couldn't wait to tell his conspiracy theorist network, some of whom were hackers of extraordinary skill, about these ideas. Maybe he'd get Roy to work on that smart dust after all.

"All right. Hey, thanks Raj."

"Any time, my friend."

Chapter Thirteen

THE SWORD OF CYRUS NANOTECHNOLOGY
PROGRAM

Even before the goal of getting their agents into the Rossler Foundation came to fruition, Dalir was implementing the other half of his plan to destroy the West. Of course the technology coming to the Middle East would, as the public had been led to expect, greatly affect the quality of life for ordinary people in a positive way. It was the secret mission that required a hidden facility to implement. Dalir hoped that his agents inside the Rossler Foundation could find some research that would allow his scientists back in Iran to craft a use for it that would be suppressed to the rest of the world; that is, a military use. Since the beginning of the Foundation, anything that could be put to use by terrorists was buried by the watchdog committees. That meant that when his scientists got their hands on the stolen technology, only Iran would have it. Iran and any allies he gave it to.

The first task was to find a location that was sufficiently obscure that no news of activity there would leak out into the world. He found what he was looking for in the Zagros Mountains, four hundred kilometers from the Persian Gulf, a city named Esfahan. Farming was the economic base, but the modern industries of steelmaking and oil refining, along with the traditional textile, food and metalwork, provided enough commerce in the bustling town of three-quarters of a million inhabitants to camouflage the comings and goings of strangers. Esfahan was recuperating from the devastation of the 9th Cycle virus that had cut its population and economy in half. Dalir's henchmen located a large building suitable for remodeling into several labs, one of which was optimistically designed for the manufacture of nano-nuclear materials.

The terms of employment for the scientists who were recruited to work there were highly desirable. Families would be allowed to be with them, and luxurious living quarters would be provided in addition to generous pay. That those quarters would be in a walled compound with guards around it was secondary to the fact of them. Virtually none of the scientists had previously had the wealth to provide such luxury to their families, and so the inconveniences were swept aside. Did a wife need to go shopping? An escort was provided, so that she could feel safe. The escort also supervised the outing so that she could make contact with no one, but what did that matter to any of the women? It was a small price to pay for their new wealth and luxury. Did a child need an education? Tutors were readily available, and the finest education that could be had was provided at the school within the compound. Dalir saw to every eventuality. There would be no outside contact; none at all.

A few of the scientists that Dalir wanted on board were not cooperative at first. True to his nature, he found ways. Some needed only to be bribed with extra money. Others found themselves following their families to Esfahan rather than stay behind after the family was kidnapped. One or two had to be shown film of their wives or children with guns to their heads. Sooner or later, everyone agreed to relocate and ordered to be happy.

Once the undercover agents in America began sending coded information and occasional photos, the scientists' work was cut out for them. Their task was to decode the messages and comb the incomplete information for anything useful, sharing data to build a more complete picture. Unfortunately, there were large gaps in the information. Too large to infer what was missing. In spite of pep talks, offers of bonus payments and threats, nothing was emerging that would further Dalir's ultimate cause.

A risky message was sent to each agent: *Why is this information incomplete?* The answer came back: *They have us working on tightly segmented sections of the information. No one has all of it except a security committee.*

Reza Mokri opened his diplomatically-sealed mailbag one day to find a coded message inside from Dalir. He was to find out who comprised the security committee for the nanotechnology program - they needed an insider. All of the work to find, train and insert agents into the Rossler Foundation would be for nothing if they couldn't break the security. To do so, one of the committee must be suborned, but who?

It took Reza nearly a week to search out the information without drawing attention to himself. When he had it, it wasn't good news. Most of the members were core founders of the Rossler Foundation; Daniel, Sinclair, Raj and Luke would be impossible to get to. That left the program manager, Karsten Adler, and the head researcher, Roy James. Reza made it his mission to get acquainted with both of them, to be able to make a recommendation.

Karsten was married, with two children, he learned. Not a good candidate. Reza turned his attention to Roy and found that he had a reputation of not liking women. Reza's message to Dalir was that their best bet was to approach Roy with al-fahsha', an obscene act, which was one of the three Islamic terms for homosexuality. One of the male agents would have to sacrifice himself for the cause.

Ironically, had Roy been gay, Reza himself would probably have been the best candidate based on his good looks. But, as the agent who approached him discovered quickly, Roy was not gay. His nervous demeanor around women meant that he was effectively cut off from their company in any romantic sense, but he'd rather do without than turn to a man, and he made it abundantly clear to the agent, who sported a broken nose for some time. The man blamed it on running into a doorway in the dark.

When that approach failed, they tapped the woman with the mildest personality, someone who could easily feign extreme shyness, to befriend Roy and eventually seduce him. Even demure Laleh Farshid was too much for Roy, though.

She sat down beside him in the company cafeteria for a coffee break one day, and he did his best to be friendly, but everything he said seemed to turn out wrong. By the end of the break, he was drenched in sweat and she was baffled at some of the inane remarks that had come out of his mouth. Now every time he saw her coming he practically ran the other way. Eventually she cornered him in an elevator.

"Roy, have I offended you?" she asked, her eyes downcast.

"Uh, offended? Me? N-n-no, uh, wh-why?" he stuttered.

"Do you not wish to talk with me, to be friends? I think you do not like me."

"N-no. I m-mean, yes, I l-like you okay," he said. Miserable, he could summon no other words.

Laleh reported to her handler that she may be able to seduce Roy someday, but it would not be soon. Another alternative would have to be found.

It was almost as if they had planned it exactly as it came down. Alica was the best choice for a seduction of anyone but Roy James. Since she worked closely with Karsten Adler and he was their best hope, she could make it seem natural that she would be attracted to him. All that stood in her way was his family, but, as she remarked to her handler in her report, any man can have a vulnerability. In Karsten's case, it was a wife who was satisfied with her two children and therefore no longer gave him enough attention in the bedroom, preferring in fact to sleep in separate rooms. The classic 'my wife doesn't understand me' situation worked in her favor after Alica encouraged Karsten to talk about his family. Inevitably, she learned that he was unhappy in his marriage, though he loved his wife still. He found in Alica a sympathetic ear and a shoulder to cry on, literally.

By increments, Alica drew Karsten closer to her. She did a stellar job in her duties, leading him to take her to lunch now and then as an extra thank-you. In return, she invited him for dinner at her apartment on an evening when she knew his wife had other plans. The setting was cozy, the candlelight romantic; her peck on his cheek as he left a welcome sign of affection to an affection-starved man. It was a calculated acceleration on her part. Alica knew better than to throw herself at Karsten - it wouldn't be subtle enough. When he started touching her casually whenever he came to her desk to speak with her, though, she knew the time was right.

One evening, as the workday came to a close, Karsten found Alica weeping softly at her desk.

"My dear Alica, what is the matter?" he asked, drawing her out of her seat to stand in front of him.

"Nothing. Please don't concern yourself." Alica dabbed at her eyes, a sob catching in her throat.

"No, please! Tell me. Is it something I can help with?" he insisted.

"I don't think so." She sighed, looked up at him with swimming eyes and found his tender upon her. "All right, I will tell you. This is the anniversary of my husband's and son's deaths. I miss them so much!" she finished, her voice going up in a soft wail.

"Oh, my dear friend," Karsten said. "I'm so sorry." He moved closer, put his arm around her. "There, there. Please don't cry. What happened to them?"

In answer, she laid her head in the hollow of his shoulder, still weeping. "A tragic accident took them. Oh, if only I had been with them! Thank you, Karsten. You are such a comfort."

His other arm surrounded her, and she felt his lips touch the top of her head. She snuggled closer. "I miss this, too," she whispered. "Being close with a man. I've been so lonely."

Karsten began trembling, and Alica knew it was only a matter of time before he would kiss her. Perhaps not tonight, since she was grieving for her husband, but soon. She would let him make the first move, and he'd never know he'd been seduced. He'd believe that he was the seducer.

That day came only a few days later, when Alica arrived

at work to find flowers on her desk. There was no card, so she went into the inner office where Karsten's desk was and asked him if he knew who had sent them.

"I thought you could use some cheering up," he said. That such a beautiful woman would continue to grieve for a long-dead husband was a crime against nature. To his surprise, she threw her arms around him and hugged him tightly.

"They're beautiful!" she said, beaming up at him with a heartbreakingly lovely countenance. He'd been dreaming of the way she felt in his arms ever since a few days before when he'd tried to comfort her. His automatic response was to put his arms around her, and there they stood, clinging together with her face tilted toward his. The kiss happened as if it were fated, and before he knew it, Alica was returning it with passion, inflaming his own. Who knows what might have happened right there in his office if the phone hadn't rung suddenly?

Alica pulled away and fled to the outer office as Karsten answered his own phone. After handling the caller, he went to see if she was all right.

"I'm sorry, Alica, I don't know what to say for myself." His entire body was tense with frustration that the call had interrupted what surely would have been the declaration of their attraction to each other.

"It's all right," she said, her head lowered. "It's just…"

"Just what, my dear?" Did he dare hope she wanted him? That such a beautiful woman would, when his wife didn't, caused his chest to tighten.

In a barely discernible voice, she muttered, "Just that, I think I have a crush on you."

Karsten could hardly believe the way his heart jumped in his chest at her admission. He gave not a moment's thought to his wife when he asked Alica to join him for dinner that night at a hotel between Boulder and Denver.

"You won't be missed at home?" she inquired. Inside, she was triumphant. She still had it! Karsten would never know what hit him, until it was too late.

"I will find a reason to be late," he whispered, brushing a kiss over her dark curls again.

"Then I would love to," she whispered back, a promise in her eyes that sent thrills of excitement through him.

Photos of the tryst wouldn't reach Karsten until there had been enough occasions to seriously concern his wife, but Alica's company was well worth his infidelity. Never had he known a woman so exciting, so inventive, and so giving in bed. He felt like a teenager again, all raging hormones, with a belief in his immortality. In the back of his mind, he kept suppressed the feeling that another shoe would drop. Things like this didn't happen to middle-aged corporate types. Alica was too beautiful - she could be a model, or an actress. What she saw in him was a mystery, until it wasn't.

They'd been carrying on their affair for a few weeks, spending every moment they could together, when the photos came. Karsten stared at them in dismay. Alica and him with their heads together and holding hands at the luxurious Meritage restaurant. Alica in a very revealing bikini, with him at her side, as they relaxed in a poolside cabana at the Omni. Most disastrous of all, Alica and him in bed, their positions completely compromising. How in the world had the photographer captured that one? Had he actually been on the balcony of their hotel room, while they were oblivious to his presence?

His first thought was chivalrous. How could he have allowed her to be exposed like this? The note in the package disabused him of any illusions that she wasn't involved in the blackmail, however. The note instructed him to turn over any information she asked for, unless he wanted the photos to go to his wife. Then he knew he'd been played.

The saddest part of that, to him, was the knowledge that he was head over heels in love with her, and that he would gladly betray not only his wife but also his employer and his own moral center if only she would continue to see him. Now he knew the depths of his depravity. He would turn over dangerous secrets to someone who would undoubtedly give them to a terrorist organization, and he'd keep doing it as long as she allowed him access to her body. How pathetic, how morally bankrupt, was that?

Without thought to his marriage or his job, both of which he could well lose over his actions, he called Alica into his office. Rising to meet her, he took her into his arms and kissed her with abandon. When he came up for air, he asked, "What information do you want?"

The woman who had placed him in a position of extreme danger said, as if she'd been making a grocery list instead of returning his kisses passionately only a moment before, "Everything."

By the end of February, the stream of information coming from the Rossler Foundation nanotechnology program was offering abundant ideas to the Sword of Cyrus scientists in Esfahan. Dalir and two of the other members of the Sword of Cyrus traveled there to meet with the lead scientists and receive a progress report.

"Welcome, aqa, and thank you for honoring us with your presence," began the spokesperson for the scientists.

"Thank you, Ostad Sassan. We are glad to be here.

What can you tell me of your discoveries?" Dalir stood tensely, hoping he would hear something that would accelerate his plans for the destruction of the West.

"We have considered your requirements, Aqa Jahandar, and there are several items that we believe we can manufacture immediately. These items would fulfill the requirement to be small and easy to transport. They would also wreak terror on a scale we have not thought possible, because they would be undetectable, yet cause death in those individuals you would target. Nanopoisons would fit this description. Nanobots that could enter a person's body through a natural orifice and cause havoc with organs would also. However, neither of these options would fulfill your third requirement, that is, neither would be a weapon of mass destruction. They would be deployed against an individual, or at most a roomful of individuals. Are we correct in believing that what you want would be deployed against a major part of a city?" Although the scientist spoke dispassionately, he was secretly horrified at the thought. Nevertheless, as he had when his wife and children were used against him, he kept his own opinions to himself. Nothing would do except to please this man, who had his life and those of his family in an iron fist.

"Yes, many cities. A coordinated attack of weapons of mass destruction, yet undetectable, unlike a missile strike. Can you make something like that?" Dalir had no need of caution in his demands. Everyone in this facility and in the residential compound was at his mercy; none would dare work against him.

"We believe we will be able to, as long as the information continues to come to us. We have hints of items that would do it, but we don't yet have all of the specifications. Here's what we envision." Turning to a laptop set up in the conference room, Sassan queued up a presentation. The first image was of an ordinary can of Coke.

"We believe we will shortly have enough information to build a nanonuclear weapon no larger than this. We have discussed how to get these objects to the desired destinations, and have come up with a list of requirements that we'd like you to approve, or add to if necessary."

"Excellent, better than we could have imagined! You can really pack so much destructive power into such a small object?" Dalir marveled at the idea, but doubted such a small thing could do what he envisioned. However, if they could make something so small into a bomb that would cause much destruction, perhaps something only a little larger would be easy to manufacture as well.

"We think so. There are hints that it can be done. As yet, we don't have all the information, but we are encouraged by what we do have. May I continue?" Sassan stroked his beard nervously.

"Of course."

"Naturally, we don't expect to be able to assemble something, even this small, here and get it through security clearances when crossing borders. But, we plan to design items that will attract no notice, such as buttons, or threads that can be worked into the design of an item of clothing. Once all of the components are in one place, they will be assembled into the weapon, a process even a child could do with proper instruction."

"And how will it be deployed?" Jahandar's eyes glittered. How many of these tiny weapons would it take to destroy half the world?

"Again, because it is so small, it can be deployed by small drones. They won't have a long range, so they, too will have to be assembled near where they are to be used.

Do you know which city you will attack yet, Aqa Jahandar?"

"That remains to be worked out. I will let you know how many of these nanonuclear weapons we'll need. Keep me informed regarding your progress." Even to someone whose very existence was in his hands, Dalir would not yet reveal the extent of his ambition. That information, for now, was for the Sword of Cyrus only.

"Yes, sir.

Dalir and his Sword of Cyrus lieutenants returned to Tehran very satisfied with the progress. None of them had expected to be even this far along so quickly. It was necessary now to begin to make a specific plan. Oleg Zlatovski was sent for and consulted as to the weakest governments and security systems in the West. Oleg was happy to supply the information, as well as to begin building a human network in the places where Dalir showed the most interest. Assuming there was anything left of the world after the Sword of Cyrus struck, such a network could come in handy for certain activities Oleg was beginning to consider in his own right.

A room was set aside for planning an attack that would occur at an unknown time on an unknown date in the future. All they had now was a huge world map with dozens of pins in a few different colors. Each color represented a type of target, red for primary, with Washington, D.C. full of red pins. Orange for secondary, and yellow for possible targets. They'd hit those if there were enough personnel and materiel. The reds and oranges represented the major capitals of the West. Destroying those cities would effectively destroy any ability to resist when the Sword of Cyrus declared their dominion over the remainder of the planet.

Chapter Fourteen
DÉJÀ POO

Late March, 2020; Boulder

Raj left Roy's office in a state of excitement akin to a little boy at Christmas time. In his cupped hands, he cradled a tiny object that Roy had given him. Finally! His own Spyfly! He could hardly wait to show it to his wife, Sushma. After that, he would find a way to slip it into some top-secret conferences, meetings he just knew the government was still holding to keep the appropriate committees up to speed on aliens, Area 51, and the conspiracy to hide the knowledge from the American people for more than seventy years.

Before that, he was planning to tinker with the video to make it record longer without sacrificing quality. Roy may have been satisfied with it the way it was, but Raj had more sophisticated needs for it. To test it, Raj sent the fly into a room full of translators, who, to his gratification, didn't even notice it. He was waiting for a chance to talk with Sinclair about a new routine he had written to speed up the transliteration process that the employees were now doing by hand. While leaning casually against the wall, he sent his fly to land on a few computers, on the walls, and even on the ceiling.

He kept it away from people's bodies, fearful that if they noticed it they would try to swat it away or even smash it. One significant difference between this little device and a real fly was that it made virtually no noise as it flew. Unlike the buzzing of a real insect, this little guy was virtually silent. Raj almost wished Roy had named it the 'stealth fly', but Spyfly was almost as good. Sometimes Raj still indulged his inner child.

After talking with Sinclair, Raj hurried to his office, his fly hovering just over his shoulder. Once there, he downloaded the video feed. The first thing he noticed was that he and Roy needed to find a way to pause the video while the fly was in transition. The swooping feeling he got from watching those sections of the feed wasn't pleasant, but it shouldn't be hard to fix that. The pictures from the wall were good, but he hadn't made the fly crawl far enough up the wall. It seemed there was an art to controlling the little fellow. The longest section of feed came from the vantage-point of the ceiling, and showed a surprisingly clear picture of most of the room. Raj watched as it scanned back and forth, sweeping the room from side to side and advancing the picture from the back to the front of the room.

A movement that seemed out of place caught his eye. Raj reversed the feed several seconds, and then advanced it one frame at a time. There. What was that guy doing? This could be fun checking this out a bit closer. Raj saved the file, noting the timestamp on the unusual movement, and loaded it into some video-enhancing software that he'd acquired at Luke's request.

Advancing the playback to the correct time, he stopped it and fiddled with the image until he could see the object in the guy's hand. Was it a cell phone? Maybe it was just some guy voice-texting his girlfriend, or taking a selfie. But he had the phone very close to his face. He advanced the file at normal speed, still running it through the image-enhancing software since he was already set up to do that. This time, he caught the flicker as soon as the person's hand moved to his pocket. It was a different person, also taking a selfie with the phone close to his face. Advancing frame by frame, Raj watched as this guy brought his phone up to eye level and moved his finger almost imperceptibly. He was taking a picture of his screen, not his face!

Raj sat back and thought about it for a while. Then he ran the video back to the first incident. The camera had caught the precise angle of the phone in that guy's hand, and yes, Raj could see the finger come down. It was the same move. Both of those guys had taken pictures, but of what? The only clue he had was that the phone in the first picture was clearly pointed at the guy's computer screen. There was only one thing to do. Clearing the fly's memory now that he had the first video saved on his desktop computer, he sent the fly back to the translation department, letting it crawl around on the ceiling to get a vantage point for each section of the room. By the end of the day, he had plenty of evidence of people taking pictures of their screens, but of what on their screens he wasn't sure. Nevertheless, it was unusual enough and worrisome enough to take it to Daniel.

Daniel was getting ready to leave for the day when Raj appeared in his doorway.

"Boss, I've got something here that worries me. Would you take a look?" Raj went on to explain what he had found and how he'd found it. As soon as Daniel saw the evidence for himself, he called Luke, hoping against hope that he hadn't already left for the day. When Luke picked up, Daniel sighed in relief.

"Luke, Raj has brought me something that you need to see. Can you hold up a minute and see it tonight?" His voice was tightly controlled, suppressing that old gut feeling of disaster, despite the low-key actions on the video.

"Sure, no problem. Sally's going to be late, too. She and Emma took little Nick for a photo shoot in his Easter outfit. They want the pictures to make greeting cards or something. Those women can think up more stuff to do than you can shake a stick at."

Despite his worry, Daniel had to laugh. He knew his mother-in-law and Luke's wife were spending their golden years in pursuits they'd never had time for when they were younger. He couldn't imagine Sarah doing that though, as busy as she was with Foundation business. Unless she decided to bake him into an early grave. She did love to bake!

"Come on up, Luke. Raj and I will wait for you."

Half an hour later, Luke was swearing a blue streak. He'd noticed something that neither of the other two saw. The people taking pictures of their computer screens were all Middle Eastern and all of them were new recruits!

"Raj, do you have anything that can synch these feeds up to what's on the computer screens when the pictures are taken?" Luke ran the video back again, stopping at each movement to look at the face and try to place the employee's name.

Raj hesitated, reluctant to reveal that he'd been too complacent in using his tools. "Not for today's work. We have that capability, to watch what comes across the screens, with a timestamp. But we haven't had occasion to use it." He looked away from Luke.

Luke understood Raj's feelings, but didn't address them. What was done was done, it only remained to salvage what he could. "Can you set it up for tomorrow? Sorry to ask you to pull overtime."

Raj was happy to be able to make up for his oversight. He'd make it right with Sushma, but he had to do everything he could to fix this. "No problem. I'll see if Cyndi can stay late also, if she hasn't gone already. Then what, just have my fly take video all day and hope to see this again?"

"Yours, Daniel's, mine. As many as we can get. We need to see if it's only the newer employees or if anyone else is doing it, and we need to know what's in those pictures." Luke's expression was grim. He glanced at Daniel, whose tension was making the room crackle.

"You got it. I'll see if I can remote the feeds back to my office, too, so we won't miss anything." Raj thought there was a provision for that, but he'd have to ask Roy how to do it. It was shaping up to be a long evening, and if he wanted help, he needed to make some calls right now.

He found Cyndi still in her office and willing to help. Roy was almost always in his lab, building something new or tinkering with a gadget he'd already built. Tonight was no exception. Taking his own, Daniel's and Luke's Spyflies with him, Raj met Cyndi outside Roy's office.

"Stay here for a minute Cyn. He might have a panic attack if you go in. Let me get some answers, and then I'll let you know what's going on and what I need help with. Okay?"

"Sure, no problem. Can I call Robert and let him know

I'll be late?" If Cyndi wondered about the panic attack remark, she didn't show it. Probably because many of the single women in the RF had been gossiping about the good-looking but painfully shy scientist.

"I don't see any problem with that. But don't let him come back. We need to keep this under our hats for a bit." Raj had his hand on the doorknob, ready to enter Roy's lab.

"Under our...? Oh, you mean on the down-low," Cyndi said, snickering.

"Whatever," Raj muttered. Whenever Cyndi updated his slang, he felt old.

Roy was excited that his gadget was already finding a practical use. He showed Raj how to set up the fly and the remote to get live feed wirelessly streamed to his computer and save it there. Already he was working on a second-generation fly that would broadcast in color, but the black-and-white images from the first-generation models were clear enough to identify faces. He didn't ask what was going on, figuring that if it was any of his business, Raj would have told him.

It was around midnight when a weary Cyndi and Raj made their separate ways home, dreading the six a.m. wake up call that would get them back to the office before anyone from the earliest flextime shift got there. They had a long day ahead of them, with some employees coming in as early as seven and others coming in later and not leaving until seven in the evening. Working eight hours flextime between seven and seven was a perk of the company that made the Rossler Foundation a popular employer.

The next morning, Daniel and Luke arrived in Raj's office where he'd set up several extra computers so that they could watch more than one feed at a time. It was nearly nine a.m. when they got their first hit. Raj had to check another screen to bring up the right computer, and when he did, Daniel and Luke knew immediately that they had a problem – a big one. The computer belonged to someone on the nanotech translation team. What was on the screen wasn't particularly sensitive by itself, thanks to Luke's insistence that the blocks of information be broken up among the translators. But, if it were put together with what probably surrounded it, it could be. Daniel instructed Luke and Raj to continue to gather data for the next few days, so they could determine exactly what the spies were after. It would take some time to make a final determination, but they had to let it continue to see just where their problem would come to roost.

One thing they needed to be careful about was accusing the Middle Easterners alone. Who knew how many of the employees were involved in this?

It was important to let it run for a while so they could determine with more precision who was taking pictures, and what part of the nanotech program they were targeting. Furthermore, what were they doing with it? Would it be possible for someone from the outside to put it together and get a full picture of the sensitive information? If so, who would that be? Discovering the plot was a lucky accident. Getting to the bottom of it would be arduous and painstaking. Luke wasn't looking forward to the next few days.

After a week it was manifest that the translators were working blind. The timestamps on the Spyfly video and the synched screen data showed information, incomplete as it was, about nanotechnology in medicine, construction, physics and electronics, along with a bit here and there on other unrelated disciplines. The scope was bewildering, and the only thing Luke could think to suggest to interpret it was to let Roy in on the discovery and ask him to suggest ways in which the data could be used for nefarious purposes. The trouble was, now that everyone was a suspect it had to be considered that Roy could be in on it himself.

Luke solved that problem by suggesting hacking into Roy's computers and phone, and deploying one of the Spyflies in Roy's own lab. Daniel didn't like it; even Raj, as paranoid as he was, didn't like it. It didn't feel right to spy on a friend, but Luke insisted that since he was responsible for security, it should be his decision and until proven otherwise everyone except the three of them and a few of the other founders was under suspicion. He was upset over the gaps that had allowed so many undercover agents into their inner circles, and adamant that they check Roy out before letting him know that they knew what they knew. They couldn't risk that leak if they wanted to discover what was really important; who was behind this and why.

Much to everyone's relief, they didn't discover anything to be suspicious about while watching Roy. Other than some embarrassing footage of him looking in the mirror and telling himself not to be such an idiot around women, he wasn't doing anything secretive. It was time to bring him in on the problem and find out what could happen if the bits and pieces of information were somehow put together like a jigsaw puzzle. There was also some discussion of bringing Karsten into the loop, but he had less expertise with nanotechnology per se than Roy did. He was a brilliant researcher in his field and a superlative administrator; nevertheless, nanotech wasn't his bailiwick.

It looked certain that it had something to do with the Middle East, since they hadn't found any of the other translators taking pictures of it. What baffled them was what was happening to the information once a written record of it was in the hands of unauthorized personnel. None of the translators had the background to take advantage of what they did find, and it was still too fragmented to do any good anyway. Roy opined that it would take a powerful computer to try to put it together in context. If anyone did, though, it could do significant damage.

The medical fragments had to do with delivery of foreign substances through the blood/brain barrier. Engineered properly, that technology could facilitate mass poisoning or contagion just by scattering it into the air over a city, or even contaminating the water supply with it. Every other discipline represented in the stolen data had equally terrifying uses. It was critical to determine where the information was going.

Raj wanted to report to Daniel and Luke what Roy had determined, and he didn't think it could wait. He made a call and asked Daniel to carve out some private time with them. Even though Roy hadn't been very specific, he had a bad feeling about it. Maybe it was just industrial espionage; that would be bad enough. But his instincts were that it was worse. That bad feeling turned out to be justified as he listened to Roy giving details in his report to Daniel.

Daniel had cut straight to the chase.

"Is there anything in these fragments of information that could lead to use of the information for military purposes?" Raj had been through a lot with Daniel, but he'd never before heard such hardness in Daniel's voice.

"Oh, sure," was Roy's casual answer. The others waited for him to elaborate.

"Look, they have information that could, if they had the full picture, let them build nanobots, nanoreplicators, nanoviruses and poisons, even DNA-specific nanopoisons.

They'd have to have the full picture, though. And what we've discovered seems to point to them only having pieces of it." None of the nervousness or indications of Roy's shy nature were present in this statement. He was in his element, and nothing could shake him except perhaps Alica or one of the other girls walking in at that moment. Fortunately, he was spared that.

"Help me out with some of this, Roy. Tell me what you can do with a nanopoison or virus. Just to be sure I'm following you," Daniel added.

"Well, one thing is delivery of foreign substances through the blood-brain barrier. Engineered properly, that technology could facilitate mass poisoning or contagion just by scattering it into the air over a city, or even contaminating the water supply with it." Roy was so matter-of-fact that Daniel was certain he didn't even recognize the human toll that would take.

"Holy crap!" exclaimed Luke, his eyes wide.

"Yeah, you could say that. With a DNA-specific nanopoison, you could put it in, say, the water at a diplomatic dinner. Everyone would drink it, but only the person it was intended to target would get sick, or die. You could even engineer it to make it look like food poisoning, so a bunch of people would get sick, but only the target would die. No one would ever be able to figure out that it was a murder," Roy said, not without a certain satisfaction. It wasn't that he was cold. To him, it was like a videogame. Exciting, but not real.

"I think I'm already sick. Why is the word déjà vu coming up in my head? Or should I say déjà poo – I have heard this shit before?" Daniel muttered.

"All of this was filtered out before it went to the researchers by the security committee," remarked Luke. "So

The Sword of Cyrus

no one has the full picture. And you say they'd need that to make this stuff?" His only hope was that the information was too incomplete to use.

"Yeah. Of course, if they had a powerful enough computer, they might be able to piece some of it together," answered Roy, unwittingly dashing Luke's hope.

"Or they could get it from someone on the security committee," injected Raj, who could always be trusted to have the most suspicious mind of all of them.

The four looked at each other uneasily. All of them were on that committee. But surely everyone on that committee was above suspicion? It had to be someone outside that was getting the information. Looking at the list of names of those who had been caught taking photos of their computer screens, it was obvious that every one of them had been sponsored for employment by Iran. Was someone in Iran just doing a bit of industrial espionage to get a jump on the competition? Or did they have another, more serious problem on their hands? They needed more information, preferably some idea about the communications these people were transmitting, and they needed it fast.

Examining the individuals' company email was a nobrainer, but Raj could find nothing of alarm in any of the messages he intercepted. Even running it through some software that would detect most common coding algorithms failed to find a single message that was anything but professional, between the translators, or a couple of private messages. It was frowned upon to use company resources to keep in touch with friends and family, but everyone did it and as long as it didn't interfere with work no one made an issue of it.

Still, any personal messages found on company computers were about daily life in the US, how nice things were in Boulder and in their company-provided living quarters, and how much they missed everyone at home. Completely innocuous. Luke even tapped some contacts in the federal security agencies to help with hacking into the suspects' social media accounts, phone records and private email accounts of the suspects. Still nothing.

Chapter Fifteen

NANONUKES

Late February, 2020; Esfahan

Despite Roy's belief, Dalir Jahandar's scientists were indeed able to make use of much of the material being translated at the Rossler Foundation. Even before the translators were discovered taking photos of their computer screens, the lab in Iran was already in possession of some important and useful information for Dalir's cause, thanks to Alica's efforts. Research had been completed to plan the weapons of mass destruction that Dalir had ordered.

The first incoming information that lent itself to such a purpose was the notion of nanopoisons. At first, they didn't see anything useful having to do with DNA-specific poisons, and in any case it would have been both difficult and risky to obtain DNA from some of the most sought-after targets. Instead, they began to develop nano-dust applications that mimicked outbreaks of disease common to the presumed target countries. Realizing that the method of delivery would have to be tested, the first to be developed was a nasty little artificial virus that mimicked Ebola so perfectly that even the doctors on staff couldn't tell the difference.

While the infectious-disease specialists were working with nanotech scientists to develop that, epidemiologists were working with others to develop a deployment method. The most efficient of course would have been something like a crop-duster to spread the nano-dust in a precise pattern. However, that had some very obvious disadvantages. While a low-flying plane could more accurately deliver the payload, there were bound to be some survivors who noticed it and remembered later. It could be traceable. Something more subtle would be required.

Stealth bombers were suggested, but Iran had no such item, and China, which did, wasn't likely to lend them for testing. Cruise and other types of missiles, gravity bombs, all had the same disadvantage. They would be detected.

Eventually, it was settled that small drones deployed from the edge of the effective range to targets hundreds of miles away would be the best method of delivery. As early as the first year of the century, such drones had been deployed against Middle Eastern targets that the US deemed terrorists; why not give them a taste of their own medicine? However, since Ebola was not a common disease in America, the first test took place over Africa. Naturally, Dalir had no desire to harm Muslims, so it was determined that a ship would carry the drone with its deadly payload around the Horn of Africa to near the coast of Kenya, where it would find the shortest direct flight to Arua, Uganda. There, many Christians would succumb to the artificial virus, or nano-dust as the scientists preferred to call it, assuming that it worked.

The Sword of Cyrus

The first strike in Dalir's war was spectacularly successful, though the cloud of deadly dust spread somewhat further than anticipated due to winds aloft when the drone's tanks were opened. Not only Arua, with its primarily Catholic population, but also parts of the Democratic Republic of the Congo were affected. The latter were tiny villages in the deep jungle, and didn't cause much stir worldwide. However, forty percent of the fifty-thousand or so souls in Arua sickened and died, in a pattern that didn't follow the normal spread of Ebola at all. Instead of an index case, all patients became ill at about the same time. Doctors responding to the emergency were puzzled. Ebola spreads from human to human, though contact with infected fluids, or from contact on surfaces where the infected fluids have been. This illness appeared to have been airborne. Nor did infected patients infect their families, as happened with the normal progression of the disease. In addition, although there were effective treatments developed during the 2014 outbreak in West African countries, the remoteness, uneducated population as well as the poor medical facilities and lack of treatment caused more than 24,000 deaths in just a few weeks. Even those who were fortunate enough to receive the treatment died, leading doctors to wonder if they were dealing with a new strain.

In America, Dr. Hannah Price saw the memo and had a moment's curiosity. Her current project was at a critical point, so she thought no more about it, other than to forward the memo to Rebecca Rossler, a fellow researcher whom she'd met during the 9th Cycle virus pandemic. Rebecca read it, shuddered at the reminder of a deadly virus with a mysterious beginning, and thought no more about it for several days.

In Esfahan, a feast was prepared for the scientists whose

project had given such spectacular results. Despite the fact that they hadn't refined the nano-dust to spare most Muslims, and that a few were killed in the attack on Arua, no one questioned that it had been a success. They now knew how to poison thousands of people at a time in a stealthy manner, and pass it off as a naturally-occurring disease long enough to escape detection. No survivor in Arua noticed or remembered a mysterious flying object that had rained death from the sky.

The next step was to determine what diseases the nano-poisons for the target countries should mimic. For that, they needed some direction, including decisions on where the weapon would be used when the real war began.

While this victory was being planned and implemented, another team of scientists was eagerly working on the hints they'd seen in the 10th Cycle translations about a nano-nuclear weapon. Fragments of the translation were painstakingly compared, pieced together and the missing information interpolated. Their research was behind the bioweapon research, but not by far and since Alica started sending them information they were making rapid progress. Another huge leap in progress came with the fragment that mentioned a deuterium-tritium mixture. Now they were getting somewhere! However, before they could test the theory, a supply of each of the rare materials would be required. While some nuclear scientists discussed and researched where or how to obtain them, others considered how to get the resulting bombs, tiny as they were to be, into the target countries.

March, 2020; Esfahan

Before any conclusion about where to get rare and expensive tritium had been reached, a fragment of 10th Cycle information came through that made the discussions moot. Fortuitously, the ongoing recruitment efforts also brought in a new scientist who was knowledgeable in the chemistry of heavy water.

"You all know of course that deuterium can be collected from seawater, where it occurs naturally. The process to collect it is simple, whether you choose to use distillation or electrolysis. I presume that you would prefer to collect it ourselves, rather than purchasing the quantities we will need for hundreds of these small bombs?" Those who'd been working tirelessly for weeks resented the new man's arrogant demeanor, but they couldn't fault his knowledge.

"Indeed. There is no need to alert any attention to our project here," someone answered.

"The real question, then, is tritium. In the past, this substance has been collected during a fusion process. Need I ask if you have built a fusion reactor?" At that moment, the new scientist was seconds from bodily harm from some of the veterans, but the leader forestalled any violence with his answer.

"You may ask. The answer of course, is no." Spoken with a sarcastic twist, it sounded more like a slap in the face than an admission of failure.

"Of course. However, I have read the fragment of information that has come to us from the 10th Cycle library, regarding bombardment of lithium with Continuous Laser Energy Compression, or CLEC, for which we also have to thank the 10th Cycle. You have built such a laser device, yes?" Fortunately, the new man had finally picked up the subtext, and was tempering his words with a more conciliatory tone of voice.

"Yes. We thought it may become useful in our research," the lead scientist answered, curious now as to where this was going.

"Indeed. Have you attempted this bombardment?" the new man persisted.

"We have, however it has not produced tritium that we can detect." That should put the newcomer in his place, the lead scientist added mentally.

But, the new man surprised him with some truly relevant information. "Because we are missing some information, and I believe I know what it is. We must immerse the lithium in seawater before bombardment. Lithium alone does not have the required free neutrons to capture in the chemical reaction." A note of triumph crept back into his voice.

"Are you certain it is so simple?" asked the lead scientist, now understanding that the new man was indeed superior in knowledge.

He knew it, too. Now the arrogance was back. "Do you question my expertise?"

"No, no, of course not." The lead scientist backed down altogether, and thereby lost his position to the new man, an insufferable egotist. A few of the others began to plot the man's destruction, as soon as they'd obtained all the knowledge he had to contribute. It didn't pay to walk into an established pecking order and try to be the alpha rooster.

And so, miraculously, the problem of fueling the nanoweapons was solved. Massive effort went into producing the first fuels and continued after the scientists took away minute amounts for testing. By the time the date for the attack was set, they were ready to test the power of the reaction.

In a normal fusion reaction, the energy is confined and used to heat water to steam, which in turn drives turbines to produce electricity. Because the relatively small radioactive output is captured to breed more tritium, the only byproduct is helium, a harmless gas. What Dalir's scientists were trying to do would instead release the energy. Readily available information online revealed that approximately 250 kilos of fuel, half deuterium, half tritium, would release perhaps 1,000 megawatts of energy in a matter of an instant, equivalent at least to a fifty megaton nuclear reaction; more than four times the power of the Hiroshima bomb. Translating this to the power released by a nanoweapon was merely theory. They would have to test it to determine the amount of fuel needed in their bombs.

Obviously, 250 kilos was too heavy and too bulky. But half a kilo, that was more than manageable, and would require only a few dozen of the small bombs in most cities to utterly destroy the center of the city, creating confusion and panic in the outlying areas. The city centers, if hit during the workday, would contain the most important people in the region; the leaders, the heads of household. Fewer bombs still would handle military bases and any ability to retaliate.

A different strategy from the July 4th bombing of last year would have to be pursued. That attack was coordinated to take place at exactly the same moment as the eight p.m. bombing in Washington, D.C. It was designed more to demonstrate the Ayatollah's power than to do any real and lasting harm. This attack was meant to destroy the West. They would strike each region when it would do the most harm, kill the most people. After that, the rest would surrender, though of course there would be some confusion and some intention to rush to the aid of those first attacked. That would only help in the mission; since the attacks would begin in the Pacific, the US would be fully engaged in its usual white-knight race to help and would therefore not be anticipating an attack on their soil.

To test the power of the explosion would require even less material, a few grams at most. The researchers sent a message to Dalir Jahandar requesting a bunker of hardened concrete in which to do it. Jahandar sent back a message that there was no time to build one. Test a smaller amount yet of the material, he suggested. After all, this was nanotechnology. Accordingly, the test was designed. Four scientists were privileged to watch and measure the destructive power of a few grams of the fuel, all of whom were killed when the building in which they were doing the test was reduced to rubble, or, more accurately, dust, along with several buildings surrounding it. The test was deemed a success, and the dead celebrated as martyrs in the cause. That was of little comfort to their families, but they were well compensated and continued to live in contentment in their luxurious dwellings in the compound.

The owners of the surrounding buildings that were destroyed also received adequate compensation for their cooperation in saying nothing. No news of the accident of unknown origin that caused minor damage in the little town of Esfahan reached even the larger cities of Iran, much less international news.

In an unexpected bonus, the remaining scientists also determined that all electronic equipment within a mile of the explosion had been irreparably fried by the electromagnetic pulse engendered by the bomb. From this knowledge, it wasn't a large leap of logic to determine that the most destructive effect would be from an explosion *above* the target. Their recommendation, therefore, was for air strikes, rather than ground deployment.

Now it was up to the logistics experts to determine how to deliver the little packages of destruction to their intended targets, and before that, how to get them into the target countries. The scientists were tasked with finding a way to safely transport the fuels without detection.

March, 2020; Tehran

Dalir Jahandar called a meeting of the council of twelve of the Sword of Cyrus to discuss strategy, tactics, and targets. He'd heard from his scientists that they must know the targets to plan the weapons and how to get them to their assigned targets. What, he asked his lieutenants, was the objective and how would they reach it. Behind the question was his lifelong obsession with restoring the empire of his multiple-great-grandfather, Cyrus the Great. His inclination was to do it by stealth, just as Cyrus had conquered Babylon more than 2,500 years ago. He felt it would be extremely satisfying to watch infidels die in confusion. His lieutenants agreed.

Because the nanonukes would be the most expensive and most difficult to build and get to their intended targets, the council decided they would be saved for the most visible targets; capital cities, centers of industry and military bases. Anything else that needed mopping up could be accomplished with nanopoison dust, in due time. In this way, they could kill millions if the cities were by chance evacuated, or if the nukes failed to live up to their expectations.

The added advantage would be the total destruction of any country with the capability to strike back. For the minor players, countries with a majority of non-Muslim faith, they would also be conquered in the same way that Arua was devastated. That meant most of Africa and South America. The decision on Asia was postponed, since several Asian countries were allies. However, when all was done, Dalir would require all survivors to embrace Islam, without exception.

For reasons of his own, Mokri suggested that the attacks take place on the beginning day of Hajj, which would be on the western calendar day of July 29 this year. Could they be ready by late July? No one knew. It was another question for the scientists.

When they had finished these discussions, a guest was ushered in. Oleg Zlatovski stepped briskly into the room and nodded at the members he didn't know. He held out his hand to shake the hand of Dalir, who simply stared at the extended hand. Suddenly realizing his gaffe, Oleg gave a nervous chuckle and put both hands in his pockets.

"Good afternoon, Jahandar," he said, intentionally leaving off any term of Russian or Greek respect. He rather thought that anything but Arabic or Farsi would offend, and he didn't know those terms. Ordinarily, he would not care whether he offended, but this man, Dalir Jahandar, had an air of command about him that was rather intimidating. Oleg had just been given a tour of the scientific compound in Esfahan, including the destroyed warehouse at Ground Zero of the nanonuke test. With the majority of his pay for services rendered to this group still to be delivered, he thought he knew why he'd been summoned today.

"Good afternoon, Gospodin Zlatovski. I trust you are well." The precise English was delivered in tones of ice.

The Sword of Cyrus

"Yes, thank you. You required my presence?" Zlatovski was now wary, since Jahandar's tone had been less than friendly.

"We require your assistance. You will of course speak of this to no one, on pain of our displeasure."

It was such a simple thing, a threat so subtle that it could have almost been a friendly jest. And yet Zlatovski understood perfectly that the consequences could - probably would - be deadly.

"You have no need to worry, my friend. Oleg Zlatovski is very discreet. What assistance do you require?" His English was heavily accented with his native Russian pronunciation, rendering the Ws as Vs and the vowels all guttural.

"You must help us determine where best to deploy the powerful weapons that our scientists have developed. As you know, the weapons are small, and the destructive power enormous."

"What is your objective?" asked Oleg, thinking only of the mission, not yet of betrayal, though it would cross his mind later.

"To destroy any capacity of the West, or the rest of the world, for that matter, to resist Islam. We intend to kill the leaders and destroy military bases that would retaliate. We also want to kill as many civilians as we can in the first strike so that the will of the people to fight back is broken. Tell us where to best place them to eradicate city centers, and where military installations are that have long-distance retaliatory capability." The plan was audacious, world-changing in fact. Never before had such an objective been voiced, to Oleg's knowledge. He sucked in his breath.

"Very well. I trust you will have no objection if I transfer my financial dealings to Iranian banks?" A nervous chuckle escaped him before he could suppress it, and he turned terror-stricken eyes on Jahandar.

"None at all. I see we understand each other. You will not speak of it to others." Jahandar repeated the obvious.

"Certainly not," Oleg snapped. Bringing his fears to heel with an effort, he said, "We are going to need a very large world map, and some push pins."

"My friend, you are behind the times," answered Dalir. With a click of a remote control, a digital flat-screen covering the entire wall of the conference room descended from the ceiling. A few keystrokes on the laptop in front of him caused the entire screen to fill with a detailed world map, complete with countries, cities and time zones. Another click turned the United States red.

"This is our primary objective. Destroy the US, and we destroy the will of the rest to resist. They must go above all," Dalir explained needlessly.

"Just so. You will of course hit Washington, D.C., and New York City. How do I mark the targets?" Oleg asked, adjusting to the technology smoothly.

Dalir handed Oleg a remote with a laser pointer. "Aim with the pointer and click the plus sign. Do the same and click minus to remove it. Use the keypad to let us know the approximate area of the target. We'll determine the number of weapons needed."

Oleg did not answer, but instead pointed the laser at Washington, D.C. A figure of 60 square miles appeared next to the city.

"Refine it. Just the area of the most government buildings, banks and such," Dalir demanded. "Assume destructive power of ten kilometers or so." Dalir was guessing, based on his scientists' comparison of the theoretical power of the nanonukes as compared to the A-bomb that destroyed Hiroshima. They thought it would be at least twice as powerful, and Little Boy had wiped out everything within a two and a half-kilometer radius from ground zero.

"You'd do best to deploy them in the center of the Pentagon, and near the Capitol, then," replied Oleg. "That will do the most damage to government. Add targets of the White House and Union Station for the most psychological impact. But good luck getting into any of those places besides Union Station."

"Leave that to us to handle. Where else?"

"Fort Knox. The New York Stock Exchange, Cape Canaveral, Cheyenne Mountain near Colorado Springs, Los Angeles, Detroit, Chicago, Dallas." As he named major cities, Oleg rapidly marked them with his laser pointer. "You'll have to look up the area of each target, I don't know it all off the top of my head." Some, he knew, were compact pockets of extreme power and wealth, others were spread out over thousands of square kilometers. He couldn't fathom the number of bombs that would be needed.

"Wait," said Jahandar. We need not destroy every large city in the country, nor every country in the West. Which would be most effective as demonstrations? Cripple them, and the rest will crumple.

"In that case," replied Oleg, "The US, the United Kingdom, and Israel." For good measure, knowing that his home country would execute him if they knew he was alive, he added, "Russia."

"Military installations?" Jahandar prompted. These were highly important, not only to destroy the ability to retaliate, but for psychological purposes.

Oleg marked each of the largest, putting several dots around the locations of NORAD installations across the continent. He then moved to Europe and began marking important military bases there. Noting that one big US military installation was in Greece, he made a mental note to sell his holdings there as quickly as possible and move to Turkey.

The meeting went on for some hours as Oleg marked cities and military installations in the UK and Russia and important financial or industrial centers, as well as NATO-controlled military bases.

"I want you to also mark important targets in Australia. Those bastards are too close to the US, politically, and they have been fighting with the US against our people for decades now." snarled Dalir. Oleg looked at him in surprise. In all their dealings, Dalir had never before used an off-color reference in speech. He must really hate Australians.

"Okay. Canberra, of course; Sydney, Brisbane, Melbourne. Pine Gap."

"What's that?"

"We never were quite sure. Highly classified, must be something of value there. It's a military installation in the Outback and they almost certainly are hosting a few nukes there for their US friends. I'll get coordinates for you." Oleg's mind was reeling at the enormity of the plan. His admiration for Dalir grew as the other asked pertinent questions and made sharp observations.

When the targets had been finalized and agreed upon, Dalir instructed Oleg to set it up, from the transport of the materiel into the target countries, to the personnel tasked with carrying out the manufacture and launch of the bombs.

"One more thing, Oleg," he said. "Make sure that nothing can interfere. Compartmentalize the assets as before, and instruct them to continue with the plans as you have laid them out, even if they see or hear something they think might change the situation. They must execute their instructions precisely on the day and time as you have instructed, and they must understand that it is the only instruction they will receive. There will be no further communication once you have set them in motion."

"Understood," Oleg acknowledged. "You'll get the plans to me securely?"

"Of course," responded Dalir. His mind was already on a detail they might otherwise have missed. The bomb plans must include a fail-safe that would trigger them if they failed to explode after a signal was sent to them as planned. They may not reach their intended destination, but they'd do some damage. Major damage, in fact.

When Oleg was finally released, Reza had another suggestion.

"You know, I was talking with JR Rossler at a Foundation function," remarked Reza. "We should look into the geology of the western United States. He seems to believe that a vast volcanic field lies under Yellowstone Park. Perhaps a few of our little surprises would trigger it to erupt."

"I'll find a geologist to confirm that. Excellent suggestion."

Dalir carefully saved the map image with its targets marked to Sword of Cyrus servers before joining the others for prayers and then a late dinner.

Chapter Sixteen

ROY'S TOYS

March & April, 2020; Boulder

Roy was happy at the Rossler Foundation, more so than at any time in his past. He liked teaching well enough, as long as there were few women in his classes, but there were no guarantees of that. Of all the star researchers attached to the Rossler Foundation, Roy was the only one who had not gone through the stress of the first Antarctica expedition and the virus. Of course, he'd known of the virus, but it didn't touch him personally. Just as now the discovery of spies in their midst gave him only mild concern while everyone else was very upset.

Encouraged by the enthusiastic reception of his Spyfly and the immediate use it was put to, Roy went back to the drawing board to create more of his flying objects. From the tiniest insect he could think of, a mosquito, to the size of a pigeon similar to the drones that Daniel remembered from Sarah's rescue from her kidnappers years before, Roy had a suggested use for all of them. His idea was that you could equip each of them with a nano version of almost anything you could want. The mosquito, for example, might be equipped with a drug that would render the target unconscious which could come in very handy in hostage and clandestine situations. The person would never guess that he'd been drugged; he'd think he'd been bitten by a mosquito, and the inevitable slap on feeling the sting would drive the drug even deeper into his flesh.

As the flying objects grew in size, so did their utility. Video cameras such as the Spyfly had, radio transmitters, communications on a battlefield. The list was endless. Each had their special features, from the multiple-shot weapons that the pigeon-sized object carried, to the speed of the hummingbird object—over two hundred miles per hour, with a target accuracy of 99.9%, for high-speed messages when radio and cell towers were down. Some of Roy's ideas were far-fetched, but his production of the little miracles was beyond compare. He stopped exploring uses for them when Daniel pointed out that if they became much more talented, he'd have to pull the plug on grounds of potential military use.

Power sources were another big interest of Roy's. In addition to the fact that he wanted to make his flying inventions more efficient, Roy had dreamed of inventing a nano car battery. Something very small, but with the potential to power a car for a month before being recharged. Not only the cachet that would come with such an invention drove him, but also a deep respect for the environment that made him wish there were something besides hydrocarbon-based fuels and underpowered electric cars. His specialty, nano-electronics, he thought would lend itself to this development. From the time he was given carte-blanche to explore the 10th Cycle nanosphere, he'd been working on this goal.

Roy began his research by determining a common unit of measurement for the power in each type of battery's core. Expressed in measurements of watt-hours of stored power per kilogram of core, the results could be compared side-by-side. Thus, an old-style lead acid battery could store a mere 25 watt-hours of electrical power per kilo. Newer core compositions stored much more. A nickel-metal hydride battery could store up to one-hundred watt-hours per kilogram, while the state-of-the art lithium ion cores could store one-hundred and fifty. Roy's quest was to find a material for the core that would be lighter and yet store and produce a much higher output. In the 10th Cycle library, he found what he was looking for, a lithium-aluminum blend, which, when packed as nanoparticles into a battery core, this material not only represented a much smaller volume for its weight, but was able to store around two-hundred watt-hours per kilogram of core material.

In the first week of April, he had it. With JR in tow, he attached his briefcase-sized battery in place of the battery in a borrowed electric car. JR folded himself into the cramped passenger seat and Roy got behind the wheel, and they headed down State highway 93 toward Golden. There, they picked up Route 6 and turned west to join I70 as it headed up steeply on the way to Vail Pass. When the car's speedometer pegged out at 120 mph, blowing past a State trooper like he was standing still, they knew that Roy's goal had been met, and then some.

The pair crept back to Boulder by the back roads to avoid arrest for humiliating an officer of the law, and went to Daniel to tell him what Roy had accomplished. It was a bright spot in a time of stress for Daniel.

"Roy, tell me you'll ask CalTech for an extended leave of absence. What you're doing is nothing short of remarkable," said Daniel, looking up from his desk before standing up to face his brother and Roy. Craning his neck up at JR had never been comfortable.

"You ain't seen nothin' yet," Roy said, with all due modesty. He winked at Daniel before leaving, giving JR and his brother something to laugh about. Both of them wondered why he couldn't do that with women, since his unhealthy fear was now a topic of frequent gossip.

Roy had seen something that interested him in another section of the library while researching what he might do with his flying toys. It was amazing what the 10th Cyclers could do with laser technology. Just for fun, he built a handheld laser that could theoretically cut a diamond in half in seconds. Of course, he had no diamonds to test it on, but it made short work of a piece of granite that he picked up in the hills. The practical limit to the power of a laser had always been the size of the power source. Now that he'd perfected the science to create nano batteries, he had batteries that could power an extremely powerful laser beam in a very small package. He had to rig his invention with a series of safety switches, to keep people from accidentally cutting off their own legs with the device in their pocket, but that was easily done.

Satisfied with the prototype, he showed the lipstick-sized contraption to Daniel and suggested they go outside for a demonstration. They were on their way out when Nicholas passed them, and Daniel invited him along. Moments later, the two were standing in open-mouthed wonder as Roy cleaved a granite boulder ten feet or more across with the tiny laser. Nicholas looked at Daniel.

"This is how...," he started.

"They cut those blocks for the Pyramid!" Daniel finished. The two shared a high-five, with a bewildered Roy looking on. He was just glad he wasn't in trouble for splitting part of the landscaping.

"I've tested it under water, too," he remarked, causing the Rosslers to stare at him in confusion. What possible use could that be? Neither had the background to realize that having to cut steel and rock under water is a daily task for underwater construction workers.

Chapter Seventeen

ENCODED WITH FIBONACCI NUMBERS

Late April, 2020

Daniel and Sarah were talking about the security breach after work one night. As he and Raj had been doing for several days, he once again said he just couldn't figure out where the information was going. They had eyes on the Foundation computers' outside communications, and had found nothing. They'd even called in favors from government agencies to locate and hack into the employee's private computers and cell phones with no success. Daniel was beyond frustrated. Both Luke and Raj had recommended letting it go on until they could find where the data wound up and what the recipient could do with it, fragmented as it was. He had been nearly ranting about it all through dinner when Sarah had a brainstorm.

"Daniel, would any of those searches have turned up the method we used back when we were cracking the pyramid code? The one Raj told us about?" She'd been feeding Nick, with the toddler trying to help a little more than she wanted. Now she turned her eyes to Daniel and searched his face.

A speculative expression stole across the still-handsome countenance of her beloved as he considered it. "Surely Raj would have checked that, wouldn't he?"

Sarah had turned back to Nick and was trying to wipe his face, to which he was objecting strenuously. "Why don't you call and ask him?"

Daniel got up. "I think I will. Need any help there?"

"I've got it."

Daniel strolled into his home office, closed the door against Nick's increasingly vocal objections to being cleaned up, and dialed Raj.

"Raj, Sarah asked a question about our problem with how the spies are communicating with whoever they're sending the stolen info to. You're probably on top of it, but you have checked those guys' draft folders, right?"

Raj sounded tired when he answered. Daniel wondered how much sleep he'd been getting since he discovered the photo-taking. "We have for the company computers. They've only got access to one email on our network. We block attempts to establish web-based email accounts as part of our normal IT policy. But we can't access their email accounts at home unless they're stupid and keep a list of passwords somewhere on their hard drive here at work."

"Hmmm. Could they be using that?"

"Sure. It's a well-known ploy."

"The government has caught people doing it, haven't they?" Daniel was pacing, his nimble mind looking for a loophole.

"Sure, but they had to have a reasonable idea of who to look at, and the cooperation of the email services. They've got a finer net than we do, Daniel."

"I understand. Still, I think I can make a pretty good case for this being a matter of national security. Do you have an objection to my bringing in the big guns?" Raj was an old and valued friend. Daniel didn't want to step on his toes - not in the least bit.

"Of course not, Daniel. I'm as worried about this as you are. What they're accessing could mean real trouble if they can put it together."

"Good man, Raj. Thanks for the chat and the explanation. I'll see what help we can get first thing tomorrow. Try to get some sleep."

Daniel opened his door and drank in the quiet. Nick must have finally worn Sarah down, or fallen asleep. He went in search of them and found Sarah rocking a sleepy Nicholas. He was getting so big that she wouldn't be able to do that much longer. His feet dangled halfway to the floor already, and he'd soon object to being treated like a baby. Sarah was making it last as long as she could. They'd have to think about having another one, if only they could find some peace in the world.

"Raj checked our servers, but the rest is going to take government help," Daniel whispered.

Sarah nodded, without changing the rhythm of her rocking or answering aloud, which would have broken Nick's trance. Daniel walked quietly away and cleared the table, wishing again that Sarah would hear of hiring help. Maybe if they had a second child, she'd see reason.

A few minutes later, she appeared in the kitchen, where Daniel was loading the last of the dishes into the dishwasher.

"Wouldn't it be funny if they were using Fibonacci skip sequences to code their messages?" she said, taking a few things out of the machine and rearranging them.

Daniel straightened from his task and stared at her.

"Sweetheart, did I ever tell you that you're brilliant?" He put his arm around her and steered her toward the living room.

"Frequently, my love. Are you almost finished? I think we could both enjoy a glass of tawny port," Sarah said, catching Daniel's intention.

Daniel followed Sarah to the dining room where she poured each of them a cordial glass of the sweet beverage, and then to the living room. They sat close together, enjoying their port, and after a few minutes started to speak at the same time. Both laughed.

"Go ahead," Daniel said.

"No, you," responded Sarah.

"I was just wondering..." he started. Sarah's head tucked into the hollow of his neck was a sweet heaviness that sent a sudden flash of tenderness through him. "Are you ready?"

Sarah giggled. "It's been a while since we used that little code, remember Daniel? R U R?"

"I remember," he said. "I almost had a heart attack that first time I thought you were going to have phone sex with me." Daniel smiled into her eyes, remembering the excitement.

First thing the next morning, Daniel was at his desk early, leaving an internal message for Raj to see him as soon as he came in. He also sent Luke a similar message. Luke arrived first.

"You wanted to see me?"

"Yes, thanks for getting right back to me. Have a seat."

The Sword of Cyrus

Luke questioned Daniel with his eyes as he looked around for a straight-backed chair and pulled it next to the overstuffed guest chairs in front of Daniel's desk. When he was seated, Daniel started by explaining that Sarah had asked some pertinent questions. There were holes in their investigation, it seemed, and Daniel wanted to know if Luke had the contacts who could plug them.

Luke considered the question carefully. There were two ways to go about it. Hack into the records of the most common web-based email services, Yahoo, Google and a few others. Or take their request to the feds, who'd shown little compunction in doing that, had the resources to do it quickly and in all likelihood were doing it already. The latter might require a search warrant, but Daniel's idea about national security had merit. After the Patriot Act was enacted, government agencies had broad powers that some said went too far in the direction of violating privacy in the name of national security. Luke didn't care to debate it. The question was, would they find anything useful?

"I may, Daniel. I need to make some calls," he said, rising from his chair and putting it back where he'd found it.

"Come back here as soon as you've got any info, please," Daniel said. "Raj should be here any minute. I'd like you to be in on at least part of the conversation, so I don't have to repeat myself. We've let this go on too long already."

"You got it. Be right back."

Raj arrived a few minutes later. After bringing him up to speed on what Luke had gone to do, Daniel brought up Sarah's other idea, that the messages could be coded and that maybe they used Fibonacci numbers as skip sequences, just as the original Rosslerites discovered when deciphering the pyramid code.

"Those sneaky bastards!" Raj exclaimed. "I'll bet that's exactly what they're doing! I need to check it out."

Before Daniel could stop him, Raj ran out of the office and back to his own, where he methodically gathered all the emails that remained on the servers, both those that were still in the sent folder and those that had been deleted but not yet eradicated from the system. Beginning with those belonging to the first person they'd caught photographing his screen, Raj applied the first reasonable Fibonacci number for a skip sequence to it. Three was a bit too small, but in the name of being thorough, he would do it. Especially since he still had the little program that would parse a text automatically within a few seconds. Three wasn't it. Patiently, Raj programmed the routine with the next number.

On thirteen, he had it. The message was terse: '*Important. Part of plan for nanopoison production.*'

Half an hour had passed and Raj's eyes were beginning to fatigue from scanning gibberish. He almost missed it when those first sensible words came up on the screen from the decoding routine. A subconscious signal alerted him to stop the routine and back up. Reading the terse message, which was surrounded by more gibberish, he rocked back in his chair and half-yelled, "What?" He read it a second time.

"Oh, good lord," he groaned out loud.

Quickly, he queued up another message, and another, decoding and saving the messages. This was a disaster! When he'd run all of them through the correct skip sequence and saved them to a single document, he printed it and literally ran down the hall with it, leaving startled employees in his wake. Arriving breathlessly at Daniel's door, he threw the printout down in front of his old friend.

"Daniel, we're in deep shit!"

Chapter Eighteen

THEY COULD HAVE EVERYTHING

Daniel scanned down the decoded messages, noting the subjects here and there. He was puzzled, though. The messages spoke of information on a wide range of subjects, but the information itself wasn't there.

"Raj, did you expurgate these messages for some reason? Leave out the meat?"

Raj shook his head. "No, Daniel. They've been very clever. They've somehow separated the 10th Cycle data from the messages saying what they're sending. I can run the rest of the message through more Fib numbers, but I suspect that the data file is actually somewhere else." He spread his hands in a gesture of helplessness. "Where, I cannot say."

At that moment, Luke came back as well. Daniel had almost forgotten he'd sent Luke on an errand, one that was all the more important now.

Luke glanced at the two men in the room, both staring at him as he entered. "What?"

"Raj found it. He's decoded some of the messages."

Daniel handed the stack of paper over and waited while Luke scanned the first page.

"Where's the actual information they're talking about?" Luke asked.

"That's the problem. We don't know. Raj thinks it's in a different message, but what he has here is only what's on our servers. I'm sure there's much more information out there on their private computers and cloud storage such as Google Docs, Dropbox, iCloud and others - we don't know where." Daniel shrugged. "It's something, at least."

"We only keep messages from a few weeks back," Raj explained. "There's no telling how long this has been going on. Would Sinclair have records of what these guys were working on? Could we synch up the coded messages with their assignments?" He looked from Daniel to Luke, and back at Daniel.

"That's a good idea. I'll get Sinclair in here in a minute. Luke, what did you find out?" asked Daniel.

"They didn't want to tell me much. I get the idea they're still doing whatever they do, and they don't want the general public to know. That's NSA stuff, so my contacts weren't a lot of help. But I did find out that Hotmail, Yahoo and Gmail are the biggest free services. If I were going to do something like you guys did, I'd pick one of them."

"Why's that?" Daniel asked, absentmindedly holding out his hand for the stack of paper with the decoded messages.

Luke handed over the papers. "Because it's tougher to find a needle in a haystack," he said.

"So, what's our next move? I take it Big Brother won't help us?" said Raj.

"Could you hack into those services?" Luke asked Raj,

knowing the answer already but maintaining the polite fiction that he knew nothing of Raj's underground contacts.

"I could, if I wanted to spend time in jail," was the answer.

"I guess we need some hackers, then," Luke said. Daniel did a double take and peered at Luke's face. Flat expression - he wasn't kidding.

Daniel made an executive decision. "Look, I'm going to play the national security card. Don't do anything yet. I'll try to get us help to get this stuff legally. Raj, we're okay on what you've got so far, right?"

Luke held up his hand. "I can answer that. We have policies in place that warn our employees that their work email is not considered private. They all signed off on that when they came on board. It's pretty standard. As long as Raj hasn't hacked into their personal computers, he's golden."

"I would never do that!" exclaimed Raj. Turning his head toward Daniel, he mouthed, 'But I know some people who would.' He winked, and Daniel chuckled.

Luke looked back and forth between them.

"Try to stay out of trouble," he warned. "I'll go talk to Sinclair."

"Thanks, Luke. Send him up here, will you?"

When Luke was out of earshot, Daniel asked Raj if he was seriously going to activate his conspiracy theory network.

"What better time?" Raj answered. He winked again and left as well. Daniel was alone to ponder whether the end justified the means. Looking again at everything the messages claimed to have been sent to the spies' employers, he decided it had to. The bad guys could have everything that had been translated so far, about nanotechnology, especially. That was the main subject that the Middle Easterners were translating. This was bad, very bad; or it could be.

Sinclair arrived as Daniel was wrestling with his conscience.

"Hi, Daniel. Luke said you wanted to see me?" He stood just inside the door, as if he were ready to escape. Daniel wondered if he was feeling responsible for the leaks somehow, though there was no reason he should. He hadn't screened those Middle Easterners, it wasn't his job.

"Come in, Sinclair. I have a question for you." He indicated a chair, and Sinclair sank into it, sighing.

"Tired?" Daniel asked.

"Worried."

"About?" Daniel didn't want to assume anything, but Sinclair was a valued colleague. He needed to be heard.

"Why haven't we rounded up those ringers in my department and deported them all?"

"We're hoping they'll lead us back to whoever they're sending the information to. But, that's the reason I asked you to come up. Do you have any records for who was assigned to what, and an idea of when?" Daniel watched Sinclair intently, unconscious that anxiety was written all over his own face. *Tell me yes*, he willed, waiting for what seemed like an hour for Sinclair's answer.

"Yes, I think I do have what you want," Sinclair said, drawing out his words. "But…"

"But what?" Daniel interrupted, unable to contain himself any longer.

"They may not have done the assignments in the order they were assigned," Sinclair clarified. "I may not have the dates exact."

Daniel didn't ask for an explanation of why the employees would have done the assignments out of order.

Whooping, he seized Sinclair by the shoulders and planted a kiss soundly on his cheek.

"How soon can you get a report to Raj?"

"Soon as you want it, I guess. What's got into you Daniel?"

"Relief. Old man, you've made me very happy."

"Now see here," Sinclair started, mock angry. But he broke out into his normal mischievous grin when Daniel started dancing around his desk. What the devil was the boy so delighted for? They still had a huge problem. He got a better idea when Daniel pressed the intercom button on his desk phone.

"Raj? We may not need you to hack anything illegally after all. Sinclair has records."

Sinclair decided not to ask.

Raj didn't tell Daniel that he'd already contacted his network. There was no stopping them, but there wasn't any need to stress Daniel about it. He did need to ask Roy about making a few extra Spyflies, though. That was the price. His fellow conspiracy investigators were as excited about the little gadgets as he was, especially when they heard that he'd caught some spies among the Rossler Foundation employees with it. He could hardly wait to tell them what he learned about Area 51.

However, since Sinclair did have records of which translators were working on what assignments, along with an idea of when, Raj went to work to merge the information, so that he could get an idea of how quickly the compromised data had gone out after translation. There was something odd about the whole operation. Raj knew that the fragments of information weren't much good by themselves. What he needed to do was determine whether someone who didn't know the library first-hand, nor the method by which he and Luke had decided to scramble it, could put it back together to get something useful.

To do that, he uploaded the fragments, the dates, the coded emails and an algorithm to a database management program and ran a report. The algorithm was the very one he and Luke had used to break the data up. When the report was finished, Raj had an idea of how the data was received; that is, in what order. Next, he replaced the algorithm with a randomizer. When that report had run, he compared the two. As far as he could see, the original algorithm had done a satisfactory job of assigning a random order of translation to the full data set. With a code number field attached, researchers at the Foundation could put it back together as easily as a paint-by-numbers artwork. Without that, data received at random over a period of weeks would be rather difficult to put together as a whole text.

He sent a quick instant message to Daniel to that effect. However, he cautioned, if the recipient had someone who was very clever at breaking codes, they could conceivably have hit on the same algorithm Raj had used to break it up. They could do the same thing he did to reverse the process.

While Raj was engaged in this process, the most deeply hidden of his underground contacts were busy on that list of names he'd provided. They took the challenge to ferret out every email account each person on the list had set up on their home computers, and hack into them to check for sent and received emails as far back as they were available. Raj was also interested in email accounts that seemed to have few sent and received emails, but a lengthy draft folder full of unsent messages. These, he believed, would reveal what was really happening.

The next day after his request for help went out to his network, an instant message from one of them came back. Coded to look like spam, it was an innocuous offer to meet 'willing girls' online. Raj took a moment to reflect on how much trouble his friend's joke would be for him at home if Sushma ever saw it, before deleting it. He then activated a program that would conceal his IP address from the site he was about to visit, and another that would mask the location of the site from his computer's logs. Failure to adhere to these protocols would get him kicked out of his group, and that was not an outcome he wanted, ever. They had been too useful to him on several occasions, and he to them.

Once he was in, Raj located the messages in his inbox. Along with several of the names he'd sent to this contact earlier in the day, were a list of email accounts with username and password attached. It would be up to him and Luke to take a look at them and see whether what they sought was among the messages or in the draft folder. Raj sent Luke a text, asking him to drop by.

A few minutes later, Luke strolled into Raj's neat office. Not a paper out of place or a pen casually set down marred the perfection of Raj's desktop. Not for the first time, Luke wondered if the man were actually a robot, but the pleased expression on his face answered that question.

"Luke, I have some news," Raj began. A slight frown flickered before he smoothed his face to its usual neutral expression. "I trust you will not look for my sources, Luke."

Luke was well aware of Raj's peculiar hobby, and the nefarious connections he had because of it. If Daniel hadn't personally vouched for the loyalty as well as the sanity of his friend, Luke would have had a serious problem with his appointment as IT department head when the Foundation was formed. By now, though, he was used to Raj's paranoia, his secretiveness and his remarkable resourcefulness when it came to anything computer-related. He had a good idea that Raj had moved forward with the hacking project that Daniel had called off. He also trusted Raj to have covered his tracks so well that not even the CIA or NSA could discover the shenanigans.

"What have you got?" Luke asked, grinning slightly with the knowledge that it was probably something ill-gained but would help their present situation.

"Email accounts for a handful of the spies in our midst. Private, web-based and according to my source, full of unsent messages. I thought you'd like to help look them over." Raj put his hand in his pocket and jingled some change, the only thing that revealed his discomfort with bringing Luke into his secret life, even though he trusted Luke and knew that Luke was already privy to much of it.

"I won't ask where you got the information."

"Thank you, Luke, my friend. Rest assured, it cannot come back to us."

Luke believed it. He'd seen the results of Raj's secretiveness before, and knew that whoever he used to get this stuff, they'd never been discovered, even by government agencies with unconscionable power and reach.

Raj was prepared with a printout of half of the names, and had set up a computer for Luke's use at a small conference table in his office. Because the operation was sensitive, Luke closed and locked the door before he sat down to work. Raj was already into the first account, reading page after page of scientific data that seemed to start and stop with no logical order. It was certain that they'd discovered what went out - the verbatim translations that Raj had uploaded to his database once today already, and pretty much in the order that his reports indicated for this individual's work. The first account Luke broke into had the same results. After a couple of hours, Luke decided they had enough to report to Daniel. They now knew how the science was being transmitted. Now to determine who was on the receiving end.

Whoever it was, the bad news was that they could have everything the Rossler Foundation had produced in the field of nanotechnology, as well as a few other items that no one wanted in the hands of terrorists. Even worse; it was complete. Gaps had been filled in that weren't assigned to Middle Eastern translators.

The meeting with Daniel was top-secret. Raj was insistent that no one outside the core Rossler Foundation members attend; everyone else was a suspect. For once, Luke agreed with his paranoia. Luke went in person to speak with Daniel, and before he did, he made a thorough search of Daniel's office for both conventional listening devices and for any of Roy's Spyflies or other nanotech spy equipment. He all but whipped out a magnifying glass and combed every inch, every object on every bookshelf, and shut down every electronic device in the room.

Daniel looked on, speechless. Luke hadn't made a sound, merely held up his hand in a Stop! gesture and begun his search. Daniel understood almost immediately that he was looking for bugs, so he knew better than to speak. Half an hour later, the office swept thoroughly, Luke spoke for the first time.

"Daniel, we may have a worse problem than we

thought. We need to get a few key people up here, and then I'll tell you what it is. Just old friends, buddy, someone on the team isn't trustworthy."

Daniel's eyes widened, and then his lips thinned as he pressed them together. He nodded and picked up his personal cell phone. In short order, he had Raj, Sinclair and Sarah on their way to his office, at Luke's request. It may be a little cramped, but holding the meeting here would save him the trouble of sweeping another location for listening devices.

When everyone was assembled and had found seats, he addressed them, shocking everyone but Raj.

"We've made a preliminary breakthrough on what data has been compromised. I have promised Raj that we won't pry into how we got this information. All you need to know is that we obtained user names and passwords for a number of anonymous email accounts. Data we found in the draft folders confirms that there has been a serious leak of sensitive 10th Cycle information almost from the beginning of the nanotech program. Furthermore, I have reason to believe that someone with knowledge of the full, unfragmented texts has gone rogue. Sinclair, I'll ask you to read the compiled text of the draft messages and verify that to be the case. I have no doubt it's true, though."

In the pause that followed his words while Luke took a couple of steps to hand the printed report to Sinclair, questions from the rest of the group were tossed.

"What makes you think that?" from Daniel, who cast a worried look in Sarah's direction as he spoke.

"But, that would mean…" from Sinclair, as he took the proffered report.

Over the cacophony sounded Sarah's firm, clear lecturing voice. "There are only two other people who have the full translations, besides those of us here. Whom do we suspect?"

Luke was justifiably proud of his niece, not only her beauty and her accomplishments, but her keen mind was such a pleasure to know and love.

"You've hit the nail on the head, Sarah, and it's the reason for this meeting. This is the way Raj and I see it. Only two scenarios fits the facts. One, the fragmented data went out to someone who was presumably unauthorized to receive it, hence the secrecy. However, because it was fragmented, the recipient may not have been able to put it all together in a comprehensible whole. Unfortunately, it's the second that we think has happened, based on what we see in these emails. Fragmented as they are, there are pieces of information that tie the fragments together. We think the recipients have compromised one of the two other people on the security committee for nanotech. Both of those people have access to the compiled data. A third, less likely scenario is that the Foundation servers have been compromised. Raj, can you speak to that scenario?"

Luke sat down, his bombshell exploded, and listened as Raj explained why the third scenario was less likely, and what he was doing to verify one way or the other. The explanation was somewhat technical, but the bottom line was that Raj had run a diagnostics report on who had accessed what, both authorized and unauthorized. He'd found no unauthorized entry into sensitive areas. The conclusion was that it must be Karsten who was dirty, no matter how unlikely, since they'd previously cleared Roy with his own Spyfly.

"I feel terrible about it, Sarah. I thought we'd put in enough security measures to protect ourselves after the Misty and Carmen incidents," he said, referring to spies in their midst during the first Antarctica expedition. "If we can't do a better job than this, maybe it's time to pack it in and turn the library over to government control." Absently, he patted her hand with his other one, effectively keeping her close.

Sarah withdrew her hand. "Honey, we can't do that! We always said it didn't belong to the US alone. It belongs to the world."

"Then let the world protect it. Sweetheart, I'm tired. Tired of being the constant center of the storm. Tired of wondering who will try to assassinate us next, or worse. Tired of worrying about you, and Nick, and everyone else, my hostages to fortune. When will the strife end?"

Sarah ran her eyes over her husband's figure, uncharacteristically bent with concern. She put both her arms around him. "When we've used everything we can find in the library to stop war," she said. She had never lost sight of the warning that Zebulon, the builder, had given in the greeting. It was imperative to eradicate war, or the cycle of cataclysmic destruction that had claimed all previous cycle's civilizations would continue. She had a feeling that their own cycle was very near its crisis.

Raj heard the decision of the security committee for the nanotech program with concern. It didn't make sense to him to eliminate one suspect at a time. Whether his liking for Roy clouded his judgment or for some other reason, the idea that he should investigate both of them immediately wouldn't go away. Consequently, he installed keyboard capture programs on both their office computers, sent out an urgent request to his informant for any personal internet interaction he could find on either of them, and borrowed Luke's Spyfly, saying his needed repair. Within the hour, Raj began receiving video of both Karsten and Roy in their offices. Unfortunately, he didn't have enough of the devices to deploy them in their homes, but if he saw nothing in the next day or so, he'd reassign these to the homes, though it would require putting someone undercover with a Wi-Fi connection near enough to monitor the feed.

Only half an hour later, at the end of the workday, he hit pay dirt. Movement on the monitor that displayed the feed from Karsten's office caught his eye, and he turned to watch it, almost looking away when he saw it was just a visitor. The feed showed a woman entering Karsten's office, and Karsten rising from his desk, walking to meet her near the door. What happened next snapped Raj's brain into full attention, as the audio reached him.

"Darling, may I come to you tonight?" Raj did a double-take, and remotely adjusted the position of the Spyfly to see who the visitor was. Karsten's wife was a blonde, but this woman had dark hair. When he had moved the camera to see her face, he realized it was Karsten's program administrator, Alica. He watched the action on the monitor raptly.

Karsten had taken the woman in his arms and was attempting to kiss her, but she turned her head. He released her, but started to complain.

"Haven't I given you everything you asked for?" he said, bitterness coloring his tone. Raj tilted his head. What had he discovered? An infidelity? A grasping mistress? Her answer shocked him even further.

"You're holding back. My employers need information about triggers for the nanonukes. They are convinced that you have it. My life is in your hands, and you want to take me to bed? Fuck you. If you don't give me the information they want, they'll kill me and take your family. Do you want that, you miserable worm? I swear I will take you down with me."

Raj's mouth dropped. He hadn't had much contact with Alica, but she'd always been soft-spoken though efficient, the perfect personality to go with her beauty. Self-effacing, even, as if she knew she must downplay her incredible looks to get along with other women and keep men from hounding her. Where had this gold-plated bitch come from? More to the point, who were her employers, and what was that about nanonukes?

On the monitor, Karsten had fallen to his knees and clasped Alica around the thighs, burying his face in her skirt. Raj couldn't quite make out what he was saying, his words muffled by his position. He must have been begging for something, Raj figured. Alica spoke again.

"Get up. All right, you can come to my apartment. But you'd better have the information with you if you want anything from me. And if you don't have it, maybe I should pay your wife a visit, tell her what you like in bed. Won't she be shocked, the little hausfrau?"

Raj grabbed a scratch pad. He was all about technology, but sometimes just jotting something down on paper best served the purpose. He made some rapid notes to remind him what he needed to do about Alica. He'd just finished when Alica and Karsten left Karsten's office and turned off the light, plunging the monitor into darkness.

His first call was to Sushma, telling her he was likely to have to pull an all-nighter, and apologizing for not being able to come home. If she got the idea that it had something to do with Area 51, it would be best for all concerned. Besides, she was used to that. No need to worry her with talk of nano-nukes. His next call was to Luke, who'd already left the building and was on his way home. Luke said he'd turn around and come immediately. "No," he said, "don't bother Daniel yet. Let's see what we can find out."

While he waited for Luke to arrive, Raj checked the recording of the feed in Roy's lab. Since it showed nothing except Roy tinkering with tiny objects on his work bench and occasionally humming off-key, Raj fast-forwarded until he caught another person in the room. Backing it up a few frames, he played it at normal speed. Alica again! Was she playing both of them? Raj listened intently as she spoke.

"Roy, Karsten needs the plans for the gadgets you've been making for the program archives. How soon can you get us those?" As Raj watched, she made no attempt to touch Roy, but she was standing very close to him by the time she finished speaking. On the screen, Roy edged away.

"P-plans? Uh, I, I haven't actually d-drawn any p-plans. J-just p-p-put them t-together. Flying nicely ... no plans. You want some? Ah, ah ... I mean you want plans?" Raj found it almost painful to listen to, as Roy's pathetic shyness around women caused him to stammer through the sentence.

"Well, could you please draw them? Karsten insists," Alica said in the sweet tones that Raj had heard her always use before. What an actress! She turned a brilliant smile on the hapless Roy, who blushed brightly enough for the color-enhanced Spyfly camera to clearly pick it up.

"Sh-sure," he answered. *Don't do it*, Raj mentally commanded him, only to hear him continue. "It'll t-take a few d-days."

"As soon as you can, hon," Alica said, now laying her hand on Roy's arm. Raj was almost amused to see him flinch as if she'd burned him. *Good man, delay.*

After Alica left, Raj checked the timestamp and saw that the encounter with Roy preceded the one with Karsten. His attention hadn't been on the monitors, knowing that the video was recording for later use. What had he been doing? Oh, yes, contacting the man he knew as Prairie Dog to hack into Karsten and Roy's private emails. He'd better make contact again, even though PD would hate it, and give him a third name. Alica Cedric; that was her whole name. Or was it? At this point, Raj wouldn't have been surprised to find that he was someone else himself. So much deception.

Raj had just made the arrangements for complete surveillance on Alica when Luke walked in. He'd been almost home, nearly forty-five minutes away from the office, when Raj had summoned him back. Realizing the time, he'd completed his trip. Sally wasn't happy that he was going back, but because he'd taken the time to come and give her a kiss and hug, she was willing to make sandwiches and a thermos of coffee for him to take back with him while he took a quick shower and changed clothes. Raj exclaimed in pleasure when he saw that Luke had thoughtfully brought something to sustain them for a while. It was going to be a long night.

The two men worked quietly together, reading Alica's messages from the company email in the clear, and then running them through the same skip sequences that had revealed secret messages among the other Middle Eastern employees. They had discovered that Alica, too, had been hired through the auspices of the Iranian delegation to the Board. By now it looked like the entire thing had been a ploy to get spies into the Foundation. Luke would like to get his hands on that good-looking devil Reza Mokri, the Iranian member of the Board. He had gone home for a business meeting of some kind. Probably spilling everything he knew to al Qaeda or the leftovers of ISIS or some other satanic outfit.

Alica's company email was clean, nothing to worry about. No secret messages that they could discern, no love letters to Karsten, nothing at all out of the ordinary. Raj insisted that Luke watch the video footage, so he could be sure Raj wasn't crazy. Ironically, Luke already knew Raj was crazy, just not in the way Raj thought. But he had to admit the guy's paranoia and better, his underground network of conspiracy nuts, came in handy. More than once. Luke smiled when the thought came up - what would it take to convince him and his group to work for the CIA? *Nah, I have a better chance of getting pregnant.*

It was nearly midnight and Raj had gone in search of something sweet from a vending machine to go with his fourth cup of coffee when Prairie Dog's message came through. Raj performed the protocols and found the message. They were in! Personal email accounts, user names, passwords, and this time even Facebook accounts and passwords along with a couple of mobile phones belonging to Alica. By morning, they'd have what they were looking for, Raj was confident.

When Daniel arrived the next morning, he was shocked to see a haggard Raj and barely less haggard Luke waiting for him.

"It's bad, Daniel," Raj blurted. Daniel looked to Luke for confirmation and slumped when he saw Luke nod.

"Okay. Come on in. Do I need to call in the rest for this?" Daniel signaled his assistant. "Do you guys want coffee? You look like you need it?"

"I'm coffee'd out," said Luke. "But I could use some breakfast." Daniel nodded. To his assistant, he said, "Traci, do you mind running out for refreshments for a breakfast meeting? Sorry to ask you." He handed her a couple of twenties. "See if you can find something halfway healthy. These guys look like they've been eating donuts all night."

Entering his office to find Raj and Luke already seated, Daniel sent texts to the others to come to his office. "Karsten?" he questioned. Raj nodded.

Raj spoke first. "Karsten has a dirty little secret." That told Daniel most of what he needed to know.

"Oh, my God," he said. "He knows the full picture of everything we've dug up in the nanotechnology material." Luke and Raj both nodded this time.

In due course, the others arrived, including a puzzled Roy. Traci brought in the breakfast, most of which would remain untouched. Speaking in turns, Raj and Luke explained what they'd been doing all night, and why. Raj apologized to Roy when it came to what they'd learned about him - that he was completely innocent of any wrongdoing. He shrugged.

"I guess I'm flattered that anyone could think I might have an exciting life," he grinned. When no one laughed, he shrunk back into his seat. He wasn't sure why he was even here. Best to listen and learn, he guessed.

"So what exactly do they have, and who's they?" Daniel asked.

"It appears that Alica has been blackmailing Karsten for weeks," Luke answered. "I'll spare you the videos, but I'd say the man is headed for a divorce. What's worse is that the recipients, someone in the Middle East, probably in Iran, are apparently working on some pretty scary nanotech stuff. We need Roy to interpret it for us, and tell us how far

The Sword of Cyrus

they've gotten. What we have picked up is they've tested a way to deploy a nanopoison, which worked better than they planned and wiped out more than 20,000 people in a village in Africa. There's also some stuff about a nanonuclear bomb, if that makes any sense?" He paused and looked at Roy, whose eyes had widened.

"Yeah, unfortunately they can do that with the information they have," Roy answered.

"Stealth technology that seems to have a nanotech connection, and some other stuff we didn't have the background to understand. We do know that Alica was trying to coerce Karsten into supplying information about triggers for the nanonukes. We can't tell you other important stuff, like how far the development of all this stuff has gone, the names of the leaders, how they plan to deploy bombs or where their targets are. We need some help, and we need it fast, in case they're already in attack planning mode. We were lucky to find out when we did." Luke wound up his report with Raj's nod of agreement.

"I'll call the President right away," said Daniel. "I trust there's no objection to turning this whole mess over to government to investigate? After all they were the ones asking us to allow these people in here in the first place." Heads shook all around the room. They knew they were outgunned with the size of the spy network they'd already uncovered. It was time to send for the professionals.

"Luke, will you stay, please? I may need your knowledge of who to ask for. Everyone else, I don't need to tell you that this is top-secret. All the players are still employed here. We need to keep it that way to trap the folks on the other end of the information flow."

Raj spoke up. "I have an idea about that. Some of those messages from the translators are going through our servers, and we have access to the email accounts they're using off-campus. Why don't Roy and I plant some disinformation?" He shot a questioning glance at Roy as he spoke. Roy's eyes sparkled. This ought to be fun!

Daniel glanced at Luke for his opinion. Luke shrugged his shoulders. "As long as it doesn't clue them that we're onto them, it's probably a good idea. No practical jokes," he admonished Raj. Raj nodded.

Chapter Nineteen

MR. PRESIDENT

Mid-May, 2020

Before Daniel could gather his thoughts, Luke spoke first.

"Daniel, I think we have to consider that our phones may not be secure. I understand the urgency, but I don't want these guys to know we've been tipped off until we have more intel. Can you hold off on your call to the president until I can get hold of Lewis and make sure you won't be overheard? It could take a day or two."

Daniel looked up from the page with the message he was reading again, something to do with laser technology. *Why are they interested in that?* "Hmm? Oh, sorry, Luke, I was distracted. You want me to hold off on calling the president? Is that wise?"

"Maybe not," Luke said, fingering his chin. "But, neither is tipping off the bad guys. Look, I'll get it done as soon as I can. It may be as simple as going out to buy you a throwaway cell and getting you out of here to make the call. Let me check with Sam Lewis."

"Oh, sure." Daniel's expression was haunted.

"It won't take long, I promise," Luke said, worrying about Daniel's state of mind. How long could a man be under the strain Daniel had been under before he broke?

A few hours later, Luke was back, with a small electronic device he installed inside the battery compartment of Daniel's wireless phone handset, inserting the batteries into the device.

Daniel watched Luke's expert handling of his phone. "What's that?"

"Scrambler. Actually, it scrambles the analog input and sends the scrambled digital signal to the phone the president will be using to take your call. And then it unscrambles the signal from his end. The bad guys may be able to listen in, but they won't be able to understand." Luke finished his task and looked at Daniel expectantly, nodding when he heard the question he expected.

"Where'd you get that?"

"You do remember your father-in-law is a defense contractor, right?" Luke grinned. It was all the answer Daniel would get, but it was enough. Daniel sometimes wished he still had the 'cone of silence' device that had served him well when he and Sarah were dodging the Orion Society. That seemed like a lifetime ago, though it was less than a decade. Unfortunately, the device was obsolete, the design compromised not long after they used it. Nothing had replaced it yet, though he had Raj looking through the library to see if the 10th Cyclers had anything like it.

"So, I can call Harper now?" Daniel asked

"Sit tight. Lewis is on his way to brief President Harper that you need to speak with him urgently. He'll call you as soon as he can."

"Oh, okay. Good. That's better. What did you tell

Director Lewis?" Daniel wouldn't ask if that call had been secure. Knowing Luke, there was no question.

"That we'd had a serious security breach. Man, I hated telling him that! Figured I'd never live it down."

"How did that happen, Luke? I know you took all the precautions available." Daniel had been wanting to ask this of Luke for several days, but hadn't found a way to bring it up that didn't sound like an accusation.

"I've been wondering that myself. My only thought is that these agents must never have had ties to organizations we know about. They've got to be rookies, recently trained. One of them would have slipped up sooner or later." Luke couldn't meet Daniel's eyes. He knew he'd done everything in his power, but still, it had happened on his watch. Maybe it was time to retire.

Daniel interrupted that train of thought. "Tell me again how we got talked into letting the Middle East into our inner circle?"

Luke chuckled humorlessly. "Hmm, as I recall, Lewis and I talked to the president about a message we'd received from a friend and Harper leaned on you."

"It's on him, then," Daniel said, only half-joking. Just then, his phone rang. He raised his eyebrows at Luke.

"Go ahead. You'll hear whoever it is in the clear. It won't interfere with your regular calls."

Daniel answered the phone, listened a moment, and glanced at Luke, nodding.

"Yes, I'll hold." To Luke, he said, "It's Harper."

Luke stood to go, but Daniel held up his hand. He wanted Luke available in case new security measures came up.

"Hello, Mr. President. Thank you for calling so quickly."

"Daniel, why is it I never hear from you unless you've

gotten into some sort of trouble, and why do you always call me Mr. President when that happens?" Harper's jovial opener hit Daniel square in the guilt center of his heart.

"Nigel. Now, you know that isn't true. I called you to invite you to the celebration we had when we brought on three new board members, remember? That was just a few months ago."

"Okay, I never hear from you unless it's business. But, I understand. As soon as I'm done in this place, I'm going to take a long vacation, and your beautiful Colorado is the first place I'm coming."

"You'll be very welcome, Nigel. We've been waiting a long time to take you and Esther skiing." Daniel waited for his cue, knowing from the tone of the conversation that the president couldn't be rushed today.

"All right, what's this I hear about a security breach? Don't tell me we missed some of the Orion Society when we rounded them up."

"No, not them. It seems our new friends in the Middle East brought a few spies with them. Our translation department is riddled with them." Daniel had begun pacing, with Luke tracking him from his seat in front of Daniel's desk.

"No kidding! Well, I can't say that I'm surprised, in a way. On the other hand, don't you have Luke Clarke heading up your security?"

Daniel glanced at Luke, who could only hear one side of the conversation. "We do. He's at a loss to explain, too. He took every precaution."

"I'm sure he did. Just goes to show how slippery those guys are. What have they been up to?"

"Looks like they could have everything we know about nanotechnology, including how to make some nasty little nuclear surprises. We're still tracking it down. We could use some help."

"Oh, good Lord. Not nukes again! Little surprises, you say?"

"As I understand it, Nigel, these things could be as small and innocuous as a can of Coke. Our resident expert tells me that they may be able to level a city block or more. But they won't have any radiation or fallout. That's a mercy, at least," he added, with something like gallows humor.

"Yeah right, tell me about it" Harper answered, with equal satire. "So, what do you know so far?"

"We've analyzed what they likely have, and what they may be planning to do with it. I think it's very likely that as soon as they have the technology perfected, they'll deploy it either here or in Israel. I'd say it's a matter of national security and warrants pulling out the stops to intercept any further communications and plan for a counterstrike. We'd like the appropriate government agency to take over the investigation." Daniel paused to let the request sink in.

"Go on," Harper said.

"If you'll send the teams, we'll cooperate in every way we can, turn over what we've discovered so far. If and when it's appropriate to arrest the perps, that's all on your guys."

"If? You mean you haven't had them arrested?"

"All we've got is a case of industrial espionage. We're leaving them alone, hoping they'll lead us to whoever is on the other side. We expect your agencies' investigation to turn it into something else and warrant those arrests."

"All right, Daniel. I know better than to second-guess you. I'll get Lewis started on it right away. Just tell me one thing."

"What's that?"

"When is this going to end? That library of yours has caused more trouble than I ever could have imagined."

"If I knew the answer to that, I'd tell you. All I can say is it's done a shit-load of good, too. I don't see how we could shut down our research, under those circumstances. And I have to add that I am not sure any of the problems we had before and now would have been prevented if the Library was managed by government " Daniel knew full-well that the continued existence of the Rossler Foundation in the United States depended on the goodwill of the US government. He also knew that most Western governments were now thankful that they had gone back to the US to set it up. The Foundation attracted more than its share of trouble, for sure.

"Hard to argue with that," Harper answered.

Mid-May, 2020; Boulder

Director Lewis graced the investigative team with his own presence after normal surveillance methods turned up no trace of the intended recipients of the information flow. After a week, he arrived in Boulder and gathered his investigators, their counterparts in the FBI and NSA, and Luke Clarke.

"Are we agreed we've turned up nothing useful, and that we now need to stop the information from getting out, no matter what?" Lewis looked around the room to see nods of agreement. "All right, then, let's talk about the way to take the suspects down without too much publicity. Luke? Any ideas?"

"I'd say the best way is to take out the translators as they get to work. Intercept them on their way into the building, and you'll have some time to interrogate them before anyone but their co-workers know they're missing. After you round them up, we'll spread the word quietly that they were detained, so as to avoid a panic." Luke was perched on an uncomfortable chair, his elbows supporting his upper body by leaning on his knees, with his hands clasped between them. It was his favorite thinking pose.

"Karsten Adler and Alica Cindric are special cases. I suggest we arrest them with as much drama as we can, just for their eyes, and immediately separate them for interrogation. My guess is that one will roll over on the other pretty quickly."

Luke was convinced that Karsten was merely the tool, but he wanted to know how Alica had gotten her hooks into him. Before the videos, that is. How had she been able to seduce a man with a spotless record? Although, the videos did provide a clue to that. What man could resist that kind of action? Luke shuddered. He loved his wife, but what would he have done in Karsten's shoes?

"What about Reza Mokri?" asked Lewis, bringing Luke back to the discussion at hand.

"We don't have anything on him," Luke said. "But, I can't imagine that it wasn't a coordinated effort. The majority of the implicated translators are Iranian. Cindric's Croatian, but we've discovered her deceased husband worked in Iran before his death. We don't have an opinion on the other Middle Eastern Board members. My gut says they're not in the know, but that doesn't mean they can be trusted."

"Okay, we'll pick 'em all up. All at once is best. As soon as any of them get wind of what's going down, the rest of them are likely to scatter. We're talking about what, a dozen translators, the woman, the program manager and the three Board members?"

"That's about the size of it."

"How many men do you have who can help us spot the ones we want?"

"Not that many. Just the front door security guard and me. I guess Sinclair O'Reilly can help with the translators, and of course the Rosslers know the rest by sight," Luke answered, ticking off names on his fingers. "JR can help you with Adler and Cindric. Oh, and Raj knows the translators. He was the one who caught them taking photos of their screens. So, my guard, Sinclair and Raj in the translation department, and I'll ask Daniel to call the Board members in for a special meeting."

"All right. Are the Board members here at the moment?"

"As far as I know. The Board is in session, but they don't meet every day. Day after tomorrow is an off day."

"Perfect. Day after tomorrow is the day, then." Addressing the room at large, he added, "Everyone needs to be here and in place by 6:45 a.m. The early birds start arriving at seven, yes Luke?"

"Right."

By ten a.m. two days later, all the known spies from the translation department had been rounded up. Karsten and Alica were in custody, and the three Middle Eastern Board members were just discovering that the 'special meeting' was a ruse to get them in one place so they could easily be taken into custody. Reza Mokri, true to his leadership from the beginning, was the one to demand answers, but first he tried diplomacy.

"I am sure there has been a mistake, my friends," he

said, his broad white smile flashing as if he were confident of his statement.

"No mistake, Mokri," Luke said. "Your countrymen have been caught spying red-handed. You're involved; we know all about it." The last statement was an assumption, but it was a classic deception of law enforcement agents to tell suspects that their co-conspirators had already talked.

"You cannot arrest us, we have diplomatic status. What is the meaning of this?" Mokri said, changing tactics immediately.

"Oh, I'm afraid that isn't true," Lewis interjected. "You see, the Rossler Foundation is a private corporation. Nothing to do with government. Board membership is a privilege, but you aren't ambassadors. You have no status." A wolf-like grin gave him a frighteningly predatory expression. Mokri blanched.

"Where are you taking us?" he demanded.

"We'll be transporting you to the FBI Denver field office, where you'll undergo questioning."

"I demand a phone call," Mokri said, still relatively calm. The other two watched the exchange with wide eyes.

"Sorry, *friend*, it doesn't work that way. Spies, terrorists and their collaborators are handled a little differently than normal police procedure. You'll get your call when we say you do. Not before."

Still protesting, Mokri was led out in handcuffs, along with the other two Middle Eastern board members, who were wisely keeping their mouths shut. Lewis asked Luke if he'd like to accompany the party and sit in on the interrogation. After a brief discussion with Daniel, he accepted and went to get his car to follow them to Denver.

Within twenty-four hours, a discouraged investigation

team realized they had a very sophisticated group on their hands. Karsten Adler was no use at all, just a tool in the hands of the sophisticated Alica Cindric. They hadn't managed to crack her cover story, nor to get her to talk. The translators were nearly dead-ends; it seemed this network was only two people deep, and none of them reported to the same person. In most cases they had not met the person they were reporting to, let alone known where to find him or her. They weren't even aware that others of their co-workers had been doing the same thing they were. Until they could round up the second tier, the investigating agencies were at a standstill for locating the ultimate destination of the information the translators had stolen. That is, unless they'd left a digital trail.

Now the best cyber-experts in the agencies were called in to inspect the personal computers found in the translators' apartments, conveniently located in one or two buildings owned by the Rossler Foundation. Search warrants were sought and approved quickly.

Mokri and the two other Board members had been placed in separate interrogation rooms, and received visits throughout the first day and night from investigators who chipped away at their fatigue and apprehension. No one was allowed to lie down, even on an uncomfortable bed in a cell. The interrogators were running on sheer adrenaline as they began to realize the expertise with which the spy ring had been put together. This was no industrial espionage caper. They began to take the national security angle seriously. At three a.m., unable to get anything from the Turkish or the Saudi board member, Lewis himself paid a visit to Mokri. He was too late.

Mokri was slumped against a wall and had vomited down his shirt front with no apparent attempt to avoid fouling himself. Mokri's skin, previously a light golden, was ruddy. Lewis kicked himself for not having the man searched beyond a check for weapons. He suspected a cyanide capsule, and autopsy would prove him correct. It didn't matter now how he'd died; the most promising connection to the top echelons of whoever was behind the spying was now broken.

One thing stood out, though. Suicide in a leader was no small thing. If Mokri had chosen to make use of this way out before the questioning even got unpleasant, they must have a very serious matter on their hands. He left the room to notify the others and have someone pick up the body. What had Luke Clarke gotten him into this time?

Chapter Twenty

THE DEPLOYMENT

Late May, 2020; Esfahan

After the explosion that destroyed their lab in Esfahan, the Middle Eastern scientists were most interested in finding a way to carry the fuels that would be both safe and undetectable by modern security scanning. It wasn't the fuels themselves at issue, it was the container. Traditionally, radioactive materials were contained in an inert gas inside a steel container, which in turn was sealed in concrete. Clearly, it was too bulky for stealth, which was one of the reasons for using a different fuel altogether.

How to contain it in something that would pass through airport security scanners was a major undertaking. It was only after that explosion that they realized how little of the fuels they would need for each nanonuke. Someone came up with the idea of creating a carbon containment system, which he called a nanobox, just over three-tenths of a centimeter square that would hold a few grams of either fuel substance. Put together, the contents of just four of

The Sword of Cyrus

these fuel containers placed in an everyday object with a way to trigger it, like a cell phone, would be able to take out a city block. If that same device were exploded half a mile in the air above the target it would not only take out the city block and kill all the people within the perimeter, the electromagnetic pulse will also fry any electronic device within a radius of about two miles.

The scientists envisioned hundreds of the tiny bombs, looking like abandoned soda cans or lost cell phones. Jahandar urged them to think bigger. He wanted fewer chances for the bombs to be discovered while maintaining the ability to destroy a ten-kilometer radius with two or three of them. Reminding him that exploding the devices in the air was the most efficient use of them, they struck a compromise. Dozens of bombs instead of hundreds or just two or three. The redundancy made it less likely that the discovery or failure of one would keep the objective from being met. On the other hand, the need to construct thousands of them was avoided.

The objects themselves would not have to be transported through security checks, only the critical components. Feverishly, the scientists worked to create a simple enough device that an untrained person could assemble from pictures and insert into containers that could be carried by drones.

With everyone working on the problem, it took only a few weeks to come up with a plan for a device that was no larger than a carton for half a dozen eggs, but carried a charge that, combined with two or three others arrayed around a single city block, would level ten square kilometers around it and destroy all electronics for up to 20 kilometers. Detonated over the right city blocks at defined intervals, ten or twelve of the devices would take out the centers of most of the target cities, or the heart of a military base. Now to manufacture the critical components. Everything else was readily available in any electronics or home improvement store in any modern country.

Aside from the fuel, the second critical component was a trigger. They'd known from the beginning that something to fuse the fuels for the reaction would be required. During assembly of the weapons, the fuels would be taken from their nanoboxes and combined in a carbon-lithium nanotube that would breed more tritium to make a larger explosion when the trigger was activated. At first they tried traditional types of detonation devices; caps, cords, even wires connected to an electrical source. Nothing worked except the laser that had been used to detonate the explosion that destroyed their first lab. But, how would they conceal a powerful laser in a small, innocuous object? And how would they power and trigger it?

The answer came, coincidentally, from the Rossler Foundation not long before the massive effort to manufacture the end product was to begin, and well before the roundup at the Foundation took most of their communications network down. One of the translators had seen Roy's demonstration of his laser toy. From a distance, she watched as he pointed an object she couldn't see, engulfed as it was in his hand, at a boulder the size of a car and cut it in half like a melon! When she reported the phenomenon to her handler, it went up the line and back down to Alica, who got Karsten to show an interest. Within a few days, the plans were in their hands, and no one was the wiser. Even when all of the conspirators were arrested, Karsten never thought to confess to such a small event.

Roy's little toy was the very thing the Iranian scientists needed as the core of a tiny Continuous Laser Energy

Compression device, the big brother of which had created such a bang in Esfahan. Incredibly powerful for its size, the laser only required the addition of the focusing material that compressed the beam to heat the fuels to an unimaginable temperature, creating a tiny sun in the moments before the explosion. Anyone who happened to be looking at the device when it went off would be blinded a split second before being blasted into oblivion. No one on the Iranian team cared.

Early June, 2020; Tehran

In the meanwhile, Jahandar, through the expertise of Oleg Zlatovski, had set in motion the gathering of an army of assemblers. Some were found in the target countries already. They were given only such information as they absolutely needed to do their jobs. They would die in droves; it was inevitable. But, they would be martyrs, their place in Paradise secure.

Materials manufactured in Iran were being transported out, concealed as part of the clothes of the carriers. At some point, a large amount of materiel was going to have to go into the US, where security was tighter than anywhere except Israel. Then it may be best to smuggle it in as a large cargo, maybe through the same tunnels that al Gadahn had used to enter the US before last year's bombing in Boulder. A way to smuggle it into Israel was also under consideration. Many of the most important targets were there.

Jahandar thought it amusing that the method of delivery for the bombs would be purchased in the open, online. It seemed that Americans didn't believe terrorism was real, unless the bombs exploded right under them. Their security was laughable for this type of commerce. Anyone could purchase the means to make a very destructive bomb, and no one would question it. Even sophisticated drones could be had for a price. And flying model airplanes as well, though it would take a certain amount of skill in controlling them to get the bombs in place with any precision. The main advantage that the latter had was that they were quite a bit less expensive; more could be purchased.

The assemblers had been trained as carefully as the spies that were sent into the Rossler Foundation, most of whom were in custody now, a few having been sent home when nothing could be proved against them. The focus of Jahandar's program had moved to the deployment stage. Everything they needed to destroy the entire political infrastructure of the target countries, including government and military as well as much of the financial system and even the controlling echelons of major industry, was well in hand. The date was set, and only the details of the delivery were still incomplete, only because the manual labor was time-consuming. However, they had more than a month to be ready, and from all reports of the assemblers, they were on schedule.

Jahandar was satisfied with the progress. His only regret was losing one of his twelve lieutenants. Reza had been a valuable contact. A search was on for a replacement, for in the aftermath of the planned Hajj attack, Dalir believed he required at least twelve influential supporters for the rest of his plan; his own takeover of the government of Iran. His first act would be to restore the great name of the Persian Empire to his country. After that, he would follow in the footsteps of Cyrus to annex the rest of the world to his empire.

Chapter Twenty-One

IT'S ABOUT TIME

June 16, 2020; Boulder

Though plenty of Sturm und Drang was playing out within the Foundation, word of the security breach had been confined to only those who needed to know. During the entire time that first Luke and Raj and later the government security team were investigating their co-workers, others in the translation department went about their assignments unaware of the spies among them. There was little day-to-day interaction among the employees who'd been at the Foundation from near the beginning and the new translators. Their assignments were different, their cultural orientation was different, and they just didn't have much in common outside of work, though the Middle Easterners had made an effort to fit in at first. Now they just exchanged civil greetings

While Luke and Raj were finding and decoding hidden messages from the Middle Easterners, Ilse Abernathy was struggling with a difficult passage that Sinclair had assigned her. It was unlike anything she'd worked on before, written in a future tense for some reason, and it seemed to predict a disaster, though the dates were wrong for the 10th Cycle's cataclysm as it was referred to elsewhere. Ilse was certain she had mistranslated something, but the more she worked to tease out the actual meaning of the words, the stranger the document got. In the middle of it, she'd actually found references to a section of the library code that contained pictures. Nowhere had anyone found pictures. How could they, when the code was written in stone, literally? Furthermore, unless she was completely wrong, it was talking about pictures of the future. She had to be wrong, what could that possibly mean?

Ilse struggled with the document for a week before she reluctantly took her problem to Nicholas. No one liked doing that. In the first place, it called their competence for their job into question. And in the second place, it was humiliating to watch Sinclair read it as if it were written in today's newspaper. However, she had taken it as far as she could, and still had no idea what the document was actually saying. She was sure she'd taken a wrong turn somewhere, and equally sure that Sinclair could straighten her out.

"Sinclair, do you have a minute?" Ilse asked, after knocking at his open door. Sinclair looked up from his work and spotted one of his favorite employees. Ilse was a solid worker, and not too hard on the eyes, either.

"Of course, Ilse. What can I do for you?" He smiled at her and gestured to a chair beside his desk.

"I'm stuck, Sinclair. I've been beating my head against the wall over this section of the code for a week, at least. It doesn't make sense."

"Do you mean, you can't read the words? Is it perhaps written in a different language?" Sinclair doubted it, but what she'd said didn't make much sense, either. Ilse was a stellar student of the language.

"No, I can read the words. But they don't make sense. It's all in future tense, for one thing. And it seems to be talking about *pictures*!" Ilse's frustration was manifest in the pitch of her voice, which had risen so much by the time she got to 'pictures' that Sinclair could have characterized it as a wail.

"Hmm. That doesn't make sense," he said.

"That's what I said!"

"Sorry, dear. Forgive me for repeating the obvious. Well, did you bring a printout?" Sinclair didn't want to show the girl up, but his eyes sparkled as he savored the idea of a challenge for a second.

"Yes, right here. The original, and my translation." She handed the pages over to Sinclair, who took a quick glance at the page of symbols representing the Linear A language that they still called Minoan for easy reference. Scanning rapidly, he found the word Ilse was translating as pictures. He would have said images, but her point was valid. What images? How could there be images coded in the stones of the pyramid? He backed up a few lines and read again, his blood beginning to run cold as he read.

Clearing his throat, Sinclair fought to maintain control of his voice. "Ilse, I'm afraid you're going to have to leave this with me. The old brain isn't what it used to be. I see what you mean, and I'm going to have to give it some thought."

"Okay. Do you want me to keep working on this section?" she asked, twirling a strand of her long hair around her finger.

"No, no. Let me tackle it for the moment. Why don't

you pull an assignment from your group's list and get started on it?"

"Okay. Thanks, Sinclair"

Then his thoughts turned to the passage Ilse had brought to him. Pictures from the future? That's what it said, but could it possibly mean that? Was Ilse playing a trick on him? Or was someone playing a trick on Ilse? His gnarled fingers flew over the keys as he pulled up the data for the original passage she was translating. He ran it through the program that translated the stones' code to symbols, and compared it to the printout. It was identical. A tremor rattled the paper in his hand as the blood drained from his face. Could the 10th Cyclers really have been able to visit their own future? Is that how they knew when their cataclysm would occur? What else did they know? What did they know about our cycle?

Who should he tell? What should he do to be certain before he told anyone? The last question sent him searching once again through the database of every word in the original Minoan, for the word 'future'. Hit after hit populated his screen, and he read snippets of the passages around the words. Many of them referred to something he translated as 'future viewing', or a device for that purpose. Faith and begorrah, this was huge! Shaken, he reached for his bottom desk drawer, where just the medicine he required was stored for times like this. The Jameson was an adequate whiskey, and his pour was generous. Sure and a lad deserved a wee nip after a shock like this.

Questions about the nature of time crowded his brain. Fragments of long-forgotten conversations with roommates and drinking buddies while he was in college, full of his own cleverness as he tied those of lesser mental agility in knots. Deep philosophical questions, like what would happen if you visited your own past and accidentally killed one of your forebears. Would you wink out of existence in your own time? Or would it create an alternate reality? Now it seemed that those weren't idle questions after all. *Wait 'til Nicholas hears this! Wonder if the old timer's heart is strong enough for it?*

Sinclair took a chance that Nicholas was still at his desk and walked down the hall to pay him a visit. If he'd seen his own face, he would have tried to compose himself before barging in on his mentor, but he didn't get that chance. As a result, Nicholas got quite a shock when he looked up to see his friend in the doorway. The man looked like he'd seen a ghost!

"Nicholas, I've had a shock," Sinclair said, rather unnecessarily. Anyone could see that he'd had a shock. Nicholas did what any man would do when a friend had had a shock.

"Care for a drink?" Nicholas asked, pulling out his own bottle, identical to Sinclair's, and two glasses, without waiting for an answer.

"Sure and another would be good," Sinclair answered, too distracted to realize he'd just revealed he'd already had a drink, and a stiff one, too, unless Nicholas missed his guess. When they'd both intoned Slainte! and downed their drinks, Nicholas waited for Sinclair to gather his thoughts. What he heard next was completely out of left field.

"Nicholas, have you ever thought about time travel?" Sinclair said. That he said it with a straight face gave Nicholas to understand that he was serious.

"Not since my college days. Why? Is there a time-travel device in the library?" he said, in jest.

"You might call it that," Sinclair said, holding out his glass for another shot. He waited in vain as Nicholas' mouth dropped and he stared at Sinclair.

"I think you'd better explain," he said, wondering if Sinclair had lost his mind, or had rather more of the juice than he should have.

"I'm not sure I can," said Sinclair, holding out his glass hopefully again. This time, Nicholas filled it, and poured another stiff shot for himself as well.

"I think I've just experienced the future and the past at the same time, without one second of the present elapsing." Sinclair's eyes were glazed, and his hand shook as he raised the glass to his lips.

Nicholas was beginning to worry about his friend. He'd never seen him in such a state, not even when his first wife died. Would it be a good idea to call Martha? Or could he get Sinclair calmed down himself? He looked at his bottle, decided there were at least two more good shots of calming effect in it, and settled down to wait for Sinclair to say something that made sense.

To his surprise, he didn't have all that long to wait. After Sinclair had drained his glass again and Nicholas emptied his bottle for one more shot each, Sinclair was ready to talk, and this time, he was more composed. And surprisingly sober. He wondered how the Irish do it – *the more they drink the more sense they make especially if you have been drinking with them*.

"One of the translators brought me something she couldn't translate today," he began. "She had it right, she just didn't believe it. Nicholas, there are references in the library about viewing the future, and coordinates for pictures! They left us pictures of the future, can you believe it?"

Now it was Nicholas's turn to be surprised, but he wasn't as shocked as Sinclair expected.

"I've always thought there had to be alternate realities," he said, echoing the memories that Sinclair had dredged up right after making his discovery. "And I've often wondered if time is real. The physicists are beginning to dispute that, you know. They view what we experience as time more as us traveling along a continuum that exists all at once, like we're on a conveyor belt, being carried past all these events that are static. They've always existed, it's only us happening upon them that make us experience time."

"I had no idea you were such a philosopher, old timer," Sinclair said, his brogue lilting as never before. It was always more pronounced when he'd had a dram.

"Who are you calling old-timer, you Irish mug," said Nicholas, beginning to feel the whiskey a bit himself.

"Never mind. Should we call Daniel? Or wait until tomorrow?"

"If we're right, tomorrow isn't tomorrow, it's yesterday, so we might as well call him today - he won't know the difference right?" answered Nicholas, with perfect logic as far as he was concerned. He'd developed a bit of a brogue, too.

"Let's call everyone," Sinclair decided. The result was that Daniel, Sarah, and Raj, each received two crazy phone calls, and Roy received one. Everyone rushed back to the office, because clearly the two older men were drunk and needed care, or they had both gone off their rockers at the same time! While they waited for the others to arrive, Sinclair and Nicholas went back to Sinclair's office for his nearly full bottle and another couple of glasses. Security footage would later show them to be weaving down the hall, arms around each other, humming the Star Wars theme song.

By chance, it was Roy who arrived first, and stopped short at the sight of the two distinguished oldsters dancing in the halls, now singing Drops of Jupiter, an oldie but goodie favorite of his mother's. He edged away, backing into his own office and trying to decide whether to call 911 or wait for Daniel, whom Nicholas had shouted out was on his way. Just as he reached for the phone, he heard Daniel's voice.

"Grandpa, what in hell has gotten into you two? Is everything all right?" Sarah was right behind him, her mouth open in astonishment.

"More than all right, boyo," crowed Sinclair. "We've discovered the future the past and the present and time travel! You know yesterday is actually tomorrow but tomorrow could be an entirely different day or is it today? Wait let me just check that again I could be wrong … today is not yesterday you know?"

"No, no, no Sinclair you have got it all wrong. Yesterday, today and tomorrow do not exist. It is all an illusion but today will be tomorrow's yesterday or maybe…" Nicholas said in a heavy Irish accent.

"Oh, my God," muttered Daniel. Someone had to have given them hallucinogenic drugs. LSD, maybe. He dug in his pocket for his phone and dialed Raj's number, the third on his speed-dial list. "Raj, are you on your way to the office?"

"Yes. What's up, Daniel? I got the oddest call from your grandfather."

"I don't know, but it looks like he and Sinclair are drunk on their asses, maybe someone slipped them something worse. Would you stop somewhere and get a gallon of coffee?"

"Sure thing. Don't sober them up before I get there, though. I must see this!" Raj's rare laughter was ringing out as Daniel hung up.

"Better call him back and have him pick up a fifth of Jameson's," Sinclair said. "When gramps and I are done with you, you're going to need it."

Forty-five minutes later, all four of the newly-arrived members of the party were hoisting their own stiff drinks, after seeing the passages Sinclair had queued up on his screen and translated. The coffee was cooling, untasted, on a side table.

"Do you realize what this means?" asked Daniel.

"Do you mean, besides revolutionizing everything we've always known about time?" Roy asked, forgetting for the moment to be shy in Sarah's presence. Or maybe it was the Jameson's that had given him courage.

"Yes, besides that. I'll admit, that's huge. But, what if it showed us where we might go wrong, as a civilization, I mean? And helped us avoid bad decisions and bad outcomes?" Daniel wrinkled his nose as his grandpa swayed too close, bringing the odor of a distillery with him.

"Yes!" Sarah cried, grasping his meaning immediately. "They didn't have time to correct their own mistakes, and they saw the end coming. Daniel! This will help us avoid our cataclysm! Make sure it never happens! Daniel, they've saved us, or given us the means to save ourselves! And think what it would mean to archaeology, if it goes backwards, too!"

She was so excited that it was hard for Daniel to say the words that would temper her happiness. The last thing he wanted to do was that. She'd been depressed, it seemed, for a while. She'd been too busy with the Foundation and the baby to practice her profession, and he thought what she really needed was to get back to work. Unfortunately, the local campus of the University of Colorado didn't have an Egyptology curriculum, and that made it doubly difficult for her to see a path for professional growth.

On top of all that, only Daniel knew how much the warning in the 10th Cycle greeting had affected her, how seriously she had taken it to heart. War anywhere grieved her to the point of despair. He hadn't been able to talk to her much about what loomed ahead for them, given the technology that the Iranian spies had stolen. It took too great a toll on her already-battered soul to even talk about it. Reluctantly, he brought up the difficulty with his next question.

"Raj, have you ever seen anything that looked remotely like a picture in the raw data? How could the 10th Cyclers have left us pictures that neither we nor anyone else has ever seen?"

Raj paused in his own daydreaming. At last, he may have the means to prove that the government was conspiring to keep the knowledge of aliens from another planet from us! He already had a listening device the size of a fly! Now he may have the means to travel in time, and observe the landing for himself. He barely heard Daniel's question, but enough sunk in to know he was being addressed.

"Sorry, Daniel, what did you say?"

"I said, have you ever seen anything that looked like a picture? If they left anything, wouldn't it be in the nature of an art gallery?"

"No," Raj answered. "I haven't. But you've just made me think of something. Remember how no one knows what the Great Gallery is for? We've found lots of data there that doesn't make any sense. No words, just random data, no matter what skip sequence we use. Could that be it?"

"I don't know. It's worth a try. Or maybe some of what Sinclair has found will give you the key. I'd like you and him to get started on it first thing tomorrow. Assuming he's in any shape to come in tomorrow." Both Raj and Daniel turned to watch Sinclair, who was trying to get Sarah to do an Irish jig with him. Daniel smiled. "If not, I guess day after tomorrow will be good enough. He deserves the celebration."

Daniel got taxis to take them all home – no one was in a state to drive a car. He also called Bess and Martha to warn them to expect their very happy and relaxed husbands' arrival.

Chapter Twenty-Two

PICTURES FROM THE FUTURE

June 17, 2020; Boulder

On the morning after the rather unorthodox celebration begun by Sinclair and Nicholas, the two were understandably a little late to work. When they did arrive, neither looked fit for duty, but both were determined to learn more about the astonishing discovery. They found Raj already at work, searching for the phrase that Sinclair had pointed out the night before. He'd celebrated a little more decorously, and had been at work for hours. A list of references awaited Sinclair, and he got busy immediately. For the time being, everyone who had been at the party last night had agreed to keep this discovery quiet until they knew more about it.

Sometime around noon, Raj hit pay dirt with a passage that contained directions for building the viewing device. This validation of the reality of the discovery was cause for another celebration. They kept it sedate this time, though. While Raj continued to work and Sinclair went right to work on translating that passage, abandoning what he'd

The Sword of Cyrus

been doing before, Nicholas went to notify Daniel. The two returned to Sinclair's office, where he was finished translating the description of the purpose of the device, and had begun translating the plans for making it.

As soon as Daniel walked in his door, Sinclair spoke without looking up.

"I think we're going to need Roy for this." Daniel and Nicholas exchanged glances, and then Daniel went to Roy's lab.

"Can I interrupt you for a minute?" he asked, leaning against the doorway with his arms crossed.

Roy put down the new gadget he was working on, an insect-sized flying device that could detect minute quantities of any substance for which it was programmed, and mark the location with an intense red flare, tiny, but visible for yards. He thought it would come in handy for automatic detection and marking of toxic waste spills.

"What can I do for you?" he asked Daniel, who was eying the new toy with interest.

"Raj found the directions for building that future viewing device. Sinclair wants you to take a look at his translation and see if you think you can build it." Daniel deliberately kept his request low-key. He didn't want to touch off a celebration like they'd had last night, as much as he enjoyed having the chance to blow off steam.

"Sure. Let me put things away here, and I'll be right down." Roy began to gather his tools and spare parts, swiftly putting them into their places with sure hands. A moment later, he followed Daniel back to Sinclair's office. Daniel regretted that the crowd was beginning to draw some attention; however, if they could build this thing, it would revolutionize just about everything. If it could be made to look backwards far enough, it might even speed up the monumental task of translating the library. And looking forward - there was no end to the utility of that! When Daniel put his musings into words for the others to hear, they were silent and awe-struck by the possibilities. Until Sinclair's flip remark set them laughing again.

"Well, if this gets out, there'll be no more betting on the horses and no more lotto to play!"

Roy had finished studying the description of the device and the principle on which it worked.

"Yes, I think I can build this, if Sinclair's translation can give me plans for a few key components." His quiet delivery of the good news almost made them miss the significance of what he'd said.

"You understand the principle, then?" Daniel asked, his question suddenly urgent. It had just occurred to him that the device may make it possible to find out why the Iranians were designing nanonukes, and when they intended to use them. Time was of the essence.

"Oh, yes. It's rather simple, really. Just as we were talking about last night, time isn't something that starts and rolls along for us when we're born. It's more like, like plasma," he said, struggling to explain to the laypeople around him. "It flows, all right, but not linearly. Certain events create the potential for alternate timelines, and even those can rejoin themselves at some later date. We travel along, and our decisions dictate which timeline we follow. People who are closely linked by physical or emotional ties are swept in the same direction as each other, and if someone follows a different timeline, his memory disappears, usually, from the collective knowledge of the others. I'll have to study it more to understand that part."

The others were held in thrall by his explanation, so inadequate for such a profound subject. Every one of them was searching his memory for a long-forgotten friend, with no luck. The alternative would have been very painful, Nicholas realized. To remember someone who had disappeared from your life, and never be able to find out what had happened to them. Come to think of it, that did happen to most people. And when the memory resurfaced, it was more painful or less painful, depending on how close to the other you'd been. More often than not, it was just a brief episode of melancholy. People you were close to didn't vanish like that, most often. They were still traveling your same timeline. It would bear some thought to discover who pulled whom with them.

Daniel was the first to recover his wits in the pause that followed. "But, what about the viewer?"

"Oh," said Roy. "Yes. You can view events in your own timeline, for as far back as it's been in existence, and as far forward as it stays stable. You can also view other timelines, but only very recent or close future events. It relies on nanotechnology, by the way. How fortunate that I'm right here." Roy said the last without the least bit of self-consciousness for the statement of the obvious. He was possibly the only person in the world with the hands-on expertise with nanotechnology to actually build the device. Some of the best quantum physicists in the world may understand how it worked, but there wasn't another man alive with the experience he had in actually building the devices that had previously proved theoretical only.

"How long will it take you to build it?" Daniel asked, his expression carefully neutral to avoid letting Roy know that it was critical. Roy wouldn't need any incentive to work faster on it, it was the most important discovery ever to have come out of the library, and the fact of it alone would urge rapid development.

"I can't say for sure. Depends on how long it takes for Sinclair to get me the critical components' plans. Maybe a week, maybe two," Roy answered. Daniel had a feeling that wouldn't be soon enough, but for now he'd let it go. There were still pictures to be seen, if the other references meant what they thought they did.

"Okay, everyone, let's keep chipping away at this one. Sinclair, a word please?" As everyone else filed out of Sinclair's office, Daniel asked Sinclair if he thought that any of the translators could be trusted to remain calm and not have their heads turned by the secret. After careful consideration, Sinclair reluctantly said that he'd rather not take the risk. He'd pull some long hours to get all the passages referring to the viewer or pictures at least skimmed. And, if possible, coordinates within the physical blueprint of the pyramid, so they could try to take a look at those.

June 19, 2020; Boulder

For two days, Raj had searched and re-searched the library for any phrase he could think of to indicate a remote-viewing device, as they'd been calling it. Remote, in the sense that the time was removed from the present. It made it simpler than to say future/past/alternate timeline viewing device, though that would have been the most accurate.

Today, having found the plans already and now that he was certain he'd located every reference, and turned them over to Sinclair for processing, he began searching for a way to render the data in the Great Gallery into pictures that made any sense. The Fibonacci skip sequences had already been applied to the large number of blocks there, with no comprehensible result. Now Raj had the idea of assigning a shade of gray to each of the blocks, according to their dimensions, and lining them up in rows, much as a black-and-white TV screen painted a grayscale picture with tiny pixels.

The first attempt revealed that there was a picture there, but it didn't make much sense. Raj wracked his brain for the key to giving the right weight to each different symbol. Then it hit him. The largest concentration of a single dimensional result; that is, the number represented by the multiplication of the height, width and diagonal measurement of the block, seemed to be in the upper corners. This must represent either white or black on the color scale. Everything else must line up in numerical order, based on the experience they'd gained of the rest of the pyramid. Everything was a mathematical equation, the results of which were Fibonacci numbers.

Taking a guess that in a gray-scale picture, the upper corners would represent sky, he assigned a light gray to the symbol that had the largest number of instances. With each new dimensional result, he gave a small increment of darker gray, until he had assigned values to all the numbers represented. Then he ran a simple switch program to replace the numbers with blocks in shades of gray. Again, he had a picture, but not a sensible one. The thing to do was to figure out the width, in pixels, of the pictures. He was off by a few, it seemed.

A little more thought brought him the inspiration. He'd use the highest Fibonacci number represented in the symbols as the width of the finished picture. The idea held a certain symmetry that he thought would have appealed to the 10th Cyclers, whom he'd come to know through their work as well as anyone could know someone who was more than 26,000 years dead. Adjusting the switch program, Raj held his breath as he 'painted' the picture on his screen one more time.

This time, it made a weird sort of sense, but what was he seeing? It looked like a ruined city, broken buildings standing tall above miles of rubble. What looked like human bodies were everywhere, too charred to tell much about them. In the bottom left-hand corner, there was a caption embedded in the picture itself. It looked to Raj like the date references he'd seen, first in the greeting and later on many library documents. He still couldn't read the data like Sinclair could, but he was curious enough to instant message Sinclair with a copy of it electronically snipped from the picture, asking for a translation.

The answer was not long in coming. "It translates to July 29, 2020. Where did you get that?"

All color drained from Raj's face. What city was this? The date, marked on a picture more than 26,000 years old, was a mere forty days from today.

When Raj didn't answer, Sinclair was worried enough to intercom Daniel and ask him to meet at Raj's office. The pair found Raj frantically pounding his keyboard, 'developing' picture after picture and printing them out. All had the same date reference on them, they realized as they picked up the printouts and tried to make sense of what they were seeing.

"Raj, what the hell is this?" Daniel demanded, when his friend ignored his presence and kept at his task.

"I'm trying to find out what cities these are," Raj answered, with a little less information than he thought he was conveying. Daniel walked over to his desk and put his hand down on Raj's flying fingers.

"Raj. Stop. Tell us what these pictures are," Daniel said, catching and holding Raj's attention. He was worried about his friend's color, a peculiar gray under his usual brown tones. It made him look ill.

"Is it not plain to see?" Raj answered. Taking up the first picture, he pointed to a familiar-looking spire surrounded by rubble. "Is that not the Washington Monument?" Seeing his friend's blank stare, he pointed to the caption in the lower left-hand corner. "It is a date; I had Sinclair confirm it." Now Sinclair looked thunderstruck, and Raj continued. "The date is 29 July, just forty days from now. The 10th Cyclers captured an image of what the Washington Monument will look like on that date."

Daniel stared at it, unable to process what he was seeing. It looked damaged, like someone had taken a bite out of one side. And where was the reflecting pool? He handed it to Sinclair for his opinion, just as Raj found another picture of a famous landmark.

"Is this not Buckingham Palace?" Raj asked. Daniel stared at the image. No, he couldn't make it out to be Buckingham Palace; it was leveled, just a pile of debris to mark it. But the famous Victoria Memorial stood, virtually untouched, in front of it. A wave of grief went through him for King William and his young family, who had become avid supporters of the Rossler Foundation even before William ascended to the throne after his father's unexpected death. Daniel devoutly hoped they hadn't been in the Palace when this happened. Or wouldn't be when it happens. How the heck was he supposed to talk about time, now? And, could they change this outcome by warning them? Sure, they could, couldn't they? Had to.

Raj had continued pulling out pictures and naming landmarks where he could. Slowly, the three of them came to see the big picture. On a date forty days from now, a terrible cataclysm would take place that would level many of the major cities in the world. Daniel couldn't help but remember all the times Sarah had brought up the 10th Cycle prediction that unless a civilization could learn to live without war, each cycle would have their own cataclysm. This certainly looked like her belief in its accuracy come true.

He couldn't bear to tell her of it, but how could he not? Should they take little Nick and the rest of their families and head for some sanctuary away from the larger cities? What would be left for them if everything were destroyed? He didn't notice the tears streaming down his face until Sinclair put a hand on his shoulder and squeezed.

"Buck up, boyo. We've work to do." Seeing that he had Daniel's full attention, Sinclair clapped him on the back. "I think it's time to get the rest of the translators working on the time viewing stuff. And you'd better give your friend President Harper a call."

Daniel agreed; the president would have to be informed first thing. But before that, he needed a few minutes, or hours, to get his own head around the information. He'd have to present it in a way that was believable, and this was the most unbelievable thing he'd ever discovered in his entire career. Furthermore, he'd better have both an explanation and an assessment of the total effect. He was going to have to identify as many of the cities in Raj's printouts as possible.

"Raj, you've identified most of these places, right?"

"Yes, Daniel."

"Can you write the cities in the margins? I need to

figure out how extensive this attack is going to be, and then we'll need help in stopping it."

"I can. And I found a text file in the gallery as well. It was small, we must have overlooked it before. I'll send it to Sinclair for translation."

"Do that, and tell him to put a rush on it. Maybe it explains these pictures." Daniel had a number of other people to talk to before he contacted Harper. He had to get started, because there was not a second to waste.

However, his top priority was to let Sarah in on what they'd found. It was true that her field of research was far removed from much of the 10th Cycle data. On the other hand, she had been with him from the beginning, and had been instrumental in discovering the meaning of the Great Pyramid at Giza. Furthermore, she had a good head on her shoulders. As much as he wanted to protect her from this knowledge, she had a right to know. He instructed Raj to keep at it, stared down the hallway at Sinclair's receding back, and then made a beeline for Sarah's office.

Daniel, Sarah, Raj, Roy, Luke and Sinclair worked tirelessly to ferret out every bit of information they could about the images Raj had found and the technology that had produced them during the 10th Cycle. While they worked on a presentation for the president, Luke discovered that Raj had found coordinates on each picture. They now had a list of the targets represented by the pictures, and he worked with Roy to determine what kind of weapon of mass destruction would be required to destroy them so thoroughly. They were operating on the assumption that it was Iran deploying those weapons, or a consortium of Middle Eastern countries led by Iran, based on the information that the translator-spies had stolen, and the location of the computers they'd traced so far as receiving the information.

They were a long way from discovering the ringleaders, but the stakes had just gotten higher.

To Luke's dismay, Roy was of the opinion that the destruction could be carried out by bombs no larger than a briefcase; or a series of much smaller bombs if they were arrayed correctly.

It wouldn't take that many bombs to level the city centers or important locations in each city. With the centers devastated, governments, police agencies, commerce and banking would all be in chaos, if not utterly destroyed as well. Furthermore, some of the pictures Raj had found after he called Sinclair and Daniel in looked a lot like military installations. Hit those, and you eliminated any ability for counterstrike. This was even worse than it looked at first, and that was the worst thing Luke could have imagined anyway.

This news couldn't wait until tomorrow. Luke checked with Daniel to be sure he was ready, and then called Sam Lewis's private cell phone. It was nearly midnight, Boulder time.

"Do you know what the hell time it is?" demanded the angry voice on the other end of the line.

"Sorry, Sam. I do. If it could have waited, I wouldn't be calling." Luke didn't identify himself. Sam knew his voice.

"Luke? Oh, shit, now what?" Lewis wished that Luke would just once call him at a reasonable hour and invite him to go fishing. Every time he heard Luke's voice, a new crisis loomed. This must be a bad one, if it couldn't wait another four or five hours.

"You're not going to believe it, old friend. We need to come and show it to the president. But it can't even wait until we get there. Can you pave the way again? We need to talk to him tonight." Luke was aware of what he was asking, and of what Lewis was thinking. It didn't take a genius to know that if you called a guy over and over again with bad news, he was sooner or later going to wish he didn't know you. But Sam was good folks. He'd do what was asked of him, because he knew they'd never cried wolf.

Chapter Twenty-Three

FASTEN YOUR SEATBELT

4 a.m., June 19, 2020, D-day minus 39; Washington, D.C.

"Daniel, if I didn't know you so well, I'd say you'd slipped a cog," Harper said. "Are you absolutely sure?"

"Mr. President - Nigel - would I have gotten you out of bed if I weren't absolutely sure?" Daniel was bone weary, and not in the mood to verbally spar with Harper. He was as certain as he could be. The evidence was overwhelming. Pictures from a future that was too close for comfort, showing every major city in the US, in a state resembling Hiroshima and Nagasaki after the bombs. And they hadn't identified every image, much less determined whether they'd found all of them. Raj and Sinclair were hard at work identifying those that had recognizable landmarks, and it appeared Jerusalem, the first non-US target they'd found, was at equal risk. That set them on a quest for other US allies' identifiable cities, in case the attack were a widespread, even global effort.

"We'll be on our way to you in a few hours, to show you the evidence. But we don't have any hours to waste. Lewis's investigative team has dispersed, and we need them back on the job immediately. We've got to find the organization that's behind this, and we've got little over a month in which to do it. That's if we can do anything about it. Maybe its fait accompli and all we can do is participate in the end of the world as we know it. Please, brief Lewis now and let him get started." He looked at his watch as he spoke. He had just two hours to make his flight, and he still needed to go home and pack for a day or two. He wasn't going to make it.

"No need to brief him, Daniel. He's been right here all along, and you're on speaker. What do you want him to do?" For an intelligent man, the president was asking a foolish question. Lewis would have a far better idea of what to do than Daniel could suggest.

"I don't know, Nigel. Pull out their fingernails? He's got to find a way to make them talk!"

"Okay, Daniel, settle down. I'll see you in a few hours." Harper had detected the desperation in Daniel's last remark and knew he couldn't push him any further. Rossler would be in his office as soon as he could, and he could tell Lewis then if he had any suggestions they hadn't already put into place. "Wait, Daniel, how are you getting here?"

"Commercial flight if I can make it." Daniel's delivery was impatient. The clock was ticking away, and he needed to end this call.

"You have an executive airport nearby, don't you?"

"Yes, Rocky Mountain Metropolitan, why?" Daniel was fidgeting, so anxious that he was considering hanging up on the president of the United States.

"Ever wanted to catch a ride in a fighter jet?"

"What are you saying?"

"New Lockheed model is being tested in Colorado Springs. I'll send it to pick you up at your convenience. Luke Clarke is coming too, right? Just get yourself to that airport as soon as you can. It will be waiting for you."

The long drive to DIA now off the table, Daniel had time to brief those who were staying behind to continue work on the viewing device and any further information they could gather.

After doing so, Daniel took Sarah home. It was three a.m., and they'd been up since early the previous morning. While Sarah made coffee, Daniel went to the baby's room and gazed at him for a moment, before carefully picking him up and holding him close. Daniel didn't know what the next hour would hold, much less the next days and weeks. The comfort of holding his boy wouldn't last very long without another chance to do so, but it was all he had for now. After a moment, he laid Nick back in his crib. He was getting too big for it, Daniel observed. When this was over, they'd need to get him a big-boy bed. He refused to think further than that.

It took him only a few minutes to pack a couple of days' changes of clothing and throw his shaving kit into the bag. Shouldering it, he went to the kitchen, where his coffee was already waiting for him.

"We'll find them, Sarah. We have to. We'll find them and stop them. Sweetheart, I can't stand to leave you right now, but it's imperative I be on hand to help Nigel understand he has to throw everything the USA can muster at this with no delay. I'll be back as soon as I can."

9 a.m., June 19, 2020, D-day minus 39; Washington, D.C.

Daniel and Luke stood at attention and under Secret Service scrutiny in the anteroom of the Oval Office, waiting to be summoned. Daniel thought that if he looked as bad as he felt, it was no wonder the security agents didn't trust him. Both he and Luke had been subjected to very personal searches, a new experience for Daniel, and not one he'd care to repeat. The laptop he'd brought with him and the map case that Luke carried with the photos printed out in folio size had both been confiscated. He only hoped that they'd reappear when Harper was ready to talk with them. For the hundredth time, he looked at his watch, surprised to see that they'd only been waiting about ten minutes.

At last, the doors opened and they were ushered in. Harper barked at the agents to leave them alone, and under protest, they withdrew. Daniel looked around the office and found it strange that it was only the three of them, no sign of Sam Lewis or any other high ranking official. But he dismissed it, there was no time to think or ask about that.

"Daniel, I can't tell you what a hornet's nest you've poked this time. I've just had the head of the Secret Service telling me you don't seem to have had a mental breakdown, but I have my doubts. There's nothing on the radar, nothing at all that corroborates what you told me this morning." Harper's slumped shoulders told the story of what had been going on since Daniel's early-morning call.

"You had me investigated?" Daniel asked. He couldn't really blame Harper, but it still felt like a stab in the back.

"You, Luke, your wife, your father-in-law, and a few others. I've had a meeting of the National Security Council, every member of which believes you to be insane. Why should I think any differently?"

"Nigel, you know me!" Daniel began. Then he reconsidered his approach. This was a waste of time. "Have you looked at the photos? Seen the presentation?" He thought it unlikely; the Secret Service had probably just made sure the laptop wasn't wired to explode. He was right.

"No. Why don't you show me?" Harper said, a little less angry now, but still sounding weary. "I'm sorry, Daniel. I know you believe what you've told me but I have nothing that is convincing me of what you are saying."

Daniel looked around and spied their confiscated items on a side table. He opened the laptop and queued up the hurriedly-created presentation to keep him on track with his narration.

"Okay, Nigel, fasten your seatbelt. You are in for a very rough ride. This started a couple of days ago. One of our translators had reached an impasse on a passage she was working on. As it turned out, she had it right, but didn't believe what it was saying, so she took it to Sinclair O'Reilly." He stopped and looked at Harper questioningly. Harper nodded. He remembered who Sinclair was.

"So he translated it, and realized they'd made a very important discovery. Nigel, the 10th Cyclers had technology to view the future, and the past."

Harper made a strangled exclamation, but Daniel ploughed on, determined to have his say before Harper threw him out. It was their only chance.

"To make a very long story short, we also found pictures, coded in the stones of the Great Gallery of the Giza Pyramid. We have printouts. They show cities, *our* cities, in rubble. They're dated a little over a month in the future, and there are coordinates that prove they're our cities. The 10th Cyclers saw our cataclysm, and recorded it, before their civilization was destroyed."

When he was finished at last, Daniel dared risk a glance at Harper. The president's eyes were wide and staring, and he'd grabbed a fistful of his iconic white hair in either hand, giving him the look of a child who'd seen a ghost.

Daniel had rightly suspected that drawing out the story would only make it harder for Harper to respond. By dumping it on him in a few short sentences, he saved time. Harper would ask for the details that he needed.

"How can this be possible?" Harper asked after a long silence during which his eyes darted everywhere in the room, proving Daniel correct. The question had several potential answers, all of which would have been correct. Daniel chose to interpret it to mean that the president wanted the science behind the existence of the pictures.

"I don't fully understand it. Probably there is no one in the world who does," Daniel said. "Our resident nanotechnology expert thinks that quantum physicists might understand some of it. But understanding it will make no difference to the fact that we are about to be destroyed in thirty-eight days. These are pictures of one possible timeline of many, and we seem to be on that timeline that leads to disaster. Our nanotechnologist believes that we can jump off it, to an alternate reality that doesn't include this outcome, if we act quickly enough to find whoever plans to do this and stop them. But that is only a theory; for now we have not discovered anything that says that alternate reality exists. It isn't magic, or science fiction. It's an investigative challenge, but we need to get on it right away. It's going to require the manpower of the US government, and possibly our allies as well."

Harper made a visible effort to pull himself together. "Mind if I have some of our experts take a look at this?"

"Not at all. Just don't let them take too long. We don't have much time," Daniel said. Luke hadn't yet said a word. Now he had a suggestion.

"I brought some references for Roy James, our nanotech guy. We borrowed him from Cal-tech when we started seeing some nanotechnology stuff coming out of the past. He's at work on a device that the 10th Cyclers left a plan for, one of these remote-viewing things. I've also brought those plans. You might want to get some people from MIT or some of the national laboratories to look it over. Roy's the one who's telling us we can stop this."

Harper looked at Luke for the first time. He liked what he saw. Luke was standing tall, no hint of deception or craft in his expression or his body language. He'd heard good things about this man from Sam Lewis, his head of the CIA. The suggestion was a good one, he'd put it in motion. One other thing crossed his mind.

"Let's assume for a moment that this is real, and it's happening, or going to happen. What guarantee do we have that you've discovered all of the targets?" Harper asked.

"We don't," Daniel answered. "We need National Security advisors to help us refine our searches. The library isn't like Google; we have to ask very specific questions. Your people would know far more about potential targets than we would.

Harper nodded slowly in assent. "Can you two stick around for a day or two?" he asked. Both nodded, and Daniel answered.

"Yes. But Nigel - there are only thirty-eight left. There aren't any to waste."

"I get that. But going off half-cocked won't do us any

good. I'd like you to stay handy. I'm going to have my Chief of Staff stash you in an office and send in some refreshments. Anything else you need?"

"If you're going to hang onto the laptop, we could both use access to a computer with an internet connection," Luke answered for both of them.

"You'll have it. I need that laptop to convince some of the skeptics on my advisory council. I'll see you soon."

Chapter Twenty-Four

BY EXECUTIVE ORDER

Harper was a shaken man and he fully intended to have all this checked out and verified. But, he was convinced enough to call Sam Lewis back in as soon as Daniel and Luke left.

"You heard?" he asked. Lewis had been listening to the meeting between the president, his old friend Luke Clarke, and Luke's nephew by marriage, the famous Daniel Rossler, via a live feed from a listening device the president was wearing in his lapel. It looked like a small depiction of the American theme of white stars and stripes on a red and blue background, a symbol of his patriotism, perhaps. No one would suspect that it could transmit the drop of a pin anywhere in the room to the listeners at the other end of the signal.

Lewis nodded.

"What do you think?" Harper asked.

"I've never had a reason to doubt Luke or the Rosslers I'm convinced and also scared," Lewis responded. "Unless they've been duped, this is for real." It scared him to say it. He knew that it was going to be on him to find the conspirators and stop this madness. He didn't have enough time.

"I agree. I'm going to issue an executive order putting every investigative resource at our disposal under your command. Find these bastards and take them out. I don't care what it takes." Harper may have just signed his own impeachment, if Congress believed he'd overstepped his bounds. It didn't matter. He was tired, and this was the last straw. If his last act as president were to be saving the world from certain destruction that was fine with him. The US had a long-standing policy of not striking first. That was about to end, if only Lewis could give him a certain target. And damn the consequences.

Executive order in hand, Lewis wasted no time in assembling the heads of the agencies over which he'd just been given authority. He wanted them to hear it from Harper, and Harper agreed. There was no time for resentment or rivalry between the agencies. When he addressed them, he spoke as if the information had already been confirmed, and swept away all expressions of doubt.

"It doesn't matter whether you believe this or not. As your commanding officer, I'm ordering you to put yourselves and every resource of your agencies in the hands of Sam Lewis to direct the search for the bastards who are planning to nuke us into oblivion. I don't want to hear any excuses about why your agencies didn't pick this up, or any doubt that it's real. The only priority now is to stop it. You have one hour to put your networks on alert, then reassemble here for a briefing by Rossler and Clarke."

The room as a whole stood stunned for all of five seconds. Then Lewis barked, "MOVE!" and they scattered like cockroaches. Lewis had already briefed his own team. Every operative the CIA had was already putting out feelers to see if they could pluck a string and hit a true note. Someone, somewhere, knew about this. They'd find them and roll their networks up, or leave a bloody trail trying.

After the briefing with the other agencies, Lewis locked himself in his office and drew up a counterintelligence plan to most efficiently use his resources. First, he secured space for a command center that would accommodate all of them as necessary. He didn't want to waste time communicating among the agencies; everyone would use his Joint Operations Command Center as a hub, and all intelligence would be entered into a database there. After consulting with his IT specialists, he made a quick call to Luke's cell phone.

"Are you guys still here?" he asked.

"Yes, for now. What can we do for you?"

"I want to borrow the Foundation's whiz kid IT guy. Raj, is it? Can you spare him?"

"I'm sure we can. You don't have your own?"

"We do, but my guys tell me Raj can set this network up to work with all the agency's proprietary software quicker than anyone else. We need a central database."

"Done. I'll tell Daniel what you need. Does Raj need to get here?"

"Doubt it. Why don't you ask him? He'd know best."

A few minutes later, Daniel was on the phone to Raj, explaining what Lewis wanted.

"No, I can do it from here," Raj said. "They'll have to live with that. I'm not putting myself in their custody." Daniel had a moment's amusement of Raj still worrying about the CIA and FBI finding out about him, when the whole world was about to blow up. Not to mention the fact that everyone *did* know about him, and he hadn't been arrested yet. No doubt it was a bitter disappointment to him.

The Sword of Cyrus

"What do you need?" Daniel asked.

"Nothing at the moment. I'll let you know if I run into a problem." Raj used a throwaway cell to contact his hacker network and explain what he'd been asked to set up. Within an hour, he had a dozen assistants hacking into the agencies' networks and reporting back on the protocols. By the end of the day, the JOCC computers all lit up with a large new icon on their screens, depicting the reverse of the Great Seal of the United States, complete with truncated pyramid, occult Eye of Providence and the two mottoes: Annuit Coeptis and Novus Ordo Seclorum, which Raj insisted roughly translated as "May the Almighty favor our bold undertaking."

Daniel knew it to be Raj's joke, an allusion to his conspiracy theories and the theories surrounding 'secret societies' that controlled the US government as well as world finances. However, the motto was apt, and no one could object to the icon referencing the Great Seal. He kept his opinion of it to himself. It didn't matter, what mattered was that Raj had succeeded in tying together the software that each of the agencies used, to create a super-database for the urgent investigation at hand.

Daniel also suspected that Raj had called in help. This, too, he kept to himself. They needed all the help they could get, and if Raj's network had eluded discovery for this many years, they must be very good. He sent Raj a text saying, "check email". In a Gmail account that had lain dormant ever since the pyramid code days, he suggested that Raj use his hackers to locate communications the previous task force might have missed. He was particularly interested in Reza Mokri's communications. The only Middle Easterner to have committed suicide while in custody, Reza must be a key player, Daniel reasoned. Raj didn't mention that his hackers had already been through all of that.

While Raj was setting up the IT side of things, Lewis was directing the NSA to again interrogate the spies that were already in custody. "You'll have to transport them offshore," he explained. "What you may have to do would be illegal within our borders." His counterpart in the NSA nodded. He knew exactly what Lewis alluded to. Methods that fell outside the Geneva Convention, and that the president couldn't know about in the name of plausible deniability. Such methods were inhuman, but then the future of humanity was at stake. If it took waterboarding or a bamboo manicure to get anything out of them, then that's what would happen.

In a stroke of brilliance, he also spoke to the head of the FBI to assess whether it would be worthwhile to employ their profilers to develop an idea of who or what the leader of the conspiracy might be. As a result, FBI Agent Salome Lane was assigned to go to Boulder and interview key members of the Rossler Foundation leadership and staff, as well as to sit in on the interviews of the spies who were still being held, for the moment, in Denver. For the latter task, she would have to hurry. Plans were to take the spies elsewhere for harsher questioning as soon as possible.

Harper was busy as well. It fell to him to inform the heads of state in the countries where the photos showed devastation. He chose to inform only those whose cities were depicted in the images of destruction. There was no sense in robbing the others of potentially their last few weeks of peaceful ignorance, nor in giving many of them any ammunition to say that he had lost his mind. He called Israel first.

"David, I trust I didn't wake you?" Harper said, when

he was connected. It was disingenuous, for he knew it was nearly midnight in Tel Aviv. Surprisingly, Yedidiyah denied being asleep.

"I fear I don't sleep as well as I used to, my friend. To what do I owe the pleasure of speaking with you?"

"Ah, David, you have such an elegant way of saying 'what the hell do you want at this time of night'," Harper remarked. Yedidiyah chuckled.

"And you, my friend, have such a direct way of translating my eloquence. What the hell do you want at this time of night?" The mirth in his voice softened the words.

"I'm afraid I'm calling to make sure you don't sleep tonight," Harper said, his tone turning somber. "I have something to tell you that you won't believe at first. Rest assured, I've had it examined, and it's all too true."

Yedidiyah matched Harper's tone when he said, "Tell me, my brother, and let me judge for myself."

Harper poured out the story, how Daniel had woken him in the wee hours of this morning, which seemed a lifetime away. What Daniel had told him, and the evidence he presented. How he'd set the investigation in motion and what had been done so far. Yedidiyah listened without interruption.

When Harper wound down, he asked the question that most interested him. "And Tel Aviv? Was it on this list?" His voice was quiet, belying the emotion behind it.

"Yes, David, I'm afraid it was. Also Jerusalem."

"It can't be the Arabs, then. The Dome of the Rock is sacred to them, too."

"All evidence points to Iran at the moment. We haven't determined for sure yet. We could use your help, the Mossad, and any other agencies you think may be able to help."

"Of course. I'll notify the appropriate men as soon as we're done here. But, what would you have them do?"

"We're going to give it everything we have, to stop it at its source," Harper answered. "But, and you must do this, too. Some of our effort has to go into finding the couriers in the countries that will be destroyed, and getting the bombs out, disarming them if we can, or taking them where their destructive power will be less important. My experts tell me there'll be no radiation. I'm thinking we sink them in the ocean, or bury them in a desert. We lose a few pilots, maybe, but we save millions of our citizens."

It was only then that the true enormity of the situation hit Yedidiyah. "Of course, my friend. Detonate them where they'll do the least harm. If you can."

June 20, 2020, D-day minus 38; Washington, D.C.

Harper had spoken individually to only one of the people whose images were arrayed in his monitor, David Yedidiyah. The other two were about to get the shock of their lives. Thank goodness some cool heads were with him to validate that they'd seen and accepted the evidence. Otherwise, this was going to come off like a monumental joke, and one in poor taste at that. Harper remembered hearing about the panic caused by Orson Welles' broadcast of "War of the Worlds" during his grandfather's lifetime. Unless it was handled properly, this news could have the same type of impact, but multiplied many times and worldwide if the wrong people got hold of it. Hence the short list of leaders who would hear it from him today.

At the appointed hour, he spoke into his microphone for

The Sword of Cyrus

the benefit of the people he'd gathered on the videoconference for that purpose.

"Gentlemen, thank you for taking time out of your busy days to gather with us today. What I have to say is of the utmost importance. Rest assured, I would not have presumed to call you together for less than earth-shaking information. You will at first believe that what I'm about to tell you is a hoax, if not a cruel joke on my part. In fact, I wish it were.

"Yesterday, news was brought to me concerning one of the greatest threats in recent times. I took the time to verify it, before setting an investigation in motion that is designed to flush out the perpetrators and prevent what we know without doubt will happen otherwise. At the end of this presentation, I will ask you to put your best assets under the direction of my Director of the CIA to be deployed against our common enemy. It will take all of us, ladies and gentlemen, to avert the coming disaster."

By this time, the Prime Ministers of the UK and of Australia were squirming in their seats. What was this? Who did Harper think he was, to suggest such a monumental favor of trust? They were soon to learn. Harper nodded at Daniel, sitting at his side, to start the slide show.

"What you are looking at, my friends, are pictures of cities in each of your countries, devastated by a new type of nuclear weapon. These are not simulated. Through a technology that is even now being examined and tested by experts at the Rossler Foundation, these pictures of the future were recorded by the historians of the 10th Cycle. Yes, you heard me correctly. The destruction you see here has not yet happened, but most surely will unless we are able to stop them."

Gasps were heard through the speakers as each head of

state caught sight of his or her own capital city, now captioned with its name, in rubble. There was no need to tell them how urgent the task ahead was. The date was also prominently captioned. July 29 of this year. It was already June 20. When the slide show ended, cacophony broke out on the videoconference. The UK and Australia, both pledged immediate and full cooperation.

Gradually, the noise died down as each individual grasped the enormity of the situation. David Yedidiyah was the first to break the ensuing silence.

"My friend, you already know that you have the full cooperation of the Mossad and others of our agencies. What would you have us do in addition?"

"We may need help to track these bastards down and we may need special forces to take them out when we find them. I'm leaving these details to our joint investigative team. I'll have Sam Lewis, the head of the operation, brief you through your own agencies every eight hours, as I've asked him to brief me. More frequently if necessary, and as we get closer to the date. I don't need to tell you that we have very little time to get this done. I'll let you know personally if we need anything else from you. Other than your prayers for our world, that is all."

When the call had ended, Harper slumped with exhaustion. He hadn't slept since four a.m. the previous morning, and was running on pure adrenaline. Daniel knew how he felt.

"Nigel, can you get some rest? Neither one of us is going to make it to the end times if we don't recharge," he joked.

"Don't even say that, buddy," Harper said. "You're right. Do you want to go home?" Harper signaled his Chief of Staff, who nodded and left the room.

"You know it," Daniel said, fervent anticipation in his tone.

"I think we can communicate by phone or videoconference now. Go to Sarah, and try to get some sleep yourself. I'm for a nap," said Harper, knowing that no such thing was in his immediate future.

"Thank you, Nigel. I'll be out of your hair as soon as we can get a flight." Daniel stood to go.

"Never mind that. Your fighter pilot is standing by to take you and your uncle home. How was that, by the way? I've always wanted to catch a ride in one of those things."

Daniel, who was halfway to the door, turned and smiled.

"Out of this world, Nigel. Literally. Mach 3 is a rush."

"Always the joker. Daniel, in all seriousness, I can't imagine what would have happened if your translator hadn't happened on that passage. When this is over, I'm going to ask for extra funding and security for you. My heart won't take many more of these surprises. We need to get that library fully translated sooner rather than later."

"I won't turn it down, Nigel. I completely agree with you." With that, he saluted his friend and went to find Luke.

June 20, 2020, D-day minus 38; Washington, D.C. and Boulder

Daniel found Luke in consultation with Sam Lewis.

"President Harper is sending us home, Luke. The helicopter to take us to Andrews will be here any minute. Are you ready to go?" Daniel's eagerness to get back home was betrayed in his rapid speech, and the nervous jingling of change in his pocket.

"I'm going to hang around here for a couple more days, Daniel," Luke said. "Sam needs my help with some retired agents we're tracking down to reactivate them. You go on ahead." He turned back to the papers he and Sam were perusing.

"Does Sally know?" Daniel asked. He dreaded having to tell her, so he was relieved at the answer.

"She will, before you get there."

Relieved, Daniel acquiesced. "But get on home ASAP. We need you, too." Luke nodded without looking up. Whatever he was doing had him fully engrossed. "Okay, then, bye, Luke." Luke waved, still without looking up. Daniel retrieved his bag from Security and found an escort to take him out to where the helicopter was waiting.

When he got there, he was surprised to find a woman waiting in the chopper for him. No uniform, so she wasn't Air Force. "Hi," he said. "Going my way?"

Agent Lane gave him a heart-stopping smile and replied in kind. "Sinatra fan?"

"Not really," Daniel said. "A bit before my time. Just seemed apropos. I'm Daniel Rossler. I don't believe I've had the pleasure." He extended his hand across his body to the woman, who was seated on his left.

"Salome Lane. FBI," she replied. "I'm a profiler. Sam Lewis requested that I go to Boulder and interview a few people, so we can get a line on whoever's behind this planned attack."

Daniel was impressed. Not only was she easy to look at, which even Sarah would have to agree, but if she could do the magic that her extended team seemed to do easily, they had a shot at finding the leader in time. And she seemed very confident that she could.

Before Daniel could ask more questions, their conversation was interrupted by the roar of the engines as the pilot lifted off. A few minutes later, both ducked and scurried out from under the rotors on the tarmac where the same Lockheed model Daniel had flown here in stood waiting for them. It was another few minutes before they could make each other hear, when they were seated behind the cockpit with headphones on for communication.

"Ever taken a Mach 3 flight before?" Daniel asked. Salome shook her head. "Get ready for the ride of your life. That first acceleration is a bit rough." He felt like an old hand at this, though aside from choppers, this was the first VTOL he'd ever flown in, and definitely the fastest. They would be in Broomfield in under an hour, just a few minutes' ride in the car from Boulder. But, the Mach 3 acceleration would make them think they'd left their stomachs in D.C.

Daniel dropped Salome off at Foundation headquarters, turning her over to Sinclair for a briefing on what they'd found in the 10th Cycle library since the presentation the president had seen. He counted on Sinclair to introduce her to the others who knew about the pictures. The fact of the looming crisis was still not being released to the public. Harper and his counterparts had agreed that there was no purpose for doing so. If they averted it, then there was plenty of time to inform the press. If they didn't, it wouldn't matter anyway. No one in the target areas would be alive to worry that they hadn't put their affairs in order.

Daniel had asked, what about people in outlying areas. Surely there would be some survivors. Had he ever read a post-apocalyptic novel, Sam Lewis had asked in return. It would be like that. People banding together to survive, looters taking food by force. 'Affairs' would have no meaning. Daniel began to consider what he would do if it came down to the final day before the destruction. Would he take Sarah and the baby and flee Boulder? Would they be able to survive as a family, with all the people they loved working together? Or would it be better to just wait for the bombs? Which would be worse, immediate annihilation, or a life of hardship and danger? He and Sarah would have to agree on the answer, just in case.

They'd also have to decide when to tell the family, to give them a chance to decide for themselves. As Daniel thought about it, he realized that the responsibility of sharing news of that sort had no boundaries. Was it right to inform his family and leave out his employees and their families? Where did it end, and how could he live with himself, if his family's survival meant letting another family die without the choice? The questions helped him understand, as nothing had before, how great the burden was that Nigel Harper carried. No wonder he'd aged while in office. The moral dilemmas were unanswerable.

Salome liked Sinclair O'Reilly immediately. In spite of the dire nature of the problem at hand, he had an insouciant Irish personality that tended to make everything a joke. And he was an incorrigible flirt. He had to be more than twice her age, and she spotted a wedding band on his left hand, but he couldn't stop making innuendo about pretty FBI agents. Instead of being creepy, it was funny. They were on their way to meet the nanotech genius when Sinclair warned her.

"The boy you're about to meet has some kind of problem with women. Don't make the mistake of thinking he's not all there, even though he'll stammer through any sort of conversation with you, if he's able to talk at all. He's actually quite brilliant, and if you can put him at ease, he'll be a good resource for you. He can tell you everything there is to know about the use the Iranians can make of the information they stole."

Salome stopped in mid-stride, effectively halting their progress down the hall. "How do you know it's Iranians?" she asked. No one had mentioned that they already had suspects.

"Stands to reason, doesn't it? It was Iran that pushed to have the Middle East included in the 10th Cycle treaty. Most of the spies in my department were Iranian and those who were not Iranian were proposed by them. And the Board member who killed himself was Iranian. Who else could it be?" Sinclair reached for Salome's elbow and turned her once more in the direction of Roy's office.

Who else indeed? Salome gained a new level of respect for Sinclair in that moment. The old man was sharp, that was certain. The buffoon act was some sort of defense mechanism. It would be interesting to study him and figure out his secrets, but her focus was on stopping a world-ending event. Her private interests would have to wait for another time.

Sinclair signaled with his hand that Salome should wait outside Roy's lab for a moment, so that he could prepare 'the boy' as he called him for her entrance. Salome had a few ideas about how to treat a desperately shy man, as her brother had a similar personality. In a moment, Sinclair poked his head out the door and invited her in. Roy James was standing with his arms crossed defensively over his chest, on the other side of a lab table where an array of what looked like tiny models of birds lay in various stages of completion.

"Roy, this is Salome Lane; Salome, Roy James," Sinclair intoned. Then, with a mischievous smile on his face, he stepped back to observe the fun.

Salome stepped forward, *glided*, Sinclair would have said. She held her hand out to Roy, whose eyes had grown round as he beheld the lovely woman in front of him. She was tall, almost as tall as he, and from the top of her shining blonde head to her shoulders, she was stunning. His eyes refused to travel further, lest he embarrass himself. He found himself taking her hand without even noticing.

"Pleased to meet you, Roy," she said. Roy swallowed a lump in his throat and said "M-me, too." Then he grimaced. What a stupid thing to say!

While Roy had been stunned by her beauty, Salome was assessing him as well. Well-built, with broad shoulders, an open, boyish look in a very pleasing face. Brown, slightly wavy hair and she thought brown eyes as well. She wondered if he always wore the safety glasses he hadn't taken off, or if it was an oversight.

Sinclair was right, it wouldn't be easy to find a way to converse with this man, but she'd lay odds it would be well worth the effort.

June 21, 2020, D-Day minus 37; Denver

First thing the next morning, an agent from the Denver field office picked up Salome from her hotel in Boulder and drove her to Denver. It was inconvenient, but the suspects would be transported to a secret location outside the borders of the US later today. After that, Salome would be in Boulder for the duration, learning everything she could from the Rosslers' staff and the 10th Cycle library. She would drive herself back from Denver in an Agency car and keep it as long as she was there.

Little was to be learned at the field office. She started with the youngest translator, a woman who the FBI minders told her was scared to death and might talk. She did, but she knew no more than she'd already said. She was to pass on any 10th Cycle document concerning nanotechnology, and she knew no one else in the network except her handler, whom she'd never met in person. She had already given them all the email addresses she was aware of. Unfortunately for the woman, that would all be verified by harsher questioning. Salome believed her already.

Nothing else of note was to be learned from any of the others, either. Except for the revelations about spy training they'd received. This was new information, skillfully extracted from reluctant detainees by Salome. The men evidenced fear when she came to question them and extended her hand to shake. None of them accepted the gesture. Sinclair would have been very surprised at her predatory smile as she sat down to question them at her leisure. Salome was a beautiful woman, blessed with a figure made for men to drool over, and she knew exactly how to exploit it in questioning these Muslim men. Her button-down blouse was unbuttoned from the top just one button too far, revealing a cleavage that made them sweat.

However, it was all in vain. They didn't know much more than the women did. Salome was beginning to believe that an expert in very sophisticated networks had put this one together. Her discussions with Sam Lewis by phone between interviews led her to believe that such a thing was rare with radical groups from the Middle East. As an FBI agent, rather than a spook, she had to believe him; she had no other experience with them. She did say, more than once, that she didn't understand why the Rossler group had trusted them. She wouldn't have.

According to the agents who'd already had a crack at interrogating these detainees, the most interesting of the bunch was not a translator. She was the program administrator, assistant to Karsten Adler, the program manager. Salome learned from her colleagues that the woman was clearly more intelligent than anyone else in the group, someone who had easily turned Adler. That he was spotless before attested to impressive tradecraft. That she wouldn't talk about any of it, not even her handler or how she communicated, had frustrated them from the beginning. They were looking forward to breaking her down by any means necessary. Salome saved her for last.

Observers would later tell the story of the two beautiful women sparring with words as if it had been an epic battle. Salome, with a degree in psychology and several years' experience interviewing serial killers, knew how to ask a question without seeming to ask. Alica was equally good at turning questions around on her interviewer, frustrating most of them into quitting the game.

Salome was made of sterner and more patient stuff. Each time Alica deflected a question, Salome returned to the subject at hand. She noticed that Alica was most agitated when the subject was her family. After two hours of back and forth, she came out of the interrogation room, saying she wanted to talk with Alica more before the woman was transported.

She also wanted to talk with Karsten Adler. Though he was little more than a victim of Alica's wiles, Salome wanted to question him about how he'd been seduced. It would give her better insight into Alica's background, she thought. She sensed that Alica may know more about the man who'd trained the spies and built the network so expertly that no thread they pulled unraveled it. Find him, she told her colleagues, and he would lead them to the real leader.

While these investigations were going on, Raj was working nearly around the clock to locate any other pictures associated with the coming disaster that he could, and learn the locations they depicted. So far, only a few sites in Israel, the UK and Australia had been identified, along with a good number of sites in America. It was puzzling to Raj how the choices had been made, but he realized that with so much data to go through, it was possible that others would be included for destruction, too, that he just hadn't found yet. He was therefore not surprised when he did locate more. What surprised him was the targets. He could explain the US, Israel, the UK, even Australia. But why Russia would be a target baffled him.

Chapter Twenty-Five

THE NETWORK

June 22, 2020, D-Day minus 36; Boulder

Since Salome Lane was on her own with regard to agency colleagues while she was in Boulder, Daniel suggested to Sarah that they should have her over for dinner. Sarah had responded favorably. She didn't mind cooking for an extra, and besides, Daniel said the agent was a looker. She wanted to see for herself.

To make her feel more comfortable, as if this were a dinner party instead of a way to fish for information from her, Sarah decided to invite JR and Rebecca. Then she wracked her brain for a suitable sixth, to balance the party. The only single man of the right age that came to mind was Roy James. With little expectation that he would accept, she called him at his office and invited him. Surprisingly, he did accept, although Sarah thought she detected some nervousness in his speech. It was all right. She wasn't trying to fix him up with the FBI agent, she just wanted to balance her table.

The Sword of Cyrus

Salome was the last to arrive, apologizing for being late due to the long commute from Denver. Sarah liked her immediately. The woman seemed completely unaware of her looks, and was a scintillating conversationalist. JR and Rebecca peppered her with questions about profiling, while Sarah put the food on the table, aided by Daniel.

"You were right, honey," she said. "She's stunning." A small gleam in her eye was Daniel's only warning that he'd better take care with his answer, even though Sarah knew beyond all doubt that he loved her and was a faithful husband.

"She's all right," he said, suffering a poke in the ribs for his understatement. Man, he couldn't win. If he played it cool, Sarah knew he wasn't being completely honest. If he said Salome was a knockout, that wouldn't go well either. Wisely, he decided not to rise to the bait anymore. For her part, Sarah was just kidding. She didn't mind that Daniel appreciated a beautiful woman. After all, he came home to her every night.

JR was fine, too, with Rebecca right by his side making conversation with Salome as much as anyone else. The topic seemed to be the medical science behind some of the accepted techniques of profiling. Apparently, Salome was published on the subject. The real surprise was Roy. Normally he would be hanging back, shuffling his feet and trying to avoid conversation. Tonight he was hanging on Salome's every word, even though he wasn't contributing to the conversation. She was including him in her smiles for the group, and he didn't even blush. What kind of magic was this?

At dinner, Salome had a chance to ask Daniel the question that had been bothering her all day.

"Daniel, why did you trust these people? Particularly

with such sensitive information as the nanotechnology discoveries?" She took a delicate bite of Sarah's' grilled salmon and flashed her a smile of appreciation.

"That's a good question. One I've been asking myself. It was mixed up in the aftermath of the 9th Cycle flu. Someone that our security expert trusted was referred to us by the president. He felt it was imperative that a gesture of goodwill be extended to the Middle East, as I recall. Next thing I knew, we had three new Board members and a couple of dozen Middle Easterners on staff, mostly in the translation department. They all passed their background checks." He gave her a rueful look, inhaled the aroma of the chardonnay in his glass, and took a sip. With a smile that excused the cliché he was about to use, he said, "It seemed like a good idea at the time!"

"And the assignments?" Salome pressed.

"The idea was to bring the Middle East up to speed, especially in scientific development. We thought if they could start right in on nanotech research, which is cheaper and packs a greater economic punch for the seller, they'd catch up with the West sooner. Also that whole idea of helping Iran and other Middle Eastern countries fit right in with the Rossler Foundation philosophy, which is that the information in the 10th Cycle library must be used for the benefit of everyone, not just a privileged few. In retrospect, it was the worst thing we could have done." Daniel's plate was empty. He placed his silverware across it and sat back with his wineglass in hand.

"Don't beat yourself up too badly. It probably would have taken a trained psychologist to discern that these people were hiding something. And in truth, most of them didn't know the extent of the project. They are remarkably dispersed. They didn't even know that others in their same unit were doing the same things they were. Someone very clever, very experienced and very sophisticated put this together. We need to find that person."

"Agreed," said Daniel. "Will you have time to meet with Luke this week? He should be home from Washington soon."

"I'll make time," she said.

June 23, 2020, D-Day minus 35; Boulder and Denver

As soon as Raj understood what they were up against, he made an executive decision to let his network in on the secret. Whether anyone else realized it or not, he believed that they were the best shot at finding the physical nexus of the conspiracy leadership. It didn't take long for them to bump into other hackers on the trail; government IT specialists who were tasked with the same goal. Naturally, the two groups were aware of each other. A spokesman for Raj's group approached him with a complaint.

"You didn't tell us that the Feds were doing the same thing," he said, a plaintive note in his voice. Raj wasn't sure whether it was his friend's paranoia or a matter of pride that was at stake.

"I wasn't sure, but it wouldn't take a rocket scientist to assume it," Raj said. "What is the problem?"

"They'll trace us back, dude." Now Raj was certain the man was whining.

"Aren't you using your usual methods?" Raj asked, impatient with the conversation.

"Well, yes. But still. They'll get too close to us."

Raj thought for a minute. "Listen, they asked for me.

They know all about me and they haven't made a move to pick me up. Are you sure you are as hidden as you think? What if I ask to have the whole group included in this project? They may even pay you. And we could make it a condition of your cooperation that you have immunity for anything you've ever done before."

Raj was carefully not mentioning hacking or any other keywords that would endanger his friend. Both were well aware that the metadata mining the government indulged in would pick up this conversation between them, and that keywords such as hacking would bring down federal scrutiny.

"I'll poll the others. That may be an incentive. I'll get back to you."

Raj went back to work on his own personal project; locating more pictures, hopefully this time with a later timestamp and intact cities. His theory was that if there were two timelines, as Roy had suggested, the 10th Cyclers may have recorded both of them, assuming that the effort to stop the original outcome would be successful. If he found them, that would have to mean it was, wouldn't it?

The FBI, who had physical custody of the detainees, weren't happy that Salome had pulled rank and demanded that they keep both Alica and Karsten where she could question them further. Anyone who'd been involved in the questioning knew that Alica was the key to the whole mess, though they doubted she was the mastermind. The others were being flown to a classified location, outside the borders of the US, for questioning. They would be subjected first to psychological torture; for example, their questioners would threaten to wrap them in pigskins and kill them in that condition, which would deny them their place in Paradise. Salome was convinced that none of them knew any more than they had already given up, and argued in vain that it was unnecessarily cruel to put them through such things, much less even more painful physical torture. Since she couldn't prevent it, she put it out of her mind and concentrated on discovering what they needed in time to stop the worst of it.

Karsten was her first target on this day. After talking with Daniel, Sarah and a couple of others who'd been instrumental in bringing him in as head of the nanotechnology program, she was curious about the evident ease with which Alica turned him. She instructed the agents who'd been assigned to protect her as she questioned Karsten to stay outside the room. Based on everything she knew about Karsten, he posed no danger to her.

"Karsten, my name is Salome Lane. I'm with the FBI. Do you know why you've been arrested?" Salome laid a plain white lined pad and a pen on the table before taking a seat across from Karsten.

"Yes. I turned over sensitive information to my program administrator, information that I understand has been used to develop dangerous weapons by someone who intends harm to the US and other Western countries." Karsten's affect was robotic; he didn't make eye contact with Salome, nor was his speech inflected. It was as if he'd been hypnotized and was speaking against his will.

Her first task was to break him out of his shock and make him reveal some emotion. It didn't really matter what - if she could make him angry or regretful, sad or even frustrated, it would give her clues to his motivations. That in turn would tell her something about Alica, perhaps enough to break through her refusal to speak.

"Do your children know that you've been unfaithful to their mother and will likely not return home?" Salome couldn't afford to regret her bluntness. Making him react was her immediate goal. Pushing that button didn't do it.

"My wife has already taken them home with her, to her parents in Switzerland. Our divorce has been coming for some time. They will not miss me." Salome heard these words as his resignation to the situation. No doubt he was not close to his children, a fact that was inconvenient, but not necessarily unexpected. Not all men were.

"Do you blame your wife for driving you into the arms of another woman?" Again, a provocative question, and again, it didn't have the intended affect.

"No. She is a good mother, but a loveless wife. I was simply tired of my life with her, but I wasn't looking for an affair." Salome congratulated herself for asking a question that at least got him to open up a bit. So, he was an accessible target when Alica was aimed at him. Salome began to realize that perhaps Alica's talent wasn't so expert after all. Then, surprisingly, Karsten spoke again.

"You wouldn't be able to understand. A woman. You can't know how boring the marriage bed becomes when your wife is more interested in the children than in keeping your love fresh. Before I met Alica, I often wished I'd married a whore, so that at least she would know some tricks to keep me interested."

Salome kept a neutral face. Karsten was both more and less than he seemed on the surface. He had a fantasy life that his bland, unblemished work record wouldn't have revealed. Perhaps he'd just never had the chance to indulge his baser nature. Given that chance, he'd revealed himself to have a weak character. And what he said revealed something about Alica, as well. Salome wondered just how much she enjoyed her work, and whether she'd had assignments like this before.

"So, you weren't angry when Alica threatened to reveal your affair to your wife?" By now, Salome realized she had most of what she needed from Karsten.

"I was upset at first. Then I realized that I didn't care. As long as Alica was willing to grant me sexual favors, I was happy to pay for them with information. The more interesting the information, the more interesting her techniques. I'd have given her anything, as long as that didn't stop."

Salome had just one more question for Karsten, and then her FBI colleagues could have him and welcome. As far as she was concerned, he deserved what was coming to him. "Karsten, did Alica ever reveal to you where the information was going, mention a name, or even a group? Did you know that she was connected to a terrorist group?"

"No," he said. "I never knew what she was doing with the information, but yes, I assumed she was a terrorist. I didn't care, as long as I could hold her and make love to her."

"That's too bad," she said.

If Karsten wondered why Salome said that, he wouldn't have long to wonder, she reflected.

June 24, 2020, D-day minus 35; Denver and Boulder

Salome's next target was Alica. She rather looked forward to matching wits with the woman again. It would be a welcome change from Karsten, who held about as much interest for her as a dead fish. She despised weak men. With a father and an older brother in military service, she knew strong, honorable men. If she had one failing as a profiler, it was that once she determined that her quarry was a coward or morally weak, the quest lost interest for her. Even a bad man could be strong, and those she hunted with a will. The others were too much like the game that was driven in front of the hunter's blind to be shot down with no chase. It wasn't sporting and it wasn't fun.

The Rosslerite men she'd met so far were of the strong variety. Daniel and his brother JR were so much like her brother that she'd felt instantly comfortable with them. Even Roy was a strong man. Shy, yes, but she knew how to handle that. Her younger brother was like him. So focused on the science that interested him that he hadn't learned to relate to other people without discomfort. But, he could be counted on to do the right thing, no matter what. She was certain Roy was the same. Kind of cute, too, she recalled with an inner smile.

After only a few minutes, her musings were interrupted by the arrival of Alica in the interrogation room. Salome had elected to remain there, ensconced in the seat facing the door, when Alica was brought in. That made it her turf, a slight psychological edge that Alica wouldn't notice at first, unless she, too, had training in how people reacted under various types of stress.

Alica looked as if she'd had a bad night, but perhaps it was only that she'd been denied her makeup. Dressed in a plain orange jumpsuit, her hair lank and with no makeup, she hardly looked the part of the Mata Hari that Karsten had described. Nevertheless, she had a defiant air that Salome could almost admire. That took some spirit, certainly. Salome decided to give her the surface respect that men would, if she looked her best. Perhaps it would disarm her enough to cause her to slip and reveal more than she otherwise would.

"Karsten Adler is still very much under your spell," she opened, an admiring note in her voice.

"Adler is a fool. He was too easy," Alica answered. She tossed her head, and gave what would have been a stunning smile, if her lips hadn't been cracked and dry from several days without lipstick.

"You must be used to more challenging prey," Salome offered. It wasn't subtle enough.

"I don't have any idea what you're talking about," answered Alica, looking away.

"Oh, I think you do. Adler described your sexual expertise. You don't get that from a book, you know," Salome said. "I almost envy you. It must be a feeling of power, to be able to wrap men around your little finger like that."

Alica started to speak, thought better of it and examined her fingernails, still bearing traces of the red she usually painted them.

"Alica, we know you aren't the mastermind of this plot. As good as you are at what you do, the mind that put this network together is clearly a masculine one, and expert at his craft. Do you know him? Did he train you himself? Did you practice your wiles on him? How was that? I imagine he's older, and maybe not in the best of shape. Did you enjoy it?"

The rapid-fire questions had Alica blinking, and the last one offended her. "No, of course not! He is..." She stopped, just before blurting out something that might have been useful. She pressed her lips together and stared defiantly at Salome.

"Alica, I don't know how long I can protect you. You're

safe from harsh questioning here, but if you give me nothing, I won't be able to prevent them from taking you where they've taken the others." Salome looked pointedly at Alica's long, elegant fingers. "You may not be so beautiful, after they get through with you."

Alica paled, but refused to speak. Salome pressed a button that summoned the guard and had Alica returned to her cell to think about it for a little while longer. What she'd said was true, she couldn't stall much longer.

While Salome was making only a little progress, Raj's crew was making the most of what little the rest of the detainees had given them unwittingly. Armed with the addresses and passwords for the most hidden of the email accounts, those that hadn't been discovered in the original investigation, they'd managed to track down a few IP addresses and locate the handlers who had passed on the information from the translators. After the people were arrested, their computers were searched as thoroughly as if Raj's network of hackers had been forensic IT specialists.

It was the work of only a day to pinpoint the location of the lab in Iran. They now had their definitive answer; it was definitely Iranian terrorists behind the spy network. And what a network it was! With the hackers assured of their safety, they and the government IT specialists were able to tell the joint investigative task force that it was an extremely sophisticated operation.

Many of the handlers were everyday people with no idea of what they were passing on. In fact, many were women or teens, non-Muslims, innocents being used in a sophisticated plot to destroy the very cities they lived in. As they were questioned, it became clear that they wouldn't know their contacts on either side by sight, didn't know what the information pertained to, and didn't know what they were doing was illegal. Vast numbers of FBI and Homeland Security agents were tied up, interviewing the suspects with no progress in locating the person who'd put the network together. He may as well have been a phantom. The database in Washington was filling up with extensive bios and contact maps of people who were nothing but cogs in the machine.

June 25, D-day minus 35; Washington, D.C.

Lewis was having a drink with Luke at the end of the day, expressing his frustration with the situation.

"Sam, you know what this reminds me of?" Luke said, after Lewis had vented. "This has all the earmarks of an old KGB operation from the Cold War era. They don't make spooks like that anymore." Luke's tone was almost nostalgic, remembering his heyday so many years ago.

"I hear that! And thank goodness. Those guys led us a merry chase. You know, you're right, Luke. I can think of only one person that could have put this together in any kind of hurry. Oleg Zlatovski, remember him? The one that we never got ahead of."

"I do. But, if I'm not mistaken, he died a few years ago."

"Boating accident," Lewis supplied. "Five years ago. His yacht blew up. No survivors."

"I don't suppose you believe in reincarnation," Luke joked, savoring another sip of his Scotch.

"No, but I do believe in faking your own death," Sam said, thinking as he spoke. "You know, it was the only way to retire from the KGB, back then. Do you think?"

"I think we'd better find out. We can't leave any rocks unturned." responded Luke, who'd just realized they could be onto something. He was already planning to speak to that profiler, Salome Lane, the following day.

Raj's search was complete. He had manipulated the data by slicing, dicing and tying it in knots, and then he created a query of the index with the names of every country in Europe and Asia as the 10th Cyclers had known them. It was when he came to the areas now occupied by countries of the old Eastern bloc that he found a cache of pictures he'd previously overlooked. To his surprise, there were over fifty targets in Russia alone. This was so unusual that he took the information to Daniel even before he finished the rest of that query.

Daniel immediately bumped it up to Luke and Director Sam Lewis, who informed Harper. The ball was now in the president's court, but he elected not to inform his Russian counterpart for the moment. If Raj found anything else to be alarmed about, he'd do a videoconference with everyone involved. If not, he would inform the Prime Minister of Russia individually.

Harper had a beef with Russia, stemming from the aggression of Russia that had taken place under Putin's watch, when they tried to annex the Ukraine a few years back. But, he was also a realist. It was six years later now, a different time and a different leader. Besides, sometimes your enemy's enemy is your friend.

Chapter Twenty-Six

NOW IT WAS PERSONAL

June 26, 2020, D-day minus 34; various locations

By eight a.m. Boulder time, Salome knew a name to spring on Alica. If the name Oleg Zlatovski didn't shake her, Alica would be on a plane to join the rest of the Rossler Foundation detainees. The hackers had turned up new IP addresses by tracing the lab communications back, and the people at the locations these addresses revealed were a different group from the spy network handlers. They were completely baffled, most of them, by the agents who pounded on their doors and arrested them. What had they done? Someone in their former country had asked a favor of them, perhaps delivering a shirt or jacket to a college student, perhaps buying some electrical supplies for the local mosque. Why would that be illegal? Some had family that contacted lawyers, who argued the same thing. These people had done nothing illegal. The authorities must release them, or what was this freedom that they'd come to America to obtain?

With the threat of having the crisis revealed prematurely, Lewis directed his teams to release anyone who had done nothing more than deliver something, as soon as they gave up the information of what and where they'd delivered it. Chances were they knew no more than the others that had been questioned to no avail. There was no use tying up the courts with false arrest complaints and having to explain to judges that some science fiction device had predicted the end of the world in about a month and these people were part of it. Harper would have his head if that happened. A few, however, answered questions with a furtive look or body language suggesting they were hiding something. Those were detained without benefit of legal counsel and questioned more closely.

It was slow and tedious work, even as the investigators felt the stress of time passing too quickly. Someone had delivered a shirt to someone else? What did it look like? Why wasn't it sent directly to the recipient? What was special about it? Where did the recipient live? Next task, track down the recipient. Question him, or her. What did you do with the shirt that so-and-so gave you? We know that they gave you a shirt, don't ask what shirt. Where is it? Why are there no buttons on it now? The more questions they asked, the more questions arose. What was all this? There was no reason for these deliveries, and yet they were uncovering hundreds of them. Literal armies of agents, combing the streets of every major city in America and Europe, finding actions that made no sense and people who couldn't explain why they'd been asked to do them. And all the time, the clock was ticking.

Salome arrived in Denver at nine a.m., ready once more for a battle of wits with Alica. She took her place in the interrogation room and again waited for Alica to be delivered to her.

"This is your last chance to help me, Alica," she began.

"Why would I do that?" Alica had made good use of her night of rest. She was as confident and uncooperative as ever. Salome wished she'd questioned her all night, without allowing her to sleep. That was a sword that cut two ways, though, and her main goal was to find the author of the network.

"Because, Oleg Zlatovski is known to eliminate people, even in custody, if he fears they may talk. We can protect you." Salome had no idea if that were a trait of the Russian whose name she'd been given, but the slightest widening of Alica's eyes at the mention of his name told her that they were on the right track.

"Tell me about him, Alica. Did you meet him in person? Is he as fearsome as they say?"

"I have nothing to say." Alica had regained her composure, and was stonewalling again.

Switching tactics, Salome let that subject go. "They tell me you lost your husband and child in a car accident. That must have been very difficult for you," she said. The husband was a minor official in an embassy in Tehran, she understood. "Is that why you took this job? Why didn't you go home to Croatia?"

"There was nothing to return to," Alica muttered, disarmed for the moment by her memories.

"Did you do this type of work before?" Salome pressed. Alica started to answer, but Salome interrupted. "Spying, I mean."

Angered, Alica flushed, and Salome pounced. "Is Alica Cindric your real name? What would we learn about you if we checked Interpol?" As quickly as the flush had begun, it disappeared as Alica paled. Salome sat back, satisfied. There was something there, she was sure of it. She had a reason to keep Alica here for one more day.

Salome didn't waste time returning to Boulder, even though she'd lined up a few interviews there for the afternoon. She called Lewis first, and told him what she'd learned. "Check with Interpol, but also check with the Russians. I have a feeling I know what she's hiding, based on her age." Lewis agreed to get right back to her.

While she waited to hear back from Lewis, Salome called the Rossler Foundation and made her apologies to the people she'd planned to interview that day. There was a very good chance that she wouldn't have to bother them at all, if Oleg Zlatovski could be found.

June 27, 2020, D-day minus 33; Denver

Due to the time differences, it was morning before the FSB got back to Lewis. Salome had spent the night in a ready room that the Denver FBI office kept for agents working on time-sensitive cases like child abductions. The cot was adequate, but probably no more comfortable than what Alica had slept on, Salome figured. When Lewis called, though, all thoughts of her stiff back fled.

Alica was a well-known figure to the FSB, it turned out. Known as the 'Beautiful Widow-Maker', she was high on their wanted list for her role in the Chechnyan Separatist movement. She was linked to some very ugly bombing incidents that killed Russian civilians, even women and children. They'd tracked her to Iran, where they couldn't touch her because of her husband's diplomatic status. Then, during the virus crisis, they lost her. Her husband and child had died of the 9th Cycle flu, not a car accident after all. This, Salome intuited immediately, had given her the motive to involve herself in the spy network when Zlatovski recruited her. She suspected that Alica knew Zlatovski very well, and possibly even knew who was behind the project.

Salome quickly ate a fast-food breakfast that one of the agents brought her and grabbed a cup of almost decent coffee. She knew it would be lukewarm and bitter the next time she wanted a cup, so the fact that it was drinkable now was a welcome surprise. Alica would be enjoying a travel-sized box of cold cereal with skim milk. Salome wasn't sure she wouldn't agree to a trade, if it were offered. Cases like this were ruining her stomach, and would eventually ruin her figure if she ever stopped running in her spare time. *Who am I kidding?* she thought. There were no cases like this.

Setting the interview up as she had twice before, Salome waited for Alica and wished she'd gone back to her nice hotel bed in Boulder the night before. She needed some rest, preferably in a comfortable bed. She gave a moment's thought to the idea that when it was over, she and a lot of other people would be dead. She sat up, alert, as the doorknob turned and the guard ushered Alica in.

"Well, well. Beautiful Widow-Maker, huh? You must have been quite the thing in your time." Alica hadn't even sat down when Salome threw the nickname at her. Alica's only response was to falter a bit as she drew the chair in beneath her. She stared at Salome, saying nothing.

"You seem to have made a few enemies in your time, Alica," Salome continued. "I understand some people in the FSB have a burning desire to get reacquainted with you."

Alica was watching Salome's every gesture, but remained silent.

"I have a small problem, hon," Salome said in as kind a voice as she could muster. "You see, you are of no more use to us. We know who put the network together, now. You apparently don't know anything else to tell us. I suspect that the FSB won't treat you very well, but we have no choice. They're our allies now. We're going to have to turn you over to them."

"No!" Alica said, the first word she'd spoken since coming in. "Don't! They'll kill me."

Salome shrugged. "Sorry. No choice."

"I know more," Alica said. "A lot more. Keep me here, and I'll tell you everything I know."

"It will be in a prison," Salome warned. "You won't like it."

"Make it a high-security prison, where they can't get to me. At least I'll be alive."

Without answering, Salome got up and left the room, with Alica sitting in despair and wondering if she'd missed her chance to save her life.

Salome called Lewis while she was out of the room. "Our little bird is singing," she said. "The threat to turn her over to the Russians did the trick. I want to send her to you, but make her think she's going to be interrogated like the others and then turned over. She'll be begging to tell you everything she knows."

"That works. I'll arrange for transport. Good job, Dr. Lane."

"Call me Salome. Dr. Lane sounds so stuffy."

When the details had been worked out and the connection ended, Lewis turned to Luke. "Do you think she was flirting with me?"

"Not a chance," said Luke. "I'm sure she has better taste."

The Sword of Cyrus

Salome went back to the interrogation room to twist the knife just a bit more before turning Alica over to the CIA to be escorted to Washington and Sam Lewis's interrogators.

"I've done all I can," she told Alica. "I'm afraid it wasn't enough. My boss agreed that you're of no further use. I think they'll take you to where they're holding the others, and after you tell them everything, they'll give you to Aleksandr Chustikov." Chustikov had been the head of the FSB since 2008. He was not a nice man.

"Please, please." Alica repeated her plea, even after Salome had left the room. By the time she landed in Washington, she would be, as Salome had predicted, begging to tell her story.

Salome hoped that the information she had would help the joint task force track down Oleg Zlatovski. There was no doubt he'd put the network together, Alica's reaction to the name virtually assured it. Finding him may very well give them the information they needed to stop this diabolical plot. However, even he wasn't the mastermind. That was someone else, and figuring out who it was had been Salome's directive. She still needed to interview the Rosslers and their staff after all.

Since there was no time to waste, she drank a cup of the cold sludge that remained in the FBI break room coffeepot and set out for Boulder again. It was time to come up with a profile of a man who could conceive of a plot to destroy half the planet and get so far in the execution of it that it may not be possible to stop him.

June 27, 2020, D-day minus 33

The FBI didn't rate a fighter pilot to transport two guards and Alica Cindric to Washington, D.C. for interrogation by the CIA, now that it was believed they had most of what she could give them. They caught a commercial flight in the afternoon after Salome was finished with her, her handcuffs covered loosely by a jacket. She was seated between two brawny FBI agents in a three-seat coach row, an uncomfortable three-and-a-half-hour flight ahead of her. Her request to be released from her handcuffs once they were seated and the exits sealed was denied. She resigned herself to taking her refreshment awkwardly, lifting both hands to sip at the plastic cup of ginger ale. Neither agent seemed willing to talk with her, so she closed her eyes and tried to sleep, concealing her fear of what was going to happen when she could no longer provide new information to the authorities.

If they turned her over to the FSB, she wouldn't survive, she feared. Maybe not even long enough to be consumed by the nanonukes that the Sword of Cyrus would deploy in a month or so. To survive that, she would have to find a way to get to Iran or Turkey. Even if she were to escape custody and make her way out of a target city, the chaos in the countryside would be difficult to manage after the cities were destroyed. Alica drifted to sleep while planning how to use her feminine wiles to escape her FSB captors, for she was certain that it would be the only way. Once she escaped, she'd make her way to the Middle East by whatever means required, even if that meant sleeping with lorry drivers or taking someone's car at gunpoint. Whatever it took, she would survive.

Shortly after five and a poor excuse for a meal that the FBI agents provided her, Alica was turned over to Sam

Lewis at JOCC headquarters. Alica examined him to read his vulnerability, and found little to go on. His face revealed no emotion as he led her to a chair and handcuffed her to the arm of it.

"Luke, would you come in, please?" Lewis said into an intercom speaker embedded by a button on the wall that probably would summon help if Alica were to attempt escape. Nevertheless, she made a note of it. Perhaps it would come in handy. This detour from being given to the FSB afforded another opportunity to attempt escape. While Alica was looking around the room, another man came in, presumably the Luke that Director Lewis had addressed.

"Look familiar?" Lewis asked the man.

"Yeah," Luke answered. "She worked for the Foundation; I've seen her around the building. Never met her in person before, though. Is this the famous widow-maker?" He put his hands behind him and leaned back against the wall, intending to intimidate Alica by his physical presence, which was impressive, she had to admit. Though his graying hair revealed him to be some years her senior, he was physically fit and still retained the looks that surely turned heads in his youth. Alica turned the full force of her sultry gaze on him and gave a slow smile.

"I can help you. I know what the Iranians are planning," she said. "And I know who the leader is, at least one of his aliases." She glanced at the other man, CIA Director Lewis and smiled at him as well. "I'll tell you if you guarantee my safety from the FSB."

Luke and Lewis traded glances. Could the woman be playing them? They had no compunction about lying to her, but before they guaranteed that she wouldn't be turned over to Russia, they preferred to hear what she had to tell them. If it was good enough, they might even be able to keep her out of the hands of the FSB. But her willingness to talk had to be tested first.

"I'll do what I can," said Lewis. "But I'm going to need something to guarantee your good faith." Negotiations would probably continue for some hours, with Alica demanding something in writing with a powerful signature on it, and Lewis working to get some idea of what the woman really had. "Tell us who trained you, and I'll take your case to my boss."

"And who is your boss?" Alica demanded.

"The President of the United States," he said. "Nigel Harper is a man of his word. Even you must know that."

"I've heard that," she said. "The man who trained me is a dead man. How, you ask? Because he is not really dead, but you believe him to be." Lewis leaned forward. He knew who she meant. Would she give a name, or only these silly riddles?

"His name," he said, schooling his voice to remain neutral.

"Oleg Zlatovski," she replied. The only expression of emotion in the room was Luke's slightly raised eyebrows. Alica wasn't looking at him, so he had the luxury of this silent communication with his old friend. Lewis sat back.

"Can you validate this?" he asked. "Are you able to give us something to prove you're correct?" He turned slightly away from Alica to conceal the twitching of his eye, a response to the distress of confirming that the wily old spy was still alive after all.

"I think so. I'll require a computer," she said. Lewis sent for an IT specialist to bring in a laptop and stay to be certain that the woman pulled no tricks of subtle communication to her network.

With all three men looking on, Alica accessed a private

website with nothing but a number to identify it. Using a password that she provided, the IT specialist signed in for her after warning Lewis that just accessing it could identify their whereabouts to the website administrators, and signing in would identify who it was, of course. Lewis considered the implications and decided that seeing what Alica had to show them was more important than worrying about a rescue effort, especially since they were deep within the Pentagon basement structure and any attack would be easily defended. The specialist made one more attempt, saying that wasn't the danger. The danger in alerting the administrator would be the sudden disappearance of the site, locking them out of any hope of recovering the information it held.

"We'd better look quickly, then," Luke answered. "It's already done."

They turned the keyboard back over to Alica, who made an adjustment to the keyboard software and then typed in a greeting, in Russian. "Wait!" shouted Lewis, but Luke put his hand on the Director's arm.

"It's okay, I can read it. It just says hello."

"Switch to English," Lewis directed. As he spoke, the screen filled with Cyrillic characters. Luke read them with ease, a result of his years of assignments that required him to learn the language.

"What does it say?" Lewis asked.

"Do you want me to read it?" Alica asked, directing her gaze to Luke.

"I'll read it," he answered. "It says '*Why are you logging in from Washington, D.C.? What has happened? Communications compromised.*' We'd better answer quickly."

Alica moved her hands quickly to the keyboard and typed. Luke read as the characters appeared. '*Operation in

Boulder discovered. Escaped, came here to find transport home. My darling, let me come to you.'"

Lewis nodded. For now, she was cooperating, but the tension was awful. At any moment, she could clue the person with whom she was communicating that it was a trap. Sweat began to roll down from his hairline. He was getting too old for this.

'*Alica?*' appeared on the screen.

'*Yes, of course. Oleg?*' she typed.

'*Affirmative. Can you get to Canada? I can bring you home from there,*' was the answer.

'*You'll come for me in person?*'

'*Yes. Meet me at the place where we danced, in Montreal.*'

"He knows something is wrong," she said to the others. "We never danced in Montreal."

"Answer that," Sam directed her.

'*My darling, you jest. We never danced in Montreal,*' she typed.

'*Thank you. I'm sorry, I had to verify it was you. Do you have a clean passport?*'

'*No, everything lost in Boulder. Running out of money.*'

'*Stay there. Contact me tomorrow at this time. I'll have instructions.*'

The screen went blank as Zlatovski disconnected Alica's access. Everyone in the room sat back, exhausted with the tension.

"Do you think it's gone?" Lewis asked the IT specialist.

"It is not gone," Alica answered. "He would not have told me to contact him if he intended to take the site down. It is my only way to contact him now. Do you believe me now? Will you take my request to your president?"

"One more item I need first," Lewis said. Alica turned huge, liquid brown eyes on him and accused him with them of bad faith. "Do you know who Zlatovski reports to?"

"I am not certain of his name, but I think I can find a picture of him on the internet," Alica answered. She pulled the laptop back to a comfortable position, and typed in a query, hitting the enter key before Luke had a chance to translate it. A series of pictures appeared on the screen, and she clicked on the first one. It was a Wikipedia article on the newly-created Directorate of Reconstruction in Iran, with a picture of the director. Luke and Sam stared at her pointing finger in dismay. The leader of the plot to destroy the world was none other than their old employee and crony, Arsalan!

"It calls him Ahmad Ahmadi here," Alica was saying, "but Oleg calls him Dalir Jahandar."

Alica could not have made a bigger impact if she'd exploded one of the nanonukes in the room.

"*He's Dalir Jahandar?*" Lewis yelled. Luke knew why he was so agitated, but neither the IT specialist nor Alica understood his agitation. Luke dismissed the IT guy, who went without protest despite the fact that Luke was a civilian. Luke checked Alica's handcuffs, and then dragged the speechless Lewis out of the room. Behind the soundproof door, he whispered urgently to Sam.

"We're in deep shit if it gets out that we hired the most elusive al Qaeda spy in history as a CIA operative." He gave Lewis a little shake, to snap him out of his stunned state.

"We're dead men, Luke," he answered. "Harper will personally gut us."

"Maybe not. This could give us an edge, as long as no one else knows it. I think you'd better get the woman her protection deal, and then we'll figure out how to deal with this." Luke was already making his excuses in his mind to Sally. He wouldn't be home for a while now. Maybe never, if they couldn't stop this thing. But there was no question that Sam Lewis needed him. After all, he was the recruiter and handler for Arsalan, aka the infamous Dalir Jahandar, number one on the CIA's most wanted list. No one had ever seen a picture of him, though his name was easy to hear when interrogations of Islamic terrorists were conducted. There wasn't an adequate swear word in any language to express his rage at the trick Jahandar had played on him, on them, on the USA on the world. Now it was personal.

Chapter Twenty-Seven

THE TIME PUZZLE

June 27, 2020, D-day minus 33; Boulder

Ever since the passage containing the plans for the remote time viewer, as Roy was calling it, had been translated, Roy had been busy attempting to build one. The stumbling block was that several components had to be fabricated, and the plans for those were elusive. Roy had lost the undivided attention of Raj, whose expertise was required to search the database for the words and phrases that held a clue. Raj was busy looking for more pictures, hopefully some that would show the world coming through the looming threat unscathed after all. Only that would prove that the fate depicted in the pictures they had so far could be averted. It was frustrating, because Roy felt that they could get direct proof, if only he could build a viewer for themselves.

Stymied in that effort, Roy sought and received permission to gather the best minds in quantum physics and a few related subjects and reveal the discovery to them. He was directed to conceal if he could what the discovery had shown them about upcoming events. However, if they could explain or even postulate a viable theory about how to go around the cataclysm rather than through it, it would be Plan B, with Plan A being stopping the attack altogether.

It had taken only a couple of days to arrange, since the respective governments pressured their scientists to drop everything and heed the call to assemble in Boulder. Not everyone who did so was pleased to be there.

Salome asked to be included, not because she expected to understand everything that was discussed, but because observing would give her insight into Roy's mind. Daniel said quite frankly that he thought all this interviewing was a funny way to go about profiling the key players, the instigator, and the author of the spy network. All Salome could tell him was that this was her process, and she had a pretty good track record. Daniel's call to Sam Lewis's office, where he was unable to reach either Lewis or Uncle Luke, revealed that the record was more than pretty good; it was stellar. One hundred percent of Salome's cases were solved.

On the day after she cracked Alica's calm exterior, Salome slipped into the conference room at the Rossler Foundation with the intention of staying low profile. She found a seat in a rear corner, and kept her head down as a dozen or so men ranging from their mid-twenties to mid-forties assembled, a few at a time. She observed their youth with a little surprise, having assumed that they would all resemble the pictures she'd seen of Albert Einstein, with a shock of unruly white hair and a crazed look in their eyes. So much for assumption, she admonished herself. She knew better, after all.

When the last scientist had taken a seat, Roy took the podium to explain why he'd requested their presence. Salome remembered her reaction to the news that the 10th

Cyclers had some kind of time travel, and she'd observed the reactions of her colleagues at the briefing. Compared to the pandemonium that had set loose, the reactions today were minuscule. It seemed these men and women were already aware of the concept, or at least could grasp the principles as Roy explained them. Salome paid close attention to Roy as the presentation progressed.

True to her observations in the previous few days, Roy was in his element when discussing all things science, and his social anxiety was at a minimum even when women were in the audience. As long as he could view females as scientists and colleagues rather than as women, he was fine. No stutter, no awkwardness at all. It gave her a way to approach him and get intelligible conversation out of him that she hadn't been sure would work, until she saw him interact with the women in his audience. Strict professionalism, ask precise questions, even when they were of necessity open-ended. She'd have to dig out her glasses, to help him view her as a fellow scientist, she noted, amused that every face in the room sported a pair.

The conversation was fascinating, if a little unsettling. The first discussions centered on what the 10th Cyclers had seen. Roy was unable to hedge enough to satisfy them, so the full story had come out, with varying expressions of disbelief, dismay and eventually acceptance. After their initial reactions, the scientists put their natural fear aside, and addressed the practical questions.

Assuming that you could indeed see an event in the future, what did that mean about the nature of time? Were the 10th Cyclers only observers, or would they have been able to change the future, or for that matter, the past? If so, had they been complicit in this outcome? If not, was there any benefit in knowing what was going to happen? If you know what's going to happen, and do something in reaction to that knowledge, will it change things enough to make that thing not happen?

The consensus was that physical time travel into the past could not exist, or if it did, we can't know it for certain. If someone were to travel back in time, actions taken in the past would affect the future to such a degree that we wouldn't know our past had been changed. Because of the quantum nature of time, the physicists argued, there wouldn't be even a ripple in the time-space continuum; those who were affected would simply be traveling along a string of events that would adjust to the change seamlessly. Salome noted that it was difficult to even express these ideas without using words that had no meaning if time were indeed what the physicists claimed it was. Or is. She was beginning to get a headache from trying to grasp the concepts.

What she could understand with no difficulty was that only major events would likely to be viewable. Minor events would be under such a constant state of flux that the ability to capture a photo of an instant would be impossible. The photos that the 10th Cyclers left, in fact, had to have been the result of a viewer moving past the event in the time continuum, and then looking *back* on it as if it had been in the past, rather than far in the viewer's future. The only way to affect such a large event would be for some large changes in the immediate future to be accomplished. Some physicists insisted that there were actually new timelines, for lack of a better word, created at every major event. In some world, that nuclear destruction was going to take place no matter what we might do to stop it. But the consciousness that we experience as a continuing existence will not have that event in our timeline.

Salome couldn't bear to think of her doppelganger, alive and aware in another world, experiencing the effect of a nuclear weapon, much less the same fate befalling her loved ones. She put it firmly out of her mind. This was something she could not solve. Her task was to save *this* reality.

She was still trying to follow the discussion when Raj burst in, printouts in hand, shouting "Eureka!" It was so incongruous that she almost laughed. Roy, however strode to meet him and take the photos. He turned them toward the audience with a joyous expression. "Here's the proof!" he cried. "Raj has found time stamped pictures that show the cities undamaged. Perhaps we are already affecting the future!"

Roy's mini-conference was interrupted long enough for Raj to fetch Daniel, who sat in on the rest of it with scientists who were overjoyed to see their theories proven in such a way. When it was done, Daniel made haste to inform Luke and Lewis, who would brief the president. It was the first positive thing they'd found since the pictures were discovered. They just needed to find a way to make it happen.

Chapter Twenty-Eight

WELCOME TO MOTHER RUSSIA

June 28, 2020, D-day minus 32

Alica had been stashed in a safe house for the night, while Lewis reported his progress to Harper and subsequently to the other heads of state through his security agency liaisons. In the wake of the news that the other pictures had been found, it was more urgent than ever to track down the planners of the catastrophe. Harper's understanding of the situation was in the form of an analogy. He and his country, along with several others, were on a train hurtling toward a destroyed bridge over a deep ravine. The only way to avoid falling into it was to switch tracks, early enough that the bridge was no longer on their route.

Harper had drawn up a limited pardon for Alica, covering only the activity she had perpetrated in the US. He didn't have the authority, he explained, to pardon her for her previous crimes. If the FSB, or anyone else who wanted her, were able to find her, she'd be on her own with them. Bitterly, she realized she'd been outfoxed. It now remained to stay valuable enough for the US to give her its best effort at protection.

A thought occurred to her and she asked Luke if they knew what Zlatovski looked like now. Luke requested that pictures from his file be showed to her, and she laughed. "He looks nothing like this now. You could walk down the street and pass him with this picture in your hands, comparing everyone you see. You would not recognize him."

To check her veracity, the same pictures were passed around among the other Rossler Foundation detainees, at an undisclosed location outside of the US. No one recognized him, and no one admitted to knowing his name. When that was reported back to Lewis, he extended a little more trust to Alica. So far, she was shooting straight with him, and as long as that continued, he'd do his best to protect her. It was going to get dicey, though, because he needed to communicate with Chustikov regarding Zlatovski.

Lewis called Luke in to witness his next communication with Alica. Despite the fact that she'd earned a limited amount of trust, the woman was dangerous.

"Alica, we've verified that you're telling the truth about Oleg Zlatovski. None of the people who worked for your organization, did you call it the Sword of Cyrus? None of them recognized the picture or the name. We'd like your cooperation in getting an updated image. Are you familiar with the work of police artists?"

Alica nodded slowly. "Yes. We, the organizations I have been associated with, have not such advanced methods as yours, but I know what you mean. I can do this. You must know that they did not recognize the name because it isn't the name he uses now. Only I know his true identity."

Sam glanced at Luke to find a skeptical look on his face. Luke spoke up.

"How do you know that?"

"What, his true identity? Or that only I know it?" Alica had a smug expression, and Lewis feared the revelation that was surely coming next.

"How do you know any of it? In fact, how do you know the name of the organization, and who's in charge? None of the others know. What's so special about you?" Lewis's voice had taken on an edge, and now she was staring at him with an expression he was afraid to read.

"Do you know what I am known for? What my specialty is?" Her expression turned sultry and inviting. Lewis began to thank his lucky stars that Luke was in the room.

"Seduction?" Lewis ventured.

"Precisely," she said, her voice now a low purr that even Luke found distracting. "I would never put myself in the hands of a man I couldn't control. While Oleg trained me, I made certain that no matter what happened, he would put my safety even above his. You'll see. I will hand him to you without any hint that he is walking into a trap. As soon as I contact him, we'll know where he is going to pick me up. You'll be waiting for him."

They should have named her the Black Widow, instead of Beautiful Widow-Maker, Luke thought. She was certainly poisonous enough. What sort of control did she think she could exert over Sam Lewis?

"What name is he using now?" Lewis asked.

"Andreas Dimitriou," Alica answered. "He was living in Greece when Jahandar's organization contacted him. Let us proceed with the police sketch. I have an appointment to keep with my dear Oleg, you know."

At the appointed time, Alica attempted to log into the site where she was to contact Oleg and lure him into a trap. Her first attempt brought a screen full of suggestions for the correct site name. Impatiently, she tried again. This time a 404 Site Not Found error filled the screen. Luke listened in astonishment as she swore colorfully, first in Russian, then presumably Croatian and finally English. The last made him blush at the foul nature of her name-calling. Oleg had smelled the trap.

Lewis left Alica under guard with an FBI sketch artist and Luke to watch her interaction with the artist.

Harper pushed back his next appointment to accommodate Sam Lewis, who had urgent business with him.

"What can I do for you, Sam?"

"Mr. President, we've learned the name of the man who put together the spy network for this Sword of Cyrus group. According to our informant, he's an ex-KGB double agent thought to have been dead for the past five years or so. We need the help of Aleksandr Chustikov if we're going to track him down in time."

Harper had no need to ask what Lewis meant by 'in time'. Everything about this crisis meant they should have been on top of it yesterday. "Have you contacted him?"

"No, sir. I wasn't briefed on whether you've informed the Russians of the threat. Besides, it would be better if I spoke to him in person."

"Okay, Sam. Give me a few hours to speak to the Prime Minister, and then you can set it up. Take any resources you require."

"Thank you, sir."

"Sam, you're volunteering to enter the lion's den. I don't need to tell you that what you're doing by going there in person is dangerous. Thank *you*." With a clap on his back, Harper dismissed Sam and immediately made the preliminary arrangements to speak to Prime Minister Shvernik.

Once more, Harper was faced with breaking unbelievable and devastating news to a skeptical hearer. This time, he did it alone, since there was no love lost between Shvernik and the other great men who were privy to the classified information. It was not an easy nor a friendly conversation. In the end, Shvernik conceded to meet with Sam Lewis as Harper's envoy, with Harper apologizing profusely that urgent domestic affairs dictated he must not leave the country at this time. Only when he saw the pictures for himself would he believe this nonsense.

Lewis waited for Harper's go-ahead and then made a call to his counterpart in Russia, FSB chief Aleksandr Chustikov. His objective was to determine whether the FSB knew of Zlatovski's subterfuge five years ago.

"Zdravstvujtye, my friend," Chustikov answered, when the appropriate assistants had synched up the calls and the two were on the line with each other at last.

"Hello to you as well, Aleksandr Tomasovich. I have news that may distress you, a lost sheep that we must find very soon."

"Sam, don't try to match a Russian for eloquence. What do you want?" The mirth in Chustikov's statement took the sting out, and Sam answered in kind.

"What do you know about an Oleg Zlatovski?" he asked.

For a moment, Chustikov considered denying any knowledge. Knowing Sam Lewis, though, that would not be believed. "Dead," he answered. "Boating accident, five years ago. We were sorry to lose him."

"I'm sure you were," Sam said. "We believe he was responsible for many of the networks that gave us such trouble when we were tracking the Orion Society. Care to tell me whether that was work he did on the side, or under official sanction?" As he spoke, Sam stared out his office window, seeing nothing but the faces of operatives he'd known, dead at the hands of the OS.

"You know I cannot comment, my friend. Why do you bring up this man?" Chustikov was tired of the game already. Sam remembered that the time difference meant the man was ready to retire for the night. Too bad, this took precedence over sleep. He hadn't slept more than a few hours at a time in several days.

"Would you be surprised to know that he has surfaced, this time at the head of a sophisticated network of Middle Easterners?"

A long silence on the other end of the line meant one of two things. Either the Russians were involved, as unlikely as it seemed, or it would indeed surprise Chustikov.

"Where did you come by this information?" came the cautious response at last.

"That's classified. I can tell you this - the network we believe he put together has been instrumental in getting some dangerous information to some very nasty players. I'd like to show you what we've got so far. Can I count on a face-to-face with you if I come to Moscow?"

"When?" Chustikov became more alert. It was almost unheard of for an active security head to visit another in a country that was not always friendly. In the past, a man in Lewis's position setting foot on Russian soil would find himself held in a Siberian prison camp indefinitely for spying.

"Immediately. There is no time to lose."

Lewis was serious, then, Chustikov realized. "I will look forward to your visit."

"Get some sleep, Aleksandr. It will be the last you have for some time to come." Those words sent shivers down Chustikov's spine.

June 29, 2020, D-day minus 31; Moscow

Sam Lewis considered taking Luke with him to Moscow, but thought better of it. Luke had been operating as if he were still CIA ever since this case began, but in fact he was still a civilian. He happened also to be still wanted by the FSB for his activities years before when he was active CIA. Diplomatic courtesy may not be extended to him, and Luke knew it. Sam would have to do without his extensive knowledge of the man he was going to see.

Twelve hours after he commandeered one of Air Force One's backups, Sam stood face-to-face with Aleksandr Chustikov, a man he'd recognize anywhere from his pictures. Far from the stereotype of a beefy, vodka-drinking middle-aged Russian man with grizzled hair and a beard, Chustikov was trim, almost ascetic-looking. His receding hairline and piercing blue eyes gave him the look of a college professor of religious studies perhaps, until his grin softened it into a mass of crow's feet at the corners of his eyes, and deep smile lines framing his thin lips and a glimpse of teeth. Lewis liked him immediately, despite years of professional discord. He held out his hand to shake the hand of his old enemy.

"Aleksandr," he said, leaving off the patronymic after the man's taunt on the phone.

"Sam, welcome to Mother Russia," Chustikov said, displaying again the grin that humanized his otherwise grim face. Lewis's eyes were drawn in spite of himself to a large mole on Chustikov's left cheek. Why wouldn't he have had that removed? Recalling his urgent errand, Lewis forced himself to look Chustikov in the eyes.

"I have urgent news, and a favor to ask," he said. Chustikov raised one eyebrow at the word favor, nodded, and gestured for Sam to enter his car.

"I have made arrangements to discuss it in the office of Prime Minister Shvernik's offices," he said. "You did not inform me that you also had official business with the Prime Minister."

"I apologize, Aleksandr. I learned of it only after I spoke with you."

Inclining his head in acceptance of the apology, Chustikov said, "Security, I assume, is of importance?"

"The utmost," Lewis replied. On the way, they discussed his unmarried state and the fact that he had no children, in contrast to Chustikov, who had been happily married for thirty years and had two children.

"We felt no need for more, after a son and then a daughter," Chustikov explained.

Polite questions about what age his children were and what they studied occupied the rest of the short journey to Shvernik's office. As soon as they entered his doors, Chustikov's banter stopped.

"All right, Director Lewis. To what do we owe this visit?"

Sam noticed he left out the usual 'the pleasure of' in the phrase, and that Chustikov had assumed the role of an interrogator, while the Prime Minister, after a few words of introduction, remained silent. Sam handed Shvernik an envelope holding the pictures of the Russian targets as he answered Chustikov.

"You know of the Rossler Foundation, of course," Sam began. At Chustikov's nod, he continued. "Nine days ago, Foundation staff found disturbing references to future pictures. They followed the references and were able to decode data in the 10th Cycle library that looked like pictures when they were processed by computers. Those pictures showed most of the major cities in the Western Hemisphere in ruins. They were date stamped July 29th of this year." Lewis paused as he took in the startled reaction Chustikov displayed at the mention of the date. "Do you have a question?"

"I take it that you have verified the authenticity of these pictures? How long have you known that our cities were targeted?" Surprisingly, Chustikov had taken in the information and accepted it, pending Sam's assurance that it was real. He glanced at Shvernik, who appeared engrossed in the contents of the envelope Sam had handed him.

"Verified and re-verified. It happens that the Rosslers recently discovered spies among them, plants from the Middle East, mainly Iran. The pictures were discovered in a separate incident at about the same time. It has taken up until just yesterday, when President Harper phoned Prime Minister Shvernik about them, to search out all such pictures. We informed you as soon as we knew," Sam said. *Or, as soon as we deemed it necessary,* he added mentally. "We assume that these pictures confirm a threat from that quarter. Just yesterday, we also discovered the name of the man who put together the network, and we'd like your help in tracking him down. He's one of yours."

"Oleg Zlatovski," Chustikov supplied. There could have been no other reason for Lewis to bring up the name yesterday, he realized. "I told you what we know of him. He is dead."

"He isn't dead," Lewis said, handing Chustikov a copy of the sketch artist's work. "He goes by Andreas Dimitriou, now, and he was last seen in Bulgaria, by members of the network that he personally trained. We have a reliable eyewitness who knows him by both names and who helped develop this drawing. I understand he has changed his appearance dramatically."

Chustikov gazed at the picture of a youthful-looking Greek man, blonde, green-eyed and physically fit. "Indeed. I knew Zlatovski well. If this is he, I'd like to know who his plastic surgeon was. I wouldn't mind sending my wife to him," he joked."

"We need to find him urgently," Lewis said again. "He put the network together that stole the technology we believe to be responsible for the state of the cities in those pictures." He shuffled through his own stack of them, looking for one in particular.

"Listen Lewis, we have managed to stay out of your wars with the Arabs for many years," Chustikov said, beginning to chuckle. "We don't want to become part of them now. I can't help you." Shvernik looked up at that, but remained silent. Chustikov hadn't seen the pictures yet. He'd come around.

Lewis glanced up from the picture he'd found. "No? You've had your disputes with the region yourself, as I recall. Not to mention your country's persecution of Muslims for centuries. I think you'd better take a look at this picture, and this," he said. Chustikov took the proffered prints and looked more closely, turning pale as he examined them. Meanwhile, Shvernik, who had yet to say a word, pulled a bottle of Kors vodka and three glasses out of his top drawer. The first picture was of the famous onion-domes of St. Basil's Cathedral, recognizable in spite of the black-and-white image that failed to display the colorful and fanciful architecture at its finest. It didn't matter, however. The domes and the spire in the center of them were horrifically damaged, as was the entire surrounding area of the Kremlin and Red Square.

If this hadn't been enough to convince him, he turned to the next picture, showing an equally fabulous cityscape of St. Petersburg, equally in ruins.

"You are certain these photos aren't a hoax," he said to Lewis, in a surprisingly firm voice. Shvernik poured the three glasses to the brim and pushed one glass to Lewis across the table without asking if he wanted it. Chustikov picked up another without invitation.

Lewis answered, "Absolutely certain. The weapons that will create this destruction are already in the hands of an Iranian militant group, known as the Sword of Cyrus and we suspect the bombs are actually already in or at the very least on their way to the target countries including of course your Mother Russia. The technology comes from the 10th Cycle, and knowledge of it was stolen over the past several months by a dozen or so translators at the Rossler Foundation. If you have anyone who can help track down Zlatovski, we believe he may be able to locate the leadership of the Sword of Cyrus for us."

Lewis's cards were all on the table. If Chustikov refused, he had no other recourse but to attempt to locate Zlatovski on his own. However, he suspected that Chustikov was playing *his* cards close to his vest. Lewis found it almost impossible to believe that the FSB had lost one of its own under suspicious circumstances and failed to follow up. Maybe they were worried that if they chased him he would run to the CIA for protection and tell them a few stories in exchange, so they allowed him his "retirement." He hoped with all his heart that there was a lead, somewhere, that could be exploited quickly.

Chustikov spent several more seconds tossing back the vodka and pouring another stiff one, while gazing from one picture to the other. "There is someone. I will assign her to your operation, but every other asset we have needs to be tracking down this network in our country. Do you have someone to work with her?"

Lewis didn't understand the dynamic between the two Russians. It was almost as if Chustikov were running the show, and Shvernik merely a pawn. "I'll find someone. I'd like to take her back to D.C. with me, show her our operation and let her interview our witness for herself. Can she be ready to go by tomorrow?"

"She'll be ready within two hours and will meet you at the airport. We must waste no time, my friend." Chustikov said, downing the last bit of vodka.

"Director Lewis, hello. My name is Tamara." Her cool hand felt delicate in his, but her grip was firm. When he stood to greet her, Sam was surprised to see that she was almost as tall as he, maybe 5'10" or so. She had the slim body of an athlete, too, he noticed. Realizing he still had her hand captured in his, he hurriedly released it.

"Call me Sam," he said. "We don't have time for titles in this project. Did Aleksandr tell you about your assignment?"

"Briefly," she answered. "He told me to make you aware of why he has assigned me. I am acquainted with Oleg Zlatovski. He may be able to change his appearance, but I will know his voice when we find him." The cool assurance in her manner was enough to give Sam confidence in her. He wondered why Chustikov hadn't mentioned the connection himself, but decided it didn't matter.

"Excellent. Did he mention why we want him?"

"I understand I'll be accompanying you to your capital," she responded. "Perhaps you can brief me more thoroughly on the way."

June 30, D-day minus 30; Washington, D.C.

On the long flight back to D.C., Lewis filled in Tamara on what they knew, what they surmised and what they assumed at his headquarters, before finally falling into a fitful sleep a few hours before their arrival. Tamara, like her boss, was at least pretending to be stoic about it, insisting that until they could find Zlatovski and verify it the assumptions were not to be believed. Nevertheless, she told Lewis that she was fully committed to finding Zlatovski. For the first time, he heard the real reason that the FSB would take this so seriously despite being skeptical about the pictures. Zlatovski had constructed all of their networks, at home and abroad, for twenty years before he disappeared. Recognized as a genius in his field immediately after matriculation at Moscow State University, he'd been groomed for the FSB since the KGB days. He knew every node on every spy network that Russia operated. If he was indeed alive, they wanted to find him before someone else did.

Tamara was frank with Lewis about her brief. She was to work with him and his outfit until they located Zlatovski, stand by as they extracted the information from him that they needed to stop this presumed attack, and then take custody of him without further ado and transport him to Russia. This she would do with or without Lewis's consent.

Sam was entranced by the woman's confidence even though he had her pegged as young, probably no older than her mid-twenties. He had no doubt she intended to do exactly as she'd been instructed, and that she may indeed be capable of taking a prisoner from him without his consent. Still, such a dedicated focus was valuable. He'd go along with it for now.

The discussion gave him some insight into the type of agent he'd need to partner with her, though, and he had the man in mind. Jack Johnson, an eight-year veteran CIA agent was big, tough, smart and had the looks to match the woman's, which would serve them well if they had to pose as a couple. Lewis had seen him at JOCC headquarters only yesterday, or was it the day before? He was losing track of time, and that wasn't a good thing. He needed to know just how much time was left on any given day.

Among other things they needed to know as soon as humanly possible was the exact location of the lab that had received the stolen technology. IP addresses that they had sniffed out put it somewhere in central Iran, but they'd yet to pinpoint it. How much of the nanonuclear fuel had they manufactured, and was it in place in the target countries already? And where could they lay hands on Dalir Jahandar? Presumably he was in Tehran, carrying out his duties, but it would be very tricky to snatch him there. A better plan was to find him at an obscure place, maybe even the lab, and pick him up. Lewis knew enough history to understand that it wouldn't be that simple. After all, it had taken more than ten years to get Osama bin Laden.

As soon as Tamara had been given a chance to freshen up, Lewis accompanied her into the JOCC, where she immediately got the impression of a beehive. One that had been attacked by a cricket bat. On one wall was an enormous world map, with pins of different colors stuck in many cities of the US, and strings of different colors stretched across the map to other pins, all red, in Iran and a few other Middle Eastern countries. Lewis noticed her looking at it and explained that they were painstakingly searching out operatives in the US, and some of them had been found to have communications with locations in the Middle East recorded in their computer history. All innocent communications, those to family that had been thoroughly checked for potential coded messages, were eliminated from the map to avoid the clutter. Part of her assignment would be to get information from Zlatovski to help them identify what sort of assets were located where the red pins indicated.

"How are you doing that?" she asked.

"As soon as we get an email address, we send a message that the person we got it from needs to meet. An agent arrests whoever shows up, and then we get all their email addresses."

"That's a slow way to do it," Tamara observed.

"True, but the network is so dispersed that it's the only way. None of the people we've arrested so far have but one or two connections. It's been a nightmare, too. Sometimes it's just a kid that shows up, and maybe his parents have no idea what he's doing. A lot of the time, the person has no idea what he or she is a part of. Some of them aren't even Muslim, or Middle Eastern. Crazy."

Jack Johnson was waiting in a small conference room, having received a message that the head of the CIA had a special assignment for him. Glad to be taken for the moment out of the tedious task of arresting and interrogating one mostly ignorant conspirator after another, he jumped to his feet when he saw the doorknob turning. He expected to see Sam Lewis as the door opened. The vision that he beheld instead nearly took his breath away. Consequently, when Lewis appeared behind her, Jack was caught with his mouth open and his eyes wide. Lewis had an inner chuckle at the sight. At least he wasn't the only one to be affected by Tamara's beauty.

"Jack Johnson," Lewis said, "meet Tamara..." He turned in confusion to Tamara, realizing for the first time that he didn't know her last name.

"Don't worry about my last name," she said, accurately guessing the reason for his hesitation. "It's unpronounceable anyway. I'm Tamara," she said to Jack, holding out her hand. "May I call you Jack?"

"Please do," he said, taking her hand and nearly deciding to kiss it rather than shake it. *Unless you'd like to call me lover*, he added mentally. This assignment was going to be fun, whatever it was.

Lewis briefed Jack quickly, knowing that he was already privy to the reason for locating Zlatovski as well as the urgency. Handing him a black credit card with silver letters and numbers and no logo, he said, "Get going. Your first stop is Athens, and if you can't get a line on him there, try Sofia, where he trained the translators. I trust your passports are in order?" he asked, looking back and forth at both of them.

Jack nodded as Tamara said yes. Lewis handed the case folder to Jack. It contained all the information they'd been able to collect on Zlatovski.

"Alica Cindric is available for you to interview before you leave. Let me know if you need anything else from me." With that, he strode out of the room to check on the data mining operation and get an update from Luke Clarke.

June 30, 2020, D-day minus 30; Tehran

Dalir Jahandar paced the floor as he waited for his twelve lieutenants to arrive. The twelfth was someone he didn't know personally, only by reputation. He was to replace Reza Mokri, martyr to the cause. It was the reason for Reza's death that brought the Sword of Cyrus together in one room again, a circumstance they had avoided since the last meeting with Oleg Zlatovski. One by one, the Sword lieutenants filed in, silent in the presence of their leader. None would speak until Dalir spoke.

"My brothers," he began. "You have been made aware of the death of one of us, our brother Reza Mokri. Reza died bravely rather than be questioned by those we seek to destroy. He will long be remembered as one of the first martyrs in our jihad." Dalir looked at his folded hands, observing a moment of silence for his friend and co-conspirator. Reza had done a great job of fending off suspicion at the Rossler Foundation until a mishap revealed others to the foundation's security team.

"It is no secret that we lost the entire team at the Rossler Foundation. Our plan goes forward, however. We have now reached the point of no return. Whatever happens now, nothing can stop it or change it. The operators will receive their final instructions in the next few days. All communications will then be broken and they will not be contacted again. There WILL be no changes, this WILL happen as planned. Our scientists have been able to create small, portable nanonuclear bombs to be assembled in place in our target cities. They will be inserted into innocuous objects, some larger than others, in a pattern that is already determined. Our materials are already in place, except for some parts that are readily available in the target cities and will not excite comment when they are purchased by our agents. Only a few dozen cores still await assembly. All is in readiness, my friends. Our plan will see fruition at the appointed time."

Dalir looked around the table as he finished speaking, inviting questions or comments with an open face and raised eyebrows. One hand went up, the new man's.

"Our leader, I do not question your information. However, I am curious. I understand that the Americans, in particular, have found a way to flush out some of our assets and arrest them. Does this not leave us vulnerable to a break in communications before we are ready for it? Do the assemblers know what to do?" Dalir regarded him steadily for a moment, and then decided that it was a fair question.

"It is true that we are not always in direct communication with the hundreds of operatives who are tasked with assembling and placing the bombs. In many cases, we do not even know who they are. This is the genius of our spymaster, Oleg Zlatovski. He has constructed the network in such a way that the capture of one man does not bring down half a dozen others. But rest assured, the plans went out weeks ago. There should be no mistakes. Even if a few bombs do not serve their intended purpose, we have built in enough redundancy to thoroughly destroy the targets."

His questioner bowed his head in assent and no one had any other questions. It was as it had been thousands of years ago. The world went about its business, secure in its hubris that nothing could disrupt it. Meanwhile, the chosen, the progeny of Cyrus the Great, would breach its walls and conquer.

One thing Dalir would not share with the others. He had lost touch with Oleg Zlatovski. Messages to the secure email address went unanswered, and this was not an acceptable state of affairs. It had come to his attention that Sam Lewis had been seen in Moscow twenty-four hours ago. He could think of no reason for this, unless they were perhaps looking for a certain rogue Russian agent in conjunction with the spies that had been picked up at the Rossler Foundation. This was just too much of a coincidence to ignore.

When the meeting had ended, Dalir slammed his fist on his desk. 'Unable to deliver message' came up every time he attempted to email Zlatovski. It was an unacceptable turn of affairs. The man had disappeared from his surveillance as if he'd never existed. Private email addresses were gone, and so was the website Zlatovski had set up for his network. No more messages were arriving at the lab's email address, from anywhere, and Dalir needed to know why. That Zlatovski had disappeared as well was serious. Had he been captured? Was he even now giving away the secrets of the grand plan set for less than a month from today? Worst of all, were international security service agents holding him in the sights of their weapons? When he found Zlatovski, he was going to make sure the man would never again cross him. Just as soon as he had all the information he needed.

An international search for Oleg may be mounted, and

Dalir intended to find him first. Only Oleg had the names, positions and roles of everyone responsible for placing the bombs and everyone controlling the detonators for each array of bombs. Oleg knew more about the whole operation than anyone else. If he fell into the hands of the enemy, it could compromise some of the operation. But, not all of it. Not even Oleg would be able to reverse this event. Dalir knew that everything was already in order, because Oleg had reported it so before the arrests at the Rossler Foundation. But it would be best if Oleg were not arrested too; it would be best to make sure he got to Oleg first.

Chapter Twenty-Nine

THE MASTERMIND

July 1, 2020, D-day minus 29; Boulder

With the news that the spymaster had been identified and a couple of agents, one of whom knew him before he staged his death, had been sent after him, Salome turned her attention to the ringleader. They knew his name now, too, and both Sam Lewis and Luke Clarke were acquainted with him somehow. The plot to destroy half the world didn't mesh with his public persona, though. To understand whether he would really go through with it or merely blackmail the West for some unknown agenda, she needed to apply her best skills to understanding what that agenda might be. After long discussions over the phone with both Sam and Luke, she began to get a picture of a highly capable and patient man. He'd engineered his recruitment to the CIA over fifteen years ago, and had gone underground at least ten years ago. What had triggered his emergence from obscurity?

The most obvious event was the 9th Cycle virus, but Sam and Luke had both heard him say his family was safe. Was that the truth? Finding the family was crucial, but the two names by which he was known made it difficult. Was either name the real one? How could she reconcile his life as Ahmad Ahmadi, political science major, CIA sleeper and Director of Reconstruction in Iran with Dalir Jahandar, al Qaeda leader and among the most-wanted terrorists in the Middle East, whose face had never been identified until Alica Cindric fingered him? He was either a superman, needing no sleep and more brilliant than she could imagine, or he had help.

Salome no longer had access to Karsten Adler, Alica Cindric or any of the translators, who, in any case, didn't know much anyway. She wanted to get an idea of who Reza Mokri had been, and why he would have committed suicide upon capture. Of all the conspirators, only he had taken that route. There must have been some reason that could be key to her investigation. She made a call to Lewis, who promised to open that line of inquiry with Alica, now that she was fully cooperating. Salome had her doubts about how full the cooperation was, but short of flying back to D.C. herself to question Alica, she had little choice in the matter. She wasn't through here in Boulder, so she didn't want to fly back and potentially get stuck at the JOCC.

One of the lines of investigation she wanted to pursue was whether the secrets stolen by the translators truly had the potential to wreak the kind of havoc she'd seen in the pictures from the future. The only person who could adequately answer her questions was Roy James. Salome considered her approach, now knowing that Roy suffered from crippling social anxiety around women. She had some experience with that, because her younger brother had a similar problem, if a less intense version of it. The key was trust and relaxation. If she could gain Roy's trust, and then keep the interactions with him low-key enough for him to relax in her presence, she could avoid triggering his anxiety. Then they could communicate like normal human beings.

Ordinarily, her trust-building efforts would take place over a longer period of time. This time, she had no such luxury. Four weeks from today, they would see the end of the world as they knew it, unless they could stop the inevitable. She didn't have time for Roy's fears, but she couldn't risk alienating him, either. She started by asking JR Rossler what Roy liked to drink in his lab, after learning that JR had become a friend. With a cold can of Dr. Pepper in each hand, her black-framed glasses on for the academic look, she knocked at Roy's lab door.

"Roy? It's Salome Lane. May I come in? Oh, I've brought you something to drink. Do you like Dr. Pepper?"

Roy was standing at a counter in his lab, frozen in indecision, a look of terror in his eyes. Salome put one of the cans of soda down in front of him. "Oh, I'm sorry if I startled you. I'll just sit here quietly until you finish what you're doing, and then maybe you could help me out?"

Salome didn't expect, nor did she get, a response. She took a seat on a lab stool, as far away from Roy as she could get in the lab, and began to look around the lab. Surreptitious glances at Roy from under her lowered eyelids revealed that he had picked up the soda and was holding it in one hand while poking at something under a Plexiglas hood on the workbench. Absently, he took a swig of the cold beverage, then put the can down and used both hands to do whatever he was doing under the Plexiglas.

Salome stayed quiet, not even clearing her throat of the sickly-sweet soda she'd sipped. The sooner Roy forgot she was there and relaxed, the sooner he would understand that she wasn't there to get in his space or interrupt him. It amused her that the way to make a shy man trust her was very similar to the way she'd gain the trust of a dog or a cat...through his taste buds. She sat, unmoving, for more than half an hour. Her back was stiff from sitting on the backless stool, when at last Roy spoke to her.

"Th-thank you." When she looked up at him, he was holding the soda can up, as if in a toast.

"Oh, you're welcome. I've heard you are the inventor of that amazing little robot, or, I guess it's called a nanobot. The Spyfly?" she ventured.

Roy blushed and nodded, but didn't speak.

"That was so clever," Salome said. Then she fell silent, knowing that too much too soon would undo what she'd accomplished so far. She sat for another ten minutes or more before Roy spoke again.

"Would y-you l-like to see my l-l-little d-d-dog?" he struggled to get out.

"I'd love to, if you want to show me," she said fighting the urge to smile. Roy nodded and beckoned her to come closer. *Score*, she celebrated silently. She moved smoothly and gracefully toward him, making no sudden moves, until she was side-by-side and could see what was underneath the Plexiglas hood. It looked like a tiny model of a dog. When Roy pushed a button on the remote control in his hand, its little head moved to the ground and it started moving forward, seeming to sniff at the ground, until it stopped and assumed the stance of a hunting dog, tail straight out, head up and nose in the air. Salome suppressed a giggle. This was cute, but she had no idea what it was for, and she didn't dare ask.

"He found the potassium cyanide," Roy said, without a trace of the stutter that Salome had come to expect. She looked at him in surprise, not only because he wasn't stuttering, but because potassium cyanide could be dangerous in large quantities. She didn't see any of the crystalline substance on the workbench, though.

"There were only a couple of grains," Roy explained. "I've been refining the identification process so that tiny quantities of dangerous substances can be detected. Naturally, they won't let me experiment with anthrax."

"I can understand that," Salome blurted, too startled by his statement to guard her tongue.

"Miss Lane, what can I help you with?" Roy asked, changing subjects as naturally as if he were a normal man with normal social skills.

"Well, I do have a few questions but please call me Salome," Salome started, slowly. This had been too easy. Carefully, in order to maintain the fragile connection, she began to question him about nanonuclear technology.

Chapter Thirty

VOLUNTEERED FOR MARTYRDOM

Early July 2020; various target cities

Hundreds of more technologically savvy assemblers were taking delivery of kits that would become drones under their ministrations. Representatives of the Sword of Cyrus had purchased them over the past few months, a few here and a few there to avoid suspicion. That the drones were readily available from many online sources was a stroke of good fortune of which Sword of Cyrus logistics experts had taken full advantage. No need to smuggle them into the target countries, when anyone with the means to purchase them could simply have them delivered to their doorstep. The perfect model, already capable of delivering a larger payload, they each had to be specially prepared to avoid detection by police or air radar. For this purpose, a set of scientists separate from the nuclear specialists in Esfahan had developed another use for nanotechnology.

Current stealth technology had not advanced much past the generation of military aircraft that deflected radar signals in unpredictable directions rather than echoing the signal back to the radar location. What if, the scientists postulated, that instead of deflecting the signal, they could find a way to absorb it? No reflection of signal meant to a radar installation that nothing was there. If it could be absorbed, the signal would go nowhere - not back to the radar installation, and nowhere else, either. It would work both for the very low-flying mini-drones as well as the much larger ones that could otherwise be detected by air traffic controllers in airports near the targets.

After weeks of work by a large team of scientists all focusing on the same problem, they came up with a special paint infused with non-reflecting carbon nanoparticles. The nature of carbon made it an ideal absorption medium. Furthermore, the paint could be easily mixed on-site once the nanoparticles were delivered. No known inspection technique could detect the carbon as anything hazardous, so it was shipped to various locations within the target countries, from whence agents distributed it as needed. Some of the assemblers got a kick out of having their children paint the drones with it.

The next task would be to synchronize the radio signals that would control the drones, so that at the appropriate moment each would receive the trigger signal. For this purpose, agents were designated to operate MCUs, or Master Control Units. Once the drones had been flown into place, the MCU, at the appointed time, would activate the signal that turned on the lasers, which in turn triggered the fusion reaction. The MCUs were instructed to place themselves in such a way that their targets were arrayed around them in rough circles.

The maps they were given showed the expected radius of destruction of the bombs, and all showed a small area in the center where the destruction wouldn't reach. Unbeknown to the operatives, who were reassured by the maps that they could find safe haven in the centers, those maps were deliberately very conservative in the expected destruction radius. In fact, all operatives would be killed by overlapping detonations. Because the Sword needed expertise in flying the drones and the other technical issues, they had decided that hoping to find enough voluntary martyrs for the purpose would be unlikely. Therefore, they did not tell their operatives that they would be 'volunteered' for martyrdom.

Chapter Thirty-One

HE'S MY UNCLE

July 3, 2020, D-day minus 26; Piraeus

Oleg Zlatovski gazed out at the Mediterranean, wishing he could change what was about to happen. If only he hadn't...but no, if it hadn't been he, it would have been someone else. Besides, there would be somewhere just as beautiful on the coast of Turkey. At least there would be no drifting radiation to rain on him anywhere he went. He heard a step at his front door and then the door knocker. The people to whom he would sell his beach-front property in Piraeus. That they would be able to enjoy it only for the next few weeks was his secret. It was his last property in Greece. He had cashed out of the rest and stashed his fortune in an Iranian bank.

In an hour, his business concluded, Oleg made his way to an outdoor eating establishment to enjoy the sea breezes of Greece for the last time. Tomorrow, well ahead of the planned nuclear attacks, he would fly to a safe haven. Today, he had to consider where that might be. He knew that Alica Cindric had been compromised and was attempting to soften her fate by luring him into custody in the United States. That was the last place he wanted to be when the bombs went off. On the other hand, the fact that his network had been pierced couldn't be pleasing to the Sword of Cyrus. Oleg wasn't sure that turning up in Iran wouldn't be just as dangerous as ground zero of one of the infernal bombs. He had taken down all communications links that led to him and was considering where to go for another change of identity.

A conversation in English a few tables away caught his attention when he heard his Greek name spoken in an American accent. Looking up, he froze at the sight of his niece, Tamara, and a clean-cut American that he would probably peg as CIA anywhere in the world, speaking to the maître d'. Oleg immediately turned his head away and, moving in a leisurely manner to avoid drawing notice, put some cash on the table and stood to leave. With his ears tuned to the sound of pursuit, he slipped down the street and into an alley, taking a circuitous route to a house he knew of, where he could obtain sanctuary and female company for the night. Now he would have to find a way out of the country that didn't involve public transportation. How the hell had this happened? Then, he knew. Alica. If he ever saw the bitch again, he'd slit her throat. Along with that of his lovely niece, if he could manage it.

Safe in a room in the bordello, Oleg considered his options. How had Tamara and her escort tracked him to Piraeus? It was true he'd severed his communications, even with those he relied upon to give him early warning of anyone looking for him, but the last he knew, Tamara was still in Russia, and that had been only a week ago. Alica must have given her the Athens information, and from there it was a matter of public records search to find all of his properties. He'd held onto the beach-front villa for too long. Obviously, he couldn't fly to Turkey, his original destination. Driving to Istanbul would take eleven hours, a trip that would require several stops. With someone else helping her drive, if Tamara got wind that he was headed there, it was possible she could catch up to him. He needed a red herring of some sort.

Oleg looked at his phone, and decided to use a public telephone to call his estate agent. It was only a matter of time before Tamara found his property, along with the agent's For Sale sign, and called him. Maybe she already had, and that was why she'd been nosing around the restaurant. There weren't that many in the area, so it had been a stroke of luck that she hadn't spotted him there. A timely word in the estate agent's ear might send her in the opposite direction if she hadn't already called him. Of course, it wasn't foolproof. Tamara knew Oleg well. Very well, in fact, he reflected, as he took a moment to savor a distant memory. His plan could backfire. Nevertheless, he had to try.

Oleg dialed, and then addressed the man in Greek. "Nikolas, Dimitriou. I wanted to let you know that I'll be moving to Paris. I'm not able to wait until the transaction clears for the sale today. When I get to Paris, I'll let you know what bank to wire the funds to." Accepting Nik's congratulations on the sale and expression of envy for his Paris sojourn, Oleg ended the call. He hailed a taxi and asked to be taken to the nearest car rental establishment, where he rented a car, gave Paris as his destination there as well, and drove the late-model Toyota Corolla north, following a route that would skirt the Aegean and end in Istanbul. From there, he would decide what to do next.

It was too bad he'd had to miss the night of rest and relaxation in the arms of a beautiful Greek courtesan. Turkey would not have so many opportunities, he thought.

July 3, 2020, D-day minus 26; Piraeus

Jack Johnson gazed at Tamara across the breakfast of koulouri and graviera cheese with fruit. He'd have preferred an American breakfast, but Tamara insisted he try a traditional Greek meal, and at the moment he was happy to do whatever Tamara wanted. He only wished she wanted to extend their professional relationship to a more personal level. From his first glimpse of her, Jack had suffered from a very non-professional opinion of his new partner. Far from the stereotype of a stout Russian woman in a babushka gleaning in the fields, this woman was spectacular in his eyes. Aside from a slightly too-prominent nose, she was perfect. Blonde hair that she styled in a chignon reminiscent of movie stars of the nineteen-fifties, ice-blue eyes and high cheekbones made her look cool and elegant and very European. She was tall for a woman, nearly as tall as Jack, who at five-eleven wasn't the tallest agent around. But, where he was brawny in a way that bespoke long hours in a gym, she was lean and smooth, with a slender figure that he'd like to explore sometime.

"Jack, what are you thinking?" Tamara asked, an amused smirk on her lovely face. She'd caught him staring and wanted to see how quickly he could think.

"Huh?" he answered. Not quickly, then. "Oh, uh, I'm

just wondering if we should be lollygagging here when Zlatovski is probably halfway to Paris by now." As Oleg had anticipated, Jack and Tamara had quickly tracked down the estate agent and received the information that he was heading for Paris. The agent had assumed he was flying.

"I don't think he's headed for Paris," she said, giving Jack that cool, appraising look that he'd come to recognize as her expression when she was thinking out loud.

"Why not?" Jack asked.

"It's something he'd do, leave information that he was going in one direction when in fact he intended to go in the opposite direction. Sam Lewis told us if we didn't find him in Greece, try Bulgaria. But, I suspect he's gone to Turkey."

"Why?" Jack asked again. Damn, he was turning into a six-year-old, with nothing to contribute but unanswerable questions. Surprisingly, Tamara did have an answer.

"Trust me, I know him. He would always leave false information, so I know he isn't going to Paris. If he is working for these Middle Easterners, why would he not go to them? And, if he suspects someone is looking for him, he wouldn't use public transportation. Turkey is the closest Middle Eastern country he can get to by driving."

"Makes sense," Jack said, mulling it over.

"We know from his estate agent that he has sold all of his Greek properties. He's going to ground somewhere else. Do you have the authority to get confidential records from a Greek bank?"

"Not in a hurry," he answered.

"Then we'll have to do it by the gut as you say." Jack almost smiled, charmed by her attempt at American slang.

"So, you're thinking he what, bought or rented a car and headed for the closest Middle Eastern country by road?"

"Exactly. Probably rented. And he probably told the company he was going to France." Her logic was impeccable. If she was wrong, they'd miss their chance to catch him in a few days, and the cataclysm would be that much closer to happening. But, Jack couldn't shake the feeling that she was right. She seemed certain.

"Tamara, can I ask you a question?"

"Certainly. Whether I answer will depend on the question."

"Fair enough. Sam told me you know this Oleg character. What's the backstory there? What have your dealings with him been?"

Tamara stared at him for a moment. All color had drained from her face when he asked the question, and Jack held his breath, hoping to get a real answer and dreading what it was, based on her reaction.

"He's my uncle," she said, her face a mask of neutrality and her voice flat. Jack knew there had to be more to the story, but unless he missed his guess, now was not the time to pry for it.

"I see," he said. "So, what are we going to do, try to find the rental company?"

"There should be a central record with the police department, or perhaps the state police, of anyone who is taking a rental car out of the country. Let's try there."

It was the first he'd heard of such a thing, but if Tamara thought it was a possibility, he wouldn't question it. That made a lot of sense, actually. They ought to do that in the US, too, he thought, for cars that were going out of state. Then he realized it would be impractical. You didn't need a passport to get from state to state. And most of Europe would fit in just the Eastern half of the US, if you didn't count Scandinavia and points north and east. Tamara was already on the move as Jack paid the bill and ran to catch her. If they didn't find him her way, they could always take the condo he'd just sold as a central point, and canvass the car rental places nearby.

Chapter Thirty-Two

THE POWER IS INCREDIBLE

July 4, 2020, D-day minus 25; Boulder

Independence Day, a holiday, and a Saturday as well. No one but a few store clerks, fast food workers and gasoline station attendants would be working today, and Roy could hear fireworks going off now and then. It was a good day to test his theory.

Roy had a pretty good idea of how the bad guys were going to design the nanonuclear bombs, and with his help, Raj and his hackers, under the auspices of the joint operation to stop this thing, had been sending out false instructions to any email addresses they could find. However, it was of limited value, since they also arrested the people on the receiving end as soon as their IP addresses had been physically located.

They were also monitoring incoming communications, but nothing much was flowing in that direction now. Evidently the arrest of the Rossler employees and the arrest and death of Reza Mokri had made the group behind the conspiracy cautious. On this morning, though, a recently-discovered email address had received a message containing full details of the fuels, their proportions, and the trigger mechanism for a bomb. It was what he needed to do an experiment that would tell them how many bombs would be required to produce the effects they'd seen in the picture.

Roy started cautiously. He calculated a minuscule amount of the fuels, as little as he thought might create the desired reaction, and found an empty warehouse that he thought would be perfect for the purpose of testing. Before he tested, he calculated the potential destructive power of a briefcase-sized bomb and compared it to the destruction wreaked by the Hiroshima bomb. As small as the bomb was, he thought it might still be about equal to the monster bomb that destroyed Hiroshima. Amazingly, that bomb had flattened buildings for only about two miles in diameter, though most people envisioned a much broader area of destruction. Between 600 and 850 milligrams of uranium had created that destruction when it released its heat and energy. The resulting firestorm had finished the job. The very thought of that tiny amount of matter creating destruction of that magnitude boggled Roy's mind. Therefore, he was very, very cautious of the blast he was about to set off.

From a distance of over a mile, he detonated his tiny replica of the nanonuke bomb, intending to measure the effects with a variety of objects he'd placed in the warehouse. When he removed his blackout goggles and looked toward the warehouse, his jaw dropped. The warehouse was gone. When he whipped out his calculator to figure the power in megatons, it dropped again. If his calculations were correct, the full-sized bomb he'd postulated was powerful enough to equal about five of the Hiroshima

The Sword of Cyrus

bombs. Everything from five to ten miles radius of ground zero would be flattened and further destroyed in the firestorm. Just one of them would take Manhattan off the face of the map. He didn't want to think about Washington, D.C., or some of the smaller European capitals in terms of land area.

Roy needed to report this result to Sam Lewis immediately, as well as notify someone that the warehouse owner was probably going to want some compensation for his building, the landscaping surrounding it, and the parking lot, which was now melting in the extreme heat of the firestorm. Sirens sounded in the distance, making him understand that not only firefighters but probably police would be there any moment. Now would be a good time to leave.

When Roy returned to his office, he found Salome there waiting for him. Startled at first, he regained his composure unusually quickly considering there was a woman involved. Something about Salome was different, relaxing him instead of making him tense. Not only was she a knockout in the looks department, she understood him when he talked about science. He'd never met a woman like her.

"Hi, Salome. Were you waiting for me?" As soon as the words left his mouth, Roy kicked himself for being a dork. Of course she was waiting for him - she was in his lab. But, she didn't seem to notice his gaffe.

"Roy, I'm glad you're back. I need your help, if you aren't too busy." She gave him a questioning look, and he forgot that he had an important message for Sam.

"Not at all! What can I do for you?" Roy blushed, wondering if she'd get the double meaning. Again, Salome didn't seem to notice.

"Since the Agency seems to have a line on the guy that

set up the comms network, I'm shifting my focus to the scientists that must be involved in using the information they got from the spies here at the foundation. I sort of understand the science, but you may be able to help me nail it down better, and suggest some names who could be involved in the Middle East. Until we find the spymaster of the network or someone else who can help us locate the mastermind, I have to turn over every rock I can think of."

"Sure! Where do you want to start?" Roy was all for helping to stop what he'd just proved was entirely too real for his taste.

"I'd like to know if you or anyone you know would be able to give me a list of the most likely scientists in the Middle East to be capable of this kind of research. And where they are employed if possible. The first thing to do is determine if they're missing, and if so, see if we can find out where they went." Salome watched the wheels turning in Roy's brain as she spoke, and had the thought that he was actually very attractive when he wasn't falling all over himself in shy confusion.

"Okay, let's do this. Got a pen and paper handy?" Salome nodded, removing the objects from her shoulder bag that was combination purse and briefcase.

"I'll name everyone that I know, and then give you some other names here to call for the same info. They'll want to know why."

"I'll deal with that, make up some kind of cover story." She made herself as comfortable as possible on one of the high lab stools and prepared to write as Roy began reciting names.

When Roy had given Salome every name he could think of, he excused himself to report to Daniel on his little experiment. It didn't occur to him until he saw Daniel's red face on his phone's screen that taking the time to help Salome before reporting to Daniel had been a bad idea.

"Do you have any idea what I've been going through in the last hour?" Daniel said, barely restraining himself from shouting. "The police have been here asking what we thought we were doing. The warehouse owner is threatening to sue, and the nearest neighbors have been informed that we caused that explosion, so I've received a dozen calls *at my home* about broken windows. I'm sure that on Monday, there'll be a shit-storm. Where the hell have you been?"

Roy blinked, taken aback. "Sorry, Daniel. Salome needed my help, and I guess I didn't realize it had taken so long."

Daniel took in the lanky scientist's hangdog posture and regretted his anger. "Never mind. What do you have to tell me?"

Roy perked up, eager to report the awesome power of just a gram or two of the nanofuels. "These bombs are incredible, Daniel! I used the smallest amount of fuel I could accurately measure. The specs of the ones these guys are actually making are going to create some major damage."

Daniel did a mental double-take. Hadn't Roy seen for himself the damage they'd cause? He was talking as if he admired the plan. "How much fuel to do this?" he asked, holding up the photo of the destruction of Boulder.

Roy sobered immediately, reminded that this was not just an interesting scientific experiment, but a matter of life and death. "Not much, Daniel. Less than you could fit in a waist-pack, I'd guess."

"Oh, shit," breathed Daniel. He needed to report this to Sam Lewis right away.

Chapter Thirty-Three

I WANTED TO CAPTURE HIM

July 5, 2020, D-day minus 24; Istanbul

Jack and Tamara had been in Turkey for just over twenty-four hours, and Jack was growing tired of the woman always assuming the lead, no matter how much he wanted to get her in bed. It had been her idea to let Zlatovski get to his destination by car while they flew there to intercept him. Since they had no idea who his contacts were or where he'd turn up, the two of them had wasted most of yesterday just sitting in outdoor coffee shops and eating establishments that she insisted were the type of places where her uncle would hang out. The trouble was, there were hundreds of them. At nearly midnight, they returned to their hotel and turned in, unable to go without sleep for another night.

By now, Oleg could be anywhere in the world, while they cooled their heels in the city Tamara insisted Zlatovski would have run to. Jack wasn't at all certain their quarry hadn't gone to Paris, as he'd told people, or Budapest, where Sam Lewis expected him to go. But, his orders were to follow Tamara's lead and protect her. While he was doing that, who was running Oleg down so that they could save the world? That was Jack's question.

It was true that Tamara was beautiful. It was also true that she was a pain in the ass. Just like Jack's ex, always right, in her own eyes. Emasculating. He'd far rather work with a male partner, as an equal, than kowtow to an opinionated, calculating bitch like Tamara. Now, if there were other benefits involved, he could deal with it. He'd love to crowd her until she admitted she wanted him. Jack had seen the looks she gave him when she thought he wasn't noticing. Smoldering eyes, if ice-blue eyes could be said to smolder, appraised his body, taking in what he knew was an appealing build that he showed off in well-cut slacks and ever-so-slightly tight shirts. If it ever happened between them, sparks would fly, he was sure of it.

"Tamara..."

"Jack..."

They spoke at the same time, after a long silence in which each had been lost in his or her own thoughts. Jack laughed nervously, while Tamara gave him another of those cool, appraising looks. When he didn't speak again, she continued.

"I need to make some calls. Stay here and text me if he shows up. I'll be right back."

There it was again, the way she directed him as if she alone were in charge, and he an assistant of some sort.

"Yes, your majesty," he muttered under his breath as she strode off. Bitch.

As soon as she was out of earshot, Tamara ducked into an alcove and checked her cell phone signal. Three bars, good enough. She dialed, and when she heard the greeting, spoke in Russian.

"Hi, Dad. It's me, Tamara. Did Chustikov tell you he sent me on a mission?" Her father, also an operative, though retired, of the FSB, may have been privy to the mission, she thought. She wondered what kind of a shock he'd received when he learned his brother was alive. *If*, she amended, Chustikov had told him.

"Tamara, it is good to hear your voice. Are you staying safe?" Her father would eventually answer her question, but not before he'd fulfilled his own agenda.

"Yes. The Americans saddled me with an over-developed jock, but so far he's staying out of my way. What did Aleksandr tell you?" Tamara's eyes darted around as she spoke, always on the lookout for danger. Because she was tucked into an alcove, she wasn't worried about danger from behind, but it could come from either side or directly in front of her, so she kept a careful vigil.

"I know who you're hunting. It's hard for me to believe he's alive." The voice was anguished.

"It's hard for me to know it and not be able to get my hands on him. You know I'll kill him, yes?"

"Of course. What he did to you, my dove. I should die for not protecting you from him, too. Your mother died of sorrow. Her death is on my head as well."

"Dad, he made sure that no one would know. Told me he'd kill me and both of you if I ever revealed what he was doing. That's why I only told you after he was dead, or after we thought he was. Now I'm glad he isn't. I'm old enough now to defend myself, and to take my revenge. I'm going to enjoy it." Tamara's voice shook with the savagery she felt whenever she remembered the monstrous abuse her uncle had put her through as a child. She hoped that she could make his death long and very, very painful. The last indignity she'd inflict on him would be removal of the offending part. He'd never rape another little girl, not even if she failed to kill him. But that wouldn't be likely. She'd kill him all right, unless she decided it would be worse for him to leave him alive.

First, she'd have to get Jack Johnson out of the way. They had different missions, Jack and she. His was to bring him back for questioning. She intended to question Oleg all right, but she intended to extract his information in the most painful way possible. Then, she'd take her revenge, and would laugh in his face as she did so.

"Listen, Dad, I can't talk any more. I called to let you know that I need your help if he gets in touch. We're in Istanbul. Let me know if you hear from him, okay?"

"Yes, daughter. I will help you. I'm sorry that I can't be there to help you punish him."

"Dad, I want to do that for myself. Thank you for understanding." Tamara rang off, and sauntered back to the cafe, where she found Jack fuming at having been left behind. Honestly, he was like a child. Always pouting about something. She'd like to spank him, but he'd probably enjoy it.

July 5, 2020, D-day minus 24; Istanbul

Deeply concealed behind numerous draperies in a souk on the outskirts of town, Oleg considered his options. He could feel an itch between his shoulder blades that he interpreted to mean that his sixth sense was warning him of his niece's proximity. Should he fly to Paris after all? What if there were a world-wide APB for him? He'd be walking directly into a trap. No, he'd better stay in the Middle East, but where should he go next to avoid being pursued by Tamara?

Oleg knew that Tamara had grown up to be as beautiful a woman as she had been a child. His peculiar tastes ran to all ages, from twelve or so to women his own age, but the sweetest of all had been his niece. It was particularly enjoyable to ruin her because he'd always been jealous of his younger brother, the darling of his mother and so much more popular among their peers. Faking his death and cutting all ties hadn't been a hard decision for him. He hated his family, and would gladly do again what he'd done to Tamara, even though he knew she would now hunt him to the death.

She'd become a talented operative, and to the best of his knowledge, a very competent assassin. The best thing for him would be to stay out of her way and hope she died in the coming catastrophe. Afterward, if she survived, he'd have to do something about her. For now, it was best to lie low until the day of destruction. Both Tamara and her handsome escort, not to mention Dalir Jahandar, would like to get their hands on him. His intention was to stay invisible.

If this had happened a few years ago, he'd elect to take a train to Syria, but the trains no longer crossed the border. Syria's civil war had been reduced to weak strikes between the government and the rebels. Nevertheless, the ban on trains crossing from Turkey hadn't been lifted. He looked in a mirror. Before he went anywhere else, he'd need to change his appearance. A blonde Greek would be notable anywhere in the region, probably.

With his plan in place, Oleg sought a beauty salon where he could get a professional dye job to change his hair color and advice on what makeup to use for his skin. His host knew of a discreet one. The rest of the day would be devoted to transforming himself into a reasonable facsimile of an Arab. He'd need colored contact lenses as well. His eyes matched those of his niece, which wouldn't do at all.

Late in the evening, Oleg strolled through the district where Jack and Tamara still sat, people-watching and changing restaurants now and then. Had Tamara not been deep in an argument with her stubborn American partner, she might have recognized the gait of the robed Bedouin that crossed her path. For his part, Oleg also missed seeing his niece, as Jack Johnson suddenly surged forward in his seat and, to her astonishment, kissed Tamara hard before sitting back down to stare a challenge at her.

July 6, 2020, D-day minus 23; Istanbul

Tamara was still shaken by the turn of events that started on the street-side patio of a bar outside their hotel. She had been fending off Jack's questions about her relationship with her uncle, growing increasingly angry at his insistence on knowing. Despite her assurance that it had nothing to do with their current mission and that no, she would not hesitate to take Oleg into custody, Jack was adamant that he had to know the history or he'd contact Sam Lewis to complain that she was endangering the mission.

At last, exasperated by his persistence, she'd spat that her uncle had sexually abused her as a child and she hated him. She expected Jack to recoil, having had plenty of experience with men who didn't know how to handle the revelation. Instead, a fierce look had flashed from his eyes and he'd leapt up and kissed her over the table. Then he sat down and waited for the consequences. She was so startled that she didn't quite know what to do next. Certainly she hadn't expected to dissolve in tears, or to allow him to lead her gently to her room, where he comforted her like a child before tucking her into bed fully dressed and then leaving.

Now Tamara had no idea how to react to Jack, and was therefore cowering in her room, trying to figure it out. She'd ordered room service rather than have breakfast with him. This was disastrous. He'd taken her edge and she wasn't sure she could go through with her plans now. Something told her that Oleg had slipped through their fingers. Where would he go next?

A knock at the door signaled her breakfast arriving, and she threw open the door to find, not room service, but Jack standing there. Tamara froze.

"Tamara, I'm sorry. I need to apologize for pushing you last night. You were right, it was none of my business. Having said that, I want you to know that I'm ready to follow your lead now. When we catch him, I'd like to beat him senseless for what he did to you. No child deserves that." He looked away, unable to bear the expression on her face. He'd abused her in a way, too, by prying. Now she had every right to hate him, and he wouldn't blame her.

"Come in," came the cool voice he was accustomed to. Jack looked back at Tamara, startled. She nodded. "Come on, breakfast will be here soon. Let's sort this out." He stepped into the room, half afraid she'd fly at him with her fists. He had no doubt she was at least a black belt. He could defend himself, but he wouldn't be able to hurt her. He found a chair and sat, head down, waiting for her to begin.

"Jack, come on, you look like a whipped dog," she said. "I'm not mad. I was last night, but it's okay now. Apology accepted." Tamara was picking up random items from the bureau that crowded the room with its size and eclectic collection of objets d'art. When he could bear to look at her, Jack noticed that she was almost as nervous as he was.

"God, Tamara, I would never... If I'd known..." He still didn't know what to say to her. He had to admit to enough curiosity to want to know when it had ended, but he wouldn't ask. As if she'd read his mind, Tamara volunteered the rest of the story.

"He told me he'd kill me and my parents if I tattled. It went on until I was eighteen, and only stopped when he was reported dead after the boating accident. Only then did I tell my parents. My mother never recovered from the shock, and died two years ago. My dad knows I'm hunting his brother and will kill him if I can. Now you know, too."

"Tamara, I can't let you kill him. Much as I'd like to, and maybe help you do it, we have to have the information he has about the network he put together. We have to dismantle it, or send it new instructions that will stop the bombings, and we only have a little over three weeks to do it."

"I know. I'll get all the information he has before I do it, but I will kill him. I won't let you stop me. If I must, I'll kill you, too." The words, shocking as they were, were delivered in a soft voice devoid of the sense of command she'd used before.

"Can we put this aside until we catch him?" Jack pleaded. "Neither of us will complete our mission if we keep fighting like we have been."

"What do you propose we do?" she asked.

"Let's at least try to work together. Now that our cards are on the table, I'll do my best to let you satisfy your requirements, if you'll let me satisfy mine first."

"That sounds strangely like a proposition," she said, "and not a nice one, at that." Jack had the grace to blush.

"No, when I'm ready to proposition you, I won't need words," was his retort. A long stare kept their eyes on each other until it was interrupted by another knock on the door. Room service was there at an inconvenient time, as far as Jack was concerned. But, it was just as well. They had work to do.

July 6, 2020, D-day minus 23; Istanbul

After sharing her breakfast with Jack, Tamara felt composed enough to let him stay while she explained why she thought Oleg was gone. Jack had to agree that what Tamara had been through probably gave her an inexplicable connection to the man they sought, and that if she felt he had been in Istanbul but now was gone, she was probably right. The only question he had was, did she also know where he'd gone? That they had no proof he was ever here was a nagging doubt in the back of his mind that he wouldn't voice.

Tamara was thinking out loud. "Okay. We believe he knows what the leader of this Sword of Cyrus group is doing, yes? So he knows he'd better stay in a Middle Eastern country, or risk being killed, either in the attack or in the unrest that will inevitably follow. Let's assume that we almost caught him in Greece. He was there the day we arrived, we know from the estate agent. He wouldn't have gone to Paris, and probably not to Budapest, which is why we came here. Where would he go from here? Iran?"

Jack had already been in touch with Washington, D.C.,

and ascertained that all cooperating airports, train depots and bus stations were on the lookout for Zlatovski. However, Turkey was not among the cooperating nations. It was entirely possible that Oleg had flown to Iran. However, he had a thought.

"What would a maniac like Dalir Jahandar do if someone he relied on to do a job failed to do it? Or got caught doing it?" He and Tamara had been fully briefed on the exploits of the elusive al Qaeda terrorist that was now believed to be the mastermind behind the coming attack. It stood to reason that someone as ruthless as he'd been in the past would not take lightly a failure on the part of a contractor.

"Kill him, I wouldn't doubt," Tamara answered, beginning to catch the drift of Jack's thoughts.

"So, wouldn't he make himself scarce until everything settled out? Before he decided which way to jump?" Jack looked to Tamara for an answer based on what she knew of her uncle, rather than logic that may or may not apply.

"I'd think so. He's gone to another city here in Turkey, or maybe to another Middle Eastern country," she answered. Then she continued. "He'd stand out as a foreigner with his last known appearance."

"So, we won't find him by showing his picture around. How would he get there? Rent another car?"

"I don't know," she said. "Let's make some inquiries."

They left the hotel, and found a few street urchins who, for an American dollar each, promised to bring them news of the blonde man with ice blue eyes like the lady's, shopping for hair dye or utilizing the services of a salon. They handed out copies of the identikit drawing made with Alica's help, and sent the youngsters on their way. While their little assistants efficiently combed the city, they went first to the airport, inquiring about a man who looked just a little off as a Middle Easterner, but could have been a European posing as someone he wasn't. They spoke to porters, snack bar operators and any airline employee who would talk to them. Around noon they went back to the hotel for lunch and a report from their young spies.

One lad told of a blonde man with eyes like the winter sky who had purchased much makeup at a salon after having his hair dyed black. When he mentioned an odd accent, they knew they had their man. Would the young man take them to the salon? There was another dollar in it for him. Questioning the hairdresser who'd performed the services for the stranger netted even more information. The customer had carelessly let it drop that he needed to blend in in Syria, where fighting was still taking place and a blonde man could be at risk. Jack and Tamara exchanged glances, tipped the hairdresser generously and went back to the airport with a new description and a question about how someone might get to Syria. To their surprise, the answer was, you can't.

That is, unless you have the means to hire a private aircraft. The other question, which no one but Oleg could answer, was what would possess him to flee to a country where he could be killed just by being in the wrong place at the wrong time? And almost anywhere in Syria would be the wrong place. Tossing conjecture back and forth, Tamara and Jack decided that Oleg had probably made that remark to throw off pursuers, and was heading for somewhere else. The most likely safe haven was either Saudi Arabia or Egypt. They were going to need help in canvassing every place where he could have chartered a plane and everywhere it could have landed.

Jack made the call to Sam Lewis, while Tamara called

Chustikov. Neither took the news well. Chustikov reminded Tamara that Zlatovski couldn't be allowed to live. Lewis heard Jack's report with disbelief.

"You need to find him before she does," he said, upon hearing of Tamara's relationship to their quarry, and her determination to kill him. "That damned Chustikov doesn't know what he's done, sending someone like her to kill the only lead we have to the leader's whereabouts."

"Don't worry, boss. We have an understanding. We'll question him thoroughly and then I'll hold him while she guts him. She deserves the opportunity."

Lewis slapped his forehead and rolled his eyes. "Johnson, you bring him back here alive or I'll gut you!" he snapped.

Then he promised Jack that he'd request help from the Mossad and other European security agencies. They'd modify the identikit image to disseminate. It wouldn't take long to determine where Zlatovski had gone. Meanwhile, he recommended that they return to their hotel, or somewhere else that would allow them access to the internet.

"Since she knows him so well," Sam said, with a twisted expression of disgust, "let's take advantage of it. I'll have all the agencies start sending airport security footage to her. Maybe she can spot him through a disguise."

July 7, 2020, D-day minus 22; Washington, D.C.

Strangely, the inexorable march of the days without appreciable progress had slowed the activity of the JOCC. There was an air of hushed anticipation, not unlike that of refugees from a hurricane waiting for the leading edge to strike at last. The situation room no longer resembled a beehive, but instead people spoke in hushed tones, walked more slowly from here to there rather than near-running as they had when the crisis started. Sam Lewis observed the room on this morning and knew that the difference was dangerous. He needed something to shake these people up again. There was no time to waste, didn't they know that? Had they all given up? Or decided it wasn't going to happen, despite all evidence to the contrary?

"Listen up, people," he roared, causing several nearby individuals to jump nearly out of their skin. "If you don't have something urgent to pursue, go over everything we've gotten in the last week. Make sure we haven't missed anything. You saw the pictures - this room is at ground zero of one of the worst areas of destruction. Find something and find it now, or you've got just three weeks to live. No one leaves this facility until we've got the bastard."

The resulting stir was sufficient to make Lewis smile. That shook them up. Hopefully he wouldn't have to repeat the performance.

Minutes later, a nervous analyst approached him.

"Director Lewis, you'd better take a look at this. It looks like we missed something." With a shaking hand, she handed him a printed slip of paper, the contents of an email that had been intercepted on its outbound journey on the previous day. Where the time of arrest should have been printed underneath, it was blank, as well as the place where the receiving IP address should have been recorded. Lewis frowned.

"What's the meaning of this? Why isn't there an arrest timestamp or IP?" he asked.

"I guess it slipped through the cracks," she said, immediately regretting her flippancy when Lewis's face changed.

The Sword of Cyrus

It now looked like a thundercloud, and the analyst was certain Lewis was about to rain all over her parade.

"Lefkowicz," Lewis barked, summoning a uniformed MP to his side. "Pick up anyone you find at this address, and bring them here for questioning. Yesterday!" he barked. The MP scurried out of the room, tapping another to accompany him as he left.

Lewis whirled on the analyst. "I suggest you fish the location of this recipient out of 'the cracks' immediately," he said. If his voice had been any colder, it would have frozen the unfortunate analyst on the spot. As she hurried away, Lewis looked again at the message.

'Confirm will not stop will go-ahead; deploy on schedule. No further communication.' This had to be an acknowledgment of an order from Zlatovski. If they could trace the IP, they had him, or at least they'd know where he was yesterday. Damn it, why was this message the one that was overlooked? He paced rapidly as he waited for the location of the receiver of the message to be traced.

The suspect and the information about the receiver arrived at about the same time. The trace had taken longer than expected because several redirects through European black-hat proxy servers were employed. However, the suspect readily admitted with whom he'd corresponded, a man he only knew as Mr. D. He'd been receiving information about a massive practical joke involving a number of fake bombs disguised as discarded soda cans and a drone that was supposed to set off some firecrackers. When close questioning and threats of bodily harm failed to shake his story, they told and showed him the real one. That's when he fainted.

As soon as he heard 'Mr. D', Lewis made the leap of logic to Zlatovski's Greek cover name. That had to be Oleg

Zlatovski, he reasoned. With no more evidence than that and the IP address location, he reached out to his Mossad contact.

"He's in Dubai," he said, with no introduction. Lewis had no doubt that the Mossad had operatives in Dubai, and that their quarry would soon be in custody. He'd give the Israelis the chance to make the capture before trusting Jack Johnson to rein in his new partner's murderous intent. When he was through with Oleg, though, he just might turn him over to her. It would serve the bastard right.

The Mossad in Dubai were very efficient. Before kidnapping the suspect, they got several good pictures with a long-range lens and sent them to Tamara. Taken as he was sunning himself on a five-star hotel's balcony, it was unfortunate for Oleg that he'd taken out his contacts to soothe his eyes. Tamara would never forget those eyes, so much like her own, but containing such cruelty and evil!

"That's him," she snarled. Jack wasted no time in communicating to their counterparts: pick him up.

"I wanted to capture him," Tamara said, when Jack had finished and sent his text message. Her expression was blank, but the pain in her voice led Jack to kneel at her side and put his arms around her.

"I know, Tama," he said, coining a name of endearment on the spot. "Let's fly to Washington. They may need you to persuade him to talk."

She nodded. All fierceness had gone out of her, it seemed, and it was left to Jack to make the flight arrangements, help her to pack and get her to the airport for their flight. On the long flight, her head nestled on his shoulder as she slept, emotionally exhausted.

Chapter Thirty-Four

MAY I ASK WHERE YOU GOT THOSE PICTURES?

July 9, 2020, D-day minus 20; Washington, D.C.

Oleg gradually regained consciousness, at first believing that he'd merely fallen asleep. However, the bed on which he rested was not what he'd expect in a five-star hotel. As he struggled to open eyes that seemed glued shut, his senses all began to come back to him. The sense of smell told him he wasn't in Dubai anymore. At last, frightened, his eyes flew open. Around him stood several uniformed men, and, most alarming, a white-coated and masked person that looked like a doctor. The person held a syringe.

"No!" he shouted, jerking wildly to avoid being injected with whatever was in the syringe. "What is this? What do you want?"

"The truth," one of the uniformed men said to him. Squinting against the bright light in his eyes, Oleg thought he recognized the man. But, it was impossible wasn't it? Where was he?

"I'll tell you the truth," he managed to say, though his

mouth was very dry. "Please, may I have some water? And to know where I am?" He knew, though. Against all odds, they'd found him. And they knew he knew, because he spoke in heavily-accented English. Unless he was hallucinating, he was in America. And that was his old enemy, Sam Lewis, speaking to him.

Someone gave him a swab for his mouth. "No water. You have a saline drip, you'll be fine." The swab was merely to make his words more intelligible, not to offer him any comfort. There was no time for that. Sam waited only until Oleg nodded his understanding.

"You're in Washington, D.C.," he said. "You are in federal custody, suspected of international terrorist acts. Don't bother to deny it," he interrupted himself, seeing Oleg begin to shake his head.

"We know almost everything already. We only need you to confirm a few things, and tell us the location of Dalir Jahandar." Lewis paused, hoping that was enough to make Oleg talk, though he didn't expect it to be.

"I don't know what you speak of," Oleg growled.

"Don't be stupid, Zlatovski," Sam said. "No one, not even the president of the USA, knows you are here. The men in this room know what you've done in your KGB career. Some of them lost colleagues to your schemes and they will not tell anyone what happened to you. But if that doesn't concern you, let me show you who else is here to question you."

At his nod, someone opened the door, and in walked a woman that took the breath of every man in the room, including Oleg.

"Hello, Uncle," Tamara said, ice dripping from the simple syllables. Jack had slipped in behind her and now put his hand on her shoulder to steady her. In contrast to the ice in her voice and in her veins, fire sparked in her eyes.

Lewis noted the sudden fear in Oleg's eyes as they spotted the dagger in his niece's hands. She was toying with it as if it were a mere plaything. It was as good as a confession, in Sam's view. There was no doubt Oleg had abused this woman, somehow, sometime. Now his past had caught up with him, and he was terrified. It was time to put the questions to him again.

"You have a couple of choices, Oleg. You can tell us what we want to know, now, with no further foolishness. Or, I can leave you alone with Tamara, here. I'm sure you'll want to cooperate with your niece; after all, she's family. Or, I can turn you over to the FSB. They seem to have an interest in you as well. I'll let you choose." Sam noted with satisfaction that the man blanched when he heard he might be turned over to Tamara. If possible, he turned even paler when the third choice was put to him. The correct answer was forthcoming.

"I'll tell the truth. But, how did you discover the plan? My network was flawless!" It was almost pathetic, the defeated spymaster still trying to take pride in his handiwork.

"Two things. First, a genius nanodevice that someone in the Rossler Foundation invented. It caught your operatives on film, taking pictures of their computer screens. That made the Rosslers' security team curious. And second, we've seen the pictures of the destruction. We know what will happen and when." Lewis tossed the last sentence out casually, but closely observed its effect on the prisoner.

"Nonsense," Oleg spouted. It was a bold gesture, considering his predicament.

"You think?" asked Lewis. "Ok let me give you a few

quick pointers to help you think straight" Lewis pulled out a document and started reading the exact targets, time and dates of the planned attack.

"Stop! I can see you have figured out the targets. Who talked?" asked Oleg.

"Your ghost from the future. Said Lewis with a big smile causing an expression of utter confusion on Oleg's face.

"Let me put you out of your misery." He showed the most revealing picture of Washington, with its timestamp of July 29th, to Oleg, whose eyes widened. "You're right about here," Sam said, pointing to an area that was smashed beyond recognition, although a few partially-destroyed landmarks gave a good indication of the location of the picture.

"How…" began Oleg, but he stopped. It didn't matter how. He knew very well that Washington was a target, and he couldn't help but believe that's where he was. The choices arrayed before him were unacceptable. They had to move him, somewhere far away from a major city. Sweat began to roll down his brow as he said the truth as he knew it. "You can't stop it. There's nothing you or I can do."

"He is of no further use," Tamara said suddenly. "Let me kill him."

"Not yet," said Sam, further alarming Oleg.

"Then how about allowing me to take a little souvenir? His middle finger?" Tamara said, still playing with the dagger and playing along with Lewis to scare the shit out of Oleg.

"But you said, if I cooperate," Oleg sputtered. "Please, let me tell you what I know, and then for God's sake, get me far away from here!"

"Hold your horses," Sam said. From another pocket, he produced a picture with a later timestamp, showing Washington unharmed. "We *can* do something, this proves it. But we need your help to do it. Get him up," he said to the doctor. "Bring him in to the situation room. He's going to tell us everything, aren't you Oleg?"

"Yes, yes, of course," moaned Oleg. "May I ask where you got those pictures?" he asked, with a puzzled look on his face.

"All in good time," Lewis said to Oleg. To Tamara, he said, "Miss Zlatovski, may I escort you somewhere? I don't think you'll be having that private chat with your uncle just yet."

Pouting, Tamara turned her back and took Jack's arm. Jack looked over her head at Lewis and shrugged. In answer, Lewis handed him a card with an address and a key ring. Tamara would have the use of a nearby safe house until the crisis was over. Then Oleg would be given into her custody for return to Russia, or whatever her mission was. Jack couldn't wait to tell her, but getting Oleg's cooperation required that the revelation not reach his ears yet.

Chapter Thirty-Five

HAVE THEY BEEN TOLD?

July 10, 2020, D-day minus 19; Washington, D.C.

In the situation room, Oleg was surrounded by analysts and chiefs of the various involved agencies alike as he began his narrative concerning the network he'd set up for the terrorist group. Within a few sentences, Sam interrupted him.

"Stop. We know a lot of this already. We'll hear it later, but the top priority is who is behind this. We have information that an al-Qaeda operative named Dalir Jahandar is behind it. Are you able to confirm this?"

"Da. Yes. Jahandar is my employer, and to my knowledge, the leader of the group called the Sword of Cyrus." Oleg shifted in his seat. The words he'd just uttered would ensure his death if Dalir ever heard of it. However, death was certain in any case if he didn't cooperate.

Lewis held up a picture of the operative he'd known as Arsalan. "Is this the man?"

"Yes. That is Dalir Jahandar. You know he is also known

The Sword of Cyrus

as Ahmad Ahmadi, yes?" Oleg was eager now to please his captors. Perhaps they would have mercy on him and spirit him away from the murderous intent of his niece. He was already plotting how to disappear again, assuming he survived.

Lewis signaled an assistant, who hurried away to begin the process of notifying allies that they had identified the leader. "Where is the lab where they're developing the weapons located?" he asked.

Oleg named the small town, Esfahan, where he'd been given a tour of the facility. Another assistant was dispatched to redirect satellite observation to the area. Oleg continued. "Jahandar is not there, though. As far as I know, he is continuing his duties as Director of Reconstruction, in Tehran."

That was good to know, but allied assets in Tehran would confirm it. A third assistant left to contact the Mossad. Now it was time to return to the details of the plot.

Lewis let Oleg talk, telling the story as he wished. He confirmed that the network had been built in such a way that operatives who had no need to know their counterparts, or even in some cases their true mission, knew no one other than their handlers, and those knew no one except their single operative and a superior. The superior in turn may handle ten or twenty handlers, but the network was so distributed that arrest of one person put no more than twenty others at risk.

This the JOCC knew, since they'd been picking up spies in ones and twos for several weeks now. It was like a ball of yarn that had been sliced up inside by a knife. Pulling an end netted only an inch or two of yarn; it didn't unravel the whole ball. Oleg didn't recall all the names, although he knew a few of the top-level people. To no one's surprise, he named Reza Mokri as one of the twelve followers of Jahandar who called themselves the Sword of Cyrus. Others did surprise them. Oleg named half a dozen well-known wealthy men known to reside in the US and Europe. Their holdings would be devastated if the plan weren't stopped. How could they be all right with that? Still more assistants were dispatched to look into their finances and see if they were pulling out of their holdings.

All of that was a matter of curiosity only. Knowing who they were wouldn't stop the attack, Oleg insisted. In the most shocking revelation of all, he confirmed that all of the fuel and components for the hundreds of bombs that were planned were already in the target countries, and for the most part should have already been assembled. As of this date, nothing remained to be done but connecting the triggering devices to the delivery mechanisms - drones that would be undetectable once they're launched. Even if some of them were intercepted or the signal interrupted, the majority would get through. In addition, he explained why he'd said it couldn't be stopped.

"All operatives have received final instructions and will proceed as planned, on schedule. They expect no further communications, and indeed, all communication infrastructure has been destroyed." Oleg now regretted that decision.

Lewis was no longer interested in the network, only in the logistics. "How close would the mobile control units have to be to trigger the bombs?" someone asked.

"About two and a half miles," Zlatovski answered, having asked the same question during his tour of the facility.

"Aren't the diameters of destruction up to seven miles?"

Lewis asked, aghast that so many of the terrorists were committing suicide.

"Yes," said Zlatovski. "The drone operators will be martyrs." His offhand answer offended Lewis and several others in the room. As if the lives were of no value.

"Have they been told?"

"No, of course not. Many are not even aware of what they are detonating. They think it is a large joke. I told you," he said. "Nothing can stop it now."

His questioners kept Oleg for hours, by the end brainstorming even the most unlikely solutions to the problem. Jamming the signal? Maybe, but there could be hundreds of signals. And how were they to know what it was? Zlatovski could not help them there. He wasn't privy to those details. What he did know was that a nanolaser device was being used to trigger the bombs. Most likely the one Roy James had invented, Lewis realized.

Another revelation was that the bombs were to be detonated four hundred to five hundred meters above the targets, so as to get the maximum EMP damage as well.

Evacuate the cities? Lewis envisioned panics like those of some old movies he'd seen, of thousands of cars gridlocked with hapless victims awaiting whatever disaster the screenwriters had decided upon. Or, worse yet, throngs of thousands of people all fighting to get away and trampling each other in the process. Nevertheless, he asked Oleg if he knew how far that effect would be spread, mentioning that if they evacuated the cities, they couldn't have tens of thousands of dead cars littering the highways. Then came the worst shock since the pictures had been found.

"Evacuating the cities will not help. Operatives are even now standing by with drones that will deliver anthrax over everyone fleeing the suburbs in the aftermath of the bombs.

The Sword of Cyrus means to kill as many of your people as they can, by whatever means are the most efficient. You cannot escape your fate."

After hours of questioning and brainstorming, an exhausted Oleg was returned to a cell and locked in. An even more exhausted Lewis, operating on no more than catnaps since the crisis had begun, presented himself at the White House. News of this kind could not be conveyed over the phone.

Chapter Thirty-Six

NO WEAPON THAT IS FORMED AGAINST YOU WILL PROSPER

July 10, 2020, D-day minus 19; Washington, D.C.

Harper glanced up at his Chief of Staff, who'd just interrupted the study Harper had been in since Sam Lewis left in the early hours of this morning. He couldn't have told anyone what he'd been looking at for hours, nor what thoughts circulated in his exhausted brain. What he had to think on was no less than who would live and who die on his watch and by his decision. The responsibility was greater than he ever would have believed, more than seven years ago when he took the Oath of Office for the first time. He'd weathered more, and more serious, crises than any other president before him, but this was the last straw.

The information from the interrogation of Oleg Zlatovski was disturbing and depressing. Yet he knew there was an alternative. He had seen the pictures that showed his cities intact; but at this moment it seemed as if there were nothing they could do.

The Chief cleared his throat. Harper had forgotten him almost as soon as he'd acknowledged him.

"Mr. President. Do you wish to speak to Daniel Rossler, sir?" He waited respectfully for the answer, expecting it to take another moment or two for his question to sink in. President Harper was clearly operating on his last reserves of strength. His appearance was alarming. The Chief resolved to convey his concern to the First Lady as soon as we was dismissed.

"Rossler? Of course. What's he doing, calling so early?" The question made the retreating Chief of Staff smile. When didn't Daniel Rossler call early? More often than not, it was around two or three in the morning. At least he'd waited until a decent nine a.m. today.

Harper picked up the ornate antique phone that graced his desk. As old-fashioned as it was, it nevertheless had the latest electronic inner workings. The appearance was just to blend in with the historic room in which Harper conducted the business of the nation. The Oval Office held too much history to be modernized.

"Daniel?" Harper's voice came out in a croak, not the firm tones of the leader he wished to be. He tried again.

"Daniel? I'm glad to hear from you. Have you got some scheme to pull our bacon out of the fire?"

Rossler's voice sounded odd, as if he were on speakerphone. "Good morning, Nigel. Sarah's here with me."

"Hi, Nigel," Sarah interjected.

"Oh, hi, Sarah. Good to hear from you, too. What can I do for the two of you?"

Daniel was the one to answer. "Nigel, we're calling to put ourselves and the Rossler Foundation at your disposal. We heard from Luke last night that we're literally sitting on a time bomb. I know it's horrifying, but how can we help? We will not give up until it's over, one way or another."

Nigel was touched, and his state was such that it put him near tears. He'd been through much with these people, supported their formation of the most advanced research facility in the world, attended their wedding, and even almost had to give in to pressure to nuke Daniel's position during the 9th Cycle flu pandemic. But, there was nothing they could now do for him. He said so.

Sarah's voice began soft, but grew stronger as she spoke. "Nigel I have a message for you. *'No weapon that is formed against you will prosper. This is the heritage of the servants of the Lord, and their vindication is from Me' declares the Lord.'* Nigel, please don't give up."

The quote, which Harper recognized was from Isaiah, gave him heart. "Sarah, thank you. Daniel, you have already done more for me than I can ever thank you for. We'll talk again, before... Well, we'll talk again. I hope you'll excuse me, because I have work to do."

Harper was already remembering another verse from the Old Testament, Deuteronomy this time. *'Do not be afraid or discouraged, for the LORD will personally go ahead of you. He will be with you; he will neither fail you nor abandon you.'* Discouragement passed away from Harper. If the Lord was with him, and he firmly believed that He was, then he need not fear. He would be up to the task.

Only a handful of his advisers were ignorant of the looming crisis. All the military and national security heads were involved in the operation that Sam Lewis headed up. The rest, those not directly involved in areas where Sam needed their expertise, had not been told. Given the hair-raising nature of the news, it was a near miracle that it hadn't leaked, not even to the families of the men and women who were frantically working to avert the bombings. It was now time to inform the most senior members of government in the other areas. There was no doubt that they'd react with anger that he'd kept it from them.

Harper was prepared to defend himself. The words panic and no need floated through his head. There had never been any need to prepare for the worst, since the worst wasn't something anyone could adequately prepare for. No movement of funds or troops, no diplomacy, no press conference would help if it weren't stopped. If it were, then creating a public panic would serve to create more harm than good.

Should he have allowed time for people to put their affairs in order? Why? No one would be left to be affected afterward by disorderly death. Only those who already lived on the fringes of society. Perhaps a few other hapless souls who found themselves accidentally outside the area of destruction and completely unable to fend for themselves without the modern conveniences they'd always had. But he now knew that even those would be wiped out by anthrax within a few days after the bombs. This was truly a case of nowhere to run and nowhere to hide.

Now, though, Harper had realized that there was indeed some need to prepare. He wasn't going to run away, and evacuation of the cities was impractical, but what if Lewis and his crew were able to stop some but not all of the bombs? What if the Sword of Cyrus didn't bother with anthrax in truly rural areas or minor cities? Then there would be a need for the citizens who were unaffected to be policed, and the survivors of any devastated areas to be aided. Harper kicked himself for not thinking of it before. FEMA was going to be completely overwhelmed, whatever happened. There was no time to lose; last-minute preparations had to begin immediately.

Handicapped by not knowing where the bombs could be stopped and where they wouldn't be, Harper knew he had to put the preparations in the hands of experts, and hope that this time, as before, he and his friends, advisers and his government would come out on top. As he explained the news to the horrified men and women in the conference room, he ended with a bold statement.

"We are not accepting this as fate, ladies and gentlemen. Good will prevail over evil. As I dismiss you to attend to your own areas of responsibility, remember this. Whatever you need to prepare as well as you can, you have only to ask. My next address will be to Congress. I promise you that the funds you require will be available, or I'll know the reason why not. In this matter, we need to all work together, regardless of partisan differences. God bless you. You may go now."

Some took pride in their leader, while others grumbled and muttered about not having enough time. No one had yet fully taken in the enormity of what they'd just heard. Nevertheless, all got to work immediately to answer this unheard-of threat.

Chapter Thirty-Seven

STRIKE AT THE HEAD

July 10, 2020, D-day minus 19; Washington, D.C.

Late in the afternoon of what had been a very long day with no sleep for Nigel Harper, he reconvened the National Security Council. Satellite imagery had located the lab, but word was there was little or no activity to indicate it was still in use. The question on the table was whether to strike at it or not. Harper was of the opinion that there was little to be gained if the informant was correct. If the bombs were already in the US, hitting the lab would do no good, could be a danger to innocent civilians in the area, and would alert the enemy to the level of intel that the US had.

His military component, though, were hard to stand up to when their ire was raised. They'd had to stand by and let the spies do all the work so far. They wanted a piece of the action. They reasoned that failure to act would imply weakness, something the US had never been willing to admit to. In the end, the vote of the military advisers reinforced by the ones who'd been left out of the

The Sword of Cyrus

loop until this morning prevailed. A ship in the Persian Gulf was tasked to take out the facility, with the caution that the strike must be pinpoint accurate. Two FA-19G Super Hornets catapulted off the carrier and flew in low to avoid Iranian radar, lifted just high enough to clear the mountains surrounding Esfahan, and swooped in for the kill.

The facility was destroyed, but along with it several surrounding businesses took damage as well. Twenty innocent civilians were killed, the collateral damage that the president and his security agencies had feared. It was a PR disaster.

The news that a widespread nuclear attack on the West was imminent had not been given to the public. As far as the world was concerned, the US had carried out an unprovoked attack on a foreign country, killing civilians in the process. The outrage was instantaneous.

The most vocal of the critics, of course, was the Ayatollah Khorasani, who was also in the dark concerning Dalir Jahandar's plans. He immediately summoned the state TV station to his palace to film an enraged speech accusing the US of backstabbing. Not six months ago, Iran had led the Middle East in attempting to make peace with the West, and to extend the hand of friendship. They had kept their end of the bargain, and now the US had perpetrated an uncalled-for attack on the sovereign soil of Iran.

All the while Dalir Jahandar was secretly smiling – the infidels had played right into his hands. They had killed innocent people and restored the hatred for them which was absent for so many months.

Khorasani called for an immediate sanction of the US by all civilized countries of the world. "Stand with us against these bullies," he said. "For as soon as they destroy us, they will also destroy the rest of you. No one can be friends with a nation that seeks to dominate the world."

The cry was soon taken up by every other Middle Eastern nation, and then the smaller countries whose leadership had not been made aware of the coming nuclear holocaust.

Harper was devastated. By giving in to his advisers, he'd allowed a media disaster that would be surpassed only by the attack that could still occur in a little over two weeks. Now, rather than focus on helping his government be prepared, he must spend time mending fences with skeptical governments who demanded an explanation for the attack. What to tell them, which of them may denounce him after receiving the information and prematurely release it to the world, weighed heavily on him. No matter how he was viewed by whatever population was left afterward, he couldn't allow widespread panic to cause more damage than the nanonukes would.

Chapter Thirty-Eight

STATE OF THE MISSION

July 15, 2020, D-day minus 14; Washington, D.C.

Early on the morning of the fifteenth of July, Sam Lewis convened a meeting of his counterparts in the other agencies, the representatives of the security agencies of Great Britain, Germany, Israel and a handful of other countries who were let in on the secret, and his science advisers. Raj, Roy, Sinclair and Daniel had flown in the previous night to sit in. With just two weeks to prevent the holocaust, they were there to assess the state of their mission.

Sam began by stating what they knew. It was quite a lot, considering the short time they'd been gathering intel since the photos had been discovered. They knew the date of the attack, and that it was just two weeks away. They knew most of the targets, or so they thought. Sam cautioned that the Sword of Cyrus could have changed some after Oleg's capture, which had surely been discovered by now. It was also possible that the 10th Cycle library had never had pictures of all the targets. However, the sheer numbers of targets that they did have, based on pictures, intel gathered by hackers and Oleg's interrogation, made them believe that they had 99% of them.

With Roy's help, Sam explained how the bombs would be assembled, probably already had been if Oleg's information was accurate. In addition, Roy detailed what components were in each bomb, including the fuels and the fact that they would be triggered by the CLEC device, for which they'd stolen his own invention of the nanolaser plans. Photos of the destroyed warehouse where Roy tested the tiny replica of the device were passed around along with charts of the calculated power of varying amounts of fuel according to the sizes of the devices they'd found out from hacked emails.

Now Sam took over, talking about the rest of the information they'd extracted from Oleg, who was still in custody awaiting his fate. He'd told them that drones would be used to deliver most of the bombs. To places like the central courtyard of the Pentagon, behind the fences at the front door of the White House, to courtyards or other protected places at Buckingham Palace, even, shockingly, the Dome of the Rock. By the latter, they knew that this was not an operation mounted by religious Muslims, but an act of overwhelming terrorism meant to utterly destroy everything in the path of its leaders.

Sam told the hushed assembly that Oleg had revealed the origin of the name of the group, the Sword of Cyrus. In telling the story of the Persian emperor who'd nearly conquered the entire world, he came to the realization that this wasn't about Islam at all. It was about restoration of Persian supremacy. The audacity of the scheme nearly crushed him at that moment. His presentation unfinished, he sat down, momentarily overwhelmed. Daniel, seeing that Sam needed a moment, swiftly stood up and took over, though his part of the presentation had been slated for a little later.

What Daniel had to say was a bombshell in and of itself. Gesturing to Raj and Sinclair, he revealed that they had learned, by closely studying the ancient images of the future, the GPS coordinates to within perhaps one-hundred yards, of the center of each explosion. This information could serve to evacuate much of the endangered population, although where to send them remained a problem. According to their informant, Oleg, evacuation would not save most from death due to the second wave of attacks, with the anthrax virus. Or even from complications arising from the EMP, which Zlatovski had told them would be maximized by the altitude of the detonation.

They also knew, Sinclair having decoded a problematic bit of data from one of the pictures, the time of each hit. Once Sinclair discovered the purpose of the bit of data from one picture, the rest were quickly decoded as well. It appeared that, rather than strike everywhere at once as they had on the previous year's Fourth of July, the strikes were timed to catch the most people at ground zero as possible.

By the time Daniel's news had been discussed and all questions that Raj and Sinclair could answer asked and answered, Sam had recovered his composure and was ready to go on. He went back to the method of delivery and the problems they would have in stopping it.

Several of the intercepted messages had given the formula for a paint mixture that didn't make sense until the investigators had raided and confiscated material from a house where a drone was being readied for the attack. With most of the components available at any Home Depot or Lowe's, the paint became stealth technology with the addition of carbon nanoparticles smuggled into the country and delivered to the conspirators. Any paint that was high in silica and zinc oxide would do as the medium for what he called the active ingredient, the carbon nanoparticles.

Tests confirmed that the stealth paint rendered conventional radar and other detection systems useless. Even if they could risk shooting down the drones, not being able to find them was the real problem. The one advantage they had, if they could find a way to exploit it, was knowing also from Oleg that the drones would be controlled from a mobile control unit that would have to be relatively close to the target, within two to five miles. If they could locate the MCUs, they may be able to stop the signals that would detonate the bombs.

It was probably too much to hope for to find them all. Even though each MCU would control several drones for the detonation, the insurmountable fact was, there were hundreds of bombs. No one doubted that no matter what they did, massive destruction would take place somewhere. That was because of some critical gaps in their knowledge.

The final thing to think about was the anthrax drones. That posed a bit of a problem because there were no know targets and no pictures from the library. Furthermore, in all likelihood they would be different types of drones than the bomb carrying ones. Sinclair posed the opinion that if there were no pictures of it, that most probably meant it was not going to happen, whether the bombs exploded or not.

Quite a philosophical argument ensued, with some insisting that Sinclair was right, and others insisting that relying on it was foolhardy. The most practical response came from Roy, who said, "Why not work on the assumption that those drones will be deployed, but plan to use the same method that will stop the bomb carrying drones to stop the anthrax bombs as well? There has to be a trigger for either event. Why would they have bothered to invent two? It's probably the same method, either way."

Chapter Thirty-Nine

THREE THINGS WE NEED TO FIGURE OUT

July 15, 2020, D-Day minus 14; Washington, D.C.

After a short break for dinner, the meeting at the JOCC continued. No one would sleep until they had a plan of action that seemed it may have a chance of success, or until they dropped, whichever came first. With the deadline looming and the practical matter of getting personnel and materiel in place, there was little more than a week to find a solution.

The group now had a firm grasp on what they did know. What they didn't know was what type of drones would be used, though inquiries to online vendors had urgently requested their cooperation in providing records of all drone purchases over the past six months, arranged by date of order. National Guard units would be dispatched to the addresses where the drones were delivered, with the full realization that those addresses could have been just the first step in getting the drones to the places where they would be assembled and loaded with the nanonuke payloads.

The Sword of Cyrus

There had been some push-back at first. The biggest online vendors didn't want to be seen as invading their customers' privacy. An in-person visit from a CIA emissary to the CEO of each firm quickly overcame the objection, though it left some board members puzzled as to why the CEO had changed his or her mind so quickly. Tracking down the deliveries was ongoing. There was a strong doubt whether they'd all be found.

Meanwhile, in the JOCC, the other questions were being discussed and the challenges laid out. One of the most important questions was how the CLEC would be triggered. It was one thing to control the flight of the drones with a single smartphone controller, but another to signal all of the bombs being triggered at the same time. The most hopeful answer was that a single frequency would trigger all of the CLECs at the same time. If that were the case, then finding the mobile control unit and disabling it would be all that was required to prevent the bombs it controlled from detonating.

The first suggestion was to use the same type of electromagnetic pulse that had killed the nukes the Ayatollah had tried to deploy. The SEMP, or sustained electro-magnetic pulse, would also kill all other electronic devices in the area, but that was preferable to allowing the nukes to go off. They would have to ground all air flights on that day, of course, so they wouldn't have planes falling out of the sky, too.

However, Roy nixed that solution by saying that nanofuels often took on unexpected properties. He cautioned that a SEMP could just as easily set off the reaction as not. In reality, that solution wouldn't have worked anyway. It was only built into a few of the satellites orbiting the Earth. There weren't enough of them to protect every target city. It would require more thought.

The second, and just as important, was could they determine the location of the MCU based on the pictures? Sam was rather incorrectly calling it the epicenter, but no one called that to his attention, since it was as good a word as any other for what they were facing. Each MCU would set off overlapping explosions from the central location where the unsuspecting trigger man would be controlling it. To find him before he set off the bombs could prevent him being able to trigger it. Sending people to hunt him down could be a suicide mission, since they'd be caught in the blasts if they didn't find him in time. On the other hand, everyone faced certain death anyway, unless they got far enough out of the target cities. No one in this room expected to survive unless they could prevent the detonation.

The discussion had circled the table, each person there putting in his or her thoughts about the riddles they needed to solve. Roy, who'd been scribbling on a notepad as they talked, summed it up.

"Okay. This is what we're facing. We have to figure out a way to pick up the drones, probably at the very last minute. I don't see them testing their stealth technology with a dress rehearsal. Second, we need to discover what frequency the MCU will use to control the drones, whether it's a cell signal, RF, or what." Seeing the nods around the table, as well as some others making notes, he went on.

"We also need to know what the trigger mechanism for the CLEC will be, and determine whether we can jam that or not. Finally, we need to figure out where the trigger-men will be. Raj, I suggest you and Sinclair can help greatly in that effort. We already know where most of the bombs will hit, correct?"

Raj nodded, his eyes intent on Roy. He was beginning to get a glimmer of what Roy was going to suggest.

"It should be a relatively easy matter to triangulate the center, and have several operatives in the area to apprehend anyone using a cell phone. One of them will likely be our trigger-man." The simplicity of that plan struck Sam as quite brilliant. He put several of his top navigational experts at Raj's disposal and they immediately went to work on pinpointing the probable locations of the trigger-men.

By now, they'd all been at the table for a long twelve hours except for a short break for a meal. Sam, who hadn't slept much at all since the crisis started, was beginning to look like a ghost with big black circles around his eyes. His top aides persuaded him to take a nap while they continued looking at all possible solutions to the challenges Roy had named. The rest of the Rossler Foundation people were also encouraged to rest and let the experts in military and espionage operations take the lead now. Reluctantly, they left the JOCC for their hotel. Roy's mind was still buzzing, though.

Chapter Forty

NO TRACE OF STUTTER

July 16, 2020, D-day minus 13; Washington, D.C.

Roy James thought of himself as a simple man, though he was among the most brilliant scientists in the world. That is, his desires were simple. All he needed to be happy were a comfortable place to sleep, food that he liked to eat, and the opportunity to do experiments to prove his theories. Lately, though, another desire had begun to intrude on the three basic ones. He often wished he could enjoy the company of a woman, and it was probably the fault of the only woman who'd ever made him comfortable other than his mother, Salome Lane.

He recognized that she was both someone who could soothe his nerves just by her presence and a major contributor to his self-esteem, at least as it concerned his social anxiety. It didn't seem to be such an outrageous hope that she could feel the same about him. He'd been with the Rossler Foundation for over six months now, long enough to see that close relationships between Daniel and Sarah Rossler, JR and Dr. Rebecca existed. Even the older men, Nicholas Rossler and Sinclair O'Reilly, enjoyed female companionship.

None of this was a conscious thought in his mind as he tossed and turned in his hotel bed, his mind refusing to let go of the challenges he needed to solve in the next week or so. As he fell asleep, the last conscious thought he had was of Salome, left behind in Boulder. That thought fueled a dream that woke him up a couple of hours later-a very pleasant dream of Salome in his arms. What time was it in Boulder? A peek at his clock informed him it was three a.m. local time, therefore one a.m. Boulder time. She was probably asleep, but he needed to tell her something. Would she come to him if he asked her? In the past, he wouldn't have dared. Now, though he was in denial born of his expectation to solve the puzzle before D-day, his survival instinct drove him to do something he would never have expected of himself.

Roy fumbled with his cell phone in the dark, eventually managing to light its screen. Despite the hour, and the fact that he had no idea what he was going to say to her, he found Salome's number and dialed it. A sleepy voice answered.

"Lane." Salome Lane was a consummate professional. If her phone rang at one a.m., someone must need her in her capacity as an FBI agent. She didn't waste time berating the caller for the lateness of the hour, but instead waited for him to tell her where she was needed. If she was surprised that the caller was Roy, she didn't reveal it.

"Salome, can you come to Washington?" Roy asked. His voice was confident, and the request sounded official.

"Of course. When?" She'd recognized Roy's voice

despite being woken from a sound sleep, and assumed he'd tell her why in a minute.

"Now," he said, and hung up before she could ask more questions.

Salome took a moment to stare at her phone as if it could provide answers. Then she got up, packed her bags and called for an airport shuttle. She would take the next available flight to D.C., following an instinct that her presence was vital for something Roy needed to do. It didn't matter what. The scary-smart brain in that handsome head was likely the only thing that stood between the Western world and nuclear extinction, but that wasn't the reason she would fly to him with no understanding of why he needed her. The reason was simply that he needed her, and somehow the ultra-shy man had gotten under her skin. If he needed her, she would be there. End of story.

For his part, Roy was no longer in sleep mode. Once his brain was awake, so was his body. Knowing that Salome was on the way comforted him in a way he didn't quite understand, but that wasn't what his brain fixated on. The first challenge he'd laid out for the analysts at the JOCC was how to detect the drones. Radar wouldn't do it, so he had to find a different way. Until someone knocked at his door the following morning and told him where to get some breakfast, he would think about that challenge.

The second challenge was to find the frequency of whatever means the controllers would use to communicate with the drones. The simple answer to that was to collect information about what type of drone they were using. It stood to reason that, even though the bombs were of different sizes, just one manufacturer's drones would be used. That would make it simpler to control them, since using different drones would require a much more complex control system. Roy was aware that operatives were trying to track down where the drones had been delivered, but he didn't need that to figure out this problem. He just needed Raj to help him analyze the purchase data. He'd lay money on the idea that the data would show them the secret.

Roy had been up since three a.m., but the expected knock on his door didn't come until seven. It was room service, delivering a breakfast he hadn't ordered, but that didn't matter. He sat down to eat it, unsurprised by its appearance. The Rossler Foundation had been taking care of his every need since he started with them. He took it as a matter of course that they'd provide his meals away from home as well. Half an hour later, he got in the shower and was toweling his hair dry when another knock came on the door. He wrapped the towel around his waist and went to answer it.

There in his doorway stood Salome, looking as beautiful as if she hadn't taken a red-eye to D.C. in response to his summons. She took a look at his bare chest and the towel supplying his modesty and walked straight into his arms. The words he murmured into her hair had no trace of stutter.

Chapter Forty-One

THEY'LL ONLY USE ONE TYPE

July 16, 2020, D-day minus 13; Washington, D.C.

Roy and Salome were late to the conference, not having heard the third knock at Roy's door that morning. The rest of the Rossler group left word that as soon as he was available, the hotel would call a car to deliver him to the JOCC. When Salome walked in with him, the table was deep in discussion about how to quickly learn to detect the movements of the drones.

"I think I know how," Roy announced, his manner calm and his voice steady. The unexpected statement served to distract anyone who was curious about Salome's presence at his side. The two of them sat down, a chair pulled up for Salome by an analyst who was coming back to the table with a cup of coffee.

Once they were settled, Sam asked the obvious question. "How?"

"Well, first I need to get a drone like the ones they're using," Roy explained. "I'll paint it with some of that stealth paint we found, and then I'll run tests to see what we can use. I expect there'll be an electromagnetic field, and there may be some other detectable aspects besides visibility."

Disappointed that the answer was to do tests, Sam was a little acerbic in his response. "And how do you intend to determine all the types of drone they'll use?" he asked, sarcasm dripping from his tone.

"They'll only use one type," Roy stated, oblivious to the sarcasm. "Otherwise the control would be too complicated. I need to borrow Raj for an hour or two, then we'll know what type. But, I suspect it will be the same ones that Amazon and the pizza shops have been using for deliveries. They're ideal for the size and weight of the nanonukes, and even have a built-in place where the payload can be mounted."

It didn't even take Raj an hour to determine he was right about the type. Digging into the online catalogs of a couple of the largest vendors easily showed him they were the drones with the highest sales rankings. That was driven by numbers of sales. That the rank number wasn't supported by reviews was an even more tell-tale fact. Lots of drones were being bought, but the buyers weren't getting online to review their new toys.

Roy made arrangements for several to be delivered to him by courier from Pennsylvania, where the manufacturer had its closest facility. Once he figured out how to detect them, he still needed to figure out how to take over their controls, and what to do with them. The danger remained that the MCU could still trigger the detonation even if it was no longer controlling the flight. Sam brought up that if he were a terrorist, he'd detonate his bombs as soon as he knew he'd lost control of them. They were a long way from a solution that didn't still get a lot of people killed.

The questions about the anthrax bombs still remained unanswered but the strategy to counter them would remain the same as for the other drones until they received information to the contrary.

Once the drones were delivered, Roy was provided with a lab in which to do his experiments on them, and was no longer at the table where they were still discussing the potential triggers for the bomb. It was a critical error in judgment. Although Roy had been the one to suggest the methodology, other scientists could have carried out those experiments. His expertise was in the nanotechnology, and it was needed in the group that was attempting to determine the best trigger and the best way to avoid pulling it. That error lost them a week before Roy was available to lend his expertise to the right task force.

During the next three days, Roy worked tirelessly, first assembling and painting one of his drones, and then applying every measurement he could think of to detecting it. He was able to detect a weak electromagnetic signal, but then realized that the signal would become lost among all the other electromagnetic noise if it was deployed in an open area. A distinct and unmistakable method was needed. He tried motion detectors. That worked, but how would they deploy large enough ones and in all of the target cities?

Roy's busy mind turned to considering a protective dome of some sort over each of the cities, even knowing that there may not be time to build it. Besides, the current technology relied on radar, and with the stealth paint, radar wasn't going to pick the drones up. What would work, would be quick to disseminate to all the target cities, and would reliably pick up every drone? Because if it let some through, there would still be wholesale destruction. As he paced, muttered to himself and then stopped to try out one new idea or another, Salome silently supported him, bringing him coffee when he seemed to flag and holding him in her arms when he seemed discouraged. The more Salome told him he was the most brilliant man she'd ever known, the more he brainstormed for the answer. In the meanwhile, she offered a profile of the MCU personnel to those who were working on hunting them down.

On the third day, Roy received a message from the group that was working on interrupting the control signal. Had he determined what frequency would be used to control the drones, so they could figure out a way to jam it? That was when he realized that he knew something they didn't, and that it was the answer to both of those challenges. These drones were controlled by cell phone apps that relied on a local Wi-Fi hotspot that the drones themselves established once launched. The app latched onto the hotspot's network and took over the drone's navigation by linking with Google maps. All they needed to do was hijack the hotspot, disconnect the trigger-man's link and establish a link of their own. Then they could fly the drones wherever they wanted them, probably to a remote location where they'd do little or no harm if they went off.

As Sam Lewis had mentioned, though, they still had to figure out the trigger and how to disable that. Sam was right; as soon as the controller lost control, he was likely to detonate the bombs anyway. Millions would still die, even if the explosions didn't take place in their intended spots.

Chapter Forty-Two

IF YOU CAN MAKE IT TEN, WE'RE GOLDEN

July 19, 2020, D-day minus 10; Washington, D.C.

Raj had by now trained several of the analysts to triangulate the 'epicenters' of the bombs. They started with the targets in the US, but were now working on those in the rest of the target countries, and were well on their way to having all of them calculated. Therefore, when Roy tapped him to help hack the drones' control programming, Raj was free to collaborate.

To their delight, there was already some software available on a hacking site that would serve the purpose with a few modifications. The terrorists had made a major mistake when they picked their hardware. These particular drones had a media access control (MAC) address that fell within a specific range of possible addresses allotted to them alone. Those addresses were publicly specified, which had given the hacker the ability to search for those devices via a program he wrote for the purpose. The app even had the ability to sever the connection between the

The Sword of Cyrus

drone and its controller and insert itself as the drone's new operator.

The software had been made available on the hacker's site. There was just one problem - the site had been blacklisted and they couldn't find it online. Articles pointed to it, but the links led to a Site Not Found error. Roy, having been on the right side of the law all his life, was discouraged. Raj knew that he was probably already acquainted with the hacker. Once again, he activated his network and asked for help finding the right guy.

Within the hour, an email with no header appeared in Raj's mailbox. He activated a software kill switch, and then opened the strange email. In it was nothing but an IP address, appearing as a web link. More confident now, Raj clicked on the link. On his screen appeared a simulation of a Las Vegas-style billboard, with the words 'click here for drone hack'. He clicked. Immediately, his screen filled up with Python code. Raj's network had come through and the code was theirs. But, although he recognized the language, it wasn't one that Raj used. They'd need to bring someone in to help with the tweaks.

Even though they'd been working alongside the federal investigation for several weeks now, Raj didn't expect any of his hacker friends to be willing to walk into the lion's den. However, he was wrong. Only minutes after he sent out a message asking for someone familiar with Python to step forward, he got a call on his cell phone. It always spooked him when that happened. He knew he was among the most intelligent of hackers, but he took great caution with burner phones. How they always managed to find him was both a mystery that concerned him and, oddly, a comfort. At least he knew that if the aliens ever kidnapped him, his friends would be able to track him down.

Raj's caller was one of his guys, as he assumed. The man he knew as Sombra, pronounced sahm-bra and meaning Shadow as he now learned, was willing to come in, in return for full immunity. And tax exempt status for the rest of his life. Raj didn't know what he'd done, and it didn't matter now, these were reasonable demands in his opinion. He was confident that Sam Lewis would make it happen. Raj gave Sombra directions to their location and told him to get as close as he could without exciting suspicion and wait for a call-back. Then he rushed to the conference room where Sam and the others were still convened, discussing contingencies and taking analysts' reports as they came in.

"I've got someone who can help us with the software to take over the drones," he said, interrupting Sam in the middle of a sentence. "All he wants is immunity from anything he's done up to now and tax exempt status." Raj wondered if he should have pushed for immunity for life, too. But, as it was, Sam was looking at him as if he'd demanded someone's head instead.

"Wait outside, Raj, please," Sam answered. When Raj had stepped out, Sam turned to Luke. "Is he a brick short of a load?"

Luke, barely able to contain a guffaw, admitted that Raj sometimes came across that way. "You wouldn't believe what his hobby is. But you know as well as I do that his shady contacts have been working as hard as anyone here. They're the best – even better than the guys on the payroll."

"All right then, he can have his immunity and tax breaks. IF he solves our problem and we all manage to stay alive. Do you mind letting Raj know, Luke? Now, where were we?"

Half an hour later, Sombra had been issued into the building, given a VIP pass, and introduced to the important men around the table, a few of whom would have happily arrested him and thrown away the key if they'd known who he was. Instead, Raj collected him and took him back to Roy's lab, where the hack was queued up on the screen.

"As far as we know, the articles that described what this does were accurate," Roy told Sombra almost before he'd had a chance to sit down. "We need to know for sure, and we need to know everything it will do. We may need you to fix it to do some other stuff."

That rather vague statement was all Sombra needed to get started. First, he read the code from beginning to end. Then he explained how it worked to the other two.

"This searches bandwidth that's allocated to these drones and locks onto Wi-Fi signals if it finds them in that range. I guess that's how you're going to find the drones that are carrying the bombs?"

"Yes, but where does it search from?" Roy asked.

"Oh. You have to deploy the software on a drone of your own, and fly it around where you're looking for others."

Roy and Raj looked at each other in consternation. They were going to have to have hundreds, maybe thousands of these things, all running this software and all controlled by someone who knew what he was doing. Was there time? Doubtful. Did they have to try? Absolutely. But first, they needed the rest of the story.

"Okay, so what does it do once it finds one?" Raj asked, with Roy looking over his shoulder at the screen where Sombra was pointing.

"This section severs the connection. Basically, it interrupts the Wi-Fi signal, so it drops, just like when your router goes down and you lose connection to the internet." Okay, that was simple enough. Then what, they asked.

"Then it pings the drone's Wi-Fi and picks up the connection itself. Now the operator can control the slave drone from his cell phone or computer, using his own drone as a relay link." Sombra's finger traced down the lines of code as he showed them what sections were responsible for capturing and then controlling the other drone.

"Can it go and find another one after that?" Roy asked.

"Nah, one slave drone per hack," was Sombra's answer.

"Okay, that's the first thing we need to change. It needs to capture at least five others in the same vicinity. If you can make it ten, we're golden."

"I'll see what I can do."

While Sombra got to work on the software and Roy went off to think about the stealth problem, Raj went to report their progress to Luke. He found Luke in Sam Lewis's company, both drinking yet another cup of coffee.

"Sombra is confident he can get the software modified to Roy's specifications," Raj said, without bothering to go into the details.

"Raj, thanks for trusting us enough to bring your contacts in to help," Sam said, smiling for the first time in days. "For the first time, I believe we may be able to win this battle.

"Just make sure he gets what he asked for," Raj said. "When this is all over, I'm still going to need my friends."

Raj had barely returned to the cubicle where Sombra was working when Roy was back.

"Guys, I need to run something past you. You've looked at the specs of those drones. If I'm not mistaken, those MAC addresses are unique, am I right? Only one device with the same MAC address anywhere in the world?"

"Of course. It wouldn't work any other way." Sombra's almost condescending answer embarrassed Raj. It was true he was one of the most brilliant programmers in the world, but Roy was THE most brilliant nanotech engineer. He deserved some respect.

Roy didn't seem to notice. "So, this routine you're working on, it's going to look for the specific range of MAC addresses that are assigned to these drones, and when it finds one operating in that range, it's going to take over the controls, am I correct?"

"Yes. What are you getting at?" Sombra was now impatient, as well as condescending.

"Then, there is no stealth problem." Roy strolled away, lost in his own analysis of what he now knew, leaving the others to stare after him in confusion – a state in which he often left people.

Chapter Forty-Three

WHERE THE DEVIL WAS OLEG ZLATOVSKI?

July 20, 2020, D-day minus nine; Tehran

Dalir paced, worrying at the problem he'd been unable to solve for over two weeks now. Where the devil was Oleg Zlatovski? His last communique was that he'd been forced to leave Greece, but the fool hadn't said where he was going. Applying a little logic, Dalir assumed he'd stay away from any and all target countries, which meant he must be in the Middle East somewhere. The question was, where?

Dalir had put his anger over the discovery of parts of the network away. Yes, it was a serious failing, but from what anyone could discover, Oleg had built the network well. Failure in one part didn't compromise another. Now that the remaining scientists of value, those that were most expert in the nanotechnology on which their bombs were designed, were gathered in Tehran, Dalir could see for himself that most of the network was intact. True, hundreds of operatives had been picked up, but so far not one single drone operator had been arrested and one of the last messages Oleg sent to the operators had been to proceed as planned, with or without a go-ahead signal. Even if they managed to arrest and stop a few they were not going to stop all of them. The wheels were in motion; nothing was going to stop them.

The Sword of Cyrus lieutenants, the twelve advisers that Dalir kept around him at all times, urged him to move up the timetable if he believed that all was in readiness and that their plot had been discovered. He didn't tell them that it would be impossible, because he'd lost touch with the one man who could make that happen. Instead, he told them that he'd chosen the beginning of Hajj for a reason, and that he would not strike early. A few accepted it; others urged him to reconsider. And a couple privately wondered if they had created a monster. Rather than accepting their counsel, Dalir was acting as an emperor would and doing exactly as he pleased.

Stuck between a council of twelve that believed him foolish or stubborn and the immutable fact that he did not have the means to move the timetable up but couldn't tell them so, Dalir bluffed it out. If anyone questioned his decisions, he would teach that one, and the rest, that crossing Dalir Jahandar bore serious consequences.

Privately, he sent operatives who answered only to him throughout the Middle East, searching for Oleg. Perhaps the man was merely hiding from Dalir's rightful indignation that his network was developing holes. Perhaps something had happened to him that left him unable to communicate. Dalir hoped it was not that. Whatever the cause, he wanted to personally teach the spy a lesson – that you cannot hide from destiny. Nor from the Sword of Cyrus.

Only a little more than a week remained. The day would come none too soon for Dalir. He wished he could move up the timetable, but it would be all right. Nothing would interfere with the plot as a whole. Sure, a few bombs may not go off as planned, but nothing could stop the great strike from happening in most of the planned targets. They could always clean up what remained with conventional aircraft and bombs if necessary, and of course, the already-planned anthrax attacks. The Army of Cyrus could not fail. He, Dalir Jahandar, future emperor of the new Persia, would not allow it.

Chapter Forty-Four

WE'VE ALREADY SCREWED UP

July 23, 2020, D-day minus six; Washington, D.C.

Daniel was worried about Sam Lewis. Luke had gone home for a few days to check on security operations at Foundation Headquarters, admonishing him to take care of Sam Lewis until he got back. Even though Daniel had persuaded Sam to divide his resources to allow them to get some rest, Sam drove himself until he literally fell asleep any time he was left alone in a chair for more than five minutes. No one could persuade him to get in a real bed and get some real rest. Daniel considered calling the president and asking him to pull rank on Lewis. Then, a better idea crossed his mind.

"Luke, good morning, it's Daniel," he said, when his phone call was answered. He'd waited until nine a.m., knowing that even though retired, Sarah's uncle would be awake early. He didn't want to alarm Aunt Sally, though.

"Daniel. How's it going?" Luke was careful on any phone call, but this one he knew called for the utmost care.

"Fine, fine. Listen, an old friend of yours is having some

trouble sleeping. I was wondering if you knew of any home remedy. He won't take medication for it." Luke thought fast. This had to be some kind of code, but Daniel wouldn't entrust anything important to something too obscure to figure out.

"So, he's being his old stubborn self?" he asked, going along with the misdirection.

"He sure is. We're afraid he's going to start making mental mistakes," Daniel said. Luke was fairly certain he had the gist of it now.

"I'll give him a call, see if I can talk some sense into him," Luke said.

"That's what I hoped you'd say," said Daniel. "Hey, I've got to get back to work. Talk to you later." Daniel expected Luke to call Sam and make him listen to reason. He didn't have to wait long.

Luke took the time to go to the office first, where the scrambled phone in Daniel's office for his calls to the president provided enough security to speak clearly to Sam. After a short wait while his identity was confirmed by the switchboard at the JOCC, Sam came on the line. Daniel was right to call, Luke understood, when he heard the familiar but tired voice on the other end of the line.

"Sam, I'm calling as your friend first, and an experienced field agent second. How long has it been since you went to bed and slept eight hours?"

"I don't remember, Luke. I honestly don't remember." Sam's voice was scratchy, as if he hadn't spoken in a while, or, conversely, had been talking for days. It was the latter that made it so. Sam had been recapping what they knew, didn't know, and were going to do about it, for days, any time new intel came in.

"Buddy, you've got to get some rest. You're going to

make mistakes. And you know as well as I do that we can't afford mistakes. Do you need me to come and help you somehow?"

"What, you're going to sing me lullabies?" Sam joked. That was a good sign, Luke thought. At least he wasn't delusional. Humor didn't follow into hallucinations caused by sleep deprivation. That was more likely to manifest as raging paranoia.

"Yeah, buddy, if I have to. Seriously. Daniel called me. He's ready to sic Harper on you with an order to stand down. You'd better get some rest."

"I can't, Luke. I can't sleep with this thing hanging over my head."

Luke tried another tactic. "You remember what we used to say to each other in the field, Sam?"

"We said a lot of stuff. What do you mean?"

"We used to say we could sleep when we're dead."

Sam laughed. "Yeah. And as I recall, that was when we'd decided *not* to take some rest. Why bring it up now?"

"Because if you and your geniuses that are trying to figure this out make a mental error, we'll all be sleeping, for a very, very long time."

"All right, I hear you. I'll take some time to rest. We've got everyone with anything at all to contribute working on one of three or four challenges. I guess the most urgent one right now is how they're going to trigger the bombs."

"What does Roy think?" Luke asked.

"I don't know. He's working on how to capture the drones and fly them somewhere else," Sam said.

"Sam, what the hell are you saying? You've got the world's foremost nanotech expert working on a scheme to divert the drones? That's nuts! Besides, the pictures show the explosions taking place in the cities, or not at all. There aren't any pictures of bombed-out countryside. That's not going to work."

Hundreds of miles away, Sam's eyes flew open and a jolt of adrenaline hit that drove all thought of sleep from his mind. "Oh, shit, we've already screwed up. Luke, I've got to go. Thanks for your call."

Chapter Forty-Five

TURN OVER YOUR PROJECT

July 23, 2020, D-day minus six; Washington, D.C.

As soon as he hung up, Sam sent an aide for Roy, who arrived breathless on the heels of the returning aide. "What is it, Sam?" he huffed. The aide had practically run his legs off.

"Turn over your project to Raj and his guy immediately," Sam said. "Have you slept?"

"Yeah," replied the bewildered Roy. "Why?"

"We're using you in the wrong place. They need you in the bomb-trigger think tank. Go take over that project. I've got to get some sleep, but I'll see you in a few hours."

Roy nodded. "Okay, whatever you need. Have a good nap."

Roy asked the speedy aide to guide him, slowly, to the room where the trigger was being discussed. On the way, he thought of a solution for the need for so many drones to take over the bomb-laden ones. He asked the aide to send Raj to him as he entered the room he was being shown to.

When he walked in, the six men and two women looked up. Uh-oh, he thought. Women.

"I'm Roy James," he said. "Sam sent me here to help you." That went pretty well. All he had to do was focus on the men. Before Raj showed up in response to his summons, Roy was discussing the properties of the nanofuels, no stutter in evidence. He excused himself to tell Raj what he'd thought of.

"We don't need the same kind of drones, just a computer program that can reach out from the air. Tell Sombra that he needs to find a way for that program to handle a hundred or more slave drones at a time. We'll install it on a computer and use an E-3D Hawkeye aircraft to get that aloft. From a couple of miles up, we should be able to capture every drone above a given city. Sam Lewis is taking a nap, but see if someone from the Navy is available to scramble the fleet to where they need to be on the day, okay?"

The E-3D Hawkeye was the latest in a long line of surveillance and battle-management aircraft dating from the Vietnam conflict, to Roy's certain knowledge, maybe even before. He'd always been fascinated by the strange-looking planes, their radome assembly looking like a flying saucer that had captured a turbo-prop aircraft. They had multiple workstations, among other things, that would make them perfect for this mission even though their radar and friend/foe identification systems would be largely useless. He'd leave it to the experts to figure out how to install the enhanced software that Sombra was working on in the specialized computer systems of the aircraft.

When Roy returned to the conference table where the trigger was being discussed, he asked that the people who'd already been there bring him up to speed on what they'd determined. But first, he asked if the large wall clock in the room could be disabled. The ticking was all too real a metaphor for the time that was slipping through their hands. Less than a week until D-day, and they still hadn't captured a single MCU operator who could give a definitive answer to the question at hand - what triggered the bombs?

Roy now believed that they could take over the drones and fly them to somewhere other than their delivery points. But, where else would be any better? And how long would they have to divert them? It could be a useless exercise despite everything they'd done to develop that capability. No matter what else happened, they had to learn what the trigger was and how to neutralize it. Roy wanted to know what the group working on that problem had been doing while he'd been working on the drone detection problem.

A spokesman laid out their best guesses. Because the drones were controlled by cell phone, as Roy had determined several days ago, they thought the trigger may also be a cell phone signal. They hadn't quite worked out how a differentiated signal would both fly the drones and turn on the onboard laser that would start the nanonuclear reaction. However, it would have the advantage of only one control device being required. That would be the most elegant solution, they felt.

Roy discounted elegant. He knew some of the Middle Eastern scientists who'd made strides in nanotechnology studies. Elegance didn't seem to be their forte. He'd lay odds that the solution wasn't necessarily elegant. If this were the case, though, the answer was relatively simple. In the United States, at least, recent legislation had been pushed through over cell provider objections that required their systems to have a central kill switch that would instantly shut down the cell networks. Too many domestic terrorists were using cell phones to trigger bombs from a remote location where they were safe from both detection and the effects of their bombs. Now there was an effective solution for it. For this reason alone, Roy felt it was the wrong answer.

The second option they reported exploring was that the bombs could be triggered by a radio signal. It was actually the first option they'd discussed, then abandoned when they learned that the drones weren't actually controlled by radio. Roy thought it was worth revisiting, but kept his own counsel for the time being. He wanted to hear everything before he weighed in with his idea. The obvious answer to this trigger mechanism option was to override the signal with a powerful signal of their own.

Both of the foregoing options depended on the plotters having chosen an instantaneous-reaction method of turning on the laser in the nanobomb. If instead they'd built in a delayed reaction, it created a separate problem. It all depended on how long a delay the bombers had time for. From Oleg, they knew that the bombers were expected to die in the blasts, which meant it couldn't be more than a few minutes. Otherwise, they'd have time to escape. Roy couldn't conceive of the purpose in killing their own men, but Oleg's testimony, wrung from him under duress, was irrefutable.

Assume it would be only a few minutes, then. Obviously sending in people to defuse the thing, so to speak, would be impossible. Once the reaction started, there would be an explosion, period. The minute the lasers were triggered, an ultra-fast reaction would create a devastating explosion, as his experiment in the warehouse had demonstrated. If this were the method, then only diversion would help, and then not much. There wouldn't be time to divert them very far.

Straight up? It was something to explore, but not a real solution.

All this took much more time to discuss than Roy would have liked. Because Sam had ordered each group to rest between sessions, splitting them up so that the work was ongoing 24/7, this session ended and was to reconvene in four hours. Unfortunately, there was only one Roy, so the most important asset was lost to the replacement group. By the time they reconvened, there would be only five days left before the bombs began to strike. Barely enough time to inform the target nations of the solution, and as yet, they didn't have one.

Chapter Forty-Six

LET THE TRAINING BEGIN

July 23, 2020, D-day minus six; Washington, D.C.

Until the method by which the attack drones could be stopped had been determined, Sam's hands had been tied. Even as the military factions in the president's advisory council chafed because their special forces operatives would need to be trained in the counter-offensive plan, he'd resisted calling them together. There was no need to have elite military sitting on their hands.

But, as soon as Raj confirmed that they had the method, it was time to bring in the Hawkeyes, their pilots and the best IT technicians to be found. One American team, consisting of a Hawkeye and its usual crew, plus one special IT tech was assigned to each target city. For the targets on foreign soil, the IT tech would be a citizen of the country in question. Any error or failure to respond in time would mean disaster, and Harper had made it clear that the US would not accept that responsibility. The foreign IT techs were due to arrive today to begin training with the American crews.

Sam had moved heaven and earth to have enough flight simulators for the Hawkeye into an empty hangar near the JOCC so that each crew would have one. Along with them came instructors who found themselves in a beehive of activity related to a threat they'd not been informed of previously. That their simulators were immediately hijacked by a civilian to install a program with which they weren't familiar didn't sit well. The first training to be done was theirs. With Roy controlling several of the drones and Raj controlling others, Sombra trained the instructors in the use of the hack software to take them over. Once they had the hang of it, Sombra took over Roy's drones so he could return to his more urgent project.

By the time the trainees arrived, the enormous hangar resembled a miniature air battle, with the instructors gleefully capturing drones not only from Sombra and Raj, but also from each other.

The game wound down as the Navy special ops teams arrived and assembled to hear the mission.

Sam Lewis was to make the address, with the Chief of Naval Operations, Admiral Banks, present to lend weight to his words.

"Gentlemen, and ladies, you are here as the sole defense of the United States, the United Kingdom, Israel, Australia and Russia against a widespread terrorist attack that is a credible and grave threat. We do not have time to give you the background and proof of what we've discovered. You will have to take the word of Admiral Banks that what I am about to tell you is absolutely true.

"You are charged with intercepting and disarming, through means that you'll be trained on for the next five days, a fleet of ordinary drones that will be carrying modern nuclear weapons of extraordinary destructive power. You will have the tools. It is up to you to learn to use them with sufficient accuracy and speed to prevent every one of them from detonating. If you fail, hundreds of thousands will die.

"As you begin to train, it may feel as if you're playing an elaborate video game. Make no mistake, it is not a game. You must excel. You have been chosen because you are the best at what you do. Admiral Banks may have a few words for you, but I am finished here. Carry on, and thank you."

Stunned silence and not a few puzzled expressions greeted his words. As Admiral Banks stood to take the microphone, all faces turned to him.

"I'll tell you just a little more about what you're facing. This is a terrorist threat from a well-financed and very organized Iranian group calling themselves the Sword of Cyrus. It is real. We know when the attacks will begin; you will not be caught unaware. Your job is to be ready."

Somewhat reassured, the men and women gathered in the hangar began to talk among themselves, until trainers barked at them. A grueling schedule would be theirs for the next five days. Half were dispatched to their bunks, mess hall or study desks where they would read about the details that Sam Lewis had left out. The remaining half stayed to learn the 'video' game on the simulators. In twelve hours, the halves would switch places. There was a scramble for the simulators that would have done a fire drill proud.

In the coming war, only one side would be armed with lethal weapons. The other, with technology only.

Chapter Forty-Seven

EUREKA

July 23-24, 2020, D-day minus six through early morning of D-day minus five

Roy had been ordered to stand down and rest, but as he'd noticed before, his brain didn't always obey outside orders. Before he went to his hotel, he sought out Sinclair's team of navigators, to check on their progress. Raj had worked out the method to overlay the pictures on maps of the affected cities, and the location codes of the center of the explosions allowed them to precisely center the pictures on the affected areas. By turning the pictures into transparencies, they could pinpoint exactly where each bomb would be when it detonated.

It was then a simple matter to triangulate the position of the MCU at the time of the explosion, as long as it was controlling at least three drones. If not, they had a line rather than a cross-referenced location. The MCU could be anywhere along the line. The analysts had also been looking carefully at the pictures, and their conclusions were that only about ten percent of the pictures showed evidence of a single MCU controlling three or more drones. In other words, as one wag put it, they were screwed up the creek without the proverbial damn paddle.

This news only served to keep Roy's brain working even as he tried to fall asleep. Even Salome's best ideas to induce sleep gave only a temporary respite from the firing electrical signals that felt like little jackhammers in his brain keeping him awake.

By the end of his rest period, he'd exhausted all the arguments for the various methods his team had advanced. The only thing he could think of that would be foolproof was to prevent the lasers from exciting the fuel. When he returned to the conference room, he asked that experts on laser technology be sent for and put the problem to them: how do we stop a laser beam from reaching its intended target?

The only answer they had - put something between the source of the beam and the target, was laughably simple. And totally impractical. Roy was not one to give up on an idea, though.

Leaving the others to debate again the three likely scenarios, Roy went alone to the laboratory where he'd worked out the specs of the drone's payload bay. What could he do to disable the cargo after locating and taking control of the drones?

Roy hit his palm against his forehead, but didn't stop his rapid pacing. "Think, Roy, think! You built that laser device - you know how it works. There must be something you can do."

Salome, had come to the lab shortly after Roy got there, and was sitting quietly in the corner. She giggled. "Hon, you remind me of the Energizer Bunny." Roy stopped in his tracks to stare at her. The battery! Salome had done it again!

The answer was in the battery of the laser. Of course! It was easy! That battery in the nanolaser was storing almost ten times more voltage than the drone's onboard lithium ion battery. Inside the battery was a nanocomputer that controlled the battery, the same as with lithium ion batteries. The computers inside the batteries emitted electromagnetic radiation in the radio frequency (RF) range. As the creator of the laser battery, he already knew the radio frequency range of the nanocomputer.

The bomb would sit below the drone in the payload area. Within it, his nanolaser would act as the trigger, but the laser operated on one of his nanobatteries, assuming the Iranian scientists had used the plan unmodified. There was no indication in the bomb specifications they'd intercepted that it would be any other plan, so it was a pretty good bet. Based on those same plans, the bombs would be roughly rectangular or cylindrical in shape, with the nanonuclear fuel in one end, slightly larger than the other that held nothing but the laser trigger and an electrical relay to turn it on. To stop the trigger from working, all he had to do was compromise the battery in the laser. It would be a delicate operation, but it would work.

He could equip one of his hummingbirds with a laser cutter, fly it in under the drone to attach to the box carrying the bomb and cut the trigger battery, which would make it stop working instantaneously. The only challenge would be to build a chip that he would be able to attach to the hummingbird, both to detect the radio frequency and direct the laser to cut the battery.

When he found the answer, Roy ran out of his lab and down the hall toward the conference room where his team was still debating, pretty much like Archimedes did about 230 BC, except Roy was not naked. Nevertheless, he narrowly avoided being shot as an intruder by one of the security team wandering the halls of the JOCC facility. Only Salome's sudden appearance around a corner saved him, because she was between the sentry and Roy before the sentry could pull his trigger. The sentry yanked his weapon upright and shouted for Salome to get down, which stopped Roy in his tracks. He turned, saw her on the floor, and started back with the sentry yelling at him to stop. Finally, Salome's cries got through to the sentry. "It's okay, he's one of us!"

Roy looked with confusion from Salome to the sentry and then clutched at his chest. No ID hung there…he'd taken it off while working on the drone because he kept catching the drone's landing skids in the lanyard. The close call had made lots of noise, and people began appearing from both ends of the hallway. Roy, who had made it to Salome's side and pulled her up, stood in the center, holding his girl and glaring at the sentry, who glared back in return.

"I'll just step in here and get my badge," Roy said finally. To Salome, he said in a near whisper, "Eureka." Salome pushing him against the wall and kissed his breath away, to the amusement and applause of every witness. Both the incident and the aftermath were a testament to the condition of the team as a whole – they were getting punch-drunk from the tension.

Chapter Forty-Eight

WHAT IF I CAN'T DO IT IN TIME?

July 24, 2020, D-day minus five; Washington, D.C.

It was nearly an anticlimax when Roy stood at the head of the table in the conference room and explained what he'd determined to the rest of the team.

"How sure are you of this?" one of the team asked.

"No way to be sure without testing," Roy returned. A babble broke out as the team protested hearing another theory with no proof.

"Look," said Roy, "I have one of the lasers in my luggage. It won't take long to build more. I need a few more of the drones with mockups of the bombs to get it right, and then we need to figure out how to keep it from happening. But I'm confident this is the answer."

The team leader looked at his watch. Almost four, and the manufacturing facility where they'd purchased the drones they had was in Pennsylvania. He picked up his cell phone and dialed without telling anyone else what he intended.

"We need a dozen of those drones, no wait, while you're at it make it two dozen" he said. "ASAP. Send a helicopter for them." He turned to the rest of the room.

"Okay, folks, scatter. Have Roy tell you what he needs and get it. Run."

"I wouldn't run," Roy said, as everyone got up to follow orders. "There are some mean-looking folks in the halls that might shoot you."

While the others were retrieving what he needed to begin testing, Roy tracked Raj down.

"Hey, buddy, I've got an idea how we can stop those drones, and the bombs too," he said, as soon as he'd found Raj. "I need something very small that can detect electromagnetic radiation in a specified radio frequency range. Any ideas?"

"What do you have in mind?" Raj returned. He thought he might know someone who could make a suggestion, but before he contacted anyone, he needed details.

Roy explained his idea, then said, "I've got a little nanodevice that looks just like a hummingbird in flight. It's super-fast, can hover when it gets to its target, and I'm pretty sure I can attach one of my nanolasers to it. But it needs to know where the laser should cut. If we aim it at the wrong thing, it could trigger the bomb instead of disabling it."

"You've got one with you?" Raj asked.

"Nah, but they don't take long to build. I can put a few together for the tests, but if it works, we'll need a lot. Do you think Sam can find me some people to build them?"

Raj shook his head, a tiny gesture that he didn't mean for Roy to see. "Yeah, bro, I think Sam can do that. What kind of time are we talking here?"

"Well, we have to have them ready in less than five days,

right?" Roy was still moving and talking as if they had all the time in the world. Raj wondered if his brain was the only thing that moved faster than a snail's crawl.

"Yeah. So, get busy on that, and I'll try to track down something that will tell the laser what to cut." Raj walked away, his own pace far more urgent than Roy's, searching his mind for the members of his hacker network that were known for firmware.

Ten minutes later, he was on a private chat session with Rube, trying to convince him to come to the JOCC where he was urgently needed. He'd once asked Rube why he was called that, and the answer was "Goldberg, man", which wasn't an answer at all as far as Raj was concerned. But Rube did know his stuff.

"Listen, talk to Sombra. He got a sweet deal when he came in. You can, too." Raj knew his words sounded desperate, even in non-spoken form. In fact, he was desperate.

"Look, my little brown buddy," Rube answered. "I don't want a sweet deal. I want to be left alone. Once they know about me, they'll be looking over my shoulder all the time. Find someone else."

"Rube, do you trust me?"

The answer was an icon, showing a head and hands repeatedly bowing. Followed closely by 'you da man'.

"Where do you live?"

"What does that have to do with anything?"

"Humor me."

"Okay, I'm in a suburb of NYC. Why?"

"Dude, if you don't come help, you've got about four days to live. I'm serious."

"WTF you talkin' about?"

"Get here and I'll tell you, but I'm serious. This is not a joke."

"See you in a couple of hours, man. This better be legit. And if Sombra got a sweet deal, I want one, too. I want whatever he got, plus they've got to admit where they're keeping Elvis and John Lennon. I want to meet them in person. Now, what's the address?"

Raj sent him directions, and told him to bring as many programmable chips as he could grab on the way. Then he went to talk to Sam.

"Okay, I've got another one of my guys coming in. Same deal as before. Can you believe he actually thinks the government is hiding Elvis and John Lennon? He wants to meet them." Raj withdrew from Sam's doorway, having a good laugh at the expense of his friend. Sam gave Luke a look of comic despair.

"Remember I told you he had a crazy hobby? I guess all of them do," remarked Luke.

"What's his?" asked Sam.

"He thinks we're hiding aliens at Area 51." Luke started to laugh, but Sam's raised eyebrows stopped him. "Are we?" Luke asked.

Roy was putting the finishing touches on his third hummingbird bot when Raj came through the door with a hulking man of about forty. "Roy, this is Rube. Rube, Roy. Tell him what you need, Roy."

With little surprise, Roy responded. "I need something small that can detect electromagnetic radiation in this RF range and direct this laser to cut it," he said, holding up an even tinier version of his nanolaser. Raj was awed by the progress Roy had made. The man was scary, that's all he could say.

"Ah I see, something like Van Eck phreaking?" When

The Sword of Cyrus

Roy and Raj gave him identical puzzled looks, he continued. "Van Eck phreaking is the process of eavesdropping on the contents of a CRT or LCD display by detecting its electromagnetic emissions. We can do the same with computers."

"Yea something like that," said Roy

And this electromagnetic radiation - what's going to be producing that?" asked Rube.

"Why, the battery in the bomb itself," Roy said, with Raj semaphoring 'no' frantically with his hands.

"Bomb? What bomb?" said Rube.

There was no choice but to bring him up to speed, and it was a very shaken Rube who turned to Raj and said, "What if I can't do it in time?"

Raj said, "Then here will be as good a place to die as New York City, yes?"

"Of course I can do that, with a bomb about to explode in my ass, nothing is impossible." said Rube, his white face negating the sarcasm.

Chapter Forty-Nine

WE HAVE NO CHOICE BUT TO GO WITH YOUR PLANS

July 25, 2020, D-day minus four; Washington, D.C.

With an incentive like that, Rube worked through the night on programming his chips to do what Roy needed. He couldn't understand how the other man could be so calm, until it was time for Roy's four-hour break the next morning and Salome came to get him. As she led Roy away by the hand, Rube got it. He wondered if they had a beautiful woman lined up to relax him when it was time for his break. Speaking of which, he'd worked through the night, during which Roy had already disappeared for several hours. When would it be his turn?

He'd written the program and tested it for bugs, but the only proof he would have that it worked would be to burn it to the chip and test it. Since he couldn't test the chip without Roy's presence, Rube turned to the desktop he'd been shown to for his work and pinged Raj on their private chat line.

"Do I get a break? Who do I talk to?"

"Hang on, buddy, sorry, I didn't think about it. Be right there."

Roy had been gone for most of an hour when Raj appeared, with an aide in tow. "We'll get you a hotel for next time, but this guy will show you a place where you can sack out for now. We'll wake you in four hours."

"Is that how long Roy gets?" Rube asked, leading Raj to believe he was acting a bit like a prima donna.

"That's how long anyone gets. You want more?" Raj's voice had turned cold.

"No, man, I want you to wake me when Roy is due back. It's time to test these bastards."

Raj felt a little small for leaping to the wrong conclusion. "Oh, sorry, man. I guess I'm not getting enough sleep myself."

Rube was out like a sucker-punched boxer before the aide had left the room. The next thing he knew, someone was shaking his shoulder, and he came up fighting. He'd knocked the aide into the door before he was awake enough to remember where he was.

"Sorry. Is Roy back?"

Rubbing his sore jaw, the aide nodded, and silently led the way back to the lab. He'd use a broomstick or something to wake this guy next time.

The next hour was consumed in integrating the firmware chip into the hummingbird's control system. Now all that remained was to mock up a bomb in one of the drones and see if it worked.

Aside from a few hours' break in his nearby hotel room three times a day, Roy hadn't been outside in more than a week. As he followed the aide who was leading them outside for the test, he reflected on how much more pleasant it would be in Boulder this time of year. Even Pasadena was nicer than D.C. in July, from his limited experience. Boulder was the best of all. He considered whether he'd be willing to give up teaching if the Rossler Foundation made him a permanent offer. Then he realized it wouldn't matter if this experiment failed. They were out of time.

With Rube controlling the drone, and several of the key team members looking on, Roy launched his hummingbird, which was now programmed with the hacker app to locate and intercept any object generating a Wi-Fi signal in the correct bandwidth with a matching MAC address. The hummingbird went straight for the drone and hovered below the box at the bottom for a few seconds before it dropped away and returned to Roy almost like a falcon to its falconer. A small cloud of smoke was visible below the drone for a few seconds. Roy and Rube retrieved the drone and went back to his lab to analyze what had happened. The men were too weary to do anything but exchange an exhausted high-five. But, they'd done it. The device worked exactly as planned.

Roy reported to Sam. They had a solution, but it still carried the very real danger of detonating the bomb instead of disabling it. However, given the time limitation, it was the best they could do.

"We have no choice but to go with your plans then," Sam said, when he'd swallowed the fistful of antacids he'd chewed. "Draw them up and give them to Sgt. Pierce," he said, indicating one of the aides. "He'll get them distributed. Thank you for your exceptional work, Dr. James.

Roy couldn't have been prouder if the president himself had saluted him.

"That also means we have to update our training plan. Are you okay to work with the top instructor and show him how this works? I'll have someone film you, so you'll only have to go through it once.

Roy was ready to drop, but it was of the utmost importance that the training begin right away. They had only a day or two before the teams bound for the other countries would have to depart to take up their stations.

Chapter Fifty

THE DEMO

Midday July 26, 2020, D-day minus four; Washington, D.C.

Ensconced in his lab in the JOCC hangar and working in four-hour time segments separated by only four hours of sleep in between, Roy had lost track of whether it was day or night as he returned to his station. He was there to inspect the drones that others had prepared with mock-ups of the bombs. He was about to star in the most important demonstration of his life until this point.

As soon as he'd ascertained that the four drones with their bomb mockups and two others of a different type had been properly prepared, he sent them all outside with aides and followed at a leisurely pace. Roy worked quickly with his mind, but his body didn't care that the entire team leadership and the president of the United States were waiting for him – he walked to the beat of his own drum.

When he reached the assemblage, he nodded to the drone operators, each of whom sent their respective birds aloft. The object of this demonstration was to prove that his laser-equipped hummingbirds could differentiate between the bomb-carrying drones and the others, first. And then that they could correctly determine where the trigger would be within the bomb and then deactivate it. To the untrained eye, the little hummingbirds looked like flying models of the real bird. Roy was the only one who fully understood that it was the nanocomputer and highly miniaturized linked cameras inside that would rapidly assess the view, make decisions, and activate the laser cutter to accurately cut the trigger battery.

When the first drone had reached a height of five hundred yards, Roy deployed his hummingbird. No human eye could have tracked it as it homed in on the drone at a speed equivalent to two-hundred miles per hour. Within seconds, it had returned to land in Roy's hand. The drone operator returned his drone to earth as well, where Roy inspected the bomb mock-up. A neat slice through the outer casing went straight through the lipstick-sized laser inside, cleaving its battery as well and rendering it useless.

Meanwhile, the other drones had risen even higher, and began circling, the two un-armed drones among the remaining three armed ones. As the assembled team members and the president watched, shading their eyes against the glare of the July mid-day sun, an all but invisible hummingbird swooped, made its decisions and returned to Roy. When all drones had been returned to base and examined, Roy determined that he'd achieved a one-hundred percent kill rate, with the unarmed drones unharmed. He acknowledged the applause and cheering with a shy smile, meeting only the eyes of his muse and lover, Salome Lane.

Chapter Fifty-One

THE FINAL PLAN

July 26, 2020, D-day minus three; Washington, D.C.

The last training session had ended and the pilots, IT personnel and hummingbird operators were on their way to their respective stations. Some would arrive only hours before D-Day, while others chafed at the wait, eager to have their part over and done so they could celebrate being alive to celebrate. They were as ready as they could be, and confident that their missions would be successful. No one was unaware of the consequences if they weren't successful. They'd be at ground zero, or rather in-air zero when the nanonukes detonated. They stood not only between the residents of the cities they were sworn to protect and death, but between themselves and death. Many had family, including young children, in those cities. No one could beat that incentive.

Lewis met with the heads of all law enforcement agencies, the National Guard standing in for local law enforcement agencies, as well as the heads of all involved foreign agencies by videoconference. They were to meet the expected attack with a standard counter-attack, which had been worked out beforehand with a handful of elite tactical experts and Roy acting as the expert in the behavior and handling of the drones and hummingbirds.

Even before the counterattack would be required, certain measures would prevent many of the terrorist operatives from entering their target areas. National Guard units, local SWAT teams and even plainclothes officers would patrol the streets from the stroke of midnight on D-Day morning to prevent entry to the city centers. People would be allowed to leave, but no one would be allowed to enter if it could be helped. Anyone protesting these orders would be arrested; anyone resisting arrest would be subject to a shoot-to-kill order at the discretion of the law enforcement officer. At six a.m. or earlier, all streets leading to the area of destruction as determined by the 10th Cycle pictures would be barricaded.

The counter-attack would be two-pronged. First, troops on the ground would be deployed early to the coordinates that had been determined as the most-likely places to find the MCUs, and to attempt to intercept before the drones were even launched. Second, if drones were launched, the Hawkeyes above the city would take control of them and fly them to coordinates they would report to hummingbird operators who would be standing by to disarm the laser triggers.

The plans weren't perfect. If just one nuke was detonated, not only would the troops and hummingbird operators who happened to be within the blast zone be lost, but the EMP would render any electronics technology within the EMP's effect useless. The mission was simple. Avoid detonation at all costs.

Chapter Fifty-Two

WE'VE GOT ONE

July 26, 2020, D-day minus three; Washington, D.C.

Salome was shaking him awake, Roy realized, in the midst of a dream of being tossed around in a rowboat on a rough sea. As soon as he made the realization, he came fully awake and looked first at the bedside clock. Three a.m. He'd slept more than six hours. He jumped up in a panic, only to feel Salome's hands on his shoulders, calming him.

"Roy, it's okay. Sorry, but they need you at the JOCC again. They've located a drone operator."

Roy kissed Salome quickly, pulled on a pair of pants and a shirt and headed for the door carrying his shoes. Outside stood an agent of some sort, he wasn't sure whether FBI, CIA or some other alphabet soup agency, ready to drive him the few blocks to the JOCC. He put his shoes on as they raced through the darkened streets, siren silent but emergency beacons on. He barely noticed that Salome had followed him into the car at the last minute, but he did have his shoes on, without socks, when they arrived at the destination.

Remembering to keep a sedate pace, Roy searched his pants pocket for his ID badge, then picked up the pace when he found it and hung the lanyard around his neck. At the operations center, he was met by another agent, who led him to an interrogation room. In the center, strapped down to a chair and surrounded by Sam Lewis along with several other agency leaders, sat an unimpressive-looking man in his early twenties. The most remarkable thing about him, in Roy's opinion, was that he had a mop of blonde curls, along with a long blonde beard and hate-filled blue eyes. What was this? This guy was no Arab.

"Glad you could make it, Roy. Here's the guy you wanted to talk to. Our team found a drone in his apartment, complete with what looks like one of their nasty little bombs. It's waiting for you in your lab. Anything you want to ask this fuck?"

Roy had never seen Sam so distraught. Normally, he wouldn't have called the kid a name, no matter what the provocation. Now was not the time to question it, though. He marshaled his thoughts to ask an intelligent question, though what he really wanted to know was what an American kid was doing working for the enemy. That's probably what had Sam worked up, come to think of it. He'd let the spooks ask that question. His was more urgent.

"Tell me exactly how the bombs will be triggered." he demanded, his voice betraying his tension.

The kid spat at his feet. Roy jumped back as if the gob of spittle were radioactive. An agent stepped forward and backhanded the kid. Roy looked to Sam for direction. Sam was staring at the kid.

"Did you know that your friends meant for you to die?"

Sam asked. The kid's eyes darted left, then right. He spoke for the first time since Roy entered the room.

"That's a fucking lie, infidel," he said, then clamped his lips shut. Sam gave a tired half-smile.

"No, it isn't. Play the tape, Jackson." Roy hadn't heard it before, and he didn't know the name of the man whose Russian accent now filled the room, but he could guess who it was. He just hoped the kid knew, too.

'You're aware that the overlap on the bombs will kill your operators, right Oleg? Do they know?'

'Of course not. They will be martyrs in the cause.'

Jackson stopped the recording. The kid's eyes were big, with white rims all around the pupils. "Who was that?"

"The guy who's been emailing your instructions. The spymaster for the Sword of Cyrus. He's told us everything."

With that, the kid slumped in his seat. "What are you going to do with me?" he asked.

"Well, we won't behead you, if that's what you're thinking," Sam said with heavy sarcasm. "That's for your buddies in Iran to do. All we'll do is keep you here with us until the bombs go off. If you want to live, you'll answer Dr. James's question."

The kid looked questioningly at Roy, who nodded. He hung his head and started mumbling something that Roy didn't catch. "What's that? I didn't hear you."

The kid lifted his head, threw his blonde curls out of his eyes with a toss of his head and shouted. "The bombs are triggered automatically when they reach the target GPS coordinates. All I have to do is get the drone in the air and steer it to the target then it will explode when it gets there."

Roy went cold when he heard that, but then he calmed down and analyzed everything with his usual insight.

The first thing that came to mind was that if the drone

didn't reach the target it wouldn't detonate the bomb. So that was a second line of defense – if they could take control of the drone and keep it away from the target coordinates until the trigger was disarmed, they could prevent the bomb from going off. Since the coordinates were known through Raj and Sinclair's efforts, that should be easy.

He then asked the boy, "So that means if the drone does not reach the coordinates it will not go off?"

"Yes, that's right."

But something bothered Roy. He'd heard the story of what happened when the Rosslers were attacked in the restaurant and the suicide bomber who got cold feet. His handler detonated the bomb remotely. Could the mastermind behind this plot have anticipated having one or more of the drones captured? Would he have built in a fail-safe to trigger it no matter what?

Roy had the drone brought to the lab and took it apart, noting with satisfaction that his earlier assumptions had been correct. As was this one. What he found was a tiny time switch built into the trigger that would explode the bomb five minutes after takeoff. Obviously, the drone operators did not know about that either. Oleg had been right. Nothing could stop this plot from unfolding exactly as planned. Except the defensive measures that Sam Lewis's team had worked so tirelessly to fashion.

The discovery meant they had five minutes from launch to detect the drone and send the hummingbird to destroy the battery of the trigger device. It was a chilling thought, followed immediately by the realization that it changed nothing. At least he now knew how long they had to get it done. Lewis needed to know this, so it could be reported to all the defense teams.

Chapter Fifty-Three

ARE YOU SURE THAT'S A GOOD IDEA?

July 27, 2020, D-day minus two; Washington, D.C.

A major concern now was the rest of the citizens of and visitors to his nation. Harper was second-guessing the decision not to evacuate the cities. Maybe they should have. Roy couldn't guarantee that his little toys could intercept every bomb. The worst-case scenario would be if they didn't work at all, but the best case was probably that they got perhaps 90% of the bombs. That was still a lot of destruction and a lot of human lives lost. It was almost a certainty that some would slip through the defenses; however, no one knew where.

Harper thought about all of the people who didn't have concrete-and-steel reinforced shelters to hide in. Why should he survive if he let anyone harm even one of the people he'd sworn to serve and protect. He called for his Chief of Staff and told him to make arrangements for an address to both houses of Congress, as soon as possible. The man who'd served him for more than seven years hesitated.

"Mr. President, are you sure that's a good idea?" He was visibly shaking. Never before had he called his president's decisions into question. But, the reasons why they hadn't made this announcement as soon as the president had seen those pictures was no less valid now. It was his duty to remind the president of that fact, and that no doubt as many people would likely be killed by panic as by the bombs that got through. It wasn't prudent to start a stampede, and besides, it was too late.

Harper saw red for a moment. He wasn't used to having his judgment questioned, except of course in the media. He enjoyed a better rapport with the opposing party than most presidents had in recent decades, so disagreements were handled on a gentlemanly basis, privately rather than in the media. With no one else to create controversy, the Fourth Estate had sometimes willingly filled the gap, especially when any controversy involving the Rossler Foundation came up. Once the darling of the press, the Rosslers had had a bad run since the 9th Cycle virus had been discovered and inadvertently released into the world by their expedition.

Now Harper stared at his Chief of Staff, visibly defiant. Only long enough to think it through, though. When he'd come to the same conclusion, he slumped.

"You're right. It isn't a good idea, not now. The time would have been a month ago, but we all agreed, even the leaders of both parties in both Houses. All it would do is start a panic." Relieved, the Chief nodded.

"Is there anything else I can do for you, sir?" He would gladly follow Harper to the gates of Hell, if he were asked. And it was because the president had a heart and a brain both.

"No, thank you. Let me know when the Rosslers arrive."

Daniel's contingent from the Rossler Foundation and their brilliant borrowed scientist, Roy James were to have dinner at the White House, just a private affair, no others. Roy had been told he was welcome to invite a guest after someone dropped a hint to the president that a certain FBI agent had become very important to him. Salome Lane would also be joining them. Sam Lewis had declined with thanks, since he felt he needed to be with his team until the last moment.

Harper had taken a short trip to the JOCC earlier in the afternoon to get the answer to his most burning question. He waited in a private conference room for Sam Lewis, Roy James and a few key others to be brought to him. When they were assembled, he looked around and asked his question.

"Are we ready?" The answers were not the ringing affirmatives that he wanted, but given the short time they'd been working on it, they would have to do. It was Roy who'd given the firmest one.

"As we can be, Mr. President. We've done all we can." His open and honest face convinced the president that it was indeed the truth. He could only hope that it was enough.

The most maddening thing about this whole business, Harper thought, was that, since the world had not been told, he and all the other leaders whose countries were at risk had to conduct business as usual. Here he was, facing the greatest crisis in a presidency known for constant turmoil, and he had to do a stupid ceremonial signing of a popular bill on animal rights this afternoon.

The leaders of half a dozen organizations that had worked to push the bill through were due in his office at any moment to watch him sign it, with six different pens that

The Sword of Cyrus

would be distributed among the excited guests as he finished with them.

At the dinner, Harper tried one more time to convince them all to stay behind and take shelter in the bunker under the White House. But all of them said no, they want to be with their families and the Rossler Foundation staff in Boulder.

When dinner was over and the guests were about to depart, the president, convinced that nothing he could say would change their minds, thanked them all for their hard work, with a special thanks to Daniel. "Daniel, you and Sarah have been such good friends and supporters. Please tell Sarah thank you, and give her a hug from me, for that encouraging message from Isaiah she gave me on that day when I was so down."

To Roy, clasping his hand with both of his own, Harper said, "Young man, you have earned the undying gratitude of our nation, if not the world, for your work here. Do take care of the lovely woman you brought here with you. Assuming everything goes as planned, I'll see you again soon."

Chapter Fifty-Four

DON'T BE A FOOL

July 28, 2020, D-day minus one; Washington, D.C.

"Roy, don't be a fool. Let the military handle it," Daniel urged. Salome had called him in a panic, saying Roy was insisting on being in one of the Hawkeye aircraft to control his hummingbird and take over any drones that they couldn't prevent from being launched.

"I'm the one who knows my birds the best," Roy insisted.

"But you can't be everywhere. You've sent out the video that all of the radio operators in the aircraft have studied for the last two days. They know their business - they've been doing stuff like this for years." Daniel's argument wasn't winning any points, he could see.

"Not just like this. There's never been anything just like this," said Roy, with a stubborn set to his jaw.

Daniel changed tactics. "I think you just want to go up in one of those weird planes, like a little kid. What if your presence there interferes with the mission? How would you

The Sword of Cyrus

feel if you miss one of the drones and the guy whose place you took might have disabled it?"

"I won't miss, Daniel. That's the point. I'm more prepared for this mission than anyone else." With that, Roy turned and walked away, done with the conversation and his mind made up.

Daniel wasn't through, though. He patted a frantic Salome on the arm and went looking for Sam Lewis, who turned out to be on break.

"Let me know when he's available," he told the aide who gave him that information. "It's urgent I talk to him in the next few hours."

Raj had built a database of the strike zones, and had sorted them in order of time. They knew already that it wouldn't be a coordinated strike, but one that was designed to take out the most civilians possible based on traffic patterns in the target cities. Washington, D.C., wouldn't be the first to be hit; the beginning would be in Australia. The terrorists were so confident that nothing could stop this that they didn't care that it would warn the US of what was coming. In fact, they were bargaining for the opposite effect – that the US would think they would not be attacked. Of course, by now, the Sword of Cyrus knew that the CIA knew something; they just didn't know the extent of it.

Security agencies overseas had been given the keys to repel the attack, just as soon as the various steps to do so were discovered and refined. A strong worry was that they hadn't had time to assemble enough of the bird-bots to attack every bomb, just as the same might be the case in the US. As Roy had told the president, they were as ready as they could be. Satellites and high-level spy drones had been dispatched to watch as the attacks began, their operating countries hoping that there would be nothing to see.

At the JOCC, tension was high. The days of activity that made it look like a kicked-over anthill were at an end. The activity was now elsewhere. Every target city in the US was assembling Roy's bird-bots as quickly as hands could be found to help, and contingencies were being planned for tomorrow's attack. If there were a nearby military base, the Hawkeye aircraft were being staged there, with others at municipal airports to take over if the military bases were hit first. The more people who had to be briefed about what was happening, the more risk that someone would leak it to the public and cause a panic.

After the near-miss in which Harper considered informing everyone in Congress, it had been discussed at dinner, and the consensus was to activate the emergency broadcast network as soon as attacks began, since there was now no way to contain a breaking news story that hit the internet. Americans would know hours ahead of time for the attacks on their own cities that something big was going on elsewhere in the world. Even now, the White House PR department was working on wording that would be short, accurate and hopefully prevent everyone running into the streets and creating chaos just as the military was trying to intercept the bombs.

Roy had won his argument. Even after Daniel protested to Sam in the hope that he'd put a stop to it, Roy's calm reasoning was convincing. His reflexes were impeccable, and he'd been controlling those bird-bots for longer than anyone in the world. With arguably the most important man in the US, if not the world, President Harper, at stake, it should be he who was at the controls of the bots protecting the central part of D.C. To Daniel's great disappointment, Sam agreed.

Daniel was preparing to leave for Boulder within the

hour, but, along with approving Roy's desire to be in the air to defend his country, Sam had now informed everyone that he intended to remain in the JOCC. As far as Daniel was concerned, it was a foolhardy gesture. No one should be there. The entire operation should move to the deepest basements they could find, in his opinion. Sam was adamant that there wasn't time. He and his crew were still coordinating the defenses. Taking the time to move the operation would put that operation in jeopardy. Besides, he was busy also coordinating the deployment of National Guard troops.

"That alone is going to alert the populace. You'll need those guys to direct traffic while everyone flees the city." It was Daniel's parting shot, and it didn't sway Sam at all.

Chapter Fifty-Five

July 29, 2020, D-day

The mood was mixed in the Deep Underground Command Center, acronym DUCC, pronounced like 'duck' as in 'duck, bend over, and kiss your ass goodbye'. The latest in a line of hardened shelters for the use of the president and other VIPs in times of extreme threat, DUCC had state-of-the art communication and video links, along with room for everyone needed to operate the country in such times. Harper had considered riding out D-Day in Night Watch, but Sam Lewis and his military advisers had convinced him it would be better to be stuck underground for a few days in case of an EMP than to fall out of the sky in an aircraft that had lost its electronics.

Harper, the First Lady, essential members of his staff and everyone else who now occupied DUCC had been escorted there at midnight on July 27th, there to wait as D-Day commenced in Australia, some fourteen hours ahead of Washington time. Some of the occupants were like overstimulated children, fretting and exhibiting nerves, others business-like and serious. The president and Mrs. Harper spent much of the time in prayer.

D-day for Australia starting at GMT +10

It began on the eastern seaboard of Australia with Sydney and Brisbane, at eight a.m. Canberra, the capital, plus three other major cities erupted in confusion as the Emergency Alert System initiated phone messages to stay at home if the citizens weren't already on their way to work, and to turn around if they were. They had waited too long; they should have made the calls at 6 o'clock. The government had decided that the most efficient way for their military to apprehend the MCUs was to keep the citizenry out of the way. Unfortunately, with not enough prior warning, more confusion than compliance was created. With several major traffic routes in all cities in gridlock because of it, troops on the ground couldn't get through in a timely manner, and many resorted to getting out of their vehicles and running through the streets to their assigned posts.

At the nine-fifteen a.m. mark, the photos had shown the cities in rubble.

But, the first indication that the future had been changed through the efforts of Sam Lewis and his team was when forty of the 50 bombers destined to launch bombs in Sydney, Melbourne, Brisbane and Canberra were arrested before they could launch their drones. Eight of the remaining ten bombs were intercepted and disabled by the bird-bots, which the Aussies had renamed cuckoos for the real bird's tendency to lay their eggs in other birds' nests.

Two small bombs exploded in Sydney - planted by hand at two of the most iconic Australian sites the Sydney harbor bridge and the famous Sydney Opera house, putting all Australians on the warpath.

It was around seven-thirty on the evening of the previous day in Washington, D.C., when the reports started to come in. Prayers of gratitude went up that Australia had so far been spared heavy losses. Half an hour later, Adelaide reported no losses. The Australian air force patrolled the skies above the cities and also all military bases. The terrorists who were supposed to blow up Pine Gap decided to fly out there in a light airplane and were picked up by two fighter jets and forced to land and arrested more than 150 kilometers from their target.

An hour and a half after Adelaide, Perth reported that they arrested six of the ten bombers before they could launch their drones, the cuckoos took out three in the air and the fourth one they dumped in the sea after they took control of it. In that case, the cuckoo failed to launch properly from the overhead plane. The bomb didn't explode at all - it appeared that the water disabled all electronics inside, including the laser trigger. This was new and good information to be passed on to other countries - if the hummingbirds fail, try to dump the drones in water if there is water nearby.

In Australia the two explosions in Sydney caused sixteen deaths and forty-five injuries ranging from severed limbs to minor cuts and bruises.

D-day for Oleg Zlatovski

It would be another four hours before Moscow and St. Petersburg, the next targets, were out of the woods. After Australia reported their losses, Sam Lewis was in a vicious mood. He sent for Oleg Zlatovski and his niece, Tamara, and had Tamara waiting in a connecting room when Oleg was brought to him. It was ten-thirty in the evening, a little over ten hours to go before the attacks were expected to start in his city, and Russia, Israel and the UK at risk in the meantime. His orders were to cuff Zlatovski to the chair and have him wait.

By eleven, Sam considered it sufficient time to have completely terrorized Zlatovski. Now he'd see just how quickly he could break this evil man. He opened the door and strolled in, a half smile pasted on his lips.

"Good evening, Oleg. I trust you have been well cared-for during your stay with us." Sweat was rolling down Oleg's face. He'd been told nothing of the preparations that were waiting for the nanonukes.

"For the love of God," Oleg said, "we must leave here!" He apparently saw no irony at all in calling on a deity whom he did not believe in and had been officially denied to exist by his old country's government.

"Oh, I think we'll stay," said Sam, smiling a little more broadly at the desperation in Oleg's expression. "I thought you'd like to be here to get the reports when Moscow and St. Petersburg are hit by the nasty little nukes your employers deployed there."

Oleg blanched. "How did you...?" His eyes widened when Sam threw down copies of the pictures showing Moscow in ruin. "Where the devil? This hasn't happened yet, it can't have! The attacks were to take place..."

"On the first day of Hajj, yes, I know. If you'll think about it, you'll realize that it has already started, on the other side of the world. We have reports from Australia. The pictures came from the 10th Cycle Library. I'm sure you'll have questions." Sam pressed a button that unlocked the connecting door, which was behind him. He wanted to see Oleg's face when Tamara came in. It was a very satisfying experience.

Oleg went even whiter than before and the white ring around his pupils made his eyes look as if they were about to pop out of their sockets.

"You told me you would protect me if I told you everything!" he cried. Tamara had her little dagger in her hand. "You promised!"

"Oh, no, Oleg, I did no such thing. I told her she couldn't talk to you *yet*. It's time. Tamara, I'd appreciate it if you let him live until we know about Moscow." Sam didn't want to even hint to Oleg that Moscow would probably survive, and St. Petersburg as well. Let it be his last conscious thought - that he'd failed, and his fate was sealed no matter who had him. "You're sure you don't want to send him to meet with his employer, Dalir Jahandar? I have been told that Jahandar has been frantically trying to reach him the last few days. " Sam asked, bewildering Oleg further.

"No, thank you," Tamara said. "This is for me to do. I suppose you do not want it to happen here?" Sam nodded.

"I'll send an escort to take you somewhere more… appropriate, in about five hours." He left the room, with Oleg howling his terror at being left alone with the niece he'd abused so brutally as a child. It was not up to the US justice system to punish him; he was a Russian citizen and the crimes had happened there. Sam had not a moment's remorse.

D-day for Russia GMT +3

In Russia, estimates indicated they were looking for about two-hundred and fifty of the bombs in Moscow and St. Petersburg combined. Police and military ground forces picked up 60% of the terrorists in their calculated positions, about one hundred and fifty of them, before they could launch their drones.

Of the remaining drones, some eighty-five were disabled with the hummingbirds. Several malfunctioning hummingbirds failed to launch properly, allowing one bomb in Moscow and two in St Petersburg to detonate, fortunately near the ground. The rest, thanks to timely information from Australia, they managed to dump into nearby bodies of water, which prevented them from exploding

Russia tragically, ended up with about 1,500 people dead, most of them civilians, and close to 4,000 injured. The Red Plain was destroyed, The Kunstkamera, the Palace Bridge, and parts of Peter and Paul Cathedral were destroyed by one bomb in St Petersburg. The other took out the Winter Palace and other landmarks. It seemed by now that the terrorists had wanted to strike at the national pride of the target nations, as much as at their governments and population.

D-day for Israel GMT +2

The Israelis turned out to be the most efficient of all countries. From their many years of experience living with constant threat and dealing with terrorist attacks such as Hamas attacking them out of Gaza every chance they got, they knew how to handle situations like these.

Their armed forces had instructions to shoot and kill MCU operators on sight. The Dome of the Rock was saved, and the highly efficient Mossad led the Israeli Army defense troops in disarming every bomb, a remarkable feat, since there were enough bombs deployed there to wipe out every Israeli in the country.

Dalir Jahandar had hated Israel more than any other government, and his failure to wipe Israel off the map was complete.

The death toll was zero - no bomb exploded and not one hair of any Israeli's head was harmed.

D-day for the UK GMT

Across the United Kingdom, most of the three hundred bombs were concentrated on targets in London. A handful in Belfast and Glasgow proved to be no problem. London's two hundred and seventy or so were stopped before they could be launched by the arrest or shooting of their operators, save thirty, twenty-five of which were disabled by the hummingbirds.

Of the remaining five, one exploded and took the Big Ben down and one took part of Cambridge University off the map. The rest the Hawkeyes managed to dump in the

Thames. The UK's toll was fifty dead and about three times that many injured.

D-day for the USA GMT -5

For Harper and the others in the DUCC, the day had already been long, beginning with the first images and reports from Sydney hours before, and continuing with various expressions of dismay and relief as the nine a.m. hour marched from east to west across Asia and Europe.

They had only a few hours to rest before it would start again with their own city and a few others on the east coast. From then, it would be unrelenting until well into the afternoon, since the US comprised no fewer than five time zones. So far, no images of either Alaska or Hawaii had been discovered. Everyone hoped that none had been missed. Ground troops were on alert in both states, but Hawkeyes, which were already spread pretty thin, weren't posted.

As soon as they'd heard from the Prime Minister that casualties in London were under control, Harper and most of the others did their best to rest and sleep for a couple of hours before being awakened with offers of breakfast at six a.m. Eastern time. It would start soon, but the mood was now lighter. So far, the reports were good. Did they dare hope that the outcome would be the same – or better – here in the US?

Sam Lewis had experienced much of the same ups and downs as those in the DUCC had. He was with a skeleton crew at the JOCC, and by six a.m. all were alert and waiting. A few blocks away in a hotel room where they'd shared the past couple of weeks, Roy and Salome said an emotional goodbye before Roy departed for the naval base from whence his Hawkeye would take off and Salome joined the others in the JOCC.

In Boulder, the extended Rossler Foundation family had watched the events of the previous day until the wee hours of the morning and then most had succumbed to exhausted sleep. Daniel's alarm was set to wake him at five a.m., an hour before the earliest attacks were expected in D.C. He'd wake the others, and would call Roy just before his plane was scheduled to take off.

One other group in the US had also watched the way it unfolded. Separately, because they didn't know of each other, the drone operators who were waiting for their big moment to release their payloads of anthrax on people fleeing the cities realized that the big moment was not going to come. If the other countries, even Russia, with its inefficient bureaucracy, could escape their fate and prevent the nukes from detonating, surely the US could do the same. One by one, the terrorists began an exodus that would see some of them captured at airports serving major cities, and others attempting to make their way out of the country against the tide of neighbors to the south trying to get in. Their dangerous weapons were left behind to be found by landlords cleaning out abandoned apartments. By that time, though, word of the potential danger would have been disseminated, and most landlords who found the drones in their properties would know to call the police, who would send decontamination crews to handle it.

The Sword of Cyrus

By nine a.m. Eastern, hundreds of drone operators in New York, Boston, Washington, D.C., Langley, Virginia. Norfolk, Virginia and Cape Canaveral, Florida were cooling their heels in local jails. Those who managed to launch their drones before being arrested watched in awe as circling aircraft that looked like aliens in UFOs had them captured took control of the drones and sent them spiraling to near ground level, where crazy hummingbirds attacked them, each emitting a small puff of smoke before being lowered gently the rest of the way to the ground. Only a few had an inkling of what had been averted.

The same was true for the bulk of the American people. Thousands were kept home by the simple expedient of sending out Emergency Broadcast System alerts, beginning at six a.m. in each time zone. A few hardy souls were already on the road by then on the East Coast, especially near New York and Washington, but those were turned away well before they reached the cities by National Guard units barricading the highways.

Roy and his military counterparts circled their assigned cities in their Hawkeyes, running the software hack that would detect drone-generated wifi hotspots as soon as they showed up. But only a few did, thanks to the efforts of the ground troops. Along the East Coast, D-Day was, as Harper had hoped, a non-event.

The Central Time Zone and Mountain Time Zone looked like reruns. One drone did manage to detonate on the Pacific Coast. The main casualty was the Hollywood sign, with no known human victims.

Chapter Fifty-Six

D-DAY IN TEHRAN

In Tehran, the Sword of Cyrus were gathered around a state-of-the-art wall display showing satellite feeds from across the world. As the time for the first bombs to detonate drew near, Dalir Jahandar, sitting with calm dignity at the head of the table, spoke in a soft voice. "Our time has come."

Indeed, when the bombs exploded in Sydney, a grin split his face and the others cheered. But, something was wrong. Only a few of the bombs detonated. What had happened? Dalir and the others sat in tense anticipation of the others, only to be disappointed as time after time, the devastating attack that had been planned went awry with little effect.

As they waited a few hours for the next show, Dalir sat in stony silence, while the others whispered among themselves. What did this mean? Why were only a few of the nukes detonated? They'd been told hundreds would utterly destroy the targets, but in fact, only one or two in each city had done so little damage as to be laughable. A few stole looks at Dalir, reading his stony features correctly as rage. Would they somehow be blamed? Were they in danger?

When the Russian attack fizzled as had the Australian, louder murmuring alerted Dalir to the fact that he may soon be faced with a mutiny. These men had contributed millions of dollars to a global attack that was beginning to look like a cheap fireworks display for a minor holiday, on the poorest of streets. Pinning all his hopes on the devastation of Washington, D.C., he watched stoically as Israel reported nothing at all and London was barely touched.

Unable to face his lieutenants on the several hour wait for the nine a.m. hour to arrive on America's east coast, he slammed out of the room for a brisk walk around the gardens. He returned to a room that had been abandoned by half of his men. The others were afraid to look at him. Jahandar knew it was over before the hour was even done in Washington. How was it possible? It was as if the enemy had known exactly where the operatives would be and had picked them up before they could launch their drones.

Jahandar was angrier than he'd ever been, even at the time when, walking away from the hospital where his dead family lay, he'd uttered the oath that led to this day. He could feel the silent condemnation of his associates. Where had he gone wrong? How had the infidels discovered the plot and more important, how had they foiled it? He needed a scapegoat, or they would turn on him. Millions of their dollars, no, billions had gone into the preparations. They'd been promised the spoils of war, and now there would be none.

"Oleg Zlatovski is responsible for this. I will find him and behead him on world television," he declared. A snort from behind his back told him that he was losing his leadership. He turned and played his hole card.

"All is not lost. We still have the means to utterly destroy the United States, even if today's bombs fail as they have so far." A few faces showed interest, so he went on. "We will wait, assess the damage. But, I have learned that the US has a terrible vulnerability at its heart. We can exploit that with only a few nanonuclear devices and suicide bombers to carry them."

As skeptical looks began to replace the interest, Dalir hurried to the punch line. "There is a chain of active volcanoes stretching from the center of their state of Wyoming nearly to the west coast," he said. "Their Yellowstone National Park is in the center of a massive caldera that rises and falls with the magma underneath. If we were to drop a few of our nukes into the naturally-occurring fissures within the park and trigger them, it would annihilate the US. I can show you the research that their own scientists have done to map this super volcano, as they call it."

Dalir's most trusted lieutenant came to his support. "Only a fool would brag about a vulnerability under his country," he said. "Infidels are so arrogant."

"Just so," agreed Dalir. Assured that he'd bought some time, he returned to the study of what little destruction his attack had created so far. It would be quiet for a few hours now, as they waited for the nine a.m. mark in the rest of the US, but he had little hope of any difference.

By the time the day ended in L.A. the Sword of Cyrus was a defeated group of people.

Chapter Fifty-Seven

ALL CLEAR

Sam Lewis was the one who called and gave the all-clear when several hours had passed with no further incidents.

President Harper emerged first, to be whisked away immediately by Secret Service agents. A briefing was awaiting him, though communications had been ongoing throughout the attack. The nine a.m. hour had now passed in all American time zones except Hawaii's, which hadn't warranted an attack, it appeared. It had been twenty-four hours since Australia caught the first wave.

The world was still shell-shocked, and recriminations were just now beginning to come in for the relatively small number of people who'd taken it on themselves to keep the rest of the world in the dark about what they knew. Leaders of some governments would be toppled by the backlash.

Harper had already planned for it, and would address the nation at 6 p.m. to explain his actions and tender his resignation if that is what the people wanted. Before that, he would have to face Congress. Ever since the administration just prior to his, the words executive action had been highly suspect, so he didn't expect to get off lightly. Nevertheless, he stood by his decisions. He called Daniel to let him know that a grateful nation might soon be beating a path to his door.

"This evening's address will detail what we knew, when we knew it, and the work that went into saving the day. I'll also suggest that we concentrate on recovery and reconstruction, rather than retaliation. You'll probably see on the ten o'clock news how it went over, so wish me luck."

Thanks to some advance PR work among news analysts and among senior Congressional leaders, Harper's press conference received more praise than condemnation. By the ten o'clock news broadcast in Boulder, he was being praised for avoiding mass panic and handling the threat with aplomb. Harper's legacy would go down in the history books as an administration that had faced countless serious challenges and come out on top, every time.

As it turned out for the first time in many, many decades the American people rallied behind their president with a huge majority – polls showed an unprecedented approval rating of 85%. Harper had now led them through two of the worst crises in the recorded history over the last few years. There was some talk of repealing the Twenty-Second Amendment to the Constitution, so that he could run for president for another two terms. Good presidents were hard to come by and if you manage to get one why let him go? The American people wanted a man like Harper to take them into the future.

Harper himself would quash that notion. He was well aware that another crisis such as the last two would seriously undermine his health. Esther deserved his full attention in their golden years, and he would not deny her that. Besides,

The Sword of Cyrus

he was tired. He needed nothing more than a long vacation, say, for the rest of his life.

At about eleven, Daniel's cell phone rang and a familiar voice greeted him.

"Thanks for always being in my corner, buddy."

"Thanks for always being in ours, Mr. President," Daniel laughed. "When are you going to come out for a vacation?"

"You can count on seeing me for a vacation right after I hand over the reins, buddy," the president answered. "But, I'm afraid you and your associates will be needed here again before that."

"Is something else wrong?" Daniel asked, concerned.

"It depends on how you look at it. Congress would like to have a word with you." Harper had to struggle to keep his big smile out of his voice, but he succeeded.

"Uh-oh," said Daniel. "Who all do they want there?"

"All of you," Harper said. "You and Sarah, Luke, Raj, that crazy Irishman and the mad scientist...you'd better have them all bring their wives, too. They could be here for a while."

Daniel couldn't imagine why all of them would be summoned, but if the president said so, it was good enough for him. "We'll be there as soon as we can, Nigel. Will you put in a good word for us? We didn't mean to cause all this havoc."

"I'll do what I can. When can we expect you here?"

"We'll be there tomorrow afternoon. I think we might as well charter a plane, with so many of us, I'll call you when we get there."

"See you then."

Harper directed his Chief of Staff to be on the alert for

a chartered plane with a flight plan to the capital. There were arrangements to make.

At three p.m. on the following afternoon, Daniel stepped off the chartered plane first, with Sarah right behind him, little Nick in her arms. They had decided to take a trip to Asheville to see Daniel's parents when this was done, assuming Daniel was still a free man after Congress got through with him. One by one, the others descended the short flight of stairs, gathering at the bottom where a military escort in dress uniform waited with several limousines.

Daniel looked at the cars in confusion. The military escort suggested they were being taken in to custody, but he would have expected Suburbans, not limos, in that case. As Roy, the last to leave the plane, reached the bottom of the stairs, the ranking officer, a general if Daniel knew his insignia, snapped off a perfect salute. Now Daniel was baffled. That wasn't military protocol.

The officer spoke. "Mr. Rossler, please take this car." He then began efficiently directing each individual or couple to separate cars. When he came to Raj, he asked, "Where is Mrs. Sankaran?"

Defensively, Raj growled that she was due to deliver their first child any day, and he would hope to be home to welcome the baby. The general directed him and Raj into a car by themselves.

Daniel found the President of the United States waiting in his car. After an exclamation of surprise, he took Nick from Sarah and handed him to Harper, then helped Sarah in, finally following himself. "Nigel, what is this?"

"You'll see," said Harper, keeping a straight face with

difficulty. Before any further words were exchanged, the limos made a wide U-turn and fell into a line, heading for a destination that Harper refused to reveal.

Less than an hour later, they were dropped off at the Capitol building. "Straight into the lion's den, huh?" remarked Daniel, who by now had relaxed somewhat. This didn't seem to be an arrest. Perhaps Congress just wanted to know how they had allowed such an egregious security lapse. It was too bad the wives would be forced to sit and watch their husbands be grilled. Sarah, of course, would be by his side as co-founder of the Rossler Foundation. He only hoped that little Nick wouldn't start a ruckus after his long plane ride. So far, he just looked in need of a nap. The rest of the Rosslerites looked as baffled as he felt, but it seemed they would soon know what this was all about.

A Congressional page escorted them into the chamber of the House of Representatives, where a throng that looked too large for the room was gathered. A hush fell over the room as Daniel, leading his cortege, stepped in. Feeling more self-conscious than he'd ever felt before, Daniel silently followed the page toward the front of the room. As soon as the last Rosslerite had entered, the doors were shut and thunderous applause broke out, frightening Nick into crying out.

By the time they reached the front of the enormous room, the applause had died away to polite clapping. Daniel and his group stepped up and gathered center stage, directed by the page. He looked around, aware for the first time that the president had slipped away somewhere.

From the wings, President and Mrs. Harper emerged, carrying a large tray, on which were several objects that glinted gold. Daniel couldn't make them out until the president stepped in front of him, facing him and away from the audience.

"Daniel Rossler, for especially meritorious contributions to the security and national interests of the United States and world peace, you are hereby awarded the Presidential Medal of Freedom, with distinction." Daniel fought to keep his jaw from dropping as the president pinned a blue ribbon with white edges, bearing a silver eagle with its wings spread, and from it dangling a gold medal of five spread-winged eagles in a pentagon. Each eagle stood upon a red enamel over gold pentagon, with a white star superimposed. Within the star, the center was a blue circle, with a pattern of thirteen gold stars representing the original thirteen colonies.

Tears came to Daniel's eyes as the president moved to Sarah, took Nick from her and handed him to Daniel, and repeated the ceremony. One by one, he presented the medals to Luke, Sinclair, Raj and Roy. Sally and Martha each kissed their husbands right after their medals were pinned on, to applause from the floor. Raj was stunned when his medal was awarded. In one part of his mind, he wished that Sushma had been beside him for this moment, and in another, he regretted that his hacker friends, two of whom had been especially helpful in averting the latest crisis, weren't here to share in the honors. Roy couldn't keep a boyish grin off his face as his medal was pinned on. From nowhere, Salome appeared to give him a kiss on the cheek.

With no other medals to award today, though the government employees, including Salome would all receive special recognition from their agencies, Harper stood and faced the joint session of Congress, with the First Lady at his side, smiling brilliantly. On his signal, the applause broke out again and continued for several minutes. Harper used the cover of the noise to speak in Roy's ear.

"I hope I'll get an invitation?

Confused, Roy asked, "Invitation to what?"

Harper flicked his eyes to Salome, standing on Roy's other side. "To the wedding, of course! Esther and I love weddings."

As the applause died down, Roy looked wildly to his right and left, and out into the audience. Could he do it? Would it be appropriate? Would he be able to get the words out without stuttering and embarrassing himself? Almost without realizing it, he was sinking to one knee, holding Salome's hand. Her face registered shock. What was he doing?

In a fog, Roy captured Salome's other hand, and in a sudden hush, said, "Salome, w-will you m-marry me?" He was so relieved to get the words out with just a minor stumble that he was startled when she shouted Yes! And pulled him up to kiss her. The world faded for a moment, and when his ears began to work again, the room had erupted in a standing ovation for the first proposal ever to be made by Presidential decree.

Chapter Fifty-Eight

July 30, 2020; D-day for the New Persian Empire

The Ayatollah Khorasani was pacing the room, his hands crossed behind his back, when the Director of Reconstruction, Ahmad Ahmadi and twelve others were shown into his presence.

Khorasani looked gray, Dalir thought. He turned gray himself at the first words from Khorasani's mouth.

"What have you done, Ahmadi? I've just heard from President Harper. These are very troublesome accusations."

Jahandar had no doubts about their future, especially when Khorasani rang an old-fashioned hand bell and thirteen men with wickedly sharp scimitars appeared from a side entrance.

Next in the Rossler Foundation Mysteries Series

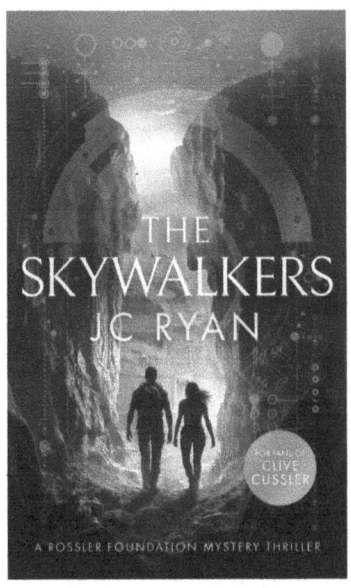

vinci-books.com/skywalkers

A 50,000-year-old letter and an ancient beast that hunts by blood.

Daniel Rossler stumbles upon a haunting letter from the distant past that threatens to reshape the future of humanity. The ancient message, written over 50,000 years ago, speaks of a beast that hunts by blood, an invisible messenger of death from the sky and a chilling warning: the freedom and very essence of humankind are at stake.

Turn the page for a free preview…

The Skywalkers: Chapter One

THE PROPHET

In the aftermath of 9/11 Western governments and their security agencies were in turmoil. Congressional oversight committees, news media and conspiracy theorists all demanded to know - how did this happen? Why did we not see this coming? What could we have done to prevent it? What can we do now? Investigations were conducted; findings and recommendations were made and heads rolled. Whether in public or in secret, consequences were felt.

To this day, only a select few people knew that the real findings of the investigations were dramatically different from the official conclusions reached by the government's 9/11 Commission.

The "chance" discovery of suspicious Wall Street activity prior to the attack, by a young whiz kid, shocked the CIA and FBI to their foundation. It took a beautiful twenty something old college psychology graduate less than an hour to rub their noses in the information that was there right in front of their eyes for years.

If they'd just bothered to look, she pointed out, they

The Sword of Cyrus

would have seen the escalation of the sale of American and United Airlines stocks over the months prior to Al-Qaeda operatives hijacking the planes that would crash into the Twin Towers and Pentagon. What she showed them was put under wraps in less than an hour and she was offered a job with the FBI on the spot.

While he rattled the American military saber in public, eventually winning consent for his plan to root out terrorism, the president's instructions in private were unambiguous. "Do whatever it takes to make sure this never happens again."

Salome James, head of security at the Rossler Foundation for the past twelve months, top FBI profiler and analyst, recipient of the Congressional Medal of Honor for her heroic actions during the Sword of Cyrus crisis two years ago, was sitting at her desk, looking at The Prophet dashboard on her computer screen.

She was busy comparing month to month data on the "Calamity Indicator", as the operatives called the part of the dashboard that indicated suspicious activities. Deeply engrossed in her thoughts, she murmured, unconscious that she spoke aloud, "That red line has moved two clicks higher since last month." In the last six months it had been going in only one direction – up. At this rate it would trigger the alarm bell in another two months. *What is causing this continuous uptick? I have to take a closer look.*

The Prophet, the most sophisticated, broad-ranging data collection and analysis software on the planet, had been developed as top priority and in ultimate secrecy in the months following the embarrassing revelations by that whiz kid.

A smile played around Salome's lips as she remembered the day that had changed her life. She would never know where she got the guts to do it. It must have been the forwardness of her youth. How could she ever forget what it felt like to walk into the FBI's offices in New York City, into a room full of experienced and hardened FBI operatives and turned them on their heads. How their faces had turned red as she showed them in a fifteen-minute PowerPoint presentation that the financial markets actually "knew" about the eminent terrorist attacks for months before it happened. In hindsight, if they'd had The Prophet available to them before the attacks, the alarm bells would have gone off fourteen days before the attacks.

Now the Prophet had been developed to help security agencies identify imminent threats to security from terrorists, rival nations, and from internal weaknesses lurking inside the global economy. It had proven itself on many occasions. It was responsible when, a few years after it was developed, the warning signs of an impending terrorist attack were picked up and again three days later in London, when a plot to blow up ten US passenger jets was thwarted, leading to the arrest of twenty four Pakistani extremists.

Salome had been part of the project team that developed The Prophet and was still a foremost expert user of the system. But, over the years, she had also realized that it had some shortcomings. She'd discussed her ideas with superiors at various occasions but by that time complacency was firmly in place yet again and her requests fell on deaf ears. With no serious terrorist attack on home soil in more than ten years, no one could see the urgency to enhance the system.

Her point for enhancements should have been driven home when The Prophet failed to alert them of the looming Sword of Cyrus crisis. Had they made the enhancement she'd been campaigning for, they would have detected the threat months before it happened and not just forty days before D-day. But again, no one had wanted to see it as urgent.

Since her permanent relocation to the Rossler Foundation a year ago, though, she'd found that she had more time to organize her thoughts about the enhancements to The Prophet. Fortunately, there was no one better than Raj Sankaran, the Rossler's resident database and computer expert and paranoiac, to help her make those enhancements.

The Skywalkers: Chapter Two

FIND ME THAT FLYING MACHINE

"I'm telling you, the man's a crackpot."

John Brideaux looked at his colleague in disgust. "So you say, but he's found some very interesting artifacts for me. I say we give him a shot."

"Ancient flying machines on the moon? Ridiculous. If you want to spend your money chasing after myths and legends, fine. I'm out."

Brideaux sat with his elbows on his writing desk, his hands tented and tapping on his chin as he considered what to do. He had no problem funding Dr. Matthew's research himself, but he did have a special group of friends and colleagues who would be disappointed at the very least if he didn't offer them the opportunity. On the other hand, if there really was such a thing as an ancient flying machine and an example could be found, he'd want to be the one to own it.

He also didn't want to suffer being the laughingstock of his friends. If his recently-departed colleague was an example of the reception he'd get, then he'd just keep the idea to himself. Act boldly, keep his cards close to his vest. That was the way to handle this. Matthews' crazy little idea had better have some merit, though. Weighing his eagerness to own the rare and unusual against the potential loss, Brideaux came down firmly on the side of the rare and unusual. A small loss, for him, meant nothing at all. He had plenty of money - more than plenty if the truth were known.

Brideaux sent for Dr. Stephen Matthews right away. The time to act was now.

"Mr. Brideaux, thank you for seeing me." Matthews approached with his right hand out as Brideaux stood to receive him.

"Of course, Stephen. You've brought me some unique pieces in the past. I'm happy to hear you out. Where'd you get this idea of ancient aircraft?"

"It's simple, really. Recently, a closely-held secret from the US space exploration program was leaked. One of the moon rocks brought back by the Apollo 11 mission had a 10-inch statue of an angel embedded in it. It's been kept under wraps since 1969."

"Extraordinary!"

"Yes, I thought so. The statue bore a remarkable resemblance to a bronze angel guardian from a medieval cemetery near Rome, but the metal was quite out of the ordinary."

"I meant that the government could keep a secret for that long."

"Oh, quite. But, as I was saying, they couldn't determine what the metal was, until someone decided it was an iron compound, found only on the moon. Do you understand what this means?"

Bemused by Matthews' enthusiasm, Brideaux shook his

head, though he had a good idea what it meant. Someone had been on the moon long enough ago for the statue to have been completely encased in moon rock. But, let Matthews tell it--he was like a small child with a new toy to show off.

"Don't you see? Someone was on the moon, *thousands of years ago*. How did they get there if ancient man didn't have aircraft? Specifically, spacecraft. And there's more."

Brideaux sat forward. More?

"Ancient Chinese texts, from perhaps 2000 BC, refer to space flight, specifically to the moon. Other accounts, long thought to be myth, are surprisingly accurate. The kicker is this. Just before landing, on the last reconnaissance pass, one of the Apollo astronauts said he had just seen what looked like a structure. His description sounded very much like a structure that the ancient Chinese texts described as having been built on the moon! Many people heard the statement clearly, but when the segment was rebroadcast, the statement was no longer there. Eleven minutes had been cut from the tapes, but too many people had heard it. NASA denies it to this day, but it's been floating around in conspiracy circles all this time."

Brideaux waited until Matthews' breathless flood of words wound down. "What's your proposal, Dr. Matthews?"

"Two-fold. If ancient China had aircraft, chances are that there are wrecked ones, or fragments of wrecked ones somewhere.

"I'd like access to the Tenth Cycle library, to see if the technology was passed down from previous civilizations. Asian civilizations have always fascinated me. How they advanced so rapidly. Since the library was discovered, I've always wondered if they had a head start based on survivors from earlier cycles."

"Interesting. Well, as it happens, I'm in a position to help you with both of those requests.

"Thank you, sir! And as for the matter of my compensation..."

"Let's start you with a grant of $50,000. That should be adequate for now. We'll revisit it if and when you need to mount an expedition."

"Thank you, Mr. Brideaux. That's most generous, most generous indeed."

"Dr. Matthews, find me that flying machine."

Grab your copy...
vinci-books.com/skywalkers

About the Author

JC Ryan is a bestselling author renowned for his intricate espionage, archaeological thrillers, and conspiracy mysteries. With over 30 acclaimed novels, including the popular Rex Dalton K9 Thrillers, Rossler Foundation Mysteries, and Carter Devereux Mystery Thrillers, Ryan has captivated readers around the globe.

Drawing from his diverse professional background—as a military officer, lawyer, and IT manager—Ryan creates compelling narratives that skillfully blend historical accuracy with thrilling adventure. He is celebrated as a master storyteller, known for crafting riveting plots, meticulous historical details, and engaging, multidimensional characters. Ryan's meticulous research lends authenticity and depth to each story, immersing readers in richly constructed worlds filled with intrigue, suspense, and adventure.

Fans of David Baldacci, Lee Child's Jack Reacher, Tom Clancy's Jack Ryan, Nelson DeMille's John Corey, Vince Flynn's Mitch Rapp, Mark Greaney's Gray Man, Gregg Hurwitz's Orphan X, Robert Ludlum's Jason Bourne, Daniel Silva's Gabriel Allon, Brad Taylor's Pike Logan, Brad Thor's Scot Harvath, James Rollins' Sigma Force, Steve Berry's Cotton Malone, and Dan Brown's Robert Langdon will find JC Ryan's novels equally compelling and unforgettable.

When not writing, Ryan enjoys spending time with his college sweetheart, whom he married in 1978. They are proud parents of two daughters, have two sons-in-law, and are grandparents to two grandchildren.

www.ingramcontent.com/pod-product-compliance
Ingram Content Group UK Ltd.
Pitfield, Milton Keynes, MK11 3LW, UK
UKHW020043211025
464173UK00003B/81

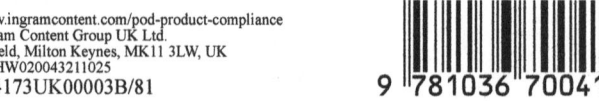